THE FALLOUT OF FALLACY

BOOK ONE OF THE PSALMS OF FIRE AND FURY BOOK SERIES

The Fallout of Fallacy

Cover Art by Rachel Mcewan

https://rachelmcewandesigns.com/

Artist Photo by Bridget Shaw Photography

https://www.bridgetshaw.photography/

ISBN 979-8-9886178-0-8 (hardcover)

ISBN 979-8-9886178-1-5, 979-8-9886178-3-9 (paperback editions)

ISBN 979-8-9886178-2-2 (ebook)

1 2 3 4 5 6 7 8 9 10

www.kristinambarbee.com

CONTENT WARNING

This book and the entire series contain threats of harm and torture of others, religious trauma, manipulation and abuse by the church, extreme violence, mentions of abuse, on page torture and bodily harm, PTSD, alcoholism, manipulation, mentions of suicide and suicide, depictions of Dermatillomania and Trichotillomania, crude language, detailed (all consensual) sexual acts, and other subjects that may be triggering or harmful to certain readers.

Reader discretion is advised.

Pronunciation Guide

Places

Aishar: ā-sh-ahr

Berren (castle): beh-ruhn

Saoirse (castle): sur-shuh

Thelimor: th-ehl-ih-môr

Character Names

Ora: OR-uh

Gerald: geh-ruhld

Ephraim: eh-fruh-m

Terran: ter-rin

Rener: rehn-air

Marion: mar-ee-uh-n

Loren: LAWR-ehn

Kathilla- kuh-th-ill-uh

Tyrrian Priscius: tee-REE-uhn   PRIHS-ee-uh-s

Nesima Mete: Nehs-ih-muh   meh-tay

DEDICATION

To the little girl whose childhood was stolen, whose life was saved by books
and stories created in her mind.

We did it.

We survived.

And we still have stories left to tell.

Chapter 1

Vernius 21, 690 AC

A threat that would crack the world asunder stalked between the shadows of the night.

Quiet steps on the cold cobblestone broke through the stillness of the hallowed Grand Hall of Archives. Father Penn guided himself with the small flicker of flame he held in his hand; the spines of the books he rushed by impossible to read in the darkness despite the candle's glow. He guided himself through the multi-storied library mostly by his memory from a lifetime spent walking the halls and pulling texts and parchments from their shelves.

As a boy bored in his studies, he had memorized each of the cracks in the floors and the exact number of stones it took to build the walls he was divinely destined to study and work within. Over time he had come to memorize many of the books and their placements, even favoring certain ladders that creaked less than others.

Father Penn quietly rushed his way down the stone steps separating him from his task and slinked into the restricted area that only those closest to the king and his Council held access to. A room Father Penn had permission to be in due to the untimely death of another High Scholar whose position he now held. While he had entry to these shelves, he was not permitted to search the codexes and parchments alone, only under the guidance and with the permission of the Master of Law and Head of the Church, Father Figgins, or the king himself.

This room contained the remaining rare records that managed to survive First King Lucarius' rage that burned libraries across the kingdom during his ascension to the golden throne, an extension of his pillaging efforts that reforged the continent in the wake of his triumph in the Great Civil War- a permanent mark on the continent's history that set education and advancement back generations.

Despite the forbidden nature of his sneaking, Father Penn meant no ill-intent. He only sought private comfort that the pages within the room may hold, confirmation that his religious teachings were not of fallacy and that the church was right to preach against those who spoke in defiance of holy texts and His Majesty's laws.

Although he only wanted to confirm what he hoped to be true, Father Penn could not silence the worry he held that those who could no longer speak their blasphemy may have been right.

His foot slipped on a crooked cobblestone and his hand jolted out to hold himself steady against a bookshelf, a quiet grunt escaped his tightly closed lips. He paused and listened for footsteps and greetings, praying for none to rise from the air, and thankful that there were no apprentices or Keepers in the hall on this night; a recently normalized peculiarity that he found gratitude in as he continued on his mission.

On a typical day, The Hall of Archives would be basked in the light of lanterns and bustling with Scholars of all levels, their apprentices, and others from The House of Scholar, all busying themselves with their research and writing at all hours of the day and night. Most scholars at night would spend their time searching through scopes pointed at the stars, deciphering their meaning; theorizing what each glimmer in the dark meant for the days to follow.

But typical days were no longer possible for the Six Kingdoms of Victarius.

Now, as the night skies grew darker with each passing moon rise, the Hall of Archives remained still as a tomb. So still that the scuttling of a rat squeezing its way into the chambers echoed throughout the halls, halting the breath in Father Penn's lungs as he moved to take another step.

Even the air seemed to still its breathing.

The amber flame of his candle paused as it came across a beaten and battered binding with a faded deep red cover that stood out among the rest, its binding repaired over time and bound in ways no longer used by Keepers. Father Penn cautiously took the book from its spot, careful not to disturb the dust around it or make a noise as he slipped the appendix into his hands.

The pages crinkled as he carefully palmed through the old records of times before The Great Civil War and First King Lucarius. He searched the ancient passages for words speaking of the Divine Houses the church preached as the destiny of each person in the kingdom; a divine calling from the stars one was born under that reshaped the world when The One True's words were brought to light. A small ping of hope glimmered in Father Penn's heart that those words would appear on the page.

But he found no words to cling his hope to.

Instead, he found psalms speaking of divinely given free will and hope for His creations to choose their own paths that led to enlightenment and prosperity. Divine Houses and destinies did not exist in his skimming of this holy text.

But perhaps, his assurances could be found elsewhere.

He placed the book back and carefully pulled another, a recording of events from the time of First King Lucarius when the peace treaty was being formed after the war. The middle of the codex was filled with scratched-out and edited holy passages and pen stains of those adding their signatures and edits to the new words. Towards the front of the log book were records of meetings with agendas related to the changes the book contained. The final passages were of pristine writing and final approvals of changes and modifications.

Father Penn shook his head slowly and his chest hardened. His lips silently mouthed the unfamiliar words that had been scrawled out and edited into passages he had memorized in his time leading sermons and teaching young lords and ladies. His mind slipped from where he stood and fell back to the last memory he had of Mother Nina, the elder High Scholar he had replaced after her death. In the church, it was rumored she had gone mad with age, a senile old crone to most in the pews now, but Father Penn heard enough of what she said to fear that her death had not been due to her age or her failing mind, especially not now that he read passages she recited under her breath when many were too busy to listen or pay her much mind.

The men of the church had efficiently replaced her legacy with reminders of her temper and her father's illness that made his mind fall too, and much too quickly, all forgot the ramblings and rants she had murmured out in her last days and paid no mind to Father Penn when he asked about what she whispered.

He remembered Father Nekaria, who had been killed a season after her death by attempted usurpers and had been Mother Nina's closest confidant, and he mournfully remembered Lord Biscile, the king's late Master of Coin, who had been killed by a bandit in the night the same season as well.

Father Penn shook his head with more vigor, forgoing the recollection of his memories and bringing himself back to this moment. There were far too many coincidences and fears to piece together tonight.

He pulled out a quill-thin knife made for opening letters and cut the parchment containing signatures and edits out of the book, then flipped the pages to cut out the note pages from meetings held by the First King. Quickly, but still cautiously, Father Penn placed the book back and stuffed the pages into the breast of his robe.

What took merely a few moments of quiet snooping felt like excruciating hours and Father Penn hurriedly took back ways through the aisles to avoid meeting with anyone who may dare wander the Archives alongside him. As he met a large wooden door leading to a back alley, he paused and turned back to the hall, his heart heavy as he let out a deep breath.

Father Penn had hoped to uncover nothing more than comforting confirmation that the foundation he had built his life upon was not a fallacy.

He blew out his candle and exited out to the atramentous back alley where the only break in the blackness belonged to the moon and stars. He raised his hood to obscure his face, and quickly set off for the asylum of his home to decipher what he was to do next once his overwhelm calmed and he could think with clarity.

Perhaps luckily, or unluckily, the streets of Isilria were not a busy place so late at night, especially on this night when most citizens would be resting early in preparation for the celebration of the Spring Equalius in the morning. The only others out were the dregs of society causing trouble or unfaithful spouses leaving Houses of Red Doors- neither of which wanted to be seen by others.

Several quick and quiet paces into the alley, Father Penn breathed a quiet sigh that was cut off by a strong, hardened hand covering his mouth and nose.

He flailed his hands as he attempted to reach for the knife in his pocket, but his movement was stopped as he was jerked back against the body of his assailant who roughly gripped his face.

Father Penn knew in his old, fragile age he was no match for anyone of the muscular size and strength of this figure. He foolishly hoped that the person who grabbed him was one of the usual drunk thieves that haunted back-alley places and he could escape with less gold in his pocket than he had before. But he knew in his heart that this was not a thief in the night, and that the truth he held in his hands would die with him before the season's dawn.

As tears began welling in his eyes and a prayer attempted to form on his smothered lips, he felt the chill of a cold blade pressed to his throat and a voice rich in deep tenor and a smooth accent mumbling into his ear, "Forgive me Father, but this is his will".

The coldness of the knife was replaced with the warmth of the blood it unleashed as Father Penn's knees hit the ground and the shapes and the shadows of the backstreet faded into pure black.

And so began the Spring Equalius; with deep red blood staining the cobblestones of the street mere hours before the celebratory day of equal light and darkness was to begin.

CHAPTER 2

The harbor at Middleton Landing was adorned with an abundance of Ayeshire banners billowing in the breeze. Armored bannermen lined the crowds of citizens anxiously waiting to greet King Ivan Scott and his family. Every citizen present was dressed in their finest attire, even the dock workers wore clothes better suited for a day at church and not the labor they were tasked with at the port.

The forest green banners adorned with leaping stags flapped alongside the waves; the movement making it appear as if the sacred animals were running from the ing's incoming boats. Gannets and sea swallows flew above the heads of the audiences, landing on posts and perches scattered about the inland area, gossiping with one another about the eventful afternoon and impatiently waiting for the crowds to leave so they could feast on unattended catches and dive into the waters currently filled with too many obstacles.

Where the long piers met the land and the thick grass began its ascension into a hill, stood the noble Montarian clan of Ayeshire with their council of advisors, including their High Scholars, Sister Ora and Father Robb, and their noble guards. Lady Belva Montarian, the Lady of Ayeshire, stood with her head firmly placed forward, her husband, Lord Theodus Montarian, held his hands behind his back a half step behind her, and their three sons Digarius, Taylian, and Samwin arranged themselves beside their father.

Framed behind them was the fortress of Middleton Landing that Lady Belva Montarian had called home since she was merely a flicker of movement inside her mother's womb and a glimmer of joy inside her father's heart. She was a stunning black woman, tall and strong in mind and body, with long textured hair that she enjoyed braiding and styling often, adding antique jewels and charms into her braids for special events as she did now. Her long sleeved well-fitted dress was deep green, her House color, and adorned in the symbols of the nature surrounding the hills of her city.

"Samwin." Her voice was firm and steady, her lips barely moving as she addressed her youngest son. "Please hold out for just a few moments more."

She had not even had to turn her head to know that he was growing tired of waiting for the king, young Samwin was always restless.

Lord Samwin let out a groan and mumbled, stopping his shuffling and shifting. "Apologies, mother."

Lord Taylian, the middle Montarian son at age seventeen, shot a quick glance and raised brows down at tthe brother half his age before adjusting himself and side eyeing Lord Digarius, mirroring his eldest brother's posture. Lord Digarius stifled a small chuckle at them both, the only evidence of the laughter being the small upturn of his mouth.

The type of anticipation felt among those gathered differed, excitement peppered the faces of innocent or blissfully ignorant citizens, while concern covered those who did not hold the king in the high regard that he demanded or who were aware of the words spreading across the Six Kingdoms of Victarius about his current fist of iron and blood.

Those concerned faces included the Lady of Ayeshire.

Beside her, Lord Theodus Montarian sighed and raised a heavy hand and kerchief to his shaved head, wiping off the sweat gathering near his brow, the humidity in the air coming to an almost unbearable index as the afternoon arrived.

Lord Digarius leaned into his father, his slim and tall frame a shadow of his large and heavily built father, "Cold beers later?"

Lord Theodus smirked, his full cheeks softening his battle worn and wrinkled face as he nodded and raised his brows in playful agreement. The underground cooling rooms beneath their fortress were filled with meat, foods, and beer and would be of great use if the predictions of a hot spring and summer were to come true. Lord Theodus had already had a lounging couch moved into the beer room in anticipation.

Lord Taylian looked up at his brother, standing a head height shorter than the heir, and opened his mouth to join in the jest between father and eldest son, but turned back to face dutifully forward.

The red bannered boat bearing the crowned lion crest knocked against the wood of the pier. The red fabric canopy hid the royal family from view as the workers swiftly tied it to the posts and laid a wooden walkway down for the family to walk across with ease. One-by-one the passengers unloaded, aided by their vassals who had already unloaded themselves from the prior, more crowded, boat.

Queen Onetta walked with ease and grace across the wooden planks, the slight bobbing of the boat giving her no issue with her smooth movements. As she settled beside her three children who had walked out before her, she turned her head back to the boat- a look of boredom painted across her hard face.

King Ivan swatted away an offered hand and exited the boat with firm and stiff movements. His head was held high, and he did not acknowledge those gathered until he adjusted himself, checking that the hem of his shirt was laid properly and his crown not crooked.

His acknowledgement of the Ayeshire citizens was simple, a quick nod to the onlookers closest to the dock, hidden behind a heavy line of Ayeshire guards, then turned back to his family. Standing among him were his King's Guard, royal aids, Queen Onetta, Prince Percy, and his two daughters- one closer to the prince's age and the other barely of school age, a kind aura surrounded the youngest as she excitedly looked around the area and took in what she saw. Glaringly missing from the royal family was Prince Elion, the Heir to the Throne, and the Hand of the King, Lord Robert Orville.

As the royals and their companions walked down the dock to meet with the Montarian family, the heads of men bowed, and women curtsied. Eyes stole glances at the passing royals despite their bowed heads. Shared whispers of excitement and commentary carried like a wave through the people.

As the king met with Lady and Lord Montarian, he gave another nod and the gathering fell to one knee for him. The king quickly dismissed the Montarian family from their kneeling, prompting the rest of the crowds to return to standing as well.

"It has been many ages since you have sailed onto our shores, Your Majesty." Lady Belva said as the group began to exchange greetings. "With such short notice, I regret that we were not fully able to prepare for your visit, but the people of Ayeshire welcome you with open arms. Middleton Landing is yours."

"Ahh." King Ivan jeered, his pale white cheeks barely tinted with color, the coldness of his skin matching the blue grey chill of his eyes. "We are not here to worry about fancy feasts or formalities, but to discuss important business and news. I come bearing an imperative proposal we will address over whatever harvest and game your kitchen can manage to scrounge up for our stomachs."

"Of course, Your Majesty." Lord Theodus Montarian replied as he stepped forward beside his wife, his closed mouth smile rounding out his full cheeks more.

"Ah! Lord Montarian, it has been some time! Your High Scholar did promise mine a fine hunt between us men on this visit." The jovial king patted Lord Theodus' arm and held his hand there, squeezing his muscle, the rings on the king's finger pinching Lord Theodus' skin. "Do not tell your wife, but that is truly why I am here."

The king looked about the lush southern town and took in a deep breath. "There is no finer hunting than in the green lands of Ayeshire."

Both men shared a laugh before King Ivan turned back to Lady Belva and spoke with more formality and firmness. "But, Your Grace, we do have a private matter to address before the ale and the game can begin."

Lady Belva Montarian bowed her head and met his eyes, "As you wish, Your Majesty."

Queen Onetta stepped beside her husband, her chin held high as she spoke and her dark eyes glaring at the Lady of Ayeshire. "Lady Montarian, Lord Montarian."

"Your Majesty." Lady Belva replied, matching the firm posturing of Queen Onetta as she bowed her head and raised it back up to match the queen's cold stare.

The queen turned her glaring eyes to meet Lord Theodus and the nervous glances of their sons. Her sharp cheekbones were enhanced as she pursed her lips as her eyes wandered. "Your sons have grown into fine young men since we last saw them."

Lady Belva's eyes flicked wide at her compliment. "Thank you, Your Highness." The Lady turned to the prince and princesses standing behind their parents. "As has your son. Your daughters look the picture of noble elegance. May I ask, where is Prince Elion?"

King Ivan replied, "The heir to the throne stayed in Isilria to take over royal duties on my behalf with Lord Orville to aid him. Elion has proven himself honorable in his duties and we thought it time he gets a taste for his future rule."

The eldest princess, Princess Arminda, stepped forward, her smile beaming across her tanned cheeks- an equal mixture of her father's paleness and her mother's deep rich tone. She bowed her head politely to the Lord and Lady and curtsied at the waist in greeting.

Both Princess Arminda and Queen Onetta wore long sleeved gowns and beautiful jewels. Queen Onetta's gown was a rich red fabric with lavish gold embroidery stitched along its front, while Princess Arminda's gown was decorated with stitched colorful flowers laid upon a bustling cream fabric. Both gowns, while quite different, would have taken endless hours of labor by a skilled fabric tradesman- labor and materials only a high-class noble person could afford.

"Hello Your Graces, thank you for the wonderful welcome to your home." Princess Arminda said, her voice soft and poetic in its flow. She tucked a loose strand of her long deep brown hair behind her ear as she stood up, turning her head to motion for her older brother and younger sister to come forward. Princess Kalia eagerly came forward, her tiny hand tugging at Prince Percy's fingers as he shyly came forward as well.

Polite greetings and formal addresses were exchanged among the upper-class families, the demeanor growing tired after repeated greetings between the families and advisors. Down the greeting line, tired of waiting for her husband to finish his talking, Queen Onetta reached where Father Robb and Sister Ora stood, awaiting their turn.

Both High Scholars greeted the queen and gave their names, neither knowing if the queen was advised on who they were.

Born under the constellations divined for House of Scholars, Father Robb, a kind man old enough to be a grandfather and Sister Ora, young enough to be his granddaughter, were the two highest advisors in the country of Ayeshire.

Father Robb spent his days advising the Lord and Lady of Ayeshire on conflicts and concerns, aiding in teaching the Montarian sons of their future duties, and leading their chapels in prayer. As the Second Scholar of Ayeshire, second to Father Robb, Sister Ora's work placed her alongside the noble Montarian family as well- the family she would be the master advisor and aid to upon Father Robb's passing. Unlike Father Robb, however, she had more time to spend on smaller, more common duties, including teaching apprentices and putting her eyes to the telescope in their tower as the generations of Scholars before them had.

"Father Robb, Sister Ora, may I introduce to you my eldest daughter, Princess Arminda." The queen said.

Sister Ora's smile twitched as her eyes flickered at the princess beaming at her with excessive joy. Princess Arminda's was bright and full of sunshine and authentic joy while Sister Ora's smile was soft and calm, not reaching her eyes. The young High Scholar corrected her faltering expression to mirror the princess'.

"Your Majesties, it is a great blessing that you are here." Sister Ora greeted, lowering her voice from its usual volume and tucking her chin in as she spoke. Her stark white dress, only worn in the church or on official business as a High Scholar, created a beam of light among the dirt and greenery behind her. She folded he hands in front of her, their callouses rubbing against one another as she straightened her back to attempt to meet the height of the royal women in front of her.

"Sister Ora, we have heard much about you. It is not common for one as young as us to be in your position, but from what we have been told—" Princess Arminda laughed and shot her eyes at Prince Percy, standing two paces behind them. "—much from the mouth of my brother, your intellect and knowledge are to be admired. It is quite a pleasure to meet you. "

Sister Ora looked back at the quiet prince and gave him a kind smile and curtsy. Her eyes scanning his tall demeanor and more simplistic attire compared to his family; subtly attempting to decipher who he was underneath his title and quietness.

"Umm, yes, it is quite an honor to meet you, Sister Ora." the prince awkwardly replied. He held an uncomfortable smile on his face as he met her eyes and quickly turned away. His black curls fell on his forehead as he moved and found interest in the gathered crowds around them. His hands wrung behind his back and his shoulders fidgeted and moved where he stood.

Sister Ora's eyes fell to the smiling young princess hiding halfway behind her brother, "And who may this young princess be?"

She smiled, curtsied, and bent down to meet with Princess Kalia as she stepped around her shy brother's leg.

The young girl giggled, "Princess Kalia."

Princess Kalia's warmth radiated through her big smile. In looks, she was every bit her mother's child. Her dark raven hair, like her mother's, gleamed and her skin was the same deep tone as her mother's. The brown eyes both her brothers and sister had were broken by bits of deep green and her cheeks were as full as the smile she happily wore.

"And Princess Kalia was due to stay at home, studying for her first season of schooling, but refused to stay behind when we all were sailing away."

Princess Arminda teasingly added, setting a soft hand on Princess Kalia's shoulder.

King Ivan and the Montarian family joined the discussing group, putting an end to the kindness that had just begun.

"Come. Let us have all have drink and get out of the humidity." the king firmly said as he stepped beside them.

The gathering moved away from the ports towards the castle. As Sister Ora began walking alongside the others, one hand aiding Father Robbin's as he walked and steadied himself with his cane, she found eerie eyes looking at her. She met the stare of an unfamiliar man who stood unmoving in front of fully armored King's Guards. She darted her eyes away from his deep glare as leaned into Father Robb.

"Who is that man?" she whispered.

Father Robb replied in kind, "Father William Figgins."

A knowing nod was her only reply. Father William Figgins was the head of the church- of all churches, the High Scholar of Britia, and Master of Law on the King's Council. His words were those of The One True, and words all Scholars throughout the Six Kingdoms of Victarius were to follow without question.

She attempted to avoid his attention, but her efforts were in vain as he and the King's Guards beside him met her steps.

"Sister Ora, a pleasure to finally meet you. I greatly enjoyed your theory on the Starfall that occurred during Lunarius that left many of us to wonder to its meaning over our winter celebrations. Father Robb sent a copy of your writings to me recently, and others you have written even before your recent titling of High Scholar. Your extensive knowledge, as well as insights were a welcomed point of view, that of which I greatly appreciated."

Father Figgins' too bright and round grey eyes continued to bore into her side as they ascended the hill to the fortress. It was not often one matched her shorter stature perfectly, let alone a man clearly older than the king's middle age, but Father Figgins height matched hers, but only due to the heeled shoes she noticed him wearing.

She kept her own look forward as he droned on, her sideview being disrupted with the continual glimmer of jewels and gold he wore in excess shining in the sun. On his small figure, there were as many jewels as there were upon the entirety of the royal family, a glaring juxtaposition to Father Robb on her other side in his simple brown tunic and pants, only accessorizing with his holy rosary and High Scholar pin.

"Thank you, Father Figgins. I do quiet enjoy a friendly discourse and discussion at times." She spoke carefully and controlled every syllable, mirroring the tone and inflection of those around her.

"It is not often that we see such young High Scholars in the kingdom, let alone young women such as yourself. I must admit I was quite surprised at how eloquent and interesting some of your points were." His tone was not sharp or condescending, he spoke as if he was stating a simple, non-offensive, fact.

Her words fell out before she could stop them, "Ah yes, because it is such a rarity for a woman to have something to say that is worth listening to."

As soon as the snark left her lips, regret punched her in the gut. But just as quickly as the emotion struck, it dissipated as she heard a small snort of laughter behind her from an offensively tall King's Guard, a chuckle from Father Robb beside her, and a more substantial laugh from Princess Arminda in front of her.

"I knew that there was more of a reason for me to like you than the few words spoken of you." Princess Arminda called back with a hint of amusement. "You must forgive Father Figgins, as I am certain he means no harm or ill-will."

"Yes, my apologies." Father Figgins replied as his lips curled into a snarling smile as he turned back to Sister Ora. "My apologies."

***

The grand stone fortress of Middleton Landing did not have tall turrets that ascended to the skies for its noble inhabitants to look down from and hide within, instead, it was built of large square towers that peaked close to the ground and were framed by long walls and walkways made of dark grey stone. The cooler temperatures and often damp climate in the town of Middleton Landing gave the dark stone spots of moss and creeping greenery, making the stronghold look as if it grew from the hills of green that it sat upon.

Along the frames of the lead glass windows and stone door frames of the interior were etchings and carvings of oak trees, freesia flowers, and the mighty stag crest of Ayeshire- the same elements and creatures that were scattered throughout the green lands and hills of the southern country and often adorned the clothes of prideful and affluent citizens.

Lady Belva Montarian sat with King Ivan Scott in one of her private receiving rooms overlooking the bustling courtyard within the fortress. She delicately picked up a wood carved honey dipper and drizzled the liquid gold into her filled teacup, setting the dipper back into its container and replacing it in her hand with a small spoon to stir the sweetener in the steaming herbal tea. The king had already begun sipping his bitter black tea, ignoring the sweeteners and additions laid out for them.

She continued reading the parchment unrolled beside her cup as she stirred. "That is an exceptional number of jewels and food lost, Your Majesty. Perhaps the sea dragons are as greedy as the legends state." She glanced up. "How did the merchants not see the rocks? They have sailed this route before, have they not?"

"Endless times. The few that survived the tearing apart of their ship claimed it was an incident. That they knew where they sailed to, that the stars they followed had *moved*."

"What?" She twitched her head up from the letter.

"Simply an excuse for poor sailing in the night." He waved it off.

She scrunched her face at his ease and slowly rested herself in the back of her chair. "Perhaps, Your Majesty, or perhaps the stars are not only falling, but moving about. You have seen what the Scholars have written when they look to the skies."

He took a deep breath and exhaled. "If that is true, then it appears the Old Gods in the skies no longer wish to look upon us and grow tired of what they see- or want a better view from where they sit in the sky."

"The Old Gods are but myths, forbidden to discuss in official means, a *sin* that the church and the crown have long forbidden anyone to speak of or lay any truth beside." she replied

The king lazily waved off her words. "The merchant guild leader in Ryanar demands payment for what the sea took. Demanding gold from a king- *His king-* who did not receive the goods ordered. They claimed if it had been their ships and not mine sailing, this would not have occurred."

"It was a cold winter and a dry harvest season last turn, the worst in many epochs for your people in particular. A loss this substantial, and to occur in such a way after everything." She shook her head. "The stars guide our calendars, our seasons, our sails. While a single glimmer in the night sky dimming or falling is not of worry..."

"My High Scholars in The Hall of Archives have their theories, as I am sure yours will as well, on the stars movements." He folded his arms in front of him and leaned forward. "Which is the reason for this visit- to ensure our allyship remains in what the stars say may be coming- dark nights and darker days. We must ensure unity remains between our two countries, and unify a stronghold with our other allies, to put an end to this brooding anger that has grown with each turn of the moon."

She nodded slowly, understanding his words and his demands of her and her country. She sipped her sweetened tea as she worked through each thought working their way through her overworked mind. Her fingers lightly tapped the delicate tea cup she held.

Scholars of all ranks, and even curious citizens, looked into the night sky often to ask for aid, information, and glimpses into the future. Stars within clusters changing their glow, star falls occurring, and seasonal celestial events aided leaders and common people in decision making throughout the passage of time. Historical records tracked celestial events and constellations in season during important events, with patterns thoroughly noted over the ages. Current dated records with ink still fresh showed the stars becoming as restless as the hungry and angry citizens waking up throughout the kingdom, the star falls mirroring that that occurred in times of war and before dark ages. Constellations shifting in the sky was a natural occurrence as the Divine Houses they symbolized came in and out of season.

But stars disappearing or moving in such unnatural ways, especially in off seasons, sent a chill along Lady Belva' spine.

"Your Majesty, I must ask, as the head of my noble House- the line that has stood alongside yours before the throne." She shot a look at him and hardened her tone, clinking her cup onto its saucer and folding her hands on the table between them. "As your longest standing ally. Is what the rumors say of you true? Of the punishments? The killings? The blood?"

King Ivan picked up a pot of steeping tea and refilled his empty cup, taking a slow sip and let a deep breath escape through his nostrils before he spoke, "Leaders such as us inherit a heavy burden, Lady Montarian. A dark weight of doing... hard things many may not be willing to do to keep our country from falling apart- to keep our people safe."

His dark glare watched her unfaltering facade before dipping itself down to the floor momentarily, the tension he held jumping away with the movement as his eyes met the grit of stone at his feet. The cold stone allowed him to borrow some of its hardness as the muscle in his jaw feathered and he glared up at the Lady of Ayeshire again.

Her eyes did not move, nor soften or harden, and held her posture firm. "That we do, sir. But many do question your name now, and many more look for ways to curse you, not just for the heavier hand you have used the past few seasons, but also believing you and those under your payroll to be the men behind the loss of many of your own advisors. That you are —" she paused to find the right words and picked her cup up again. "— cleaning up messes before they become too much."

She sipped her tea and mumbled into her cup. "Their words, not mine, of course."

King Ivan leaned in, his eyes transforming to that of a hungry lion as his blue eyes formed ice around their edges. "And what messes would those be?"

She shrugged lightly, feigning ignorance, and showing no cracks in her armor. "That I do not know, but is it not my duty as your ally to provide you knowledge of what occurs in your own commonwealth?"

Her cup returned to its place on the table and her hands returned to their familiar spot folded in front of her.

One side of his mouth curled as he slowly cocked his head and nodded. "That it is, as it has always been."

"And as your ally, would you not wish for my continued honesty and our mutual accountability as our father's had with one another?"

Their gazes separated, the king's moving to the window beside his chair, his eyes tracing the carvings in the stone, and Lady Montarian's turning to her folded hands on the table, every muscle in her forearms working to not wring and twist them until her fingers snapped.

The king held a long pause of contemplation before he spoke.

"We do not wish to be disappointments to our legacies, do we, Lady Montarian?"

She spoke to his turned face, her head lightly cocked as she held her position against the king sitting so casually and lazily in her own fortress.

"No. No we do not." She said.

Chapter 3

"Y ou have been quiet and distant since your meeting with His Majesty yesterday afternoon, darling." Lord Theodus Montarian said as he leaned against the open doorway to their large bed chamber.

He finished stepping inside, leaving it open behind him. His wife tapped the hand of the vassal that was helping adjust her braids. They nodded and bowed to both the noble leaders and left through the open door, closing it behind them.

The servant's working hands were replaced with his. His large hands resting on her squared and hard shoulders. "And you have been tense."

She felt the pressure of his fingers digging into her muscles and his fingers lightly moving her long braids over her shoulder. She sighed and rested her head forward. "I am always tense."

He leaned forward and kissed her bare shoulder, the cut of her rich purple dress left bare her shoulders, neck, and décolleté. He flicked his eyes up at the mirror in front of them to look at her through it, giving a devilish smirk. "Not always."

She meet his eyes in the mirror, and shook her head and smiled. "Theo, not now."

He softly moved to kiss her neck, keeping his eyes locked with hers as he murmured and moved a hand to gently hold her neck. "I can be quick, and it will very much relax you before our shared feast."

"He is hiding something." She murmured, relaxation and warmth loosening her shoulders just enough for her to take a breath.

"Who?" he asked, his attention still on her neck.

She shot him a look. "The king."

Lord Theodus stood up and squeezed her shoulders before turning and walking about the room as she spoke. A small look of defeat on his face as he sat on the edge of their framed bed. He fiddled with his overcoat, a well-fitted silver and dark green pattern covered his upper body, tightening around his muscled arms as he moved his elbows to rest on his knees.

"I asked him directly about the rumors of him being behind the deaths of his own men. He would not give me a clear answer, only spoke in riddles and veiled threats." She moved her braids back around her shoulders, adding charms in different sections to match the simple jewels that adorned her neck and ears.

"He is a politician, darling, that is how all of you speak in court rooms and meetings."

She nodded in agreement with his jest.

"If he did do what is rumored, where would we stand?" he asked.

Lady Belva finished with her hair, pausing in contemplation at his question. "There is only so much immorality one can watch before they too become the same."

"Ah, political riddles again." He smirked, his voice then changing to a flat tone. "But morals sway as often as the breeze, darling."

Her head snapped back to him. "Are you suggesting ours should move?"

He leaned back on the bed onto his elbow. "I am merely stating what we both know. He is his father's heir after all, and... we both have had to make decisions that we did not particularly like in the name of our people."

Lady Belva chewed on her cheek and stayed silent, turning back to her mirror to finish her braids.

"I do not agree with what he is doing," her husband clarified. "what we *know* he is truly doing from messengers words and travelers tales, but we must ask, after all this time, after all of the buildup of his actions that have led us to today, why are many of those within his own city still complacent, still loyal despite what they see occurring to their neighbors? If they are okay with this, why must we not be?"

She stood and straightened her gown as she turned for the door. "You know as well as I that the average person does not care for the nuances of politics and swaying loyalties, so long as they are fed and taxes kept low, anger and malevolence can be satiated, and peace can be bought." She sighed, "It often takes too much pain for the average citizen to strike up against those holding them in place, even if they know they are being held. And others may see the blood and punishment as what their brethren deserve."

"Then, I ask you again, what is it you wish us to do?" he asked as he stood from the bed and moved beside her.

She reached for the doorknob, holding it as she quietly replied. "We decide which side of history would grant our souls the most peace, and we write our names in it."

***

Silverware clicked and scraped on the plates as the noble families and their guests ate and their mixture of voices carried on various polite conversations between bites. Lining the room was an overabundance of servants-some from the Montarian House and numerous more from the Royal Household-holding food trays and decanters of drink while standing anxiously alongside King's Guards who stood so eerily still it would be hard for a quick eye to differentiate them from an empty suit of armor set out for display.

Each time a plate or cup teetered on the edge of emptiness, a dutiful servant jumped from their spot against the wall to fill it to the brim before quickly and quietly stepping back out of sight.

"Servant!" King Ivan gestured by swinging his wine glass in the air. "More wine for all. Now that our bellies are full, we must toast to the news I bear."

Servants hastily stepped forward from against the walls and quickly filled glasses, even those with only a sip taken from the stein. The king's cup was filled first, and he barely allowed the cup bearer a moment to step away before shoving his chair back- the harsh sound of the heavy wood scraping against the stone floors startling the nerves of the room.

A bard sat in the corner, lightly strumming a lute beside a heavy fireplace, hidden in the shadows of the stone frame protruding from the wall. She stopped her strumming as the king stood and leaned back in her chair, hiding herself more among the tapestries and torches behind her.

"Her Majesty and I would first like to extend our most gracious gratitude for receiving us so well with such short notice. Let us raise our glasses to the honor you have brought to your country and all the Six Kingdoms of Victarius." The king raised his glass. "To Lord and Lady Montarian, and the great people of Ayeshire."

Each guest raised their glass and Lord and Lady Montarian shared a look, remembering their conversation moments before dinner in their bed chamber, as they waited for the standing king to finish addressing the room. The Middleton clan sat spread about the table, intermingling themselves with the royal family and both family's highest aids and consultants who were asked to join in on the family feast.

"I am filled with pride when I think of the allyship between our people and the generations our unity has lasted, and the many generations after where our peace will continue. Your clan continues to stand dutifully by your House words of strength, integrity, and grace and are an example many in our kingdom could learn from."

Heads around the table nodded in agreement and many eyes, including the king's, drifted towards the wood painted crest mounted on the wall above the generous fireplace steps away from His Majesty. The heavy wood bore their house words on its edges and a leaping stag was centered in the shield. On the opposite end of the room was a matching fireplace and carved crest, mirror images of one another.

Tired arms still held their glasses in the air, waiting for permission to set them down.

"Your Majesty." Queen Onetta said as she jutted her sharp chin at her husband and shot her stare at him. "Perhaps we raise our toast when your words are complete?"

King Ivan grumbled as he reluctantly nodded and set his glass down. Queen Onetta smiled with satisfaction as those around set down their chalices and steins as well.

"Yes, well, as I was saying. We would be ignorant to not notice that we are on the very precipice of change. The stars have been speaking of nights as dark as they were centuries ago, and our people have become passionate in their dissonance and perilous in their actions."

Lady Belva scrunched her eyes as the king continued. In her time spent near His Majesty in court rooms and at noble events, he had always been more to the point, even if his words caused the listener uncertainty in what point he was illuding to, preferring bluntness to long stanzas. She shifted her eyes to the silver-haired and ghostly white Father William Figgins sitting across from the king, his thin lips mouthing subtly along as the king spoke. She moved her glance back to the king before anyone noticed where it had gone.

King Ivan's eyes met Lady Belva's. She offered a small closed-mouth smile and non-threatening stare as his eyes bore into her, his lips repeating similar sentiments from their prior conversation. "It would be a shame and disgrace if our history of alliance was *tainted* with anything less than the upmost continued loyalty to one another during these times. It is long past due that the throne shows its gratefulness for what your House has done for ours. Our alliance is strong, Lady Montarian, but our Houses are not as united as they could, and perhaps should, be. It is time our Houses united in a bond that will last past any death or battle. A bond of holy union."

Bodies jostled in their seats and the quiet and dutiful servants on the sidelines even shifted and gasped at the king's words. The only members in the hall to not act out in shock were the king's own kin.

Lady Belva and Lord Theodus turned to one another, her eyes quietly telling him she had no knowledge of what the king spoke of. Eyes traced around the gathered guests, stopping at the noble children who bore no betrothals- Prince Percy, Princess Arminda, Lord Digarius, new-of-age Lord Taylian, and the two youngest children, Lord Samwin and Princess Kalia.

It had been well known among noble families that Princess Arminda, while not betrothed officially, had been a carrot well dangled in front of other families wishing for power and alliance, but the king held tight to traditional royal family values- unions were not to occur for younger children when their older siblings were still unwed. Each person outside of the king's circle gave a look to Prince Percy, his eyes on his plate and shoulders slowly turning inward as he felt more stares on him.

"As we all know, Lady Montarian cannot seem to stop bearing sons, which is quite a humorous joke of God after her mother could not stop producing female heirs." The king stopped to laugh at his own joke. "Fortunately, God Himself must have known that this day would come and brought to your family not a daughter born of noble blood, but a *woman* born a Scholar, who has become so vital to your House that she may as well have come from Her Grace's own womb."

Still smiling from ear to ear, the mildly drunken king looked to Sister Ora sitting stiffly across the table from Prince Percy- eyes wide and staring at nothingness in front of her on the table.

Her heart was beating so hard she felt as if the entire room could see it palpating in her chest. Her mouth ran dry, and her body overheated, the warm red undertone of her lightly tan complexion becoming more prominent as she pulled her body into itself. If she had any words within her to respond, she would choke on them as soon as they formed on her tongue.

"Now, unfortunately, my eldest son is already promised to another but what is second best to the title of future queen for a lady?"

There were no words, only worry. Only panic.

Glares bore into one another as the Montarian family attempted to speak to another without saying a word. Eyes pleaded for a distraction to stop the continuation of His Majesty.

"A princess!" Princess Kalia's voice burst through the heavy wave of trepidation suffocating the room.

"Exactly, my darling," King Ivan jeered. "What better way to continue our long-held alliance than with a wedding?"

The king looked around, expecting joyous smiles and cheers to erupt and calls for more wine to be heard from all, but received nothing besides looks of confusion and shock. His Majesty turned to Lord Theodus who sat next to him, his grace's elbow resting on the table and his hand over his mouth, his eyes large and holding a look of turmoil.

"A marriage proposal, Your Maejesty?" Lord Theodus mumbled into his hand.

The king looked to Lady Belva, whose turmoil held anger she had no chance to hide. Her glare took turns looking at Prince Percy and Sister Ora, both of whom looked as if the news was of a death, not a marriage proposal.

"What in the bloody *fuck* is wrong? Did you have her on reserve for one of your own boys?" The king turned from Lord Theodus to Lord Digarius. "Maybe you should have had your boy over there pry open her legs and shove his cock in her first so he could lay his claim to her before mine could."

Lord Digarius jerked his head to look at the king, his anger not hidden and the fire inside him threatening to slice a dagger into the king with his words or a weapon. Quickly, Lady Belva stood and reached her hand out to halt her son's fury at the king's disrespect.

"Apologies, Your Majesty." Lady Belva cut in as she moved to stand beside her son and physically hold him in place with her delicate hand on his shoulder. "In our excitement of your visit, we all have indulged in one too many glasses of brandy and wine, our shock and emotion unable to come to the surface thanks to the fine elixirs. We are overwhelmed with joy that you would want to give our House such an honor. Sister Ora has been like a daughter to us for so long, I feel as if my own child has been gifted such a blessing."

She turned to Queen Onetta down the table. "It seems, Your Highness, that we have a royal wedding to begin planning. Do let me know how Ayeshire can lend a hand to this celebration."

"Of course, Your Grace. We will ensure that this alliance and wedding is heard throughout the entire kingdom." The queen's superficially sincere tone was laced with the same power that her words came with.

Sister Ora attempted to hold in the bile gathering in her stomach, her hands sat hidden on her lap, ripping and picking at her nails and skin, the pain of the tearing skin and nails but failing to bring her back to center.

It was too much.

She pulled at the long bit of skin hanging off her nail bed, the shock of pain at the tear momentarily distracting her from what was ripping her apart inside.

Princess Arminda leaned to the left towards Sister Ora and gently placed her hand on top of Sister Ora's in her lap, not noticing the bits of blood gathering at her nail's edges.

The princess had a soft smile, but sorrow colored her eyes as she softly spoke, "Welcome to the family, sister."

Sister Ora finally looked up to Prince Percy- her betrothed. His expression was no more joyous than hers, but he managed to give her a meager smile. If looks could speak where words would not, she would hear the deep hearted apology that his eyes were pleading to her.

***

Sister Ora did not say a word as the world continued to fall apart around her and voices clamored on late into the night. After the king dropped the shocking news at the dinner table the meal quickly concluded, appetites long lost by the Montarian family who had been left in the dark over the royal family's surprise news.

The royal family had agreed to end the meal and the night early, King Ivan from his anger at the non-enthusiastic reception of the news, and the rest agreeing that the night had grown late. Princess Arminda was the only royal family member to directly address Sister Ora before turning in.

You get used to the feeling- being a pawn. She had whispered before brightening the room with an eager smile and excitement over new dresses and jewels she and the rest of the women would need for the wedding.

But Sister Ora had already known the feeling Princess Arminda spoke of. Long ago she had perfected bringing pride and joy, not shame or anger. Of being assertive and smart, but not aggressive or intimidating. To read each change in voice and movement of body and adjust her own stature and tone to ensure she blended in properly or stood out in the only acceptable way allowed in each room she entered. She knew quite well how to be a perfectly played pawn. That was her only use in life.

Sister Ora once had a rebellious nature in her youth, but as her body grew and the pressure and people around her made her fear losing her worthiness, she gave in to what was ahead of her and, through epochs of sacrifice and overwork encouraged and pushed upon her, she found herself in the highest rankings within her Divine House at an age where many were still debating their limited paths and experimenting with their potential.

The fireplace crackled in the background, adding more warmth to the heated room the Montarian family paced in. Father Robb and Sister Ora sat on the couch, the breeze of the open window behind them cooling her neck. Emaline, Sister Ora's personal guard and close friend long before her oath was taken, was the only person bearing physical armor in the room. Her muscled stature covered beneath silver metal plates. Emaline's face was firmed with quiet rage as she stood against a wall staring across the room, watching Sister Ora hold herself together by a fragile thread.

Ora's long black hair twisted in her fingers as she rubbed the split ends, twisting pieces around her fingers as she continued to stare into nothing while the voices around her discussed what decisions to make for her on what was declared mere hours before.

"If I had known, if he had told me during our prior meeting instead of hiding it to announce to us all, I could have come up with a plan." Lady Belva snapped towards Father Robb. "We could have scoured books of law and found *something* to stop this."

"And he likely knew that." Lord Theodus replied. His dinner coat was unbuttoned and carelessly draped around him as he sat shaking his head while his wife stood firmly at the head of the room, not allowing herself to relax.

Father Robb grumbled, "A law we could use to argue against this would be that of paternal agreement. If parents are living and the betrothed is not willing to marry, all one needs is their agreement to such marriage declarations to allow it to occur and just the opposite, they could fight to forbid it."

He looked to Sister Ora beside him on the couch opposite the fire. She gave a half-hearted shrug, "My mother would have agreed to this, not caring for much else besides how this would make me, make *her*, appear to those around her. I am the only unwed child, the youngest and the only one born in a Divine House high in societal status. This marriage would give her everything she wants in life."

Sister Ora was not even meant to exist and that haunted her each day. An asked for accident by a father aching for a daughter amongst his sons from a wife content without her existence. A mother who found her own redemption and gain in what her daughter would become once she realized the worth her little girl could give her. A mother whose love always came with an aching cost and requirements to be met.

A mother that had taught her that her existence had to be earned.

She shrugged again. "And my father would have eventually been worn down by her incessant arguing and tale spinning. He always chose her side when it came to me."

"Mother, surely your title could overrule this?" Lord Digarius came forward from the open windowsill he leaned against. His glimmering brown eyes held no light tonight and his thick expressive brows stayed crumbled tightly as he ran his long thin fingers through his tightly trimmed textured hair.

Lady Belva huffed, looking again at Father Robb. He nodded. "You could always use your title to reject his proposal, it has been done before in other noble betrothals."

Lady Belva found a chair to sit in and rested her hands on her lap. The crackling flames of fire the only noise to break the silence as she held the room in silence while she contemplated the consequences of any action, or inaction, she were to take.

"Despite my disagreement with His Majesty, rejecting the king's proposal- *declaration-*" she corrected herself, "would risk a tear in the delicate fabric of our allyship. It could be interpreted as us wishing to make an enemy of him."

Sister Ora looked to Lord Digarius as he opened his mouth to retort and defend her- the sister he had recently found through friendship and not birth. She cut him off, her voice broken but understanding. "And it would not be worth it to do such a thing over something as small as this."

"Ora." Emaline found herself standing beside Sister now, resting a hand on Sister Ora's as she continued anxiously pulling and twisting her hair. Emaline moved Ora's hand from her hair and watched her. "This is not small, this is important."

"It is okay, Emaline." she quietly mumbled.

Emaline stepped forward to stand closer to Lady Belva. "Your Grace we cannot, you cannot, just sell her off like this!"

Sister Ora shook her head and reached to stop Emaline. She stood up. "It does not matter, because I agree to the proposal."

Both Emaline and Lord Digarius jolted, but held their tongues as Sister Ora looked between her two friends.

"It is the proper choice to make and if it is what is best for this country, if it would be easiest for everyone else, then I will do it."

"Sister Ora, you have power in choice in this moment. There are laws and social rules that could back your rejection." Lord Digarius shook his head at her declaration.

"No." Sister Ora sat back down and looked at her blood stained nail beds. "I do not wish to burden you all with the ramifications of that."

Sister Ora dug at her thumbnail bed, ripping another strip of skin from her finger and watching the blood pool on the edge of her fingers hidden and crumpled in her lap.

She had been a burden, a tool, an unwanted thing that killed herself each day to be perfect and deserving. She had been these things many times over in her life, and now, she was a pawn again, once sold off for another's gain, her last remaining choice in life finally ripped away from her.

She tore another nail to distract herself from the tears that wished to softly brush down her cheeks.

Chapter 4

The allied leaders walked through the garden grounds with Lady Belva leading her husband, the king, and the queen through the pathways. They had taken separate morning meals after the prior night's dinner and despite the slight friction still in the air, civility and decorum had to remain.

The garden was filled with memorials of stone and beds of greenery and native florals. Dew still stubbornly stuck to the leaves and dripped off the intricate carvings of legendary leaders lost to the ages, woodlands animals, and interpretive etchings of historical events and moments in time.

Lady Belva stopped near a statue slowly being covered in small green vines climbing from the bed it stood in; a hefty great sword etched in stone and stabbed into uncontrollable waves. Her eyes fell over each curve and blemish in the statue and traced the three lines of words etched into the white stone.

For the countless lives lost to the seas and shores of the Isles of Aishar.

For the families forever changed for peace.

The Aisharian War, 670 AC.

If she stared long enough, as she did for epochs after that war, she could hear the ocean waves crashing and the bodies perishing. The bodies she ordered to their deaths in her first epoch as their Lady.

King Ivan firmly nodded at the large statue. "Hell of a war that one was. Bloodiest in ages, but the shortest as well. Those Aisharians—"

Queen Onetta cut the king off with a firm tone, anger threatening to creep into her sentences. "Those Aisharians, *my people,* are valiant and resilient gladiators who had no option but to turn on their own. That civil war was a harsh lesson for the attempted usurpers, for Lord Priscius' own brother."

The queen looked to her husband and then held her stare on Lady Belva, both of whom had now turned to her. Her eyes were cold, and her words factual without any depth. "One that I know your countries had no choice but to be a part of, and I thank you for the aid you provided to my people."

Lady Belva nodded and continued walking down the stone path, the group following alongside her. "That memorial was the first piece I asked our House of Craft to carve for our gardens. I did not even have the ink dried on my titling papers nor my father's soul settled in the heavens before news traveled to us about the declaration of battle. We lost so many in that blood bath."

"As did all of us. Much of my brother's ships did not even make it onto dry land before the water buried those he led for my father." King Ivan said, his interest and enthusiasm waking up at the prospect of telling war stories. "And he survived to the end to only be taken by a blade's infection he refused to have treated."

"Fighting alongside the mighty Sir Stephon Scott was a memory I shall carry on with me for a lifetime, Your Majesty. Your brother was mighty as an ox but more stubborn than an ass." Lord Theodus jested.

"That he was." The king shook his head as he smirked at his brother's memory, changing his pace to walk alongside the lord. "That war may have been responsible for many deaths and families being ripped apart, but I recall it also being responsible for your redemption as a commander, Lord Montarian."

A muscle feathered in Lord Theodus' jaw, as the two men now fell in step with one another and he grumbled his response. "Yes, many have believed that."

"I for one never did. You did not need redemption for what happened at Broken Tower or for helping rid this continent of that damned Fraser Edgel." The king waved a hand in the air, "You should have been celebrated."

Lord Theodus did not reply. His mind instead fell back to what occurred in that battle and the fallout he fought against for too long.

Lady Belva cleared her throat to recatch the king's attention, her noise a command to stop the garden stroll. "I hope you know what sending an army to fight alongside the royal army was not an easy choice, Your Majesty. Especially with it having been my first official order to my people as their Lady. I do not make my choices lightly."

"And neither do I." King Ivan said, his enthusiasm now gone. He squared his shoulders and hardened his jaw, he scanned the noble woman standing equally against him.

Across the courtyard, a vassal approached, bowing quickly upon their arrival. "Excuse me, our Majesties, Your Graces. The stables and horses are ready for the hunt."

***

King's Guard and Ayeshire guards lined the perimeter of the bright green valley, framing where the king and Lord Theodus sat on small stools and conversed under the shade of overgrown oak trees. Several paces away, still within the perimeter of intermingling gold and silver-plated armor, stood Sister Ora, Prince Percy, and Lord Digarius laughing with a tall handsome man with a summer tan and long wavy blonde hair.

The late afternoon wafted in on the breeze as the king and Lord of Ayeshire snacked on a spread of grapes and olives brought from The Grovelands, meats and cheeses from the cellars of Middleton Landing, and spiced teas and ale from different parts of the kingdom all laid out on a short-legged table.

"Now *this* is God's country. This is where men like us are meant to be. Those damn halls they crowd us in and stuffy rooms where we sit at all hours- those are nothing compared to this." King Ivan exclaimed as he took his seat across from the Lord of Ayeshire- a freshly filled plate of food in the king's hand.

Both men wore similar casual attire, adorned in browns and forest green pants and vest-covered shirts, the color schemes meant to hide themselves well among the bramble and foliage of the hunting grounds.

Lord Theodus did not look up from the short table separating the two, the tabletop game in front of him requiring his concentration. "You speak as if you wish to ride away from your rule until the sea overtakes the land."

"Given what is occurring, would you blame this old man for dreaming of it?" The king casually said.

Lord Theodus lifted his head, the prominent creases around his eyes softening as he raised his heavy brows and cocked his head. "Not at all, Your Majesty."

King Ivan chewed on bread and cheese, then jutted his jaw in the direction behind the two where Sister Ora and Prince Percy were in conversation with two others. "What do you think of our pairing?"

Lord Theodus turned around in his stool, ignoring the king's word choice. "I think it will serve our counties well, that is, if she does not eat the poor boy alive. Sister Ora has been in our advisory as a High Scholar since her titling the winter before last, and as a minor Scholar before that. She may be an agreeable woman, but when needed, she has been a force to be wary of."

King Ivan let out a boisterous laugh. "She likely will. That boy of mine *is* soft. Smarter than most in our kingdom, but softer than silk. Thank the Gods old and new he was second born, or I would fear for the day the crown is placed on his dream-filled head."

The king took a large swig, blocking Lord Theodus' glare from his view.

"And what of Prince Elion? How is he holding up standing in your shadow?" the lord asked.

King Ivan removed the goblet from his lips. "He will be a fine king in his time. Strong, knowledgeable, and sure of himself- most days. So long as he holds the right company to guide him, our kingdom will be in honorable hands."

Lord Theodus carelessly moved around the wooden game piece in his hand- their friendly table game now abandoned for the conversation. His mind walked away from the king in front of him. He glanced around at the wall of red caped King's Guards, their armor thicker than his own soldiers- the silver plates of their suits lined with gold and the king's crest proudly displayed on their chests and pauldrons. Their numbers larger and, perhaps, their talents more impressive than his guards.

"I know what you have been doing, what you have been considering, Lord Theodus."

The king's words pushed Lord Theodus' attention back to him- the king now glaring across the table. "You cannot beat me; you have already lost before we've begun."

Lord Theodus adjusted himself in his seat, his free hand carefully moving to his sword sheathed at his side, his eyes quickly darting around again to the king's sworn swords. He attempted to subtly count the paces between he and the nearest guard.

"Quit stalling and play your piece so I can rightfully beat you. *Again.*"

The Lord of Ayeshire let out the breath stuck in his lungs and looked down at the table where their unfinished game sat. Relief overcame him as his nerves escaped with his breath. Too many battles and brawls over his time had made Lord Theodus too suspicious of potential enemies, made him too quick to jump to actions involving swords instead of words, and his memories still whispered their worries at him about his past commands.

Lord Theodus lazily tossed the piece in front of him onto the game board. "And here I was thinking if I could get your droning on long enough you would forget."

***

Prince Percy stood a polite distance away from Sister Ora as they conversed with Lord Digarius and their tall blonde friend, Gerald Ackley, who had accompanied them on the hunt as a lead archer. Born under the wolf and bow constellation for the House of Huntsman, Gerald had spent his life-time learning all he could of the woods and metal tipped weapons, hunting wild beasts that threatened citizens and beasts meant to food the people. Prince Percy had also learned in their conversation that Gerald's experience included military service after Lord Digarius, who Gerald trained with and befriended in their youth, had requested Gerald voluntarily enlist in service at the time when Lord Digarius gave his mandatory oath. Gerald easily obliged to serve alongside his friend the season before the two were set to complete their rite of passage of the Huntsman at the Wolfsden mountain village.

"The mountain wolf was the size of a Clydesdale; the hardest part of the hunt was skinning its hide after dragging it back down to Wolfsden." Gerald's smooth and deep tenor continued their tall tale while Lord Digarius smirked.

Sister Ora playfully rolled her eyes, then murmured to the quiet Prince Percy beside her, "It gets bigger each time they tell this story."

Gerald opened his mouth to make an inappropriate comment, already making Sister Ora stifle her laughter before he said anything.

"Gerald, *no.*" she laughed, dipping her head down and shaking it. Her long black braid moved along her chest and brushed against the dark jeweled emerald fabric of her dress.

Prince Percy's soft brown eyes fell onto her bright smile, watching her cheeks dimple as she soaked in the simple joy. The prince did not see the shared glare between Lord Digarius and Gerald.

Lord Digarius cleared his throat, his arms crossed over his chest and the sleeves of his ivory shirt stressing as he flexed his arms. Gerald kept his sleeveless arms behind his back, but lifted his sharp chin and straightened his posture as Prince Percy's eyes met their displeasure.

"Your Highness," Lord Digarius began, "if I remember properly from our times meeting one another in court, you have not been one to hunt or fight, yes?"

Prince Percy's relaxed and less stoic demeanor stiffened, preparing to go on the defense against the striking comment from the young heir. The second prince swallowed and painted on his posh court face. "That is correct,

Lord Digarius. I spent most of my studies in the Grand Hall of Archives in The Keep, even traveling to my mother's home in Thelimor for some time to indulge in their ancient library. War and weapons have only been of interest to me on paper, not in life."

"Here, here." Sister Ora replied, a smile threatened to come alive at the corner of her mouth as she looked at the prince. As their matching brown-hazel eyes locked, she shook her head. "Do not mind these two, Your Highness. Lord Digarius enjoys being obnoxious when he is bored, and Gerald has been the same since we met several epochs ago upon my arrival to The Landing."

"Well, you used to like me being this way." Gerald gave another mischievous grin; his smile and warming cheeks making his handsome face even more striking.

"You two...?" Prince Percy shifted his eyes between the two.

"Many lifetimes ago. We quickly learned that we were better off continuing our friendship." Sister Ora shrugged. "It did take a few—"

"— many." Gerald corrected, then continued and looked down at the prince. "It took many *many* tries before the friendship *without* its benefits stuck."

"*Oh.*" Prince Percy uncomfortably replied.

Sister Ora pinched her brow. "I do not believe this conversation appropriate given our audience, Gerald."

"Ah, apologies, prince." Gerald's face flatlined and his shoulders heaved up and down as he loosened his breath, the quiver of arrow on his back rising and falling with his upper body.

Lord Digarius glared between he prince and Sister Ora, then elbowed Gerald's ribs. "Gerald, I believe Emaline was calling for us over there." He dipped his chin and pointed his head to where Emaline stood in line with other Ayeshire guards, her helmet turned in their direction, watching the awkward and ill-paced discussion taking place.

Lord Digarius dismissed himself politely and left the group, without hesitation- but with annoyance- Gerald followed dutifully behind, leaving Prince Percy and Sister Ora alone.

"I apologize for them, Your Highness." she said, her chin tucked into her neck as she spoke to him.

Prince Percy shrugged. "There is no apology needed. It is nice seeing friends caring not for title and treating one another with such likeness." He looked away to the king and Lord Montarian sat stewing over their game. "It is not common, though."

Sister Ora followed his gaze. "It is more common than you think. Perhaps not friendships between ones titled like Lord Digarius and *common* —" her tone crinkled at the word used to reference people at Gerald's social status. "— men like Gerald, but outside of castles, many of us in different Divine Houses develop loving relationships. I met Gerald in a tavern when I came to town, and Emaline the same."

Prince Percy shifted. "Your guard? She and you are friends?"

Sister Ora smiled until her eyes crinkled as she watched her friends carry on their own conversation, not-so-subtly attempting to watch she and the prince from the corner of their vision. "The best of it. She was a soldier, knowing Gerald through their military training that overlapped. He introduced us, we became two sides of one coin, and when I became titled as High Scholar and a guard was to be assigned to my protection, she gained permission to turn from soldier to guardian and leave active duty. And now we are inseparable, even if we wished to be, we could not."

A pain stung at her gut and jerked her chest inward. She shot her head to Prince Percy. "She and I will not be separated, correct?" Her fingers dug at her nails and her eyes began to sheen with wetness. "Please tell me I do not have to lose her as well."

Prince Percy set the very tips of his fingers on her fidgeting hands, then quickly twitched them back as their skin touched. "Do not fret, no, I do not see why that would have to occur."

"Thank you, Your Highness. I apologize." She straightened her body and corrected the emotions on her face. and removed any inflection and tone from her words. "It was not my place to ask such a thing."

The prince's soft and round face broke into a comforting smile. "You do not have to apologize in every conversation we have. You are allowed to ask me things, to need things. I know we have just met, and these circumstances are not... *ideal* especially with the rush of all of our leave taking place in a few days but we have similar interests from what I have been told, and we have time before we must —"

The nervously stammering prince made the mistake of meeting her eyes just as the sun hit her pupils and gave them a golden glow as she looked up at him.

"Before we must— " he stuttered and paused, taking a nervous breath. "— be married. What I mean to say is that perhaps we could try being friends."

Sister Ora's face warmed with a softness and her full cheeks grew as she felt a kind smile grow. "Yes, perhaps we could."

***

Queen Onetta held the pages of her book open with the tips of her fingers. Her left hand rested in her lap under the small round table she sat at in the gardens. Nearby, Princess Arminda entertained Princess Kalia with the help of their aids. Childish giggling and light-hearted laughter came from where the princesses played- two simple sisters forgoing propriety for a moment.

Queen Onetta let out an annoyed sigh as the giggling and play continued. She lifted her chin to watch them from across the garden. Princess Kalia twirled in front of a bed of purple flowers, the ends of her deep red and orange trimmed dress in her hands as she spun.

She watched for a moment, considering smiling at her youngest daughter's happiness, but darkness fell over her eyes, and she rescinded the thought. Her eyes flicked to the walkway as a royal aid approached with a tray of letters for Her Highness. He did not speak, only requested permission to approach with a simple bow, stepped forward and set the tray on her table, then retreated, bowing again before parting.

She gingerly closed her book, properly fixing it square in place on the neatly organized and nearly bare table. The delivered parchments had already been unwound from their rolls or removed from their envelopes for her, as they were always expected to be, unless sealed with confidentiality wax seals her aids were not allowed to tear.

The first letter was easily skimmable; mere details from her staff at The King's Keep confirming information of the engagement festival being prepared in Isilria for Prince Percy and his betrothed- a proper royal festival would greet them when they came ashore, both for celebration of the holy union they had planned and for public relations the queen knew needed improved.

Being the sole heir to the stewardship over the oldest city in the world had come with extensive knowledge and experience on how one was to always appear to others and a multitude of ways to rectify the most atrocious public sentiment. While her status as Queen of the Six Kingdoms overrode her inheritance over Thelimor, her lineage and lessons were imprinted onto her very bones, so deeply that tomb raiders would find her father's words carved into her remains generations after her body decayed.

She turned the letter face down beside the unread pile on the tray and picked up the next parchment; this one worn with more travel and time, sea salt and sun aging.

"Ah." She let out a small noise as she read the familiar scrawlings of her father's Scholar. This letter had made quite a journey by bird, boat, and messenger to get to her from the grand island providence of Thelimor that he still held his clawed grip over.

She ignored the anger growling in her throat as she read yet another letter from Lord Orilion Kavistia, more unsolicited advice on how she and her husband should handle what was occurring and the gossip his ears around the kingdom brough to him. His words had always been full of little advice but always brimmed with belittling demands. Her title of Queen of the Six Kingdoms could not stop the father she was named alike from attempting to keep his control and dominance over her, despite his title as lord of the oldest city in the world being lower in status than her current crown.

She folded the paper in half and tore it before letting it join the other.

The final letter was addressed to both the king and queen from Prince Elion, written in his own handwriting and not that of a Scholar. He touted on about the comings and goings of the city under his first watch standing in for the king, his curiosities of how their trip was progressing, and his concerns over the political cleanup he was undertaking with the most recent shocking death that occurred the night before the Spring Equalius.

"I told him we should not have left so soon after." She grumbled under her breath about her husband's decision. "I warned him of how it may appear to leave the city so quickly."

Father Figgins appeared without a trace of noise and sat across from the queen. Her eyes only dancing up from the letter at seeing the movement in front of her.

"Hello, Father." She said.

"Your Highness." He replied, his voice smooth and slithering.

"What brings you and your shadow to my afternoon tea?" Queen Onetta absent-mindedly replied, not bothering to look to the spot she knew Sir Marion would be standing.

Father Figgins grey haired head twisted to look behind him at the man standing nearby, fully adorned in King's Guard gilded and silver armor with only his helmet missing from his person.

Sir Marion, the head of the King's Guard and Master of Armor, hailed from the Isles of Aishar as Queen Onetta had. A valiant and feared gladiator, Sir Marion, like true Aisharian fighters, did not enjoy weighing his body down in plates of metal, preferring the traditional Aisharian custom of only small pauldrons and essential coverings when in battle. It was only his status as the Master of Armor that prevented Sir Marion from disposing of his armor when on duty.

Father Figgins turned back from Sir Marion and faced the queen, now looking up at him. "We are awaiting His Majesty. The hunting party should be back shortly, and the present members of his Council have some manners we need to discuss."

"Oh?" She picked up her now cold tea and pretended to re-read the parchment in front of her. "Anything of importance?"

"It will be at His Majesty's discretion if I can inform you of that."

His crooked long fingers reached for the small plate of bread and accompaniments centered on the table, picked over throughout the afternoon by the queen. Father Figgins snatched up a piece of cut bread, coating it in butter with the small silver knife beside the slab of light yellow. He contemplated what accompaniments he would stack atop the bite as he covered the slice with the spread.

Queen Onetta set the letter and her teacup down, crossing her fingers together on the table in front of her. Her light movement and demanding presence caught Father Figgins' eyes for a moment as she began speaking.

"Father Figgins, do you ever tire of being second best?" she asked.

He did not stop putting together his snack, nor did he move his attention from the tray of cured meats and fruit in front of him.

"Do you?" he replied.

CHAPTER 5

The meadow foxtail and rye grasses of the field whispered and danced in the light breeze that wafted across the knoll. Tall trees bordered much of the open field; their bright green leaves and twittering feathered occupants signaling to the citizens and animals of Ayeshire that a lush spring was already underway.

Sister Ora felt her chest slowly fill with the fresh air of the field as she straightened her back and stared down the target twenty paces in front of her. Her right hand released its grip on the bow string and the air ripped beside her face as the arrow flew.

"As usual, a perfect shot, Ora." Gerald's voice congratulated from just a few steps away. "It's like you were destined for the bow, not me."

Sister Ora scoffed, "We all know that Destiny has always had different plans for me." With her last words, her round dark eyes sank down to the bow in her brown and calloused hand that she had tightly wrapped around the grip; the grip that was specifically carved for Gerald's larger hands and had taken her many training sessions to adjust to holding.

No matter how perfectly she shot or how well she adjusted to the bow, it still felt wrong in her hands; hands that were divinely destined to hold books and parchment- and now a prince's hand.

After returning from the hunt that she was mandated to attend to accompany her future husband, Sister Ora had made herself as busy as possible in her last knot of time in Middleton Landing. She had spent as many days as possible with her found family and even more time catastrophizing the chosen future ahead of her.

There would be no more stolen afternoons with friends secretly doing as they wished and learning from one another what skills and knowledge they were not meant to know and finding out who they each truly were and forgoing the facsimiles they wore in front of others.

Another light breeze whistled across the grassy field and blew her long black hair into her face, blurring her vision and interrupting her reminiscing of memories she clung to.

"Better than a life spent in the water when you get seasick every time you step on a boat." Sedrick's rich bellowing voice cut the silence and laughter trickled through the group in various snickers. "Destiny may be a bitch, but at least she has a sense of humor."

Sister Ora smiled impishly at the jest, her smile filling out her prominent cheekbones and creased her button nose as she chuckled and fiddled with the bow she still held.

Gerald smirked- his soft smile known to make many men and women swoon- as he strode across the field to sit down with Sedrick and Ephraim. Both friends were keeping themselves busy on the sidelines of the clearing, Sedrick with his nose stuck in a book and Ephraim with a pile of dark blue cloth in their lap and a needle in their hand.

The shade underneath the tree offered reprieve to Gerald's sun-kissed and freckled tone and his blonde hair shuffled around his shoulders as it caught the breeze that rustled around the group's favored picnic spot. He settled himself against the same tree trunk as Ephraim, close enough to casually peer over their shoulder at what they were sewing, and when he leaned in to look closer, almost close enough to allow the scruff on both their faces to brush.

"And what's today's project, Leaf?" Gerald asked as he settled in next to Ephraim, always choosing the intimacy of the nickname he gave Ephraim when they first became friends long ago.

Ephraim held their project up from their lap, keeping their forest green eyes fixed on the stitching they were intently finishing. "I'm fixing this cloak for Ora —" their eyes shot a joking glare in her direction as she joined the group. "— for the hundredth time."

Sister Ora fixed herself down in front of them and snatched up one of the empty steins sitting on the blanket they had covered with food and drink.

"Oh, come on, Leaf, I know how much you love stitching, so really, me burning my cloak was an act of love." She smiled over the stein as she raised it to her mouth to take a sip, leaning to her side to relax.

"Leaf, Gerald, and I are going to miss your sense of humor while you're off gallivanting around Isilria and The King's Keep, Ora." Sedrick said, closing his book with a snap. "Whatever shall we do without your wit and charm?" His joking tone was emphasized by the feigned high-class accent he spoke in that differed from his own native tone, as if he were acting out a character from one of the books he kept his nose stuck in every time others were not looking.

"Oh," Ora replied, "I think you three will be able to survive just fine, but just barely, I am sure. And if not, you can simply take a job on a trading boat and come visit me between jobs, Sedrick."

Sedrick's face lost all its warmth and paled at the mere thought of being back on the water. He shook his head. "I am perfectly content with keeping my land legs. There is plenty of work here on the docks for me."

"Plenty of low paying grunt work, Sedrick. You cannot seriously still be content living with so many others in a house too small?" she pointed at him. "Taking a sailing post on a trading boat or two would finally get you out of that pig barn you call a boarding house."

Sedrick took a large drink from his cup and ran his fingers through his tightly cut and thick hair as he set the stein down. "I am as content as I am able to be."

"Ora have you decided which of us will be the one taking over your position as the worrying mother of our group?" Ephraim mocked; their jaw stubbled with dark hair creased into a teasing smile as they broke their concentration on their project.

Everyone choked on a laugh before, one by one, their stifling attempts turned into fits of laughter. It was a sorrow filled day, and as the group had become accustomed to as they all grew in closeness, bantering and laughing were the best types of medicine for the friends in saddening times.

"Now what is this all about?" a stern voice from the other side of the clearing asked.

At the sound of Emaline's voice and the appearance of her figure, Sedrick's eyes grew twice their usual size and his tough exterior somehow managed to tense and soften at the same time.

Emaline held her helmet at her side, tucked under her arm dangling above her sword that moved against the motion of her body as she walked towards the group. Her long thick locks were pulled back in a low gathering, falling down her armored back with a stray few locks falling over her pauldrons. She smiled brightly as she approached, her smile competing for brightness against the sheen of her armor in the sun.

Gerald quickly chimed, "Just getting in our last few bouts on one another."

Emaline sat next to Sister Ora, stealing some food from her hand as she settled. "Well," she stopped chewing to say, "We best finish up. Everyone is gathering at the port to prepare for the departure. I was caught up in too many goodbyes with the rest of the Armor-born this morning when I was clearing out my space in the barracks. I am sorry I was unable to be here to see you all as well."

"You will see us again, both of you will see us again." Sedrick said, his eyes not leaving Emaline's profile. "This is not goodbye; it never can be."

Sister Ora fought against the tears threatening to burst from her eyes as her jaw trembled.

"No." Ephraim sharply said as they watched her face begin to crumple. "I know what pains your face and you are not allowed to take *any* blame for this."

Gerald scoffed. "Leaf is right, blame the fucking— "

"We have many to blame for this." Ephraim coolly cut him off. "But that will do nothing to fix what is happening. This is what has been dealt, and we will find ways to deal with it."

"We will." Sedrick added with a curt nod. "We always do."

"Well," Ephraim said. "Lucky for Ora, I have finished fixing your cloak just in time for your departure."

They tore off the last dangling thread from the fabric and tossed the lump over to her. She unbundled the deep, rich, midnight blue fabric to see a new color of thread on the sleeve edge. Where the candle burn was, there was now a brassy gold crescent moon and star embroidered over the perfectly matched patch of fabric.

"Oh Leaf, it is exquisite!" Sister Ora said as she rubbed her thumb over the embroidered spot "Thank you, and thank you all for gifting me one last afternoon of normalcy."

"You're welcome." Ephraim smiled, leaning forward towards the group's pile of belongings to put away their stitching supplies. "Now, please, do us all a favor, and keep yourself away from any open flames while you're gone. You may be destined for many things, but burning in flames should not be one of them."

***

Sister Ora finished wrapping journals and supplies and stuffed them in her bags. The casual conversations that accompanied her time with Father Robb were replaced with her sorrowful silence. She looked to Father Robb as he hobbled over with another one of her journals, messes of pages stuck out the sides and ink and drink stains decorated the pale cover and pages edges.

"Thank you, Father." She softly said as she took it from him. Her face scrunched as she worked to make space in her overstuffed bag for the book.

Father Robb faked a smile and nodded once, avoiding looking at her and keeping his wet and red-tinted eyes everywhere else. He turned and looked about the room; their shared makeshift office thrown into the center of the

Middleton Landing Archives. Both had preferred to keep themselves close to the scriptures and books when writing and teaching and found no use in locking themselves away from the rest of the Scholars or castle dwellers. Both often enjoyed the friendly interruptions and discussions to their day that being in this room often brought.

He kept his eyes on the telescope sitting on the generously sized balcony a few paces away, the doors to the exterior tucked between shelves of parchment.

"You had left it outside again." he lifted a finger from his cane to point at the balcony and turned back to her, tapping the book she was trying to stuff in the bag. "Best be sure to be careful about that. There were lots of good theories in this one. And best to be careful in general."

"I promise I shall keep myself out of trouble." Sister Ora feigned her own smile

"Good." he raised his hand and set it on her shoulder and took a deep breath. "You will be more exceptional than they could ever imagine. I know this is not what you wished for yourself, but find the light in this, Sister Ora, find a way to still be who you are and do not let this destiny take it from you."

Her throat bobbed as she swallowed. "I will be who I must and who I am told to be, as I always have."

Her eyes fell to her hands as she pulled and plucked at her nail beds and fought back tears. Father Robb moved his hand to rest on hers, squeezing her fingers to stop her picking. "My dear, be who you wish, who *you* need you to be. Perhaps this is your chance to finally find out who that is."

"Perhaps." She whispered, her voice crackling and straining.

He patted her hand and picked up one of her smaller bags, hobbling across the room to the entrance. "Come come, we must not be late, do not want to hold everyone up."

She followed closely as they both walked down the hall to the entrance of the castle. They walked in friendly silence down the long hallway full of squarely cut and even arches and crossed paths. As the entrance to the castle came into light, and the cart awaiting their arrival became more than a blurred shape in the distance, Father Robb huffs and grunts turned into words.

"Sister Ora, I must ask you a favor while you are away."

"Of course." she slowed her pace more to stay in step with him.

He paused as they arrived at the entrance of the castle, just out of earshot of the others on the carriage.

"I know you are naturally curious, and being a once young and curious boy myself, I do appreciate that, and quite enjoy our discourse and your wandering mind." He paused to gently grab her hand and look in her eyes. "But not many others share my tolerance and admiration of that. I've told you tales of my life as a young Scholar apprentice in the king's city, they do not tolerate curiosity as much as other halls of learning and knowledge. And I know you have heard the rumors about the other Scholars being killed. Regardless of if there is truth behind the gossip or not, and after this visit from His Majesty, do not test what may be hidden from us and what game he may truly be playing at."

He stepped closer and leaned in. "Even if there is no truth and no reason to worry, this king has shown what he likes to do to those who displease him, his prisons fill each day and hanging blocks have stayed bloody since the displeasure rose among his people during their harsh winter and many sought vengeance. Please be careful; keep your questions and boundary pushing inquiries to yourself and try not to draw much attention."

She squeezed his hand. "I truly did mean my promise to do my best to stay out of trouble."

A larger look of concern washed over her as she continued in a hushed tone, squeezing his hand too tightly and her breath coming in tiny puffs of too-little air that would not refill her lungs. "Do you think there is truth to the whispers? That the crown is lying to us? That those on the streets are speaking the truth?"

The questions came rushing out of her before Father Robb stopped them with a gentle squeeze of her hand and solemn look. He patted her hand and turned to leave her and make his way onto the carriage. Sister Ora followed suit, she and Emaline helping him into their transport as they set towards the port that lay at the bottom of the winding road.

As Ora helped Father Robb down from the carriage as it came to a half at the port, several servants and dock workers came to aid to unload the last of her luggage and move it onto the boats. Among the workers was Sedrick, who always made light work of the heaviest jobs.

"Hello Sister Ora and Father Robb." Sedrick greeted. "Let me get your bags and we'll get everyone on their way."

"Let someone else get those bags and help this old, hobbled man down to the greeting line, will you son?" Father Robb replied.

They both headed down, chatting away as always- with Father Robb sneaking a small book into Sedrick's pocket, while the others unloaded the luggage and Sister Ora scanned the port bustling with activity.

Father Robb had found his place comfortably by Lord and Lady Montarian and their children, all of whom expertly smiled and conversed with the royal family gathered with them. Wandering eyes on both sides of their conversations found their way to her. Looks of sadness and frustration came from the noble Ayeshire family she had made her own, curious, and suspicious glances came from Her Majesty and various eyes from the royal Scott family. Prince Percy's eyes switched between looks of worry and softened staring.

"Your future husband is kind of cute." Emaline jested quietly as she stepped beside Sister Ora; Gerald and Ephraim in tow. "Very much your type."

Sister Ora scoffed. "And what type is that exactly?"

Emaline smirked. "Slightly scared of you."

Both women snorted out a small laughter and averted their gaze away from the watching royal family.

"Emaline, I do not believe I would be able to survive this drastic change without you." she finally turned away from the gathered masses and faced her friend, craning her neck up to meet Emaline's eyes. "I regret my anger all those moons ago when you swore your sword to my protection when I gained my title. I thought you so ridiculous for giving up what you did for a life spent following me around, but now, now I am so thankful for that choice."

Emaline smiled. "As I told you when I left the battles for your guardship, I did not leave anything behind that I did not wish to rid myself of. And besides," she shrugged. "we already had what bit of friendship we could with one another, my oath gave me a duty-bound reason to continue that."

Gerald and Ephraim shared an overly dramatic look with one another before Gerald spoke up. "Are we not the ones you are saying goodbye to? Save some dramatic declarations for those of us who you two are leaving behind."

The group of friends laughed as Ephraim and Gerald demanded embraces from both.

"Invite us to the wedding, yes?" Ephraim asked Ora as they separated. "We promise to only slightly embarrass you in front of your new family."

Ephraim painted a jovial smile on their face, noting how sorrowful hers still was. They brought their hands to cup her cheeks and pushed her cheeks up into a smile. Sister Ora laughed and shoved their hands away. "Yes, of course I will invite you all. I would not have it any other way. Seeing you all again would be the only moment of joy that day."

Gerald shot a slitted look at the back of the prince as he stepped forward to Sister Ora. "He is not good enough for you. None of them are."

"Gerald, you did not even believe yourself good enough for me and that is why we are now friends. I do not believe anyone would be good enough in your eyes."

Gerald shook his head and shrugged, pursing his lips out. "Correct."

Sedrick hastily stepped over to the group. "Last of the boats are taking off with cargo and their aids in a minute. His Majesty is looking mighty antsy and —"

Sedrick's words were cut off as Prince Percy walked towards them, armored guards in tow. The group of friends bowed at his presence and quieted their conversation. Prince Percy stepped forward to Sister Ora, giving her a soft smile and held up a silk handkerchief for her glistening eyes. "I apologize for disrupting your goodbyes, but we must be taking off."

She smiled and gently took the kerchief from him. "Of course, yes I understand, Your Highness."

She turned to face her friends one last time, Emaline the only one to step beside her, but Sister Ora could not find any final words within her. Her head fell as she wiped her eyes with the kerchief.

Sedrick stepped forward and pulled her into a hug and whispered his words. "Until another time. Thank you for giving me a piece of your world that I could not have."

She slowly pulled away with a silent nod, then faced the rest. "Until next time."

Sedrick swallowed the lump in his throat as he turned his attention to Emaline and hugged her as well. "Until next time."

Sister Ora moved to stand beside Prince Percy as the group finished their goodbyes with Emaline. She felt his eyes darting over to her and his body shift as if he were to say something, but words never came.

Emaline joined them in their silent walk as they met with the Scott and Montarian family gathered closest to the piers and past the gathered crowds. Almost all of Middleton Landing stood by waving and smiling at the parting parties just as they had been upon the arrival of the royal family. Many waved to Sister Ora and Prince Percy, congratulating them on their engagement, both betrotheds' politely thanking them as they returned their words with flat smiles.

The king's and queen's impatience forced her goodbyes to be swift with the Montarian family, no long speeches were exchanged, only swift sweet words and embraces. Lady Montarian was the final one to wrap Sister Ora in a hug and say goodbye.

As they held on tightly, Lady Belva whispered in her ear. "Keep your eyes and ears open, Sister Ora. Do not let them know that we have ears listening."

Sister Ora pulled back, her brow furrowed at the Lady of Ayeshire's final words to her.

Lord Montarian slid his eyes to meet Sister Ora's, Lord Digarius shifted on the other side of his mother, his glance sharing the same devious sentiment as his mother and father's.

Sister Ora swallowed the gathering bile in her throat.

"Of course." She mumbled as she turned, taking the arm of Prince Percy, and made her way onto the dock lined in the king's sigils; trading in her home's familiar green banners for ones adorned with vicious crowned lions surrounded in red blood.

A pawn once again, by the family that took her in and promised her their care.

Chapter 6

The king's city of Isilria sat carved into the rocky shoreside cliffs that held back the great Ringhar sea. The sand brown tones of the cliffside rock clashed against the rich blue waters that brought in cooling winds and travelers from all corners of the Six Kingdoms of Victarius.

While the stone of the buildings matched so closely to the natural stone paths and walls along the shorelines, they were anything but dull. Even the poorer neighborhoods had the expectation to keep their homes lively and colorful with greenery and bright flowers planted in windows and along their walls. The homes on the main pathways in the capital, as well as those closest to The King's Keep atop the hills and ridges, had more intricately carved doorways and painted tiles decorating their entryways and windows. Deep colored clay roofs drew visual paths along the intertwining uphill streets that guided citizens and visitors along the slopes of the city.

When sailing into the city, viewing scopes would catch small glimmers of the maze of greenery throughout the highest plateaus of the city- small groves and gardens filled with various fruits and large olive trees brought from the fertile Grovelands. In fair weather epochs, the king's vineyards would also be filled to the edges with over producing vines for his family's private reserve.

This city was grand, but it was once made of gold.

The street path from the main harbor to the heart of the city was lively and crowded as wagons of goods were pushed to and from their ships and the stone hill path was filled with the sounds of energetic chatter and music dancing in the wind from the festival awaiting the royal family. An overwhelming scent of street food laid so heavy in the air that the arriving royal family could smell it as their boats made their way into the port.

Sister Ora and Emaline stood beside one another as the rest of their party members gained their land legs. Behind the wall of King's Guard armor and above the stone wall of the ridge, curious citizens looked down and observed the guests of honor. Glances and pointed fingers found their way to Sister Ora's direction, uncertainty washing over the onlookers faces as they discussed the foreign face among the royal family.

"That will take some getting used to." Emaline murmured as she leaned to Sister Ora, her voice muffled with a metallic twinge by her helmet.

She nodded her head quickly and replied quietly. "Yes, yes it will."

Prince Percy stepped up beside the two, taking his place alongside Sister Ora. He loosened a small sigh. "Shall we?"

He crooked his elbow out to Sister Ora for her to take.

She just stared at it.

The prince's eyes fell and his arm fidgeted as he debated on dropping it. "Sorry, you do not have to. It is just- it would be appropriate given what this celebration is about."

He shook his head and dropped his arm and repeated himself in a mumble. "You do not have to."

Sister Ora curled her fingers around his inner bicep and nudged his arm up. "Apologies, Prince Percy, I did not mean offense. I am just attempting to take all this in."

He let a small smile crease the corner of his lip at the feeling of her fingers on his arm. He hid it the best he could as he stepped forward to lead them in their walk behind the rest of the royal family. Emaline fell in step two paces behind them, blending herself in among the red caped King's Guard- her green cloak marking her as different among the wall of armor.

"Much of this festival is for the city, really. We just need to parade through with my family, wave at our people and accept their congratulations, and then make it through the celebratory dinner in The Keep."

Our people.

Prince Percy pretending to not notice the twitch on Sister Ora's face at his phrasing.

The congregation of citizens were already parted out of the streets for the royal family once they made their way onto the main cobblestones. Sister Ora took an unsteady inhalation and exhaled, squared her shoulders, and presented to the city the picturesque of happiness as she smiled and waved at those around them.

Despite his lifetime spent as a prince, Sister Ora felt a nervous tension in Prince Percy's arm as he waved and smiled, himself seeming to awkwardly take in the attention that was disproportionately placed upon the pair. As they continued and more faces blocked the views of the side streets, a mixture of solemn stoicism and outright displeasure came into view. While enough of the gathering was excited and gesturing happily at the royal family, particularly Sister Ora and Prince Percy, there were enough displeased faces for her to notice.

"Why do some gathered appear angry? Were they all forced to be here?" She asked out of the corner of her mouth.

Prince Percy did not reply, he simply swallowed and continued smiling, nodding, and waving.

"I see." She mumbled to herself.

The occasional flower fell at their feet and beside them on the stone. Two white tulips caught her eye as they gently flew in front of her. She gathered her skirt with her free hand, moving the billowing gemstone colored fabric out of the way, as she paused to bend down and pick them up.

Prince Percy's arm gently pulled her up before her knees were fully bent.

"Apologies, we are not supposed to take them." He explained, his tone full of regret.

"*Oh.*"

"Our aids will come gather them for us, finding the best and building arrangements for us to display tonight at dinner."

Sister Ora turned her head back to the flowers and found the face of the girl in the crowd, still holding a small bundle of white tulips. Hope was still on her face even as Sister Ora was being swept away.

Sorry. She mouthed to the now sorrowful girl before her figure was hidden by the armored guards marching behind the pair.

"I can make sure they make an arrangement of white tulips for you if you would like. They often move the arrangements into the betrothed's sleeping chambers after the celebration ends as the first official engagement gifts from the people." His eyes kept flicking over her face as he spoke.

"You do not need to, Your Highness. I do not wish to be a bother."

"*Oh.*" He turned his face back to the crowds.

Ahead of them, the grand castle came into view and the king and queen paused, now greeting- for the first time during the entire affair- members of the crowd. Polite laughter and smiles were exchanged over unheard words.

"Minor lords and ladies. Honorary ones whose titles were bestowed upon them by His Majesty." Prince Percy explained to her.

Sister Ora nodded, "Are we to greet them as well?"

Prince Percy nodded and began to guide them up to the talking royals and nobles. They had not even taken a full step before they were stopped by a rush of noise from the onlookers nearby. Both their heads turned to the right as a small ball rolled towards them, knocking gently against the fabric of Sister Ora's skirts.

She dropped her hand from the prince's arm and picked it up, smiling softly at the painted swirls and filigree that covered the wood and had chipped profusely in several places. Without thinking, she began walking towards the family- both parents quietly scolding the children who had been the culprits of the rogue toy.

Gold and silver armor moved in front of her and blocked her movement.

Sister Ora held out the ball at the unmoved guards, "If you shall not allow me to return this, then may one of you please be so kind to do so?"

They did not reply and stood firmly.

Silver armor framed in a green cape stepped between Sister Ora and the King's Guards.

"I shall do it, m'lady." Emaline stated. Her gloved hand plucked the ball from Sister Ora's hand just before her body shoved itself between the two King's Guards to the family standing nearby.

"Sorry, ma'am. We didn't mean to." One of the children, a young blonde boy, shyly apologized, his eyes at his feet in fear and shame as Emaline approached.

"It is fine, accidents happen." Emaline did her best to show kindness, despite the cadence of her voice being sharp and stern as she addressed the unknown children. She lightly tossed the ball in the air and handed it to him. His hands shook as he reached for it.

"You're not going to punish us, are you? We really didn't mean it, we swear!" The panicked voice of a little girl with brown hair asked from behind him.

The fear-filled children could not have been more than six and were staring up at Emaline in an amount of distress that she had been too familiar with when she was as small as they were. As she panned to the parents and adults gathered beside them, she saw similar looks of worry from their faces that dodged the turning view of her helmet.

Emaline bent down, taking her helmet off and sitting it on her bent knee. She met the eyes of the girl and smiled as she spoke, "No? I would never do that. The oath I swore was one of protection and peace, not of harm."

The girl softened a bit and nervously pulled at the seams of her dress as she spoke. "That's what the other people like you say here, but then they yell and hurt people a lot when they don't listen and walk around all day and night scaring us."

"Well," Emaline gently reached out to hold the girls' fidgeting hand as she spoke, "I promise that if you ever get too scared or need help, you can come find me, and I will lend you aid."

She looked up at her and smiled, wincing her eyes closed as they met the glare of the sun peeking out from over Emaline's shoulder.

"But how do I know if they are you or not? You all look the same in your scary armor?" The blonde boy asked, the ball moving between his hands as he asked.

"Just look for the noble stag and you will know you are safe." Emaline turned, showing the Ayeshire crest on her silver shoulder plate; a stag head centered in a simple shield with delicate greenery around it.

Stags in Ayeshire were considered sacred and holy and were commonly found roaming in villages and near settlements. They did not fear any person, knowing that they would never know an arrow to their flesh or threat to their life- only to be honored. Even the most dishonorable or starved man would not hunt one down and take its life.

The stag not only represented the country of Ayeshire on paintings and maps, but in their oaths as well. They represented the pillars upon which the common and noblemen of Ayeshire stood for: gentleness, integrity, and grace.

Behind Emaline, a throat cleared much too loudly and was followed by the noises of shifting armor. The parents politely pulled the children away as Emaline picked up her helmet and stood, placing it on her head as she met back with the guards she was assigned to stand beside.

"Sir Marion will hear about that." One of the King's Guards gruffed out at her.

"I am shaking in my boots." She snarked.

The other King's Guard, who stood much taller than them both, gently stepped forward to Emaline as they met with their group. "I would advise taking that threat a bit more seriously. Sir Marion is not one to —"

A slight worry coated the velvety baritone of his voice but did nothing to stop Emaline from cutting him off.

"Yes, I have met the Head of the King's Guard. I am not worried."

"You should be." He murmured as they stepped beside their charges, all of which continued in their prior conversations without pause or change as the guards retook their posts.

***

The noises of the festival carried on throughout the night, past the too long dinner that the royal family held in honor of Prince Percy and Sister Ora's engagement. High above the streets that held themselves in celebration, in a turret stretching into the starlit night sky, sat the king and his sons.

"Even the stars do not seem to desire to stay in their place." Prince Percy said, his head turned toward the northern sky as he messed with the viewing scope in his hand.

"Just like our people as of late." Prince Elion, the Heir to the Throne and eldest royal child, added while perched casually in the same window, one leg bent at the knee on the sill and the other dangling inside the stone wall. He stood and wandered over to the table of drink and parchment, fiddling with various scripts that were set out.

The second prince pointed towards a prominent gathering of stars in the north. "The Eye of The World has dimmed since last turn, and less than a fortnight ago several stars rained down into the sea while we were sailing in The Gulf."

"And what is it that the Scholars you entertain had to say of this?" King Ivan asked, moving away from the table of star maps and past Prince Elion.

Prince Percy turned his head to his father; a disheartening look on his face.

King Ivan let out a knowing sigh, his eyes moving to where stars once were and their lights once charted the sky. Where things were once held tightly in place and dared not move from where they belonged.

"All of the warnings are in the stars. It is happening, father, whether we wish it to or not." Prince Percy mumbled.

The king let out a deep breath, his tense shoulders falling with his chest. "Perhaps it is not too late. Perhaps we can stop the fire from being lit before what we fear most comes true."

"And what if it is too late? What if the fire has already begun? The signs show that it has, father." The ever-inquisitive scholarly prince questioned.

His tone careful and curious, ensuring his father knew that he was not questioning his king, but merely speculating possibilities.

Prince Elion ended his silence across the room, stepping towards his brother and father. "It *is* too late. We have all seen what our people dare to do when every night grows darker. It did not stop while you all were across the waters on your trip, and it did not cease tonight when that man gathered a crowd and shouted ill repute against us in the streets while we dined in the confines of our keep. He caused a mob of his enemies and allies to break out in the streets, fighting one another over his words against the crown!" The crown prince shook his head. "Whether any of this displeasure and growing anger have anything to do with the stars and the words of old dead men, it does not matter- our kingdom is no longer what it once was, we must continue to prepare for what is brewing. Find more allies, ensure more strongholds fly our banners, buy more loyalties."

Prince Elion's sharp tone matched the sharpness of his features. His cheekbones were sharp and chiseled as was his jawline and his eyes were as glaring and fierce as his mother's. His thick black corkscrew waves, the same that sat atop Prince Percy's head but were cut to the nape of his neck instead of kept short, were the only soft feature on his well-toned and slim body. The softness of his hair did nothing to take away from his stature.

King Ivan replied with the same sharp tone. "The words of those old dead men *do* matter, Elion. They are precisely why we are here and why we are securing our alliances. Our line has spent generations working to prevent those visions from being seen and coming true. They will not come true because of us."

The two princes looked to one another as their father repeated the same words he had shouted many times over in private company.

"If we burn and fall, then our people will, too." The king continued, "We must do what needs to be done to protect them, as we always have, despite what they believe of us. The Psalms must not see the light."

As the king and his heirs turned from the window to drain their drinks and end their night, a lone star in the southwest fell across the sky, forming a tail akin to a fire on its path.

CHAPTER 7

Sister Ora huffed and threw the blankets off her overheated body as she sat up in bed. She had not slept for a moment. Her mind chose to spend the past two nights sending her into fits of anxiety rather than bouts of rest. It had done the same for the ten nights she had spent on the king's ship, and all the nights since the dinner in Ayeshire where she was proclaimed to be Prince Percy's future bride.

The only sleep she had been able to find as of late had been brought on by heavy pours of wine she infused with the ground valerian root that she had brought with her. Insomnia brought on by chest pains of anxiety was not new for her, she had felt the weight of the thousand-pound stone sitting on her chest at midnight long before her introduction to the royal Scott family, but her panics had been more controllable then.

Normally, she rarely had to dig so consistently into her stash of valerian root that Ephraim had prescribed her long ago, but that prescription was now running low and she tried to use it sparingly even on her worst nights. While the royal family's Healers likely had their own stashes of the sleep-inducing and calming flower, Sister Ora would not ask them for aid.

Surely, they would talk.

Rays of sunlight had eased through the slits in the shutters well over an hour ago, but the silence of the castle had only broken a few breaths prior. She did not wish to be the only one awake and wandering around and had laid awake waiting for the signs of even one person beginning their day before finally starting hers. The lady's maid she was assigned knew she did not favor early mornings; the only request Sister Ora was brave enough to speak on, and would not come for her until later.

She sat up and rubbed the exhaustion out of her eyes, now sunken in shadows on her face. Her palms dug into the skin of her cheeks as if she could force her face into appearing awake and bringing back the brightness that had once been there.

She made her way across the room, opening the shutters on her way to the wash basin waiting for her on the other side of the space. The basin adorned the top of an ornately carved vanity, the soft floral carvings matching the etchings on the bedposts. Soft towels were stacked beside the bowl and a pitcher of water had been left for her last night by her lady's maid. Glass bottles of soaps, oils, and perfumes also decorated the countertop; their scent softening the air around them without even being opened.

Sister Ora poured the water into the basin and used towels and soaps to freshen for the day, choosing a soft petal scented oil to run through her hair that she braided as she looked around the room.

While this room was no chamber fit for a queen, it would still make many back in Middleton Landing, and even on the streets of Isilria, green with envy. The room held not only a large carved bed and a vanity for self-care, but also a large writing desk with an assortment of fine books on its shelves, two chests of drawers for clothing, and a small dining table that could easily fit several guests.

Atop the table sat enough food to feed her for days, so long as she had someone to come let her dress seams out after indulging. An overflowing bowl of fruit was placed next to a large decanter of wine, breads, cured meats wrapped in twine and paper, and delicious pastries under a glass cloche. Snacks laid out for late night enjoyment or aperitifs before mandatory family breakfasts.

She wished she were hungry enough to eat even some of the food that sat on the table, but her stomach still felt like a knot that could not be undone.

Sister Ora finished braiding her hair and threw the braid over her shoulder as she walked over to the chest of drawers to get dressed Atop the drawers laid out a dress picked out from the small collection she had brought over. She held it up in the light and smiled as her eyes fell over the stitching and dyed fabric of the dress Ephraim had helped her reimagine a few seasons ago.

The once faded grey gown had been dyed a rich shade of azure blue. The backside, where worn out buttons once were, was now an open back with a semi-sheer cape that capped her shoulders. Sister Ora loved the new dress as it was, but her dear friend insisted on adding even more of their personal touch and embroidered the neckline with the same filigree that the Ayeshire crest was adorned with. This dress, Ephraim insisted while helping her pack, would help her blend in, but still stick out, with the people of Isilria and the castle's inhabitants.

After dressing, she pinned her Scholar insignia on her chest, adjusted her braid, and prepared to leave the overly grandiose chamber behind. Despite her distaste for early mornings and her grumpy nature in the first moments of the day, she was to meet Father Figgins in The Grand Hall of Archives this morning for a proper tour.

She pulled open her chamber door and was greeted by an unmasked Emaline leaning against the opposing wall; one foot propped against the stone behind her.

"Morning sunshine." Emaline smirked and shoved herself off the wall, grabbing her helmet off the ground in one smooth movement.

Sister Ora grunted, and her stomach loudly grumbled.

Emaline's eyes slitted and she shoved a pointed gloved hand in the air, pointing at the door behind Sister Ora.

"*Nope.* You are too much of a grouch in the morning as is. The royal family is not breaking their fast together this morn, go back inside and eat something."

"I am not hungry." She snarked back.

Emaline set her gloves hands on Sister Ora's shoulder and spun her around. "You have picked at your plates the past three days that we have been here, even more so than you did while sailing, and you are not sleeping. You do not get to fall apart completely."

Sister Ora reluctantly obeyed and marched back into her chambers. She swiped a sweet pastry off the table and turned, then turned back and grabbed another. She held the second pastry out for Emaline as she met her at the door again.

The two walked in casual silence as they enjoyed the quick breakfast.

Emaline nodded her head as she bit into the flaky fruit pastry Sister Ora gave her. "This is so much better than the shit they feed me."

"How are you holding up?" Sister Ora quietly asked as they walked by aids and workers in the hall.

Emaline took another bite and shrugged. "Fine."

"How are you getting along with the other guards? The ones you house with now?"

"Fine."

Sister Ora pressed on, now smiling out of the corner of her mouth as she began teasing. "Make any new friends?"

"No." Emaline paused. "I don't like people."

"You like me. And Leaf, and Gerald, and Sedrick."

Emaline grimaced, her distraction of a snack now gone and her fingers rubbing together with a coin between them, "Gerald and I got on because he would not allow me to *not* be his friend. And then he introduced me to you all. And now here we are." Her replies were short and quipped, cutting each sentence off with sharp punctuation and pause.

Sister Ora stopped walking and turned to face Emaline who was still fidgeting with the coin in her hand and avoiding looking at her. "Emaline. How are you *really* doing?"

She shifted back and forth, watching the stone on the wall behind Sister Ora. She huffed. "I will be fine. I do not- I do not like change. This is a lot at one time. There are new rules, routines, new... social expectations. I do not know how to talk to them."

"Them?"

Emaline jerked her shoulders in a shrug, "The other guards. I cannot read them very well. So I cannot find a way to talk to them that is alright with them."

She let out another huff. "It took a long time for me to be okay with our group of friends."

"I know." Sister Ora softly replied,

Emaline shook her head quickly and shifted to place the odd coin she was rubbing back in the pouch on her side. "We do not need to talk about my issues. You are the one —"

Sister Ora threw her head back and groaned before straightening herself and walking aimlessly towards the wall of open windows behind Emaline.

The endlessly high stone walls were draped with fabric on the edges of the equally high windows, the fabrics alternating between displaying the insignias of each of the Divine Houses and the regal crest of the royal family. Where one would typically have simple torch sconces to light the way, vases of flowers, items of gold, and ornate sconces lined the walls and tables.

She paused to look out the large open windows down onto the lower parts of The King's Keep, out past the capital city outside its walls and beyond onto the ocean bays at the bottom of the rolling hills.

For a moment, standing among such grandiose possessions and looking down on the people of the kingdom, she understood why those who lived so high on this hill might feel above them all.

Emaline slowly stepped up beside her.

"We were just figuring out who we were, Emaline." Sister Ora said.

Emaline pursed her lips and nodded, joining her in looking down at the landscaping laid out before them, "We were."

Emaline shifted uncomfortably again, a breath escaped her as she began to speak, but she cut herself off before she said a word.

"Say it." Sister Ora said, not in a demanding tone, but encouraging Emaline to speak openly.

"We are not those little girls anymore."

Sister Ora turned, a puzzled look on her scrunched face.

Emaline continued, her voice matter of fact and flat "You afraid that even the smallest mistake would make you a failure to everyone. And me, already having lost everyone, and too scared to do it again. We are not those little girls anymore."

Sister Ora let the words hang in the air a moment before she pushed off the balcony edge and turned to continue their walk.

"But aren't we?"

***

The Hall of Archives was just as grandiose as the rest of the castle; expansive shelves overflowing with books and rolled parchments were spread across multiple floors. Plush furniture and thick dark wood worktables were scattered along all four floors, arranged into a variety of seating and studying areas. The magnificence was brought together by twisting stone staircases that begged visitors to come inside and get lost amongst the words and worlds on the pages the room was filled with.

Emaline and Sister Ora stood in awe at the double doored entrance. Sister Ora's mouth was agape as she slowly stepped inside and looked about.

"No wonder you needed a tour." Emaline said.

Sister Ora did not notice the robed Scholars squeezing inside past them, she was too engrossed in staring up at the large carved sandstone pillars and out across the floor she stood on, taking in the full shelves that were so tall that heavy wooden ladders were needed to access books on the highest shelves.

"Yeah," she mumbled as she finally closed her gaping mouth and began walking around the entry room, "it is a wonderful place."

Keepers of the Archives walked the hall in front of them, their eyes not meeting the two women's but their necks bowing politely at their presence. The Keepers busied themselves with placing books back on shelves and pulling new from their places, parchment lists in their hands being referenced as they did. Others spent their time lighting candles that had burnt out and doing their best to control the dust and dirt that danced in the rays of sun breaking through the high arching windows.

"Sister Ora! Welcome to The Grand Hall of Archives!" Father Figgins voice announced his presence as he appeared behind them. He clapped his hands together as made his way into the hall, demanding their immediate attention.

As the women turned to meet his greeting, Sister Ora noted the straightened spines of the nearby Scholars and Keepers upon his entry and the sounds of quick shuffling feet.

"Father Figgins." Sister Ora greeted, bowing her head as she addressed him. Her eyes paused on the unmasked King's Guard behind him.

"Sir Marion." She timidly added.

He held his stare behind her where Emaline stood. The sound of shifting armor plates told her that Emaline had moved from her close proximity behind her.

"I am glad you found your way here with ease this morning." Father Figgins began the tour of the library with the nod of his head as he led them forward.

He guided them around the perimeter of the open space encircled with the massive shelves, allowing Sister Ora to get a closer look at the room. "I thought it most appropriate to guide you through the hall myself after you settled into your new home."

"Will I be working here?" she casually inquired, still taking in the space. Her eyes caught on an art installation hanging above them; rods and baubles descending at various heights from the ceiling and depicting constellations that she recognized instantly.

Father Figgins cocked his head. "Working?"

She continued to look at the art piece, running down the list of constellations in her mind as she found each one, "Yes? As a Scholar? Or will I be elsewhere?"

Father Figgins let out an unnatural laugh. "Oh no, Sister Ora. You are to be the wife of a prince. You do not have a need for *work*. This is-" he waved a hand in the air, "simply a place you may come to be a lady of leisure in."

She shot a look at him, shock covered her face, the emotion surrounded by glimmers of oncoming sadness.

"Oh. But can I? Work here?" Her fingertips dug under her nails as she spoke, "Is there anything I can work on or help with?"

Father Figgins shrugged and turned his back as he kept walking. "I suppose if you wish to continue your studies you could- with proper approval by me of course. Perhaps you could hold a conference with the other Scholars here and discuss the winter star fall you wrote about. They might find what you had to say interesting and could apply your theory to their own work and research. That theory- of the star fall not being a holy occurrence but that of a natural phenomenon- did a lot more for you than you know, Sister."

Sister Ora kept up her pace beside him, hearing every few words as he drawled on.

Father Figgins extended his arm to point at the gathering of shelves they had approached, "This is the modern history section. Here you—"

"What do you mean?" she accidentally cut him off as his prior words caught up to her. "About my theory doing more for me than I know?"

He shrugged, "It is what caught my eye. After Father Robb sent it to me, I wrote him to send me copies of more of your work, of which he obliged. Prince Percy, you know how he is with his own obsessive intrigue on those topics, read them as well and found his own fascinations with your ideas. The match made sense before I even proposed it to His Majesty."

"You-" she swallowed the lump in her throat and let out a harsh breath as she tore the edge of her fingernail off, "You were the one who proposed my betrothal to Prince Percy? It was your idea?"

He shrugged again, as if everything he had said was of little importance and common knowledge that she already should have pieced together, "As I mentioned, the match made sense. And, we needed to ensure the alliance with your home country, Sister Ora. Decisions such as this are how alliances are formed or continued through uncertain times. It was a favorable proposal for all of us. Now, as I was saying, this is our modern history section. Much of the information here you may already know, although, we do have a much more diverse offering of volumes of legends as well that I doubt you have seen in your little collection back at Middleton Landing."

His voice trailed off as he moved down the aisle while Sister Ora stood still at the end of it. She watched his small frame grow tinier as he kept walking and talking, it taking a moment for her mind to remember the decorum that was required of her. She quietly hurried her steps, running quietly to meet him at the end of the aisle before he turned the corner.

They continued through the main floor, Father Figgins dumping more information onto her lap about the library's contents with continual reminders that, should she forget any of it or need aid, he had ordered all his Scholars and Keepers working in the Hall of Archives to assist her.

They made their way up one of the winding stone staircases, their armor-clad companions making light work of the steep ascent of the stone and keeping easy pace with the pair. The second floor, one she had only gotten glimpses of as she walked the main floor, held the same style of shelves and seating areas as the first, as well as several busts of figures.

"Ah, First King Lucarius." Father Figgins said as he stepped beside her standing in front of a scowling bust of a long-haired and long dead king.

Lucarius Rominia was crowned king in 407 AC after the conclusion of the Great Civil War that ripped apart the continent with bloodshed, famine, and plague. The continent was reborn into the Six Kingdoms and borderlines redrawn after the war ended. He named himself, and ensured historical records named him, The First King to delegitimize those that had ruled before him.

Her eye and jaw twitched despite herself.

"You may speak freely if you need to... You can trust me." He replied to the sharp change on her face. His voice softened as he offered his comfort.

Against the wishes of the constant voices in her head, perhaps due to her exhaustion or her unbalanced emotional state, she let her mask fall for a moment. "Do you not think it inappropriate to have his bust here, overlooking a space that he would have gladly set aflame if he felt like it?"

When the First King ascended the throne, a madness more violent than the cruelty he was historically known for overcame him. First King Lucarius sent his loyal soldiers across the continent to burn libraries as well as destroy all effigies and temples to the Old Gods. The only libraires to be spared were the Grand Hall of Archives in his castle and the libraries of Thelimor, which were too far off the mainland for the First King to reach.

Father Figgins jaw tightened. "The First King did what was required of him to ensure his true reign after the Great Civil War. Burning the libraries of his enemies and the temples of the false gods was instrumental to his righting of the course of history."

The continent never fully recovered from the loss. Today's scholars and record keepers worked tirelessly to make up for the intellectual advancements and knowledge lost in the destruction. Infrastructure, scientific, and other forms of progress had come to a screeching halt once the flames settled and were reborn from the ashes that killed them.

She gestured around at the greatness of the space they were in. "Yes, but so much history, so much knowledge was lost in what he did and now it only exists here."

"Precisely."

A satisfied glimmer shone in Father Figgins eye that sent an ice-cold shiver slithering down her spine.

Chapter 8

"I have spent more of my time comforting our people than I have been advising you as your Hand." Lord Robert Orville paused and crossed his hands on top of the table. "Your Majesty, I must remind you *again* that the last time the crown was called into question and discussed this much by its people, the continent turned to ash for fifteen epochs."

"You are not some counselor to the people, Lord Orville, you are the Hand of the King." Father Figgins snipped from across the table, his voice tired and bored. "Your job is not to provide comfort to them like you are their mother; your job is to help this council keep them under control and keep this government efficacious. We must focus on putting an end to the words being spoken of His Majesty and the church and reassert our control."

"Yes because our tactics to reassert our control through blood and beatings has been going quite well, Father." Lord Orville snarked back. "While I know your dog enjoys using the King's Guards to do so, forcing our people to live in fear is not the way to lead. We can turn the tide of public opinion by showing them that they are safe and protected under the crown and are not under a constant state of threat. Before you joined this council His Majesty and the throne were successful in peaceful ruling."

In the background, the early morning sounds of the city waking up for the day carried through the large open windows alongside beams of sunlight casting harsh shadows and bringing in bright light. Voices of citizens and servants crept into the room with the breeze and various noises of another busy day in the capital became background music to the contemplating council.

Even so high up in their turret, surrounded by decorative symbols of their prestige and elegance, these noble men could not completely escape their people.

Lord Orville ignored the searing glare from Sir Marion, the aforementioned dog that he had brought into the conversation, and turned to the king. "Living in fear of harm and abuse is not a way to live."

King Ivan ran his right hand over the top of his left, his fingers running along the small bones that had never healed properly after they were broken in his boyhood.

The Hand of the King had been a long-time friend of the royal family and had watched King Ivan grow from a boy to a man. After years of friendship with the royal family, Lord Robert Orville served King Ivan's father during the latter half of the late-king's reign. The late King Andrius' ruling had ended in more peace than it had begun with thanks to the extensive efforts of Lord Orville, and King Ivan, then just a prince, had less hidden bruises thanks to his aid as well.

The king leaned back and rested his elbows on the arms of his chair. His eyes scanned his Council. "Well, any counters?"

Prince Elion moved from his relaxed position seated beside his father. He uncrossed his legs and sat up straight, pushing his shoulder length, shaggy black hair out of his face as he moved. "An integral part of keeping this monarchy running is to assure the people that we *are* protecting them. As Lord Orville spoke of, our people have a history of rebelling when they feel they have been wronged or left helpless by the throne. We spoke extensively of this while you were away during our Council meetings."

The prince's eyes flicked over to his father, waiting for approval before taking up more time. "The aids that arranged the engagement festival for Prince Percy and his betrothed spent much of their time among the people, focusing their words on how the festival would bring them more prosperity, a small, but effective boost to their pocketbooks. *But* it was a short-lived distraction from the larger issues at hand."

King Ivan took a deep breath and nodded. "And what would you propose we do? If you were king and these were your issues to handle, how would you deal with them?"

"We must stop wasting our efforts on short term corrections for long term obstacles. Many of the recent words spoken stated that the crown was not fulfilling its duty of feeding and protecting the people. Let them speak ill of us if they choose, let us focus on our duty of proving their words wrong."

"And how will we do that? You know of the merchant ship that sunk that was full of food and goods we had tried to bring to feed them. That plan failed." King Ivan retorted in a factual tone, countering the beginning of his son's proposal.

Prince Elion had grown used to his father's testing inquiries inside and outside of Council meetings. Since his first lessons as a boy, he was consistently tested. Each answer he gave had been heavily scrutinized and ripped apart by his father or his teachers and arguments for arguments sake were normal among the king and the heir. Each mistake and incorrect idea seemed to be catalogued in the king's mind, brought out later to remind Prince Elion of how he could have failed as a king if solutions he had proposed were enacted.

"Do not send for another ship, feed them from our own hands. Show our people that we are willing to make a sacrifice just as they are. Our private reserves and the crops within our private gardens grow plentiful as the season continues, send the food they birth out to the people, use the church to distribute the meals and," Prince Elion turned to the always quiet and obedient Lord Barker, the Master of Currency. "find if there is any coin we could pull to buy goods from our own reapers to distribute or to buy supplies for them to increase harvest this season."

Prince Elion turned to his father, squaring his shoulders for an argument, already racking his mind for what to counter with.

The king pushed his lips into a thin straight line, drumming his fingers on the arm of his chair. "Any counters to that?"

Sir Marion, the head of the King's Guard and Master of Armor, finally brought himself into the conversation; his posture casual and lax with an ankle resting on his opposite knee and his body leaning against the back of his chair. Each word he spoke was carefully chosen and spoken in his deep tenor and silky accent. "Respectfully, Your Majesty, do you not worry that a softer hand may make the crown appear weak? In Aishar we —"

King Ivan held up a hand. "Respectfully Sir Marion, we are not in Aishar. And thankfully so."

Sir Marion tightened his jaw into a firm line, hardening the chiseled cut of his face.

"Yes, Your Majesty, but, as I was saying, in Aishar we did not stop the civil war with free meals, Lord Priscius had to use his armies and allies to win the war."

"Tyriann the Tyrant's own twin conspired behind his back and gained allies in rooms he sat in while the lord's back was turned. That civil war was brought on by two men believing their claim to the lordship was truer than the other and who argued their entire lives over whose head crowned from their mother's legs first. This is a different circumstance, Sir Marion." Lord Orville politely added. "There is no war here to fight yet. That is what we are trying to prevent."

"My son and Hand are correct. We have tried many tactics with minimal success. Perhaps it is time we retract our iron fist and reach out a kind hand. *For now.*" The king tilted his head to the side, "And if that proves fruitless, then we will do more of what we must. I will not go lightly into another Age of Darkness like that which King Jacquard changed our lands with after he stole his sister's throne."

The king jabbed his finger into the tabletop, moving his glare around the table. His tone intense as he convinced the room, and himself, of his words. "While I owe King Jacquard for putting our line on the throne, I will not easily become the power thirsty and cruel man that he was. Nor will I become like my father."

***

Lord Robert Orville poured two cups of black herbal tea. Ignoring the sweeteners and additives laid out on the buffet, he took the two cups with him as he sat down with King Ivan. He politely shooed away the young squire offering their aid, prompting the squire to stand quietly beside the door waiting another order.

"Thank you, Robert." The king said, still reading the parchment scroll in front of him as his Hand sat down across from him and placed their cups in front of them.

Lord Orville drummed his fingers on his steaming cup. His shoulders were hunched, and his lips were flattened into a sharp thin line as he stared down at the tea that was too hot to drink.

"Yes?"

Lord Orville looked up to see King Ivan's eyes peering at him in inquiry.

"Your Majesty. I have stuck by your side through your every trial as king as I did for your father, even before I became his Hand. I corrected the paths he was sending the kingdom down and challenged him when he needed to hear opposition, I have, without hesitation, done the same for you and challenged you when respectful disagreements were needed. But…"

King Ivan folded the parchment and set it down. He leaned back in his chair and crossed his hands on the table. "But?"

"But as of late, i I may be brash, it is as if you do not wish to be reasonable." Lord Orville's eyes flicked up at the king's stare. "I believe a change within the Council is needed to ensure that you do not become the man you do not wish to be. A king you are becoming despite your hopes." Lord Orville sat up straight and squared his hunching back. "A king is as great, or as wretched, as the Council he keeps."

King Ivan inhaled slowly and exhaled without hurry. "I know you and Father Figgins do not see eye to eye on *anything*, but it is important to surround oneself with those of differing opinion, to have advisors with different ideals. And Sir Marion has been, despite his… *nature*, incredibly effective in retraining and leading our King's Guards and restructuring our armies."

"Your Majesty, they have driven you to extreme measures this past epoch!" They both eyed the squire in the corner who had quickly averted his eyes to the ceiling as they looked at him, Lord Orville lowered his tone. "Measures that have put us in the precarious space we are in."

King Ivan did not bother quieting himself, his tone dangerously close to letting out the anger he buried within him. "Have we as a Council perhaps made mistakes in judgement? *Yes.* But have we also had to take extreme measures to stop what was rising? To prevent more whispered dissent among our people? *Yes.*"

Lord Orville threw himself back in his chair in frustration. "They only whisper so why do you have to scream in response? Every king and queen in our history has had vicious things said of them, even your wife's own ancestor, the beloved Kind Queen, was whispered about and disliked by some."

"And you saw where that got Queen Oriana! Her throne taken from her and a life exiled to the Isles of Aishar to rebuild her line!" King Ivan now shouted. "Squire! Bring me something stronger than this."

The king waved his hand in the air near the bitter black tea he had yet to touch.

As the squire poured for His Majesty, Lord Orville spoke, his cadence careful and friendly. "Perhaps, Your Majesty, we could hold off on the drinking for now."

The king and the Hand shared a quiet look while the king contemplated the liquor calling out to him.

"Perhaps you are right, we have plenty of drink and decadence for tonight's dinner, I should not spoil that palate." The king picked up his teacup, dismissing the half-poured knuckle of liquor the squire had poured.

Lord Orville continued, "The point I am attempting so poorly to make, the one that took many epochs for your father to learn as well, is that not every action by our people requires a reaction. I know you are paranoid about the prophecy of the Psalms—"

"We do not speak so freely of those words, Robert." King Ivan snapped again, shooting an eye at the squire before returning back to Lord Orville. "I agree with your concerns, which is why this morning I heeded your advice on our current situation. We shall take it and see how our people respond. And if they react poorly, then so shall we."

Lord Orville rested his chin against his joined hands. His elbows rested on the tabletop, poor etiquette that he did not care to break himself of at this moment.

In front of him sat the young boy he once knew, now a king, shaking and scared of the fresh bruises on his face and his drunk father screaming in the other room while Lord Orville blocked the door and spoke sense into the raging king. In front of his misting eyes, the boy grew into a young man, his inherited anger brewing that he worked himself into a panicked frenzy about to prevent from ever showing. The same brown haired and pink cheeked young prince who had promised Lord Orville he would never be like his father- the man he was so afraid of becoming, the cruelty he was so scared was given to him through his father's bloodline.

"You must be careful, Ivan. Power is delicate mistress, and your paranoia could be her death."

***

In times of turmoil, Lord Robert Orville, like so many other inhabitants of the royal castle, would walk the garden grounds of The King's Keep to find peace; hoping it would blossom from the beds of dirt like a budding seedling planted before the light frosts of winter would steal the life from its newly established roots. Isilria did not get much snow or frost in the winter and on this warm day, The Hand of the King did not get much peace.

The sandstone pathways of the massive gardens weaved through arches of greenery and vine, past beds of the finest flowers and most heavenly scented herbs and flora. As The Hand continued to pace throughout the lanes, quietly conversing with himself and occasionally pausing to stare at the rainbow covered flower beds hoping for them to answer his rhetorical inquiries, he glanced up to see Father Figgins casually walking in his direction.

He would much rather see The Butcher on a hurried pace coming to execute him.

"Fuckin' hell." Lord Orville mumbled. He straightened the bottom of his embroidered vest, giving his hands something to fidget with as he waited for the snake to slither towards him.

"Ahh, Lord Orville, I see both you and I had the same plans this fine afternoon." Father Figgins greeted him with pleasantry and a smile that was always incapable of reaching the ice in his eyes.

"Yes, it appears that you and I have finally agreed on something." He flicked his eyes upward, rolling them in annoyance at the feigned niceties.

"And what is that?"

"That beautiful days like today are best spent outside instead of in the castle *conspiring* around a table." Lord Orville let out a forced chuckle and glanced away again, shaking his head, and pretending to admire one of the stone carved statues near their path. He held his hands together behind his back, one set of fingers drumming against the other hand.

Father Figgins held his tongue, noticing others strolling by. Both men smiled as the two women greeted them on their own promenade before disappearing down the winding path.

The men stood awkwardly looking about, attempting to decide how much more feigned politeness was required of them before they could excuse themselves from one another's presence without sparking castle gossip spread by the others around the garden.

Lord Orville looked behind Father Figgins, noting that Sir Marion was not present, and was replaced by another King's Guard who now stood talking to Lord Orville's guard a few short paces away.

"I see you are without your shadow this afternoon." Lord Orville smirked, the wrinkles around his lips deepened as he did so. His thin blonde eyebrows- the same color as the short ponytail gathered on his neck- cocked up as he looked down at Father Figgins.

Father Figgins attempted to not show irritation and countered back. "Ah, yes, Sir Marion is quite busy with his other duties."

"Oh? Off doing his true job as Master of Armor or off doing one of his jobs for you?"

Father Figgins' eyes narrowed at the comment as he sharpened his voice into a harsh whisper and stepped forward. Despite the venom in his tone, his cadence carried the same unbothered ease as it often did. "You and I both know any job given to Sir Marion is under his duty as the Master of Armor and as a servant of the king."

The Hand of the King scoffed. "You know William, for a man of God, you seem to forget that your sins are no more forgivable than any others. The lengths you continuously go to in the name of His Majesty and the throne, and the actions you have so forcefully pushed the king to commit since you infiltrated our Council should fill you with an amount of shame that no penance could ever ease." He paused, his frustration continued to take over as his voice rose. "The messes I have continued to have to clean up to avoid His Majesty's downfall- you should be begging for mercy from God for aiding in their happening."

Father Figgins stepped forward, his steps casual and slow, until he was mere inches from The Hand of the King's face. "That has always been the key difference between you and I." He reached out a hand to straighten the Hand of the King brooch that Lord Orville wore on his chest, then panned his darkened eyes to meet Lord Orville's glare. "I never feel shame for what I must do, and I will never hesitate to put an end to *anything* that stands in my way."

Father Figgins stepped back, pleased with himself, and walked past Lord Orville.

"Your way? Do you not mean that of the king?" Lord Orville called over his shoulder.

Father Figgins paused his steps only for a moment, gritting his teeth and clenching his fists. He did not reply as he set off down his path.

CHAPTER 9

"So, how many kids?" Prince Elion asked.

Prince Percy cocked his head up from the book he was reading. "What?"

His brother smirked and laughed as he sauntered into Prince Percy's reading room. Prince Percy laid out on a sofa relaxing near the open window and looked intently at his brother in confusion. Prince Elion tapped his brothers feet, motioning for him to move so he could sit on the other end of the lounge.

Prince Elion pulled the ribbon from his tied back hair and ran his hands through the sweat dampened strands as he sat down. His appearance more casual than it should have been at this time of afternoon, but the small cuts on his tense arms- exposed by the rolled up sleeves of his thin white shirt- indicated his sweaty and worn state was due to a challenging swordsmanship lesson that had just concluded. "I asked how many kids for you and Sister Ora? How many did you negotiate for?" he motioned his hand in the air. "You know, when you met and discussed the terms of your arrangement."

Prince Percy shut the book and set it on the table in front of the couch, adjusting himself to sit properly on his side. "We have not had such a conversation."

It was Prince Elion's turn to look with confusion, "Have you discussed your living arrangements? If either of you can take another to bed? Have outside relationships? Where you will sleep?"

Prince Percy did not reply and instead avoided his brother's stare. He cleared his throat and rubbed the back of his neck and found the rug beneath his couch of deep interest.

His older brother shifted on the couch, fully facing him. "You have not had any discussions on the technicality of your marriage, have you?" Prince Elion pinched his brow, "Percy, you do recall my advice to you before you left for Ayeshire, right?"

"Yes, I do. I simply did not take it."

Prince Elion pinched his brow harder and rested both elbows on his knees. "Percy, when Lady Easter and I first met we exchanged our pleasantries and sat down at a table with a scribe to write down the terms of our marriage and came to an agreement on all of it."

"Yes, and then she went back to the Dragon's Tower in Odessin, returned for your wedding, said her vows, and you have not spoken since."

Prince Elion shrugged. "Yes that was part of the negotiation. We will speak again when she returns from her new studies. We already consummated what we were required to." the Heir to the Throne grimaced. "And as part of our agreement when needed, we will live together but separate here in the Keep when I become king. I can continue to see Jeffrey, or whoever I am with at that moment, and she can see whoever she likes as well so long as we are able to prove an heirs she births are of my blood."

The future king rested his head on the back of the sofa and held up two fingers. "Two children. That was the other arrangement. As fast as possible to get it over with."

"Yes, well, maybe my arrangement with Sister Ora will be different." Prince Percy mumbled.

Realization came over Prince Elion's face as he jolted upright and jerked his body to face his younger brother. "You like her."

"Plenty of noblemen like their wives. The Montarian's grew to love one another, and Lord and Lady Torrin of Sebern were madly in love from the moment they met one another when they were young." Prince Percy began rambling, recalling names of noblemen past and present who enjoyed, as far as the public eye knew, their political marriages.

His brother cut him off, his voice low and warning. "You barely even know her, Percy, and love is not a requirement of our duty."

"And love does not *take* from our duty." Prince Percy countered, standing up and starting to awkwardly pace away the nerves the conversation brought on.

"But it can." Prince Elion warned again as he stared up at his pacing brother.

"Just because you—" Prince Percy cut himself off as he raised his voice.

The heir stood up and tightened his chiseled jaw and cocked his head at his brother. "No, no, brother, do finish that sentence."

The two princes stood facing one another, a small coffee table piled with books brimming with bookmarks and dog-eared pages separating the two.

The younger prince composed himself. "I have a chance, however small it may actually be, to not be miserable the rest of my life in the name of duty."

Prince Elion stepped forward, his eyes wincing. "There is more to this than your imposing marriage to a woman you have barely even spoken with. What have you not told me?"

Prince Percy set his jaw and hesitated. "Mother offered me the heirdom to her inheritance of title over Thelimor. She said it is mine if I would like to take it, if not, she would offer it to Arminda if father approved it. But I do not know if I wish to have it." He sighed. "A letter bearing Lord Mete's seal arrived from Odessin just before we departed for Ayeshire, offering me a position in the citadels of Dragon's Tower when one of the High Scholars retires soon, but the lord's words spoke of conditions we would have to discuss first."

Prince Elion shook his head as he turned to pace in the opposite direction of his brother. His hand covered his mouth as his other clenched in a fist at his side. Prince Percy quickly noted his brother's anger rising and quieted his unsure rambling.

"Oh do not stop because of me." Prince Elion started to shout as he turned back to his brother. "*Please* do tell me more about how you get to have some semblance of a life, of a choice, while I am saddled with being *the fucking heir*!"

Prince Percy let the words finish their echo around the room before quietly replying. "I do ask, dear brother, which life is worse? Being the fucking heir, or the spare pawn?"

***

Excessively intense emotions had spoiled every course of the royal family dinner.

The only individual who seemed remotely interested in speaking that evening was Emaline, who held Sister Ora up in the hallway as she concluded a long conversation with another guard over what the upcoming jousting season may look like and if it were to happen at all. Sister Ora did not wish to rush her out of her conversation, knowing it was not easy for her to speak comfortably with others on her own, but the wine had poured much too freely at dinner and Sister Ora drank as much as the others to survive the meal filled with glares and snippy comments between the royal siblings and the king's quiet staring into the ether around him.

It was not until Sister Ora had left the dining hall and stood in the quieter space outside that she had fully realized how much she had indulged in.

She ran her hand along the cold stone, the texture feel fuzzy against her fingertips, mimicking the feeling running through her bones. She walked slowly down the hallway, keeping within eyesight of Emaline, who was still distracted by the conversation and with her back turned.

Sister Ora turned the nearby corner, her walking aimless and slow, her intent being to stay within earshot of her guard and friend and hope to walk off her drunkeness before slumber. She fell into a daze studying the many paintings outside the dining hall. The breeze of the open archways outside cooled her skin that had been warmed by the wine and the handful of lit torches encouraged her to continue to walk away into the broken darkness.

Armored steps echoed behind her as she stood at a cross of paths illuminated in orange.

Just as quickly as the steps broke through her minds haze, they stopped and an arm forcibly grabbed her shoulder, spinning her around much too swiftly.

As she staggered, preparing to shout at Emaline for being so rough, she was met with the glaring face of The Head of the King's Guard. She attempted to jerk her arm away from Sir Marion's grasp, but her efforts were useless against his hardened hand.

He hummed at her, his face mere inches from hers and his fist tightening even more on her arm. "Be careful, young miss, you should know that the world is a dangerous place for those who wander all alone in the dark. Unguarded. Unwatched."

She hissed as she jerked again against his grip. "Let go of me *now*."

Sir Marion's grip tightened, and his dark brown eyes and scowling face turned more terrorizing than they already were. His lips opened to retort against her demands for freedom but was held off by another voice.

"Is there a problem here?" Emaline's threatening tone said as the metallic shrill of her unsheathing sword echoed in the dark.

Sir Marion let go, forcing Sister Ora to stumble back as he did. He turned, faking an innocent smile on his face. "No, I do not believe there is." He turned to Sister Ora, who was still reeling from the interaction. "Prince Percy's betrothed was stumbling from too much drink, and I was offering her my escort back to her chambers. It is, after all, uncouth and undutiful for a High Scholar and future member of the royal family to be without a guard at their side."

Emaline slid her sword back in its scabbard and shoved forward between the two. Her gloved hands clenching and unclenching in fists as she fought the urge to begin swinging them.

"Escorting Sister Ora and guarding her is my duty, Sir Marion, not yours. I have her."

"Do you?" He smirked. "She was here alone without you. If you were one of my King's Guard this mistake would have your cloak and your head. Things are quite a bit different here in the king's city than they are in the scraps of Middleton Landing, I would suggest that if you would like to keep your cloak or your head, you learn our ways- quickly. You were signed over to my watch, Sgt. Kingery, and I do not tolerate laziness in duty."

The two glared intently at one another as Sister Ora looked on. Her eyes darting back and forth at the two, wondering which one of them would break the silence with the throw of a fist or the swing of a sword. Instead, Emaline broke it by stepping back towards her.

"Sister Ora, let us get you back to your chambers." Emaline walked with Sister Ora away from Sir Marion, keeping her body between the two and replacing his harsh grip with one of her own

When their steps were far enough down the hall, Emaline halted and roughly let go of Sister Ora.

"What in the hells, Ora?!" Emaline hissed, "I turned my back to finish a conversation and you disappear!"

Sister Ora worked hard to sober herself up more. "I am sorry, Emaline. I did not mean for you to get in trouble. Maybe I could speak to Prince Percy and ask him to talk to his father or someone, so you do not get punished."

Emaline held her hand over the metal plate on her chest, the pressure of her palm attempting to shove her pounding heart back in its place, "It is not myself that I worry about, it is you. Sir Marion- what they say is true about him. He is a terrifying, bloodthirsty man. The things the other guards say of him, they," she swallowed a lump in her throat. "they are terrifying. Do you know what they said he did as a child passing through the Blood Rite to become a gladiator of Aishar?"

Sister Ora's eyes widened as she slowly shook her head. "No."

"There is more to fear in this city than drunken thieves or angry citizens looking to use you to get some sort of vengeance the king." Emaline looked over her shoulder as if she waited for a shadow to leap from the walls and attack. "There are phantoms that will do much worse to you for fun."

Emaline did not allow her to respond as she set her arm on Sister Ora's shaking back and guided her back to her room. Sister Ora did not sleep that night, and Emaline did not allow the night guard to take her place in the residency hall.

Chapter 10

Heat radiated throughout the room as sunlight beamed in through the gaps in the curtains and onto the two bodies on the bed; both covered in sweat from the sun's heat and their hours of passion.

Sir Marion placed his hand on the center of her back and pushed her torso fully onto the bed; her face pressed in the tangled sheets as her hands clung tightly to them. He stood behind her and tightly gripped her hips, holding her in place as he continued to thrust into her.

The sounds and scents of brutal fucking coated the air as her shouts echoed out onto the street, her pain filled pleasure unable to be completely silenced by the sheets she bit into. Their heated breathing and pounding drowned out the noises of the capital city outside their window and covered up the feigned pleasures coming from the rooms around them.

Sir Marion let out a long, deep groan and pressed himself into her with more intensity and dug his hands into her skin, grunting with exhaustion as he folded over on top of her. His arms formed a cage around her as he desperately tried to hold himself up and catch his breath.

As his breathing slowly came back to him, he moved her dark waves off her back, pressing surprisingly gentle kisses down her spine as he moved himself out of her. He stumbled his way over to the washing basin to clean himself off as the woman of pleasure shuffled herself onto her back to watch him make his way back to the bed.

He handed her a towel to wipe herself off before grabbing a glass of wine from the bedside table and tossing himself onto the mountain of plush silk pillows.

She followed his movements and crawled her way to the head of the bed and rested her head on his shoulder, letting her hands wander over his sweat coated body. She let out a small giggle, tracing circles and lines on his bare chest, "It's almost unfair that you are the one to pay me for that, when I feel like I owe you a debt."

Sir Marion took another large gulp of wine before the cup was snatched from him, the nameless woman finishing off its contents. He cocked a brow and aggressively reached for her and grabbed a fistful of her hip and force-fully pulled her on top of him, the chalice of wine now thrown on the bed and the remainder of its contents mixing with the other messes on their sheets.

She squeaked in surprise at the movement then laid her head back and moaned, feeling his still hard cock beneath her, her body hopeful to feel him completely consume every one of her senses again.

"There is a reason you are every woman's favorite here, *sir*." She moaned as she began grinding against him, her body still ready to take anything he wished to do to her.

He fisted her hips again, lifting her up to set her on top of his tip, letting her sit there and feel him pressing against her entrance, he ran his thumb slowly over her clit, staring at it with his darkened eyes as she moaned. He crooned, "And why is that?"

Her stomach twitched as he pressed his thumb harder, his other hand still fisted at her hip and not allowing her to sink down onto him, "Because, because," she gasped, "Because you take what you know we both need and you do not stop. Because you fuck me like you want to ruin me."

He smirked and threw his hips upward against her body.

Her back arched as she shouted and began to ride him. His hand found her neck, using his tight grip on it and her hip to control how she moved on top of him.

Just as Sir Marion opened his mouth to make a remark, a knock at the door interrupted them.

He grunted and continued moving her body on him, his anger at the attempted intrusion fueling his aggression. Her walls quivered around him and encouraged more force, and he took what he wanted from her.

The knocking at the door returned with louder force.

Sir Marion did not stop as he shouted at the door. "Who is it?"

A voice spoke from the other side, but neither could make out what was said through the thick wood and their fucking.

Sir Marion angrily groaned and dropped his hand from her neck, reluctantly stopping his thrusting. "I cannot hear you, just come in and make this interruption quick."

After a moment's hesitation, a King's Guard stepped in, looking at the floor as he entered. "Apologies, sir, but Father Figgins stated he needs to speak to you. He said it is urgent."

Sir Marion rolled his eyes and gestured towards the woman still on top of him. She pushed her chest out and arched her back, eying the armored knight standing in the doorway who now raised his helmet at the two. She did not move against Sir Marion, despite her aching for friction, instead, she kept smiling at the King's Guard whose fists were now clenching and unclenching at his sides. She lifted her hand at him and waved.

"Well tell him that this is my afternoon off to do with what I please, and pleasure is what pleases me this day." He moved his hand from where it rested on her hip and smacked her ass, jostling her and making her laugh.

"You serve at the pleasure of the king, Sir Marion, and that has no day off." Father Figgins' voice said from behind the knight. He stepped around the armored man and into the room as he addressed The Master of Armor.

"Oh, it looks like we're having a little party." The woman of pleasure laughed as she looked around at all three men. She began grinding slowly on Sir Marion. "He did not pay me enough for all three of you."

Father Figgins stepped forward, his face coated in disgust as he pulled a coin out of his pocket and tossed it at her. The rude gesture prompted her to stop immediately. "Will that be enough for you to leave?" he sneered.

She looked at the coin tossed on the sheets, worth more than an afternoon of the most salacious activities- both legal and not- and then gave an uncertain glance to Sir Marion. He reluctantly dismissed her, tossing the blanket over himself as she got up and left the men. As she walked out the opposite door, Father Figgins turned to the King's Guard that accompanied him and dismissed him as well.

Sir Marion stayed lounging, propping his upper body on his elbow as he turned onto his side and reached for another chalice of wine on the table beside the bed. His state of undone messiness contrasted to how Father Figgins held himself several paces away- rigid and stern, dressed in embroidered clothing perfectly tailored to his body and not a single hair or thread out of place.

"What is the name this time?" Sir Marion asked.

Father Figgins inhaled deeply and flexed his hands behind his back. "Lord Orville."

Sir Marion stopped pouring his wine and looked at him. "The Hand of the King?"

"Lord Orville stands in the way of what must be done for the betterment of kingdom, for the crown. Each time he bends His Majesty's ear, the king grows softer and more hesitant. He turned His Majesty into the weak ruler he was before we stepped in and offered our much-needed guidance. His hesitation and softness will ruin everything that this kingdom has been working towards for centuries, what I and many others have been working for. Lord Orville does serve a purpose to the future of our people, but it is not his destiny to be the Hand any longer."

Sir Marion scrunched his brow. "Am I to take care of him like the others?"

"We need to be rid of him, but there is to be no blood spilled by you. The king still believes that Father Penn did escape with the stolen parchments the night before the Spring Equalius, that they were never recovered." He turned his jaw down at Sir Marion. "Use them."

Sir Marion's darkened stare cleared, and he nodded slowly in understanding. "And then the Hand of the King will be found for treason and executed and a new Hand will need to be named." He chuckled. "After all your time being second best."

Father Figgins sharpened his words into a deadly blade as he hissed. "The Six Kingdoms are fast changing and there will be no stopping the wheels of war once they begin, but with enough power I can steer them in the right direction- in *our* direction."

Sir Marion sat up and rested his feet on the floor, the silken blanket still draped over his lower half. He took a long slow sip of wine before replying. "And you believe one man can hold that much power and influence in his hands?"

Father Figgins scoffed. "Given what you have done for the crown with your own hands, I am surprised you would say such a thing. How they have choked the life from those powerful enough to turn this kingdom to ash and taken breath from those kind enough to stop it." He straightened and stepped forward. "Are your hands the only ones that can force the future to change, Sir Marion?"

Sir Marion's eyes flickered up and down at the frail figure standing a few short feet away from him, unguarded, unprotected, unable to run or fight. The craving heat built up inside Sir Marion. He quickly squandered the familiar flame within himself as he straightened up/ "No, perhaps not. What needs to be done, will be done."

"Good" Father Figgins turned to leave, reaching the doorknob before he heard a throat clear behind him. He grabbed a bag of money from his doublet pocket, then turned and tossed it at Sir Marion before opening the door to leave.

"If she is still out there, do send her back in." The jangling of coins disrupted Sir Marion's comment. "and have her bring a friend if she would like."

***

Anger gripped the air in the room with such firmness that one could choke if they were not careful with their breath or their words. King Ivan's fury paced alongside him as he stormed through the room, the glass and metal on the table quivered as he moved and the windowpanes shook with fear when he neared him.

"This *cannot* be true. Lord Orville has been a trusted friend of the family for ages and a loyal Hand since you took the crown, father. You must calm yourself and see clearly through your anger, he would never betray you- or us." Prince Elion spoke from the opposite side of the room, his own anger shoved down under layers of shock and panic.

King Ivan continued his path of rage, barely holding back more physical displays of it. Glass had already been shattered earlier when Father Figgins brought him the news of Lord Orville's betrayal; there was not much left to wreck in the room besides the people standing in it.

And King Ivan would not be like his father. His fists would never strike his heir.

His son.

"The stolen papers from the Archives were found in his home and his servant confessed to hearing him speak against the crown and this council." The king snatched the crumpled papers from the table and spit out his words. "And messenger birds were prepared to send word to the kingdoms about what he knew- confirmation of what we have done to keep this king-dom from falling to pieces."

The king dropped the papers down on the table, resting his hands beside them and hanging his head in defeat. "I do not wish to believe it, but with this evidence, this confession, I must."

"This would not be the first time in our history that a Hand of the King has stepped out of his place, Your Majesty. Abandoning loyalties is not un-common for those who are full of contempt and frustration of the path being forged." Father Figgins paused, "And we all knew how unhappy Lord Orville was with the path we were forced to go down for our people."

King Ivan poured too much wine into his chalice, draining the entire glass in one breath as he mulled over Father Figgins' words. The alcohol gave a temporary stop to his shaking and calmed his vitriol for a moment.

"I do not want to believe his betrayal any more than all of you." The king turned to Prince Elion. "Especially you, Elion. But the evidence and his aid's confession cannot be ignored or written off as hearsay. We all have seen how hesitant and tired Lord Orville has become over what this council has had to do to protect the throne."

"I just- I cannot believe he would turn on our family." The prince miserably let out.

Father Figgins sighed, his voice filled with concern and sorrow. "Even a worm will turn, Your Highness."

The chamber doors clanged open as a gathering of King's Guards led by Sir Marion stepped through the doorway. An unaware Lord Robert Orville walked in the center of them; a docile sheep trapped among a herd of lions in shepherd's clothing.

"What is happening? Why was I taken so quickly from my own home?" He began to step towards the king, worry straining his words. "Is everything alright?"

"Sir Loren, Sir Thomas, restrain this man." Sir Marion ordered as two of the King's Guards stepped forward, grabbing each arm of The Hand of the King to hold him firmly in place.

"What in the- what is going on?" Lord Orville's confusion turned into solid anger. "Let me go you fools."

King Ivan and Prince Elion stood side-by-side across the room, silently glaring, and watching the building moment. Both men silently searched Lord Orville for signs of betrayal as if it could be written upon his face for them to read.

"Tell us it is not true." Prince Elion firmly demanded.

Lord Orville shrugged against the grips on his arms. His brows furrowed more, "What is not true? What is going on?"

Father Figgins rolled his shoulders back and stepped beside the table to face The Hand of the King. He jutted his chin up, holding back a smile.

"Lord Orville, you are being charged with treason and conspiring against the crown. We have been given evidence of your transgressions and a confession from one of your servants of your misdeeds." Father Figgins picked up the paper on the table and held it up for him to see. "They admitted to overhearing you speak of treason against His Majesty and this council and found in your chambers letters outlining your attempted betrayal of the throne."

Lord Orville looked over at King Ivan. His crumpling confusion fell into pieces as he saw the glare on King Ivan's face. A glare that showed his mind had already been made. The betrayal already believed.

Still, he defended himself. "Do you truly believe that if I were to betray you, I would be so *stupid* as to put it on paper? And to leave it unguarded? Or to speak about it aloud where others could hear me? While we may disagree at times and I do worry about courses of action we have taken, betrayal is not within my bones. I have watched you grow from a babe into a king and swore to you to do the same for Prince Elion if I lived to see the day."

"Did you or did you not speak against the crowns actions in the gardens recently? In conversation with Father Figgins? Is it true that you stated that His Majesty and this council should feel shame for our sins and actions?" Sire Marion replied.

"Well, yes. Somewhat." He stammered. "I was angry and frustrated. Father Figgins caught me in a moment of quiet contemplation and took my words for what they were not. Ivan, my good friend, you must believe me. I would not betray you."

King Ivan lurched forward, pounding across the room, stopping inches from Lord Orville's face. His words spit out of his mouth in intense rage and fury.

"It is *Your Majesty*. You have lost the right to call me a friend the moment you put pen to paper to deceive me." The long-time admiration that the king felt for Lord Orville had completely dissipated, and in its place was an animosity that was so deep he was entirely engulfed by it.

Lord Orville stood in stunned silence as the king turned and stepped away. His mouth laid open in shock as his eyes widened in disbelief. "I have done no such thing."

"Then explain how it is we have been given this evidence." Prince Elion countered; contemplation covered his expression as he moved forward to stand by his father's Hand. "Show us how we are wrong."

Lord Orville shrugged and shook his head. "They are lies. Fabrications. Someone must have planted the evidence and conspired to create these crimes."

Father Figgins stepped in front of Prince Elion, separating Lord Orville from the heir desperate to not believe the betrayal. "If what you say is true, Lord Orville, then your conspirator must be in the room with us, as no one outside our chambers knows of what your letters spoke of." Father Figgins cocked a brow as he now calmly moved to stand beside the king, "Are you *again* accusing royalty of conspiracy and crimes?"

Realization dawned on Lord Orville's face much too late. The snake had already struck, his venom already had already taken over and pacified his prey.

"*You son of a-*" his entire body shook as he attempted to jerk himself free of the steel clad grip of the guards.

Prince Elion tried to quietly reason with Lord Orville as he thrashed for a moment longer. "You are not helping your case."

Lord Orville did not hear the prince's plea. He felt his sharpened mind failing him as his ire and panic tainted any logical thinking.

"You son of a bitch." He snarled at Father Figgins.

The king spoke in an unvarnished tone. "Your inability to defend yourself today only shows your guilt. As you well know, this council is a council of law, Robert. We have found you guilty of your crimes and you shall be punished in haste for what you have done. Your execution will be quick, I will not draw it out. I will give you that."

Lord Orville shouted, "I am due a trial. *A public trial!*"

"*No.* You are due what *I* deem fit for you." King Ivan snarled before turning his back. His hand shook as he reached for another glass and brought it to his lips.

"Then I demand to speak to your supposed witness and hear their allegations myself!"

"For their protection, they are not here. Our Council has already heard their testimony and made the appropriate decision based upon their words." Father Figgins cooly said.

Lord Orville spoke to the king's still turned back.

"Tell me, then, *Your Majesty.* How many more executions and assassinations will it take before you are satisfied with the bodies in the morgue? How many more lies will you tell the people and *yourself* to protect the crown that weighs so heavy on your head. *The crown that is doomed to catch fire and burn us all?*"

The glass in the king's hand shattered.

Prince Elion's chilling calmness answered instead. He would not let his anger overtake him as it did his father. "Speaking to the king in such a way is a privilege you no longer have, Lord Orville. Guards- take this criminal to the cells in the farthest, most solitary place in our prison. There is no need to prepare any decent pen for him, as His Majesty has willed it, he will not be here for long."

King Ivan inhaled deeply, slowly as Prince Elion moved to stand beside him. The filigree shaped bronze crown atop the king's head pinched every nerve and felt much too tight, much too heavy, as if it was pushing the weight of the heavens onto him. His nerves shook him again as he felt the buzz of adrenaline mix with the alcohol that he knew he should not have allowed himself to drink.

Father Figgins waited for the door to close behind the King's Guards. He handed the king another glass of wine as he poured his own, ignoring the shattered pieces on the buffet they stood beside. "You Majesty, this may be a blessing in disguise. His betrayal, we could use it to our advantage more than we think."

CHAPTER 11

"**G**et up, you useless fuck."

The prison guard unlocked the iron cell door and swung it open, stepping inside as it loudly came to a slamming halt on the dingy and damp stone wall.

"I said get up." the guard kicked Lord Orville lying in his own filth and pulled him up by his chained arm.

The shackle chains connecting the king's former Hand's wrists jangled as he was abruptly forced up and pulled out of the lone cell and into the dimly lit dungeon hallway. Just as he was able to get his full bearings of what was occurring, two King's Guards stepped forward and grabbed either arm, forcing him down the hall.

"Where...where are you taking me?" Lord Orville's voice was scratchy and barely audible, adding to his pathetic appearance. Each swallow and attempt to speak felt as if dry sand was being poured down his throat. It had been days since he had been given any water. His only determinant of the passage of time had been the inconsistent check ins of the prison guard ensuring he had not found a way to end his suffering before his punishment was due.

"His Majesty has changed his mind, you're free now. We're taking you home." the guard on the left answered.

"I am? I am free?" Through his confusion, Lord Orville's voice still picked up a twinge of hope.

"Yes, and I'm on my way to fuck the queen." The other guard chuckled. "You thought you could get away scot-free after going against the king? Oh no, do they have special plans for you."

The arch of the exterior entrance came into view as the sounds of the gathered crowds washed over the walking group. The bright sun and heat of its presence overwhelmed Lord Orville's dulled senses and forced him to close his eyes as they stepped across the threshold to the outside. A mixture of city guards and King's Guards held back the shouting crowds and created an open pathway for the walking group; the hangman's gallows awaited them at the path's end.

Screams of traitor, sinner, and much fouler language came from the crowd as they walked towards his end. Familiar faces of citizens Lord Orville had given counsel to or met during his volunteer work spit bitter words at him just the same as those he did not recognize.

The crowd grew angrier and more disruptive as the guards finished pulling him towards the center of the platform. Rotten food was pelted at the stage and shouts erupted from the crowd as the men who would carry out his punishment also took to the stage. Behind and above the display stood the royal family on an elevated and well-guarded viewing stage.

"Traitor! Bastard! Sinner! Liar!" came from the crowd as Lord Orville centered himself on the stage and hung his head in shame.

Work had been done well against his reputation while he had laid in the dungeon mulling over why he woke with his head still attached after the Council promised a swift crucifixion.

Silence fell as Father Figgins, wearing long, embellished red robes stepped forward to address the crowd, motioning with his arms for all to quiet.

He began.

"Before you stands a criminal, a traitor, and a sinner. Many of us falsely knew him as a kind and caring man, a man of honor and duty, but that was a lie he fabricated all too well. He has not only spoken words of treason against the king and blasphemy against God and His will." Father Figgins' eyes flickered down to look at Lord Orville. "But he had also hoped to inspire others to take to anger and wished to put in harm's way more innocent people.

"The now former Lord served alongside two kings as their Hand. He bent the ear and gained the trust of those two kings who had hope, in their own ways, to keep our kingdom unified and at peace, to move us onward to a prosperous future. But this man did not see fit the visions they had created. Had it not been for the confession of one of his servants who came to us so terrified to speak out, but so brave to confess what they knew about who he truly was behind closed doors," Father Figgins choked on his words and set a hand on his chest as he turned to the shy and scared servant standing alongside the royal family, "If not for them, could you imagine what could have happened had the king not stepped in and put a stop to this?"

The crowd's energy took up again as many expressed shock and worry. Father Figgins gave the crowd a moment to allow their shock to build, to create a momentous moment. He then shook his head. "My heart aches for the acts this man almost caused and the acts he *did* cause. For the lives he took along the way and framed others for."

Robert Orville shook his head, his eyes piercing through Father Figgins as the lies he spoke continued to evolve and grow. He was to be the fall for everything he stood against that the Council had done, the convenient solution to the messes he had tried to stop.

"You calculating bastard." Robert quietly snarled at the Head of the Church preaching to the crowd.

Father Figgins turned to him. His extravagant robes billowed in the breeze, the white and red fabrics creating waves in the wind as the jewels adorning his hands and neck glinted in the sunlight.

He stepped beside Robert Orville, raising his chin, his hands instinctually reaching to rest on a pulpit that did not stand before him. He folded his hands in front of him instead. "There are many crimes for which you *should* be executed for, Robert Orville, but God had asked us to be merciful and forgiving of you. To allow His Holiness to enact His Judgement on you. As

His Majesty and I are dutiful servants of our Almighty Lord, it is our hope that your penance will bring you the peace you so desperately need. As it is God's Will, you will be punished *only* for your blasphemy, the sin you hid so well from us all. As our teachings show us, blasphemy is a sin graver than the most heinous of acts."

Different murmurs came from the crowd in waves, speculation if the mercy Father Figgins spoke of was freedom or something else. Robert's eyes sparked with flames as he stood hunched beside Father Figgins, covered in dirt and filth from the prison with starvation darkening his face, the fine threads he had once worn replaced with basic prison garb.

Father Figgins raised his voice and looked down his nose at the crowd enraptured by his words. "God stands with the throne and the throne stands with God. For your crime you will kneel before us and atone in the way you committed your sin." From his billowing sleeves, he brought forth a a large metal nail, as thick as several fingers and as black as the night. "A nail shall be driven through the tongue of which you used to speak your blasphemy. You shall kneel on this platform, praying for forgiveness and redemption. After one day, your freedom shall be granted, and the nail removed."

Several gathered covered their mouths, holding back larger exclamations and noises, imagining the pain of what he was to endure. Others shouted for the guillotine while other prayers of gratitude attempted to drown them out.

Father Figgins did not pause between the gasps and loud whispers in the crowd, he continued.

"If you survive God's Will and can speak once you are granted your freedom, then know that God has given you His mercy. If you cannot speak once you are free, then know that God has not freed you from your sin, and you are to walk the rest of your days in atonement, praying for the redemption of your soul. And if you do not survive, then know that this is His judgement."

Robert said nothing.

"You have been fated with this punishment by God Himself, Robert Orville. But first, you must confess to your sins and your crimes, only then will forgiveness be considered."

Robert looked over the crowd, taking in the faces of the people he was once a friend and needed ally of. He swallowed the sand in his throat and mustered up the strength to speak, "I have served this kingdom for the entirety of my life. I have fought for peace, justice, and the betterment of our people. You all know what I *have* done, who I *am*. Let my actions that you know to be true be what is left in your heart. Not these false fabrications."

He slowly turned back to the sneering snake beside him and replied with what venom he had remaining. "And may God and these people forgive you and His Majesty for your sins, and may you burn in the fire and fury that you deserve."

From above, the king tightened his jaw at the words, his vitriol clutching at every fiber in his face. Beside him, Queen Onetta gently nudged his arm, her face stoic and unfeeling at what was occurring.

Father Figgins sneered at Robert, then nodded at the guards holding him. "And may He forgive yours." He said as he took a step backward, handing the nail to the masked executioner at the edge of the stage.

A guard knocked Robert onto his knees, slamming his head onto the small wooden table that had been placed in front of him. His chin, still covered in dirt and grime from the dungeon cell, rested on the grains of the worn table.

The guard grabbed his jaw to force his mouth open, and Robert managed to shout out his last words before he was silenced, "*And the world of men shall be made to begin again.*"

Behind him, King Ivan and both the princes' eyes flickered in panic.

The guard holding his face tightened his grip and pulled out his tongue, holding onto the tip of it with his gloved fingers. The pinches of the chainmail covering his fingers scraped against the dry flesh of his tongue, scratching the pinkness and already beginning to draw blood.

The Butcher silently stepped forward, holding a thick square headed hammer and thick black nail in his leather covered hands. His hooded face hid any expression as he wasted no time in enacting the sentence. He pushed and twisted the square nail slowly, intently, and painfully, through Robert's tongue until it ripped through the other side, its tip barely penetrating the table but still forcing out a muffled scream. The guard holding his tongue stepped away and aided in holding Robert down.

The Butcher brought the hammer above his head and arched it down on the nail with a weighted swing. At the clang of the metal colliding, another muffled shriek escaped Robert's mouth. His continued shrieks were bastardized by the streams of blood flowing from his tongue and streaming down onto the table, pooling around his chin and mixing with the tears that had carved a path down the dirt of his cheeks. As Robert tried to scream more, the air from his lungs filled with liquid as he spit red rain around him, splattering it over the stage and onto those gathered close.

The crowd shrieked, horrified at the sight and the onslaught of blood that now painted dots on the faces of those who were the closest.

The Butcher raised his hammer again and brought it down with more force, driving the nail further into his tongue, ripping it apart more. He continued his swinging until the tip of the nail broke through the bottom of the thick table and the head of the nail had fully sunken into the shredded remains of pink flesh. With each swing, the grains of the table were completely saturated with red and the white stone beneath Robert's knees were dripping with streaming puddles.

His shrieking turned into exhausted gasping cries. The crowd stilled as Robert Orville's eyes turned white and his body fell limp against the table. His head sagged to the side; twisting his tongue unnaturally as he fell silent and his cheek found its resting place in a pool of deep crimson red.

CHAPTER 12

G erald felt her fingers slowly move through his tousled hair and tightly grip his strands to hold him in place. Her back arched as she pushed herself onto his face more and he tightened his clutch on her thighs.

"Fu-" her gasp was cut off by Gerald rolling his tongue faster over her, keeping the same pressure that caused her to hold him so roughly in place. Her deep breathing became short and rapid, and her thick thighs tightened harder around his head as the building heat overcame her and shook her entire body.

Gerald smiled against her and moved his tongue over her clit again, then moved to gently kissed the inside of her thighs, allowing her a moment of reprieve before he would put her through it again.

"How many more times are you going to do that to me?" she asked between breaths.

Gerald mumbled his response into her thighs as he traced every stretch mark with his lips. "How many more times do you want me to?"

Gerald looked up from between her legs to see the satisfied smile on her face, smiling at the complete sight of her: her stomach still moving in and out to its fullest as her breath calmed to find a steady pace.

"As many times as you desire, sir."

He moved a hand from around her thigh to between her legs, his fingertips dripping with her orgasm as he ran them slowly up and down her cunt before pushing them inside her.

"Shit." Gerald jerked his head up from her.

"What?" she breathlessly asked.

"I forgot. Shit, I forgot." he said as he jumped from bed to find his clothes. "I forgot I told Dig- Lord Digarius- that I'd go on a hunt with him today."

"Are you kidding me?" she shouted and leaned her body on her elbows, tousling her disheveled hair around as she leaned up.

He turned and looked back at her, shaking his head as he bent over to grab his pants and pulled them on. "I know I am a fucking stupid man for leaving a woman like you in a state like this but I have to go."

She sat up in bed and rested her elbows on her bent knees. "Then do not. You two are close friends. Tell him no."

Gerald adjusted his shirt and tucked it into his pants. "While *yes* we are good friends and it *is* just a friendly hunt, unfortunately, saying no is not that simple."

She squinted and scrunched her brow. "So does he not let you..."

Gerald leaned over the bed and kissed her, cutting off her drawn out question. "No. It's not like that, Linette. Lord Digarius is a good man. I just- our friendship is different is all."

Linette's face tensed in an emotion that teetered between confusion and distaste.

"I'm sorry." Gerald said as he pulled back and picked up his boots by the door, barely finishing stuffing himself into them before heading to the door.

Lord Digarius stood outside the door in his hunting attire, kicking at dirt clods as the door opened and Gerald stepped out.

"Finish so quickly?" Lord Digarius teased.

Gerald glared and Lord Digarius chuckled. "Well, perhaps later you can actually finish."

Gerald let out an annoyed rumble as they approached the readied and saddled horses waiting at the tie up line down the road. "Unfortunately I do not think there will be a later with her."

Lord Digarius paused by his horse. "Oh? Again?"

Gerald shrugged, blowing off his true emotions. He untied his mount and threw his leg over the horse's back, adjusting himself in the saddle as he replied. "You know how it is with me. Always the lover never... never mind."

Gerald nudged his horse towards the mounted guards ready to accompany them on their late-day hunting trip, focusing his attention on trying to unsour his sullied mood. Lord Digarius quickly followed behind on his horse and the group rode in silence through the parish until their trail was framed by open fields and trees instead of buildings and walkways.

"Why are you so fidgety today?" Gerald asked, noting his friends' hard posture and hands fidgeting around the reins.

"Several messenger birds came from Isilria today. Some marked with the king's seal, others from common houses that we keep in correspondence with. Mother received them and she and her advisors have been locked in her office since their arrival."

"What did they say?" Gerald cocked his head over to him.

"I am afraid even if I knew what the messages read, I could not say." Lord Digarius' tone was matter of fact, but Gerald could still sense the hint of disappointment at the need to keep secrets between them.

"Ah." Gerald sighed as he adjusted and scanned the clearings around them. He had grown used to their friendship having their limits, at least from Lord Digarius' side.

"I am sorry, Gerald." Lord Digarius' eyes flicked up and down as he looked at the back of his turned head. "When you are on my council, things such as this will change."

"I am to be on your council? And what place would I have there?" Gerald asked.

"I do not know yet, but it would be nice to have you there alongside me. I may need someone to put me in my place every now and then." He jested.

Gerald smirked and nodded his head, "Wherever you need me, I'll be there, my lord."

The hunting party came upon a tree lined field known to be popular for fallow deer, wild boars, and other wildlife to gather throughout the day, especially given the foliage planted by Reapers to feed the game and encourage their return throughout the seasons. Near the parting in the foliage loomed two large oak trees with lines worn in the bark by leather ties repeatedly looped around their girth by repeated hunting parties.

The pair tied their mounts around the trees and Lord Digarius turned to their accompanying party, nodding at them down the path where they waited for the young lord. The two men crept through the tree line, careful not to snap a twig on the ground or snag a branch on a bush and came upon the opening of the tree encompassed terrain.

The golden glow of the late day sun cast yellow and orange rays of light along the wavering tall grass in the meadow. The surrounding trees drew dramatic shadows along the field and provided fair coverage for the prowling hunters standing just on the edge of the tillage. The cacophony of the forest had let itself rest momentarily while the days dwellers began their preparation to settle in for the night and the nocturnal creatures of the woods laid docile, waiting for their moon to rise and wake them. Quietness enveloped the space and provided an aura of peace and purity.

Lord Digarius and Gerald allowed themselves a moments pause to take in what the lands had blessed them with.

It took no time for them to get a glimpse of the gathering of wild boar sprinkled on the greenery of the far field. Both men reached for their bows in unison, then shared a look. They let their bows rest on their backs, and both brought a fist in front of them, hovering it over their other hands that lay open.

Like most trivial decisions between the two, they settled it as they did when they were young: with a game of rock, paper, knife. Lord Digarius won the childlike game and silently knocked an arrow and drew his bow, pointing it towards the largest boar in the rangale and aimed for the spot between its front shoulders.

At the moment of impact, the rest of the wild boar screamed and scattered in all directions, sprinting and hopping over the far back bundles of grass as the two hunters walked towards their game.

"The least you could have done for me was let me have the shot." Gerald commented, stepping over a thick chunk of grass beside the downed pig.

Lord Digarius pulled the arrow from the animal with a grunt. "And where is the fun in that?"

He looked over to Gerald's face, assuming it would be more lighthearted and jovial than it was. He let Gerald stew in his emotions for the time being, allowing him the chance to speak freely of them first.

Gerald's only emoted in a weighted grunt as they picked up the tied hog and rested the ends of the pole on their shoulders. Aside from an occasional noise of exasperation or grunt, there was silence as they made their way to their horses.

"What exactly is it that is going on with you two? Is it serious?" Lord Digarius inquired, attempting to continue friendly conversations as they huffed and dropped the pig; preparing it to mount on the back of his horse.

"I do not know" Gerald focused on pulling apart the tied ropes and retying them.

"Ok." Lord Digarius drug the two consonants out. "You have not told me much of your courtship with her, I assume it was casual. Do you *want* it to be serious?"

"I do not know." Gerald snapped back, pulling the new knot around the pig's ankles tighter than needed "Should it not be your love life under interrogation instead of it always being mine? After all, you're the one who must produce precious heirs. Where are all the women lining up at your bedroom awaiting their turn?"

Both halted as Gerald turned away and let out a drained sigh.

"Apologies, my Lord. That was unfair to say." He turned back, searching for signs of forgiveness and understanding in Lord Digarius' face.

Gerald paused and grunted. "It is just that I am not getting any younger. I should have found a wife or husband by now, or at least a promising partner. I do enjoy my time with her as she does mine, but she and I both know there is not much more there for us. It has been hard to find someone who will stay past sunrise and..."

He shook his head as his words trailed off.

Lord Digarius stepped forward and laid a hand on his shoulder, forcing him into a hug. "I am sorry, brother. I know your quest for love has been tough. Just know, that the moment you do find someone who does not fade away, I will be there for you... to interrupt and drag you away from them as well."

"You are the largest asshole I have ever known." Gerald muffled into his shoulder before shoving away from him.

The two laughed and made fast work of throwing the boar atop Gerald's mount and meeting with the rest of their party for the ride back into town. The friends parted ways at the fortress, Gerald assisting with passing off the wild game to their kitchen butcher as Lord Digarius was quickly shooed away by a noble aid informing him of his needed presence.

***

Ephraim picked up a white powder-filled vial and handed it to the young Lord Samwin Montarian sitting beside them.

"Now carefully pour this powder into this bigger vial here." Ephraim instructed as they pointed at one of the vials on the heavy wooden table centered in the study room surrounded by books, herbs, and more curiosities.

Lord Samwin, eager to see the experiment come to its pinnacle, enthusiastically jumped forward in his chair to pour out the vial. Just as quickly, Ephraim leapt out of their seat and grabbed him to pull him backward.

"Woah! I said carefully, little lord. You should remember by now that sticking your face mere inches from an experiment is quite unsafe. I do not think your mother has quite forgiven me for your singed eyebrows many moons ago."

"I do not think she has either. Every time you come to the castle to show me experiments, I swear she starts praying." He laughed as he, somewhat reluctantly, settled back in his chair.

Lord Samwin harbored no interest in anything related to being a young lord and after too many epochs of him wreaking havoc on the castle with his boundless energy and endless curiosity, he finally found a way to spend his time in his youthful epochs. Being of noble blood, and not a direct heir to a title, Lord Samwin had choice in his destiny regardless of the Divine House he was born under. Unlike common citizens, noble Houses were deemed of higher divinity and of more importance than the pre-determined fates which bound the citizens of the commonwealth.

Lord Samwin leaned forward again, this time carefully, and slowly poured in the powder. As he poured, the liquid began to fizz and bubble, eventually spilling out over the lip of the tube and onto the wooden table that bore many marks and burns from prior trials. The brightly lit stone walls around them also bore scars from experiments gone wrong or gone too well.

He moved his glance between Ephraim's face and the bubbling experiment, waiting for a big bang or climactic conclusion.

"This experiment is simple fun, Lord Samwin. A quick study in chemical reactions that is harmless. Well, so long as you do not store the mixture in a closed container." Ephraim shrugged as they casually mumbled the last sentence.

"Why is that?" he wondered, his head cocked and intently watching the bubbling foam spread and disappear on the table.

"Well, in time, it would explode." Ephraim said as he reached for a rag to wipe up the mess.

"You probably should not have told him that." Lord Digarius jested from the doorway.

Lord Digarius leaned against the doorway smiling. As Ephraim turned to greet him, they let their eyes wander just a bit longer than needed. Lord Digarius' skin tone was a bit lighter than his youngest brother's deep melanin complexion. He left his hair fuller than Lord Samwin, opting to keep the natural coiled texture in short twists and often rotated between being clean shaven and having the slightest scruff on his face. Today, he had chosen a light shadow of a beard and let his short twists relax into a more natural style.

Lord Digarius pulled himself off the doorway and sauntered into the room towards the two, his deep brown tailcoat flowed behind him with the open buttons exposing the simple linen V-cut blouse he wore tucked into his black trousers.

"Now littlest brother," Lord Digarius teased as he grabbed Samwin and pulled him out of his chair. "we are going to forget that last part, yes?"

Lord Samwin laughed as his brother set him down next to his chair. "Well, I don't know, it might be fun to remember that for the future."

"I swear your need for mischief will be the greatest trial I face when I become lord." Lord Digarius replied, shaking his head and ruffling his brother's hair.

The lord-to-be turned to Ephraim who had begun cleaning up their mess. "Apologies for interrupting, friend, but my brother and I are needed in the courtyard. Taylian and father have thoroughly beaten each other up, and apparently it is our turn to swing our swords against one another."

"No need for apologies, Lord Digarius, we were just ending our lesson with a bit of fun today." Ephraim smile then cocked a brow at the young boy standing eagerly by the doorway. "Lord Samwin, do not rush to leave so quickly. Aren't you forgetting something?"

Lord Samwin looked about the room, confused as to what they may have forgotten, "Did you need my help cleaning up today? Normally you prefer to do it yourself."

Ephraim smiled again and tapped the Healer's Guild pin on their chest, "How do we begin and end each lesson?"

"Oh, right." Lord Samwin straightened up and cleared his throat, beginning his recitation of the Healer's Guild oath that Ephraim had him practice each time they taught him.

"With my ancestors and God as my witness, I swear to carry out this oath and promise.

I will abstain from causing harm and only heal.

I will protect life, not take it.

I will prevent pain and sickness where I can."

He paused and pursed his lips as he worked to recall the remainder of the oath, the latter part coming out in stuttering bursts instead of fluid perfection,

"I swear to uphold this oath and my obligation to all; the sick and the fallen, the healthy and newborn.

May I always act as so to preserve life and the traditions of my calling and may I experience the joys and abundance of aiding those whose call I answer.

So help me God."

"Good job." Ephraim smiled and nodded, looking at Lord Digarius who also wore a smile of pride.

"Alright, off we go. Thank you again, Ephraim. My family always owes you a debt for your aid." Lord Digarius said as he guided his brother out the room.

Lord Samwin paused at the doorway beside his brother. "Ephraim, when do I get to swear it, for real?"

Ephraim shrugged. "In time, little lord. You must first face the same trials and education that all under the House of Herbs had to before choosing this guild's path, or another."

***

"Stop being so aggressive with every hit, Taylian. Conserve your energy and be efficient with your swings, not barbaric." Lord Montarian corrected his middle son as they sparred in the fortress' courtyard.

He stepped back from his father and caught his breath, his chest heaving under the linen fabric of his shirt that now lay stuck to his chest with sweat.

"How am I supposed to defeat an opponent if you keep telling me not to be aggressive? One minute you tell me to be *more* aggressive, then the next you tell me to be *less*."

His father did not answer and only moved forward, prompting him to raise his weapon and move as well. They circled each other, Lord Taylian walking rigidly with his arms tense in preparation for an attack, while his father casually moved with his sword down at his side.

"Defeating an opponent requires more than just physical strength. You need strength- of the mind and body- and to not let your emotions over-whelm your judgment so you can always stay one —"

Lord Taylian lunged forward and swung his long sword in a heavy arc. Lord Theodus casually swung his weapon and deflected the hit, shoving his son's sword down, and forcing the blade to strike at the ground.

Lord Theodus raised his sword and rested it against his son's neck.

"— one step ahead of your enemy." He finished speaking as he sheathed his sword. "Take a break, Taylian. Catch your breath and calm yourself."

Lord Taylian did not move, he glared down at his own sword and heaved his chest up and down, not only attempting to recover his breath but to control his frustration and anger at himself.

Lord Theodus stepped forward and rested a hand on his son's moving shoulder. "You know how to fight, son, but on a battlefield, your anger must be managed. A mind of chaos in moments of risk is deadly. Be as sharp as that blade you meticulously fuss over each day."

He squeezed Lord Taylian's shoulder and dropped his arm, urging him to come take a seat with him on the stone benches lining the open courtyard.

The courtyard of the Middleton Landing castle was the main stage for much activity in Ayeshire outside of swordsmanship practices and demon-strations. Lord and Lady Montarian enjoyed having the gates open during festivals and events or as they saw fit to allow their people to visit with them and tour the historic grounds. Some citizens would even find themselves observers of such demonstrations or guests at sporadic teas and prome-nades.

Today, however, the courtyard had been emptied of non-castle residents at the quick behest of Lady Montarian who was yet to make an appearance for the day, leaving her husband and her entire family on edge. Lord Taylian nodded and sat to remove the practice armor he wore, his face frustrated and disgruntled. He had heard the same lesson countless times over, and yet he still found himself struggling between chaotic fury and mental clarity when he had a sword in his hand for too long of bouts.

Lord Theodus noted the look of defeat brooding in his eyes as he took a swig from his waterskin.

"Taylian, what is our house symbol?" Lord Theodus asked.

"The stag." His son replied flatly, fidgeting with a strap on his side.

"And what is the stag framed inside of on our crest?"

"Freesia flowers and oak leaves." The same flat tone.

"Correct, and what is our house motto?" A tone intentionally ignorant of his son's annoyance.

Lord Taylian was growing quickly tired of the questioning and answered with crossness. "Strength. Integrity. Grace."

"No, those are our house *words*, what is our *motto*?"

He let out an angry grunt, frustrated and aggravated. "What is the point of this, father?"

"The point is," Lord Digarius said as he approached with their youngest brother by his side. "that he is trying to teach you the same lesson I took forever to learn myself. Our motto reminds us of what you need to remember before you are ready to go off on horseback leading soldiers or representing our family in reception halls and banquets."

Lord Taylian sighed again, then recited the Ayeshire house motto that had been burned in his mind since he was a child. "Find strength in your resilience, integrity in your actions, and grace in your heart."

His older brother smirked and shook his head at his monotone recitation of the words. He walked to the display of dueling swords, picked one up and pointed it at his brother, gesturing for him to join- of which he did promptly.

Lord Digarius took several steps back and placed his free hand behind his back and left his sword in a ready position, nodding at his brother to do the same.

"Our family's strength is found in our ability to adapt to change" Lord Digarius lunged forward and struck his sword against his brothers, who had already moved to block the strike. "and to recover from adversity."

Lord Digarius swung again in a different flair and was successfully blocked again. The two continued their exercise with Lord Digarius consistently changing his technique and striking pattern, each time being blocked by his brother's concentrated and quick hand.

"Good." Lord Digarius continued and circled around him. "You adapted. But, your posture was not as refined as it must be- you were hunched, too tense, a bit sloppy. Refining the basics is key if you wish to take in the words that Sir Rainey taught me during my epochs in training."

The brothers resumed their ready positions, facing one another.

"One" Lord Digarius commanded, and they both moved forward, taking their first lunge position.

"Two" he counted. They stepped forward again, tapping their swords together.

"Three"

While his brother obediently moved to the third position, Lord Digarius jumped forward, gently smacking his sword's tip against his brother's abdomen.

"You said three. That was *not* three." Lord Taylian quipped, stepping back and dropping his sword to his side.

Lord Digarius smiled and shrugged. "Correct, but right now, I am your opponent. While *we* always act with honesty and integrity, we must also ensure that we do not allow that to be our weakness. Enemies and opponents will use anything to defeat you, and you must always stay ready. Do not trust their words or feigned kindness."

Lord Taylian felt his anger coming up again, his agitation at his brother's tone and unsolicited teachings. His frustration at his brother's natural perfection versus his own hard-earned mediocrity.

"And then what? Am I to show them grace when they have tricked me and lied? That is part of our motto is it not? *Act with grace in your heart*, is it not?" he mocked and spat.

Their father shouted from where he sat with their youngest brother paying not a lick of attention to what they were doing. "We show grace to those who deserve it, Taylian. Those who betray us and make themselves enemies do not deserve compassion; they deserve death. Our words mean much, but they do not mean everything."

"Be as the stag is. Even the docious animal will fight without pause when an enemy is in front of them, when it has no other option but to do so." The voice of Lady Montarian came from the open archway of the courtyard.

Her husband and sons all turned to her. Lord Theodus stood up quickly at seeing her face- hardened, sharp, and angry. She took one step forward and addressed them.

"Lord Robert Orville has been executed by the king."

CHAPTER 13

"The Hand of the King is dead? Executed by His Majesty? For *treason?*" Lord Montarian paced around the war room and rubbed his jaw. "*The* Robert Orville who would apologize extensively if he forgot to send a congratulatory message to us for even the most mundane joy? Who would tip our servants any time they assisted him on his visits here?"

He stopped his pacing when his steps met Lady Belv'a firm stillness. "*That* Lord Orville committed treason?"

"It appears so." she replied in exhaustion. She took a long, tired breath and rubbed her brow. "But, possibly not. And I do not know which possibility is more concerning."

Lord Digarius continued to shift between the parchment scrolls on the table, re reading the same letters as the conversation continued. "What possibilities?"

His mother sighed. "If Lord Orville, excuse me, if the *former* Lord, did commit treason, knowing who he was, the things he stood for- if he did commit this treason then that means that His Majesty was much farther down a dangerous path than we thought, that the king was committing acts so heinous that Robert could not bear it any longer and had to betray the crown."

"And if he did not commit this treason?" Lord Digarius set down the papers and watched his mother.

"Then the king killed an innocent man on purpose and is more tyrannical than we thought him to be."

"Our House is his longest standing ally, friends before they ever sat on the throne. Are we here to stake our continued support of His Majesty and his actions?" Lord Digarius queried.

"No." the Lady of Ayeshire said.

Tightness and unease saturated the air in Lady Montarian's war room as the Montarian lord and lady, Her Grace's advisors, and Lord Digarius stood in silent anxiety.

Lady Belva quietly moved back to the head of the table. She stood behind the carved chair that once held her father and her ancestors before, straightened her spine and firmed her jaw as she rested her hand on the intricate carvings of the chair's back.

"Men have started wars over less." she said as she scanned the room. "And we shall give the king a chance to prevent one."

Lord Theodus stepped beside his wife. The couple nodded at one another; a solemn movement shared between the two seasoned leaders.

"We must find our allies and prepare in case he will choose a path of war, then." Lord Theodus began. "House Torrin will fight by our side if war would occur, I am certain of that. My former House has always been an ally and friend to Ayeshire, even before our marriage united our countries on paper."

"I hope so but," Lady Montarian interjected. "They do prefer themselves peacekeepers, not war starters."

The Lord and Lady made their way separately around the table in the room. Carvings of the landscapes and elevations of the continent glimmered in the firelight. Flags and crests were carved within the borders of the six kingdoms, their presence denoting the Major and Minor Houses that ruled over each part of the lands.

"Yes, but they are also keepers of justice. Lord Torrin keeps true to his family's words, both sides of it. If keeping the peace forsakes the upholding of justice, he will not stay quiet." Lord Theodus countered.

"*Protectors of peace, keepers of justice,* yes." Father Robb hobbled over to the table with them. "But the last true war the Torrin family found themselves involved in was the Royal Civil War. They only involved themselves to demand the end, siding with whoever would bring peace first, not caring that their aid fell on the side of the usurper king."

Lord Theodus nodded. "Then we ensure that my cousin knows that we intend to ask for peace first, and that war is only inevitable if the king does not surrender before the battlefield. If that does not bring him to our side, we give him the reminder of how the late King Andrius treated his aunt when Lady Earla was married to him. And how King Andrius buried her as a broodmare before she was able to be crowned queen."

He looked across the table at his wife, searching for confirmation that his thoughts aligned with her greater plan.

She nodded and jutted her chin upward. "Torrin blood may run through King Ivan's veins, but that alliance failed the moment Lady Earla was no longer a wife but a womb to King Andrius. We shall ride east. Visit my sister at Sandhill House and secure House Bromlyn first, then continue onward for Sebern to gather their army as well. We will ensure alliances and agreements along the way in what is to come. In what we must do for the greater good of our kingdom and the justice our people deserve. Lord Montarian, I am confident in your ability to gather an army with discretion as to not raise concerns?"

"Aye." he replied. "We can fabricate a tale of war games or training exercises and only state the truth when, and if, needed."

She looked around the room and took in the faces of the men and the advisors and aids around her. Her eyes closed for a moment as her chest rose upward and filled with a deep breath. She exhaled and opened her eyes. "Are there any present who wish to question my course of action?"

"Nay." Her advisors, husband, and son replied.

She continued. "Father Robb shall send a messenger bird to Berren Castle to alert them of our stopover, the same with Sandhill House. When our alliances are assured and we are ready for the worst, we shall write to the king and demand he do what we know he will not: that he step aside, and that he confirms he is unfit for the crown. This has gone on long enough. The execution of the Hand of the King should not have been the last straw, but it now is. I will not watch as His Majesty becomes crueler and more tyrannical and risk more lives while we wait for something much worse to happen at his order. I will not risk what may come next by his hand."

The room nodded in agreement.

Lady Belva turned to Lord Theodus. "Lord Commander, call the banners."

Chapter 14

Father Figgins stared admiringly into the gold and gaudily framed mirror, adjusting his cream silk pallium to drape properly around his neck and over his deep red chasuble. He moved his attention and fingers to the excessively large jewel on the gold pin that held the pallium in place, polishing it spotless and centering and adjusting the pin again. He ran his thin boney fingers down the tail of the pallium, ensuring it too was perfectly draped.

The very image of God. He thought as he stepped back, once again staring too long at the gilded mirror.

Outside his office door he heard the final welcoming notes of the chapel's organ bursting through the stone walls. He picked up the black covered and gilded -page scripture book that sat on the wooden chest underneath the mirror; the gold of his many rings blending perfectly with the bright gold of the page's edges.

"Let the show begin." He grinned as he walked out the door to the worship space awaiting his presence.

As the door shut behind him, the crowd of parishioners stood in the pews waiting for him to take his place at the pulpit and give the opening greeting that would allow them to be seated. He took his time settling in behind the pulpit; perfectly centering the scripture book that he would not use, pretending to scan the pages for the right text, and ensuring his attire and accessories were laid exactly as he wished.

He soaked in the moment as he did each time he stood in his place of power, letting his parishioners obedience satiate his need and their attention to his every word settle deep within his old bones. Every word he spoke, every back he stabbed, every hand he shook and every action he enacted throughout his life was masterfully crafted to bring him to this place

He deeply inhaled the smell of incense and smoke as they wafted throughout the cathedral and differing perfumes carried in the air from the pews of quiet and dutifully patient churchgoers. He looked down at them and smiled.

"May the grace of God, our divine creator, and his blessings be with you." Father Figgin's voice echoed and boomed throughout the grand hall of the luxurious church.

"And with you." The crowd replied from the intricately carved wooden pews padded with rich fabrics matching the exuberance of their own attire.

***

"It is a vintage from my own collection, Your Majesty." Father Figgins nodded towards the fresh decanter the squire set in front of them before leaving the room. "Quite exceptional."

King Ivan finished chewing the stewed lamb as he grumbled and shook his head. "Perhaps another time, Father. It is only lunch."

The king set his fork down and rubbed his forehead slowly, pushing the pain and agitation away. He cleared his throat and tried to steady his breathing. "And I am still feeling the headache from our wine a few days ago. It rang throughout the church gongs this morning and has only gotten worse."

Father Figgins uncorked the decanter of dark liquor, the scent of cinnamon, spice, and molasses whisked in the air and wafted under the king's nose. Father Figgins slowly poured himself a glass and set the decanter back down with the cork beside it between the two.

King Ivan clenched and unclenched his shaking hand under the table as he attempted to keep his eyes firmly on his cup of tea.

"It is no worry, Your Majesty. I just thought this moment momentous and worth celebrating." He watched as the king's eyes raised to meet his. Father Figgins lifted the glass to his lips, sloshing the amber inside of it around, and sipped. He closed his eyes, letting out a small moan at the burn of the liquor that wet his lips.

"Perhaps... one drink." King Ivan gave in. "It *is* a celebratory day."

Father Figgins smiled as he set down his glass. His hand, still cold from the chill of the crystal he held, straightened the new Hand of the King pin on his chest. His fingers stroked the open hand molded atop a simple circle. A crown sat centered on the palm, the edges of the crown being the focus of Father Figgins casual rubbing. The threads of his lavishly embroidered tunic matched the brushed bronze metal of the pin and the stones and metal around his boney fingers and pale neck matched in perfect aesthetic to the finesse of his new title.

Robert Orville's dried blood was still being cleaned from the crevices of the execution slab when Father Figgins was handed the pin by King Ivan. He tentatively accepted it from His Majesty, claiming he needed time to pray and ensure that God's Will aligned with what the king was asking of him.

He spent two days polishing the metal until it shone as if it were freshly forged and practicing his signature with his new title before making his way into the king's lunch today and accepting it with practiced grace and humility.

"My time in commune showed me a great deal, Your Majesty." Father Figgins said as the king drank. "The path we are on, it is His Will. It is how we shall keep the psalms from coming true. We can stop the new age from coming if we continue with our work."

King Ivan set his drink down and rested his elbows on the table. His chin sat on top of his closed hands.

"The Psalms have already begun, Father. You have seen the signs in the skies and the movement of our people." The king inhaled as he sat up and carefully recited the ancient prophecy. The words known only by those inheriting the heavy crown and those the bearer trusted with its truth,

"When the eye of the world has dimmed and stars have fallen as if made of rain,
Of solid gold and stardust rulers shall remain, forevermore until burned in fury
and in flame.

And the world of men shall be made to begin again."

King Ivan poured another drink as his mind buzzed. "The Psalms of Fire and Fury terrified First King Lucarius so much he and the church falsified the foundation our kingdom was rebuilt upon after the Great War. His fear gave birth to the deepest truth we hide about the Divine Houses and their necessity to our kingdom's future." He shook his head as Father Figgins opened his mouth to interject. "The stars fell as the snow came this past winter and two showers of star fall filled our sky again this past knot, our people grow in their fury alongside the skies. The Eye of the World is doomed to continue to dim into blackness and I have ruled in fear of it all."

"But this fear can be your salvation! Our people's salvation!" Father Figgin's preached.

King Ivan shook his head again, the headache that would not leave him only growing more as the liquor took over. "I am standing on the most dangerous edge of a blade, Father Figgins. And you now stand right beside me on it. I have spilled blood to protect the greater good of our people. I have inherited the debt of holding up a false system to ensure order and that our kingdom does not fall. I must do horrible things, the most treacherous things to ensure our world does not come to its end. And I have failed to prevent this prophecy from happening no matter what I have done."

He slung another drink back, no longer caring that he had always kept careful track of each of his drinks. "It is no wonder so many went mad." He said in defeat, his words beginning to slur as the liquor settled in his stomach atop his half-eaten lunch.

"You have not failed, Your Majesty. The night before we sent your former Hand to the dungeons the moon was eclipsed; one twin overtook the other in the sky and signaled to us that an evolution was occurring, a life changing time was gifted to us by our actions." Father Figgins leaned in. "Those who knew the Psalms and who would use them against you no longer breathe because of our work. Our people shall settle, just as the stars will. What has occurred the past seasons was a test from God and our faith in His guidance of us. It is God's Will that we continue down our path, that will lead us to the peace and evolution we seek."

Father Figgins held a pause and softened his voice. "You are a *just* king, Your Majesty. You are a good man, and a good man would do everything within his power to stop this age from ending and that is what you have done in your rule, despite what they may say of you."

King Ivan leaned back, his shoulders fell against the back of his chair and his hands rested in his lap. "The world will never understand why we have done what we have."

"It is not their job to understand." Father Figgins turned to look behind himself at the painting held in a gilded frame on the wall.

King Ivan stared intently at the oil painting that caught Father Figgins attention. Brought to life in paint strokes was a depiction of the world before God's light saved them from the hell His creations were born into. Equal parts day and night, the painting showed demons lurking in the shadows, eating the innocent who could not escape their claws while those who kneeled in prayer in His light and submitted themselves to Him found protection from the evil corrupting the land. Different iterations of the piece hung in cathedrals and grand halls throughout the continent. The piece was titled *Absolution and Salvation Through Deference*.

King Ivan nodded as he returned to his cold lunch.

***

"Emaline, there you are." Sister Ora greeted as Emaline approached. Sister Ora set down her cup and turned in her chair as Emaline approached. She pointed to a plate setting on the table beside her. "I saved you some lunch, come sit."

Emaline's face bore a heavy mourning as she stopped beside the table, her helmet tucked under her arm and her eyes avoiding Sister Ora's. Behind

Emaline, Prince Percy sheepishly approached the balcony dining table. His glance danced between both women and his shoulders hunched him into a submissive stance as he wrung his hands behind his back.

"Oh, Prince Percy." Sister Ora pushed her chair back to appropriately greet the prince. He quickly shook his head and shooed away her attempted formality as he always asked of her.

Sister Ora finished standing, forgoing the curtsy at his request, and exchanged the greeting for another as she took in Emaline's seething anger held in by the tightness of her jaw and Prince Percy's fear not hidden at all.

"What happened? What is wrong?" She stepped towards the silent and brooding Emaline. "Emaline what is wrong?"

Emaline cocked her head to the side as her jaw tightened, the words hissing out between gritted teeth. "His Highness has important news."

"Sister Ora, I—" Prince Percy carefully stepped towards her and swallowed. "I am truly sorry. I need you to know that this was not at my request, and I did not wish for this to happen. I tried to stop it, but my father would not hear it."

"What are you talking about?" Her heart pounded and her fingers twitched as she brought them together in front of her. She battled her craving to pinch and pull at her skin. "Is it our betrothal? Did you father demand it end?"

She did not miss the shot of pain in his eyes at the hope she did not cover in her words.

"No." He replied, he glanced at Emaline who still stared straight ahead, then turned back to the quite tall King's Guard standing near him. The helmet covered his face, only a slit revealed his eyes and showed the bridge of his nose and the cupid's bow of his lips. "Sir Loren, please come forward."

Sister Ora's furrowed brow lifted as she understood what the prince would not say. "You promised me that Emaline would stay with me if I so wished. If *she* so wished."

"I know, but my father feels, as do Sir Marion and Father Figgins, that it is no longer appropriate. The King's Guard are sworn to the royal family, to our protection —"

She cut him off. "— And Emaline swore the same oath when she returned from battle and took up her posting as a Noble Guard, *as my Noble Guard*."

Prince Percy sighed. "But that was before our betrothal. You are a member of the royal family now and it was deemed appropriate that you are protected as such."

"I am no member of your family, not yet." She stepped forward, her hand reaching out to touch him before she jerked it back to herself and bit back tears. "Let her stay until we are wed at least. Please, let me keep something of my life."

"I'm sorry." Prince Percy somberly replied. "I promise I did not agree with his decision. But it was not mine to fight."

Sister Ora looked to Emaline again. Emaline's own sorrow would not fall down her face in tears as it was for Sister Ora but would come later in bursts of rage and anger when no one would see her fall apart.

It was best for enemies to never see you weak enough to break.

"Emaline." Sister Ora croaked out.

Emaline turned, her jaw now trembling, and she slowly dipped her head in a bow. "It has been my upmost pleasure serving at your side, my lady, but I am afraid duty calls my name elsewhere."

Sister Ora shot her head back to Prince Percy, her movement so harsh her hair threw itself back over her shoulder. "So this is it? His Majesty's kindness has been expended enough and she is now to leave at this moment?"

"I'm sorry." Was all Prince Percy could mumble before he nodded his goodbye and turned away. "I am truly sorry."

Emaline paused beside Sister Ora and dropped her voice to a whisper. "Out of all the King's Guards, Sir Loren was the kindest I met here. Prince Percy insisted on choosing your new sword himself from his own entourage of guards. But he did not choose anything else, believe him in that." Emaline stepped away, her eyes red and glossy as she looked back one last time, "Goodbye, sister."

The title that accompanied Sister Ora's name for epochs changed when Emaline said it. Not a Sister of the church, a dutiful woman bound to books and words, but a sister by choice, a friend bound to another through something much stronger than bloodline or faith.

CHAPTER 15

Despite its name, Sandhill House was no more a simple house than the earth was born from a droplet of blood pricked from the finger of Old Goddess Atimnial while tending her heavenly gardens.

In comparison to the large grand capital citadels throughout the kingdoms, Sandhill House was much smaller and less regal, but it was still a mighty fortress integral to trading routes and passages in the south. Tower Bridge, the largest bridge in the southern lands that Sandhill House was built to defend and watch, was looked over by the lands stewards and passage on it was meticulously tracked and supply trade dutifully monitored.

It was, for those who held no care for paperwork and supply trading, a dreadfully boring place. It was such for Lady Lydia Bromlyn, Lady Belva Montarian's younger sister, who had wed herself to the steward, Lord Lucas Bromlyn, when she was at much too young an age to leave her family home, but deeply desired to hold a higher status in society and find some duty comparable to her older sister.

"Sweet sister," Lady Lydia exclaimed as she embraced Lady Belva, barely giving her a moment to acquaint her legs to the land, "It feels as if it has been eons since I have seen your face. Time at Sandhill moves as slow as the inland current."

The two sisters exchanged authentic and joyful pleasantries and Lord Theodus and Lord Bromlyn exchanged greetings as well, in such a way one would expect two brothers-in-laws who barely knew, or respected, one other would- with simple handshakes and grunts of acknowledgement.

"My Lord do show more respect, please. Our Lord and Lady are here." Lady Lydia sweetly said to her husband, her hand still holding her sisters fondly. "It is not often we are blessed with any excitement or a noble visit."

Lord Lucas addressed Lord Theodus again, his tone salty and sharp like the stone that built his ancestral homestead, "My Lord, what brings you here? It is tax season no longer, there is nothing to collect. We provided ours to your courier long before the 15th of Aquius."

"I am certain you are in good standing with your taxes to the country, Lord Bromlyn. But that is a concern my wife, *your Lady*, can address." Lord Theodus turned to his wife, both looking at one another in contempt and remembrance of how Lord Bromlyn acted.

"Your taxes are fine, Lord Bromlyn. As our messenger bird said, we come to discuss important matters and to ensure our shared understanding in the future of our kingdom." She politely said, ensuring her voice was soft, even, yet firm with no room to question her, but not so stern he would find her offensive.

"Your presence was last granted to us 13 epochs ago when you forced my hand to still when I intended to claim more land under my banners to the north, land owed to my House." He snipped. "You sent a brigade against your own people and rode with it."

She corrected him. "I sent myself and a brigade to stop a battle that had no sense to it. No one is owed land simply because they can see it, my lord."

Lord Bromlyn ignored her and turned back to Lord Theodus. "Does this visit have anything to do with the news that travelers have brought to us lately? Of Lord Orville's execution?"

"Lord Bromlyn." Lady Belva stepped forward and squared her body. "Our houses have been unified long before your union to my sister and yours has long been loyal to mine before I was titled. There is a future to discuss and I am here, as *your Lady*, to ensure continued loyalty and understanding."

Lady Lydia panicked, "What is happening sister? What is—"

The Lady of Ayeshire cut her off, noting the curious ears around the docks and hushed her tone. "Hush, sister."

She painted on her regal and stoic makeup as she spoke; straightening her stance and sharpening her face and words. "As I know you prefer his company over mine and we wish to have a friendly stay, my husband, my second in command, will fill you in on what it is your House is to do for our country." She paused, remembering his ego that required constant satiation. "Your lands are important to our people, Lord Bromlyn. What you do here is important. What your Lady commands of you will ensure continued honor on your line."

***

"Sandhill House is of the upmost importance to Ayeshire if war will truly come. We do not believe His Majesty will step down, but it is our hope he would before any battles must begin." Lord Theodus addressed the room, those gathered consisting of Lord Bromlyn, a military advisor, and his High Scholar.

"And if there is to be a war, Tower Bridge would likely be near the battles. That is, if your swords were to let the king come near our lands. "Lord Bromlyn smirked. "We have under five thousand soldiers spread from here to Wolfsden. The remaining lands to the west have over twenty thousand. Where are they?"

"Gathering still." Lord Theodus replied. "We have sent word to all throughout the lands, advising leadership that we are preparing for war games training before the long winter. Lord Torrin at Sebern has agreed to be a part of our war games and his army is preparing the same. We hope to gather in secret under this guise before we are made to strike, if we are made to, that is."

"Yes, but, where *are* they?" Lord Bromlyn asked again.

"Fifteen hundred will be at my side before dawn. Their boats were just behind ours. They will march with me to Berren Castle to meet and hold this same discussion with Lord Torrin. The rest..." Lord Theodus paused and cleared his throat. "What is of importance at this time is to ensure that these lands, which offer quicker passage between our countries, are protected and that our armies have free passage through. We have two thousand we can lend to your fortress to ensure protection and we offer our hand in case these lands were to be targeted by any enemy."

"That is all? Two thousand swords? If we are so vital, why not more?" The military officer spoke up.

The Sandhill High Scholar, wearing common scribe robes and carrying a heavy ledger, added. "And free passage? No tolls to be paid?"

"I promise you, no more soldiers will be needed if we focus our forces and Sebern's at pushing past the borders into Britia, past where they could even begin see the stone pillars of Tower Bridge." Lord Theodus assured.

"What is the plan for the remaining soldiers at The Landing and to the west? How will Iron Bay aid in this war? What are they being asked to risk?" The military officer asked.

Lord Bromlyn relaxed in his chair at the opposite head of the table, his smooth, snarkiness covered his face as he watched the frustration build on Lord Theodus' face. "As you can see, my lord. My men and I are concerned, and rightfully so." Lord Bromlyn said.

Lord Theodus hardened his voice. "You and your men seem to believe this is a negotiation. It is not."

"Then if it is not a negotiation, you may leave, Lord Montarian." Lord Bromlyn lightly gestured towards the door. "While we may be a minor house under to yours, we are not legally required to bend to your whim and bark like your dogs."

"So you would let our lands fall, then?" Lord Theodus barked.

"No, they won't fall. You have assured us that no king's army shall make it to our lands, so we will be just fine regardless of what we would do. My family were stewards of this land before these hills bore a title, a title that we were given for our aid."

"It was not your aid but your submission to a usurping king that got you this land." He growled between his teeth.

Lord Bromlyn laughed as Lord Theodus leaned into the table.

"So, the great commander Lord Montarian does still have a bite. Being second in command to your wife did not take that away as I had thought it had."

Lord Theodus straightened his posture and took a deep calming breath. "So that is what this was then? A fucking game to rile me up while we stand on the edge of a war?"

"That is what politics is, Lord Montarian. A game. A power grab. You play the same game with swords and shields, while I do so with words, just as your wife does."

Lord Theodus was defeated, the sneering snark of Lord Bromlyn had not even cracked and he was no expert in making men like that cave without being on a battlefield.

"What is it you want, Bromlyn? The land you tried to claim before? A new title?"

I want... assurances." He move forward and rested his arms on the table, moving from a casual posture to one of command. "Do you believe your battle strategy, whatever it may be, will win this war if it does occur?"

"Yes. I do." Lord Theodus squared himself.

Lord Bromlyn's advisors shook their heads and mumbled more words of disagreement. Lord Bromlyn held his hand up as he silenced them. "Would you promise your life on it?"

"Yes, of course."

"What about your wife's?" Lord Bromlyn glared.

Lord Theodus froze. "What do you mean?"

"If you are so confident in your army's plan, a plan that, again, you have not fully shared with us and ask us to bestow complete trust in, then leave Her Grace here at Sandhill under our protection. If you are right then, Sandhill, and Her Grace, will remain unscathed."

Lord Theodus snapped and slammed his fist against the table. "Dammit, Bromlyn. You cannot ask that of a man, of me."

"No?" He asked. "This is a discussion regarding battle and war, and you are the Lord Commander, are you not? I would think a negotiation such as this to ensure an alliance would be well within your jurisdiction as Lord Commander." Lord Bromlyn's tone was still cold and calm, but a sharp edge accompanied his demeanor.

"I will not be held responsible for her reaction to this insult or her acceptance of it." Lord Theodus hissed.

Lord Bromlyn's voice slithered. "So, as Lord Commander do you accept our offer to ensure our loyalty and any aid you seek? Or shall you leave it to chance?"

Lord Theodus wanted nothing more than to turn his smirk into a broken, bloodied mess. Reluctantly, he leaned forward and gave an answer that he had no option, or right, to give- an answer that he hoped his wife would understand and accept.

He was no man made for politics.

"Yes."

CHAPTER 16

Lady Belva expertly threw her shoe.

Lord Theodus expertly dodged it.

"Theodus you overstep your command once again." She snarled as she stormed about their guest quarters. "You should have stopped the negotiations, left the room and found me to fix this mess."

"I had no choice, Belva. I am sorry." He tried to step for her to offer his hand, but she shook her head and stepped away.

"You had a choice. You had a choice to have your wife, *your Lady*, negotiate when it was my autonomy on the line." She held back her angry tears. "You have no idea what you have done by this overstep. Do you not understand the words I confide in you each time men like Lord Bromlyn question me? Each time men like him turn to you for leadership while I stand holding the high command title? You have set my tireless work back so carelessly."

She sighed and sat down, resting her head on the back of the chair, and rubbed her forehead. "I have had to perfectly curate myself as a leader, as a satisfactory replacement for my father to men like him and all the others who looked down on me. I have had to speak graciously and perfectly, to make myself the right size in rooms that I should overtake, to only snap when absolutely required of me, and to hold men's egos so delicately in my hands and offer them love when, if I were a man, I would not have to worry about their emotions. With one decision you have erased that work and played right into his hand. I trusted you, Theo."

He kneeled before her and placed his hands on her lap. "I know and I am so sorry. I was trying to help our cause and I thought not of what that would do to you. I spend too much of my time trying to prove myself so capable after all these epochs, and with one stab at my ego and questioning of my manhood, Lord Bromlyn pushed me so far I could not see what he was truly playing at."

He reached his hands forward to grab both of hers and raised them to his face. He kissed her rings and rested his forehead on the back of her hands. "I will do what I must to make this right by you. I will go speak to him and rescind what I said. And perhaps punch him in the face. I would very much like to do that."

She sighed and removed her hands from his and placed them on either side of his head, kissing the crown of his head before gesturing for him to stand so that she may as well.

"I have been so centered on ensuring that my own leadership is respected above all that I feel as if I have neglected to aid in your political leadership." she said. "You came into this marriage a skilled leader of battles and I entered it so determined to remain in control and remind all that I am the one who bears the title, that I am still of Vegaria blood despite taking your name and my family's House taking it as well."

She sat down on the bed and took several deep breaths to center herself. "I will fix this. It is my seat that overrules all the lands within our borders and I shall remind those men of that truth. If Lord Bromlyn wishes I stay here, then he will learn to become comfortable with the Lady of Ayeshire needing to borrow his seat for some time."

***

"Again." Emaline heaved as her opponent fell to the ground with a clashing crash of armor.

Emaline's chest heaved with every breath; sweat and mud coated her as she angrily paced around the battle ring. "I said *again*".

Her opponent crawled off his back, barely standing up before she began charging and swinging again. The dull practice sword she wielded collided with the chest plate and pauldron of the soldier as she repeatedly swung at him while he stumbled to defend himself.

As his sword fell to the ground beside him, he signed his final yield to her. While still full of adrenaline and heated anger, Emaline stopped as he collected himself and left the ring. She caught her breath for a moment, looking around to see which of the gathered soldiers were left to challenge.

Her returning ship had landed the day prior. She did not bother sending word beforehand of her return and the king's dismissal of her duties as Sister Ora's sworn sword, she saw no point in putting quill to paper to bring faster news home of her failure. Instead, before the boat was fully tied on the dock, she marched straight to the training rings to request her re-enlistment in the active army.

She had impatiently waited all evening and after nightfall in the barracks to hear if Sir Rainey, the Command Sergeant of the Ayeshire armies, or Lord Montarian would accept her request for re-enlistment. Sir Rainey gave no word besides the news that Lord Montarian had sailed off with Lady Montarian for important business. Her mentor did, however, make a promise that he would personally request her return to his army.

She scanned the crowd, waiting for bravery to strike in the hearts of one of the other soldiers. Her attention caught swift movement approaching her peripheral. An unarmored Lord Digarius swiftly jutted into the ring, grabbing a practice sword from the sidelines as he approached her and smiling as he brandished it around.

Without wasting time, the two traded quick blows- with Emaline holding back her strength to not bruise or hurt him and with Lord Digarius barely attempting to strike, instead spending his energy acrobatically dodging in such a way that caused Emaline intense frustration. Each dodge and playful duck away from her strike was accompanied by his laughter as her strikes would alternate between meeting their target and slicing through air.

After a few moments of this game of play, Emaline stopped and stood looking at the grinning young lord.

"Are you done now?" he teased.

Emaline took her helmet off and bowed her head, huffing out between labored breaths. "I yield."

Over his shoulder, Sir Rainey stood conversing with those gathered, keeping his eye on the two in the ring as he chatted. Lord Digarius cocking his head in the Command Sergeant's direction, signaling to Emaline to follow behind. As she met his stride, he leaned in to whisper.

"You are full of rightful anger over the king replacing you with one of his own for Sister Ora, but being the face of death to your fellow soldiers will not protect her, or anyone else."

"I know." She choked out, her voice hollow and her throat hoarse and sore. She stopped as they met with Sir Rainey on the sidelines. "Hold on. Fellow soldiers, my lord? Does that mean?"

Sir Rainey responded for the young lord. "First Sgt. Kingery. It is good to see you back in the training ring. We have war games to prepare for, and this," he gestured to the brigade around her. "This is your brigade. Welcome back."

Several soldiers sat sharpening their blades or repairing broken plates of armor, others were deep in discussion, and the rest stood nearby, smiling, and listening.

She shifted back and forth and exchanged glances at Sir Rainey and Lord Digarius. "Are you certain? When I left I had only been a First Sergeant for but a moment. I would find no offense in returning as First Class, or even less if appropriate."

"It is not appropriate, and it is not how re-enlistment works, so no. We had consolidated this brigade with the twenty-first temporarily, but it is now yours- as it was meant to be." Sir Rainey had always been a stern man who believed firmly in the written rule, proper decorum, and duty. He gave her no moment to argue or speak and turned to the gathered brigade. "Twenty-second!"

All conversation, meandering, and activity stopped as each soldier stood at attention.

Emaline used all her strength to hold herself firm and adjusted her posture to mirror that of Sir Rainey.: bearing astern glare and stoicism that she had learned from over her epochs under his wing and leadership.

"Today we welcome back one of our own, First Sgt. Emaline Kingery. She will lead you all into battle as she has lead before when our land was taken in the east over three winters by those in the mountains. She will mold and train you as she has been before." He let a small smile crack the corner of his mouth. "And most importantly to you all, she will ensure you win these war games!"

The battalion around them held obedient restraint at wanting to smile or cheer. They stood awaiting her command. Emaline watched the crowd in front of her, remembering many faces from her time enlisted and seeing fresh ones on men and women so youthful she knew they had just left their war camps for the first time.

"At ease!" she commanded, then added. "Dismissed!"

The gathering of soldiers relaxed and cheered, those closest to her moved to her and shook her hand and clapped her on the shoulder in congratulations before departing back to their duties. In between overwhelming handshakes and hugs, she snuck her free hand to the weapons belt she wore and unbuttoned the small pouch stitched to the leather strip. She held her hand inside the pouch, anxiously rubbing at the old coin she kept hidden.

The familiar feel of the worn-out words and insignia offered her the centering her mind needed and the comfort she sought. The only token from her life before it was lost, the only piece of memorabilia found with her when she was left swaddled on the steps of the orphanage that raised her.

Lord Digarius stepped forward and excused the soldiers around her. "First Sgt, now that you are back, there is something you need to know. Finish here quickly and then come find us in the war room."

CHAPTER 17

S tacks of wooden discs and flag markers were strewn along the tabletop, framing the edges of the kingdom map carved into the table. The discs were of various sizes, the size related to the number of soldiers they represented and each was painted with a crest representing one of the six kingdoms: the stag, lion, eagle, bear, dragon, and kraken adorned the pieces.

The figures had been well used and repeatedly used with forgotten remnants of prior strategies still laid out on the mess covered table. The hearty fireplace centered in the room crackled as ashes of parchments flicked up from the flames and scraps with burned edges and broken wax seals attempted to escape their fate of being engulfed and destroyed.

Lord Digarius commanded the room and shocked lead military officers with his announcement. He kept his explanation brief, only giving needed information on what injustices the king had wrought upon the people that justified breaking the familial alliance. He gave little space for reactions.

"As far as those outside this room are to know, we are heading for a war game and nothing more. Your soldiers cannot yet know that we aim to take on the king if he does not remove his crown. Lord and Lady Montarian have secured our alliance with Sandhill House to ensure safe passage and their loyalty. Lord and Lady Torrin of Sebern will be brought into the fold next. As far as the Torrin clan knows, this is a war game, a friendly faux battle between allies."

Lord Digarius darted his eyes like flying daggers at each officer in the room, a silent threat and warning to keep their silence.

"The element of surprise is essential, officers." Sir Rainey sharpened his chin. "His Majesty's army, including those at Ravenhall, are nearly double our forces. If he can gather all of his allies before we are able to, then we will be exterminated quickly. A true war takes much time to plan, but we do not have that luxury and have been made to act in haste."

"He has Odessian loyalty, we can assume that, given Prince Elion's wife being the Lord's daughter, and we should assume also that the Isles of Aishar are on the queen's side given her bloodline. That gives the king almost one hundred thousand at his side. We have seventy at the most." Lord Digarius added.

"My lord, I do not mean to question Lady or Lord Montarian's abilities but, are we certain Sebern will join us in this battle? If the king does not step down we *will* go to war, are we certain we have allies to prevent a slaughter?" Emaline asked.

Her fellow First Sergeants, the only other officers brought into the meeting aside from Sir Rainey, their Commander, all looked to her. Her hand twitched at her side with nerves but relaxed when they all nodded in agreed concern.

"This concern is precisely why the king will not be written to with our demands until *after* we secure our alliance and their army." Lord Digarius' tone was hard-nosed, he again eyed the officers in the room.

"And if we don't?" Another First Sergeant asked.

Lord Digarius faltered in a response and Sir Rainey replied instead. "That is a question for the Lady and Lord to answer to *if* it were to come to fruition. We are not here to question and squabble over political concerns, but to discuss what we were all born to do- win a war. So the question is, how will we do this?"

Sir Rainey nodded at Lord Digarius and stepped back to allow the Ad Interim Lord Commander, a title bestowed on him by his father when he left, to continue addressing the war council.

"Right. Ravenhall is our first target. We march for their lands, await the command to strike and hold ourselves on the border of Sandhill House lands on the northern side of Tower Bridge. We only draw our blades or cross that border if the king does not stand down. The wardens of the land will either bend the knee or fall on them."

"Is that not an act of war itself?" An officer asked.

Father Robbins, who had remained quiet on the side of the room with Lord Taylian who was observing, raised his hand and spoke up. "Technically, no. There is no law or doctrine stating that we cannot gather our own army and stand them at the border of our lands. While the northern land surrounding Tower Bridge is on Britian soil, it is under Lord Bromlyn's jurisdiction and..."

"And being that Lord Bromlyn's House is sworn to ours-" Lord Digarius waved his hand and shrugged. "The politics of the land get messy, but our advisory council, specifically Father Robbins, have ensured that we would not be committing such an act so long as we stay where their flag flies."

Emaline cocked her head to the side slowly and leaned down to closely inspect the borders carved into the table before standing back up. "But how could we fit our entire army in such a small swatch of land above Tower Bridge? Let alone cross that bridge with such a large number? The bridge is perhaps a dozen horses wide, marching nearly thirty thousand across would not be possible if we wish to halt only thirty miles on the other side."

"We won't be marching all thirty thousand across. Under my advisement Lord Commander has determined that our best course of action is to split our army. Take the number we need and move for Tower Bridge," Sir Rainey ran his finger along the path they would march. "while the remainder continue east around Sandhill House, cross into Sebern, and march along the border to just past the hills of Ravenhall. When Lord Commander and I take Ravenhall, you all will move in, with hopefully the armies of Sebern alongside you."

"And we will sweep along the green lands right to the king's front door." An officer added, nodding in agreement, and avoiding the smile that teased at their lips.

"Precisely." Lord Digarius added. "Sir Rainey has the brigade assignments of which units will march in the morning to get a head start and move east for the borders, and which will finish preparing to head directly across Tower Bridge. He will aid the eastern units in their gathering of troops at the far war camps before returning to my side where we will move onward to Ravenhall."

Sir Rainey pulled a parchment from the pile, ready to inform each First Sergeant where they would lead. Lord Digarius continued among the shuffling papers. "We must assume the king will not go quietly and will demand a war and we must be effective and swift with our responses to ensure we exhaust his forces and land before any of his allies can gather. If they do, if Odessin and Aishar join this war too soon, we could quickly fall."

"What about the north?" Emaline popped her head up. "Have we considered asking for their aid? Lady Edgel is no fan of the monarchy; she may be inclined to raise her battle axe, if no for us, against him."

Lord Digarius shook his head. "It is unlikely. The last war that Craigie found themselves in was leading the rebellion that began the Great War of 390. They keep to themselves and their skirmishes on the borders. And," He let out a deep inhale, "given my father's history with the late-Lord Edgel, we believe it would be best if Lady Torrin asked her family and old country to fight if their aid is needed."

CHAPTER 18

Surrounding the mountain carved stone that built the Torrin ancestral home were spotty fields of green and vast walled in grounds filled with stone archways, gardens, small buildings and barns and training grounds for soldiers and upper-class citizens alike. Behind Berren Castle, a backdrop of imposing mountains stabbed through the clouds and protected the kingdom from those who hid in the mountains and in the Unclaimed Lands.

The twang of firing arrows sang through the vast training grounds alongside the crashing of impacting armor and weapons. Immune to the busting of noise was the eldest Torrin son, Cossius.

Lord Cossius stepped closer to Ella and brushed her hair behind her ear, leaning forward as he did and pushed his firm chest against her back.

"Raise your arm higher, like this." He whispered as he wrapped his arm around her and gently moved her bent elbow up higher. The deep tenor and crooning nature of his voice was emphasized by his whisper.

"M'Lord, you act as if I do not know what I am doing, when you and I both know I have been training with the bow my entire life." Ella smirked. She turned her head back to him, and felt his large hand grip tighter on her waist.

"Yes, but is it not so much better this way?" he smiled into her ear, prompting both to let out a flirty giggle. His thick red tousled hair tickled her face as he tried to take the opportunity to kiss her, only to be stopped by a flirtatious shake of her head and grin.

A few steps away, his younger brothers, Rener and Lyall both shared annoyed looks.

Lord Rener mumbled. "Can't even train one afternoon without trying to find somewhere to rest his cock."

"Rener, I am curious." The younger of the three men, Lord Lyall, asked with irony. "How many more women do you think he shall take to bed before he finally settles down and makes a few heirs?"

Lord Rener laughed and shook his head, knocking another arrow as he took an inhale.

"That is a question that I do not believe even God has the answer to." He shot and unsurprisingly missed the target and impaled the edge of the hay bale. His face crinkled in annoyance at his repeated miss, opting to blame the shot on his brother's distraction and not at his struggle to see well at far distances. He stepped back as he absent mindedly rubbed his hand along his slender jaw and the red scruff he had been neglecting to take care of.

Lord Lyall stepped forward to take aim, then turned to look at Lord Cossius and Ella again, still flirting a few paces away. He turned back to the target, corrected his stance, and shot, fixing his arrow only a few inches off the bullseye.

"I still do not understand why mum and da' do not put a stop to it and make him settle down. He has a duty to our country and his title." Lord Rener tossed his hands out and dropped them back to his sides. His mother's accent coming out with his frustration. All of the Torrin children held a slight accent from their mother's side, the occasional stronger vowels and softer spoken "T's" would come through and blend with their father's clear and brisk vernacular most prominent in central and southern Sebern.

"Lyall," Lord Rener stepped in front of his younger brother and looked down at him, placing a reassuring hand on his shoulder. "Cossius can flirt and fuck until he cannot anymore, just as you and I can if we choose to. By duty, he is not required to produce heirs until he is titled, just like any other noble or royal. And if he is not careful and makes a few before betrothing a bride, well, we have succession and marital laws for that."

"If he is not careful you will just cover it all up for him or fix it like you always do. He's never had to be responsible, and it is so infuriatin'." Lord Lyall grumbled and turned away, quickly shooting off an arrow again.

Lord Rener sighed and his shoulders fell. They were as broad as he was tall and so much fell on them that weighed him down when it came to his older brother. "Lyall, what is actually wrong?"

"I am not even participatin' in these war games and I'm out here trainin' just as much as you are. I'll be eighteen next season. Let me partake." He ran a hand through his tight red ringlets, the bane of his existence when he compared his scrawny stature and messy hair to his older brother's muscular bodies and their effortlessly wavy red hair given to them by their mother.

The conversation broke as the sounds of storming hooves echoed down from the fortress' central entrance. A clear shot and only a minutes' walk from where they stood, the billowing green stag banners waved in greeting as the surrounding courtyards halted.

Lord Cossius, who was as tall as a Clydesdale and almost as muscular as one, bellowed in excitement, encouraging all around to do so as well. He turned and jogged to his brothers, a smile beaming across his square face as he jerked his chin for them to go, "Let's go plan a fuckin' war, eh?!"

***

Lord William Torrin stood intimately close to Lord Theodus Montarian in the receiving room. The two men whispered to one another, Lord William repeatedly mumbling and shaking his head in uncertainty. Lord Theodus withdrew a paper from under his armor chest plate, shrugging his shoulders as he passed the note to his cousin, the seal of Lady Montarian's office holding in the contents.

Lord Cossius and Lord Rener walked into the room, leaving behind their younger brother to wander the halls and find a new responsibility to fill his afternoon. Their father held up a finger to silence them before they spoke, the parchment unraveled in his hand as he continued reading it.

He looked up, his hooded blue eyes and fixed deep set brows showing the urgency of his demand. "Close the door. Servants, please leave us."

"We are not here to plan a war game, boys." Lord William Torrin addressed them and walked the parchment over for them to read. His tone was sharp but controlled and even in cadence. "We are here to discuss the potential of a real war."

He took a long inhale and exhale as he turned to Lord Theodus standing beside the window. Lord Theodus nodded and held a grim and sober look.

"When do we march?" Lord Cossius shot his head up, barely reading the letter, his question carrying too hopeful of a tone.

His father held up his hand, "We are here to discuss the *possibility*. Lord and Lady Montarian seek our alliance and our army."

Lord Rener still read the long letter, tightening and pursing his lips and tapping his chin as he took in the entirety of Lady Montarian's request and explanation.

Lord Theodus stepped forward. "I would first like to apologize for our hiding of our true intent. We did not wish to raise alarms and alert the king of our plans. As the Lady of Ayeshire states in her official request, His Majesty has lynched and executed countless citizens for the simplest transgressions against the throne. He may have also done the same to advisors and aids in his service who were attempting to do the same, although, we speak not on fact in that regard. But, we do know that he has executed Lord Robert Orville for supposed treason. A man that has served two kings faithfully, who we all know to be incapable of such an act *unless* serving the crown was no longer ethical and treason was the only option for a man of morals."

Lord Theodus took a breath. "His Majesty knows that his throne is threatened because of his people's anger with him, he visited us as spring came and worked to ensure our alliance and obedience. We can no longer offer that. His lands are dividing and—"

"*Our* lands. Not his. He may rule over the Six Kingdoms, but these lands are the people's, not his." Lord Cossius spit out as he cut into Lord Theodus' words.

Lord Theodus cocked his eyebrows and nodded. "Spoken like a true son of Craigie."

"Aye." Cossius jerked his chin up and flicked his bright blue eyes. "I may not have known my uncle, but I know quite well what he and all of the north stand for."

"Cossius." His brother quietly pleaded as he finally lifted his gaze from the letter.

"Son, do not begin with this." Lord William ordered, then turned back to Lord Theodus. "Our country, our line, stands for peace and justice. No matter the path and the alliance, we seek the path of long-lasting peace and one that upholds justice. My father and those before me have ensured our standing true in our House words, and I will continue their work. This... decision, may make this path diverge. We could deny our alliance and keep some semblance of peace that we have known, or, we could demand justice, which would throw us into war."

"Is it truly a life of peace if the king is forcing us to live under tyranny?" Lord Rener queried. "Blood may spill less without war, yes, but that is only due to the totalitarian obedience he may demand of us one day quite soon, as Lady Montarian's words suggest. Word may not travel as quickly to our home as others, and we must take third hand news with grains of salt given how many mouths must pass them off, but His Majesty has been walking a dangerous line. And I do not believe we all need to rediscuss what the night skies are saying that have sent our Scholars into fits of worry."

"Our alliance with His Majesty has been fragile since the late-Lady Earla's death." Lord William mourned in remembrance for a moment, then looked to Lord Theodus again, "My father's anger almost tore it apart right then. If not for your parent's quelling his anger, cousin, King Andrius may have made us separatists with how he treated my late-aunt before she was even his queen."

Lord William ran a hand through his greying hair, the dark brown mop painted with shimmering streaks. He turned and faced the window, looking down on the green hills and chilly landscape. The rain had gently begun to fall as Lord Theodus and his envoy arrived and it was now beating against the glass window panes. The room waited for his answer.

Lord William to address his cousin. "We will follow you into war if it comes to it, cousin. But we do so in the name of justice and peace. The king must be given the opportunity to answer for what he has done, to change his ways. And if he will not, then we fight against him and name a new heir to the crown. Our people are not kings or queens, and our line holds no desire to become that. The one time our line got too close to the crown it brought my aunt a death much too young. We learned our lesson quickly when we treaded too close to that high of power."

Lord William took one last controlled breath and gave a firm nod. "When we return in victory, it shall be your line who determines who we bend the knee to."

***

"Iron Bay has been dutiful to your House for generations, my lady. Since the building of our first port, we have been true to your line, not because of duty or of title, but because your ancestors earned our respect." Lady Nilkimm placed her pint down on the table. "We are our own people, we breathe the sea air and use its salt as our medicine, our iron feeds your people's needs and in return your animals and grain feed ours. We may live within your borders, but our people are not yours to order around as you wish."

"I would never dream of demanding anything of you or your people, Lady Nilkimm. I am but asking." Lady Belva leaned back in her chair, its back and arms bearing the marks and sigils of House Bromlyn and Sandhill House. She had freed her hair from her braids and it surrounded her like a halo, covering the sigils of the minor House on the chair that was much too wide and ostentatious for its posting. "You have our coin, as much as you may need, and you have our aid to protect Iron Bay if the time comes where our people will be needed. My banners need your swords under it, Lady Nilkimm. My House needs yours."

Lady Nilkimm ran her hand down the long blonde braid she had tossed over her shoulder. Her black leather vest bore the crest of Iron Bay- an unbreakable iron chain, seemingly the only piece of her clothing not stained with salt and labor. "Aye, you put me in a hard place. To serve your House I must risk sacrificing my own." she shook her head. "Our people do not bend to any others will or their words."

"My House would never ask them to, my lady. *I* would never ask them to. Your House did not bend nor break when dragons flew over the lands and threatened fire. Instead, your ancestors chose death over obedience. They stood at the mouth of a dragon and *dared it* to burn them. And that dragon bowed to your people's strength." Lady Montarian bowed her head. "As do I."

Lady Nilkimm took a deep inhale and sat back in her chair, her sun spotted and freckled complexion clouded with uncertainty. "Any war will not be quick, nor will it only be fought by land. Iron Bay and the Spotted Isles need protection for the moment that war ships come to our waters. We know more tales than you of the king and his doings, of what he does that has caused our sailing ships to come back with more gossip than goods. We shall take your coin, and any supplies you offer to fortify and strengthen our ports and lands and we will use the rest of your *gift* to add more sails to our docks." She paused and sipped from her stein. Her face hardened like iron as she set the metal cup down. "I will allow my swords to swear to you for this war if it comes, but they must choose to do so of their own free will. I will not force them."

"Thank you, Lady Nilkimm."

She nodded and excused herself from the table, her silent advisors and aids rising in unison with her. Lady Belva stood with them to offer her goodbyes.

"And, my lady," Lady Nilkimm turned to Lady Belva before leaving. "if your House does fall to the king and he demands our loyalty, we shall remind him that iron does not bend, not at the knee, nor anywhere else."

CHAPTER 19

“Nnone of you are coming back, are you?” Lord Samwin asked, his eyes downturned as he sat on the edge of his bed.

“That is not true.” Lord Digarius strode over to sit beside his brother. “We all will come back. Mother, father, and I *all* will come back. But for now, you and Taylian” he turned to their middle brother who stood pensively by the door. “must remain here and keep our name—“

“ — Alive. Keep the family name alive in case they do not return.” Lord Taylian snipped.

“*Taylian.*” Lord Digarius hissed then softened his face and turned back to their little brother. “We will return. And while we are away, you are not to leave the walls of this fortress, you are to continue your lessons, and keep your wits about you. *Both* of you.”

Samwin nodded, his damp eyes turning away as he moved his blankets around to settle under them. “You promise to return?”

“On my honor.” Lord Digarius stood up and helped settle him into bed, ruffling his hair before turning to leave. As he made for the door, he jutted his chin at Lord Taylian, commanding him to follow him out.

The door barely latched behind the two before Lord Taylian shouted.

“I can fight. You know I can, Dig.”

“Yes, but we need you here, Taylian.” Lord Digarius continued his quick steps down the hall, Taylian a few steps behind.

“To do what? Sit around and bore myself to death? Wait for a bird to tell me you are all dead while I did nothing to protect our family or our people?”

"Taylian, *enough*." Lord Digarius continued, each step slamming into the stone beneath him.

"No! Let me fight."

Lord Digarius shot around. "No. Taylian, the battle field is no place for you, not now."

Lord Taylian's eyes glistened, his voice a crackling whisper. "Please. I must do something."

Lord Digarius let out a deep breath, resting his hand on his brothers shoulder before forcing him into a hug. "You must stay here. Lead our House, protect Samwin, and... take on the title of Lord should you need to."

Taylian shook his head into his brother's chest, holding onto him and squeezing hard as if doing so could hold him in place and make him stay.

"You must come back. I cannot be you."

***

Emaline slid her fingers down the center of the sword, inspecting each centimeter of the blade. She turned the blade to the side, her eyes running across the edge.

"There. Where the fuller comes to its end." The blacksmith beside her huffed at her critique. "That chip may be tiny, but the blade is already weakest at its point, we cannot allow for any imperfections."

She swiftly flipped the blade around, handing it to the ash and sweat covered blacksmith. "Repair this one as well, please."

He grunted as he took the sword from her, adding it to the large pile she had already deemed unsuitable. Around the exposed building, Iron-born of all ages hammered away at hot steel and shoveled coals from their reserves into the flaming forges centered in the open walled building. Outside of the forge, clashes of metal in combat were accompanied by shouts of command.

"Any more?" his gruff voice brought her attention back to the task in front of her.

Emaline shook her head. "No, that is all. Thank you, sir."

She turned to leave but his deep tenor calling at her stopped where her feet crunched in the gravel and dirt.

"It is good to see you back and in a position you belong." he called.

She slowly turned and took in his face again; the fullness of his crinkled face and sun spot covered skin marred with coal dust and fireside labor bore no hints to a shared past. "Do I know you, sir?"

"Eh, I do look quite a bit different from when you were here last, as do you. You were barely knee high to a hound dog when I first saw you comin' in with the other lost children. You were skin and bone, and barely that, when you arrived, couldn't even pick up a sword made for one of your age. And now look at ya, leading us to freedom. Well, pretendin' ta do so." He winked and his tanned face cracked in a soft smile. "Ya always had more of a fighter in ya than most of the ones that come through here."

Emaline cleared her throat, attempting to rid it of the dry lump now caught inside, her hand fidgeting on her swords pommel.

"You were the smith that forged my first sword- the one specially made for my smaller stature when I could not carry the others. And you forged my dueling blades that I trained with, yes?"

He smiled.

"Thank you, sir... Thank you."

"Leave me alone! Stop it!"

Emaline jerked her head to where the shouting came from and set off quickly to find the child the young voice belonged to. Her fast pace brought her to a hideaway alley between two buildings where a group of three boys had gathered, laughing as they shoved and kicked at another boy in blue rags.

"I said stop it!" The boy in rags shouted, finally gaining a moment of reprieve to fight back. He pounced on a taller black-haired boy who seemed to be the leader of the bullying children, tackling him to the cobblestone ground.

Emaline stood at the entrance of the alley, watching and waiting.

Watching and remembering how she had once been in his place in this same camp that was her childhood home after the orphanage dropped her and the others off ages too young to fight, claiming their mouths were too hungry to keep feeding. The buildings had not changed, each one only updated only enough to provide shelter from the changing weather. The structure and order of each day the same as it had always cruelly been.

Even the air smelt the same; of burning coals and hot metal, dirt and sweat.

The boy in blue did not have a chance to swing before another pulled him off and threw him on the ground, punching him in the face and adding to the fresh redness that was already there.

Before she knew it, her feet were moving and her hands reached for the swinging child. "*Enough* you little shits."

She threw the swinging boy off the other and placed herself in the middle of the chaos. "Do you think this makes you strong? Fighting and hitting one another? Chasing one of your own to a back alley to swing at?"

The three boys remained silent as they picked themselves up off the ground.

"He ain't one of us" the tall black-haired boy shot out. "Look at him, he's nothing."

"No. He is your *brethren* in this camp and a brother-in-arms when you leave it. He is more than—"

"First Sgt. Kingery, leave it be. Boys will be boys and boys will fight." Sir Rainey called from the street opening. He cocked his head down to the three boys. "You three, take him to the Healers to be taken care of, then go run your exercises."

"But we already did them" one of them whined.

"Then you get to do them *again*." Sir Rainey ordered.

The boys scattered out of the alley, reluctantly picking up the smaller bruised boy and taking him with them.

"If we allow boys to be like that then what kind of men are we training for battle? For life?" Emaline shot out, fury causing her to storm at Sir Rainey.

Sir Rainey dismissed her anger as he nodded for her to follow him out of the alley. "It is nothing to worry about, Kingery. They will grow out of it, the war camp will beat it out of them, and if that boy they were beating is anything like you, eventually he will beat it out of them, too and be better for it. Just like you are."

Emaline's jaw clenched. "I am not better for what I went through, and neither will he be. That boy should not have to suffer and be tormented just because others before him survived the same, or worse." She cringed at the memories and fixed her stare to the eastern war camp they had settled in ten days prior. "I do not owe gratitude to my suffering for the strength I now have."

Sir Rainey sighed and contemplated. "No, you do not. Perhaps, I will talk to their trainer; see to it they stop with the fighting and are punished until they stop. And perhaps allow you some time to show that poor boy that right hook of yours."

"Maybe." Her eyes continued to scan across the camp as they walked, now close to the building where the visiting officer's chambers laid. Her hand flexed on the pommel of her sword again.

"Still not used to being back, are you?"

"I never wanted to see this place again. I hated it here. I still hate it here. Getting out was my only good memory of this place." she said.

"I seem to remember a few happy moments you had on these grounds." Sir Rainey nodded down the pathway where fighting rings laid. "Like how you became champion of the ring several tourneys in a row. You did not seem miserable then."

"I had to pummel a boy's face until my fist was raw and almost gut another girl to get her to yield the fight." she shook her head at the memories. "I was only joyous that my blade struck when it needed to so I could survive."

Sir Rainey grunted. "All the same. You are here now and leading your own company of swords into a battle that will change the Six Kingdoms forever."

He stopped and turned to her. "You are what will be written of in legends to come."

The weight of being one destined for war glory after losing her kin to its bloodshed fell all around her. A mother killed in battle and a father too scarred by her death to watch his baby girl grow up to face the same fate. The coin in her waist pocket felt as if it now weighed a thousand pounds and the sword at her side bore the same crippling heaviness.

The glory that made her an orphan was now her glory to wield.

Her parent's phantoms haunted her even as her age turned into its thirties, but what kept her awake most nights were not their ghosts, but how great she was at being the thing she hated. From being the same great weapon that took everything from her and how many orphans she would have to create in order to survive.

"Then let us hope that the legends will be kind to my story." she said.

***

The courtyard and Place of Arms at Berren Castle were filled to the stones with soldiers inspecting weapons and moving supplies. Further out on the castle grounds, the final work of the sendoff feast was being completed in preparation for Sebern's army and Lord Montarian's convoy to deploy to the war games that all outside the Lords' inner circles believed to be occurring.

The festival lights, music, and food would be a much-welcomed contrast to the darkness looming over those knowing the truth.

While the outer halls of the castle were filled with soldiers and aids bustling with anxious activity, inside the residency area, the halls and rooms were mostly empty and quiet. The Lord and Lady of Sebern were quietly gathered in a sitting room with their two youngest children, Cletta and Ennis, and Lady Catherin Torrin's ladies maid, Lula, attempting to find a moment of peace before the outbreak. The noble couple sat together on a plush and well-worn couch, watching their two children play together on the floor- the innocence of their play softening the tightness in the space.

"How much hope do you hold that Craigie will respond positively to our message?" Lord William asked over the sound of his shuffling of parchment in his lap.

Lady Catherin sighed. "I know my people too well. It would take a miracle for them to come forward and fight. You know as well as I that they refuse to be involved in anythin' outside of their bloody clashes over the holy lands at the border. Especially after Broken Tower, we cannot count on Kathilla's heart warmin' to us ever again. But, after what you told me, I felt it worthy to try."

Lady Catherin's northern accent slipped in and out as she spoke, the harshness of her native tongue softening itself in with the fairer pronunciations she picked up over the epochs in Sebern. Her accent may have fallen over her time inside her new home, but her northern features had not. Her hair was made of rich auburn red waves and her fair skin was dotted with freckles that spread along the porcelain whiteness. The grassy green of her eyes darkened as she spoke, reflecting her sadness over the memories of Broken Tower.

Her husband nodded and grunted. "I wish we had the time to speak to her in person, your words might carry more weight if you spoke them yourself instead of sharing them in ink."

Across the room, Lula let out a near-silent scoff as she sat sewing on one of Her Grace's dresses.

"Lula, did you have something you would like to add to our discussion?" Lady Catherin snipped, her head cocked and eyes demanding an answer.

Lula looked up, stunned that her scoff was not silent as she intended. "No, Your Grace, my apologies."

"No, no, clearly you have an opinion that you feel so compelled to share since you could not hold your silence. So please, do tell."

Lula set down the dress in her lap and cleared her throat. "Your Grace, it is just that, I do not believe any amount of effort would convince those... *beasts* in the north to do anything to help. They are simply a barbaric — and I have said too much."

Her Grace spit venom as the familiar flame in her Craigie blood boiled. "I should not need to remind you that those *beasts* you speak of are *my* people and *my* family. You may not be from these eastern lands and have only been in my House's service for a short time, but the only element savin' me from strikin' the idiocy from your mouth is the distance between us right now and the presence of my children."

Cletta and Ennis sat stunned on the floor, only returning to their play when their mother halted her words and offered a small smile to them.

"I understand, my lady. I apologize for speaking such things." Lula turned back to the gown in her lap as her shaking hands moved to continue with her stitching.

Lord William squeezed her hands gathered in fists in her lap. "My love, I do not wish that the last images of my wife's face I see before war be of her deadly anger."

She smiled and leaned in and whispered, a new flame flickering in her eyes. "You do not leave for another day. I can assure you that tonight there will be far greater images of me for you to take with you."

The two shared the same look they had given one another since they were young teenagers sneaking off when their families dined together and visited each other's lands. Lucky when their young lust turned into adult love, their families approved their coupling and proposed marriage.

Not that the two would have asked for it.

She rested her hand on his cheek; his face instantly softening at her touch as he moved his head to fall into her hand. "My love, I wish I could come fight with you. I am a woman of the House of Armor and of the north. I know how to wield a sword and a shield just as well as every man and woman leaving under our banners."

"And having you at our side would make for a quick victory, as I am certain any man seeing you with anger in your eyes and a weapon in your hand would surrender without a moment's hesitation." He laughed and smiled. "But we all cannot go. We already risk much with Cossius and Rener joining my side in battle. Our House needs you here, safe within its walls."

He placed his hand gently on her stomach. "And while I am certain you are going to bless our family with another fierce warrior of a child, an unborn baby cannot swing a sword."

Lady Catherin sighed reluctantly, looking down at both of their hands resting over her faintly round stomach. His thumb absent mindedly rubbed where it rested on her, the familiar feeling of his soothing gesture relaxing her nerves.

"Then, just know, my love, that if you are to die at war and leave me alone with *six* children to raise, the afterlife will bring you no peace when I join you." They laughed into each other as her voice softened, "Come back victorious, William, but most importantly, just come back."

She squeezed his hand as she felt a familiar tiny tug at her sleeve, one that often interrupted moments like this.

"Mum, can we go to the feast now?" little Ennis asked, using her arm as a hold to pull himself onto the couch between the two.

"Of course. Let us call on your brothers and then we can all go together. Hmm?" she replied as she brushed his unruly red-brown hair off his forehead.

"Hey, that's mine." he shouted, seeing Cletta now playing with the toy he had abandoned. He batted away his mothers hands and crawled from his spot on her lap and teetered back over to where he had come from.

Both parents looked on with sorrow as Ennis plopped himself back down on the ground and pulled his toy back into his possession.

"One last family affair. One last day to pretend everything is not changing." she whispered.

Chapter 20

"Lord Torrin has chosen treason as well it seems. What a terrible disappointment." The king crumpled the parchment in his hand and tossed it into the crackling fireplace. "I must admit, the Montarian ploy was smart, pretending they were bringing back friendly war games between countries so we did not raise a brow to their gathering armies. If not for our little emissaries around the kingdom, it may have worked."

King Ivan stood at the head of the round table. At the peak of the last moon phase, he had called upon his war council as a precaution to receiving word of what the Montarian clan was planning. His Majesty had waited for more word to arrive on what their hidden canaries knew before seeking action; the letter they received today from Sebern gave him his final reason to officially call upon his own military.

His Majesty rested his hands on the table. "They have yet to officially declare war, nor have they written demanding my stepping down, as our letters stated they would first. If they wish to sneak about, then so shall we. So, tell me how we are to do that?"

A large, armored man with black hair, a square face, and dark eyes stepped forward. "If what our birds have said is true, Ayeshire's troops have long since departed from The Landing and will pass over Tower Bridge well before our own could make it halfway across our lands. They have an unstoppable advantage on our soldiers here, but not on Ravenhall's. We should stay with our idea to use Ravenhall as a wall.""

Prince Elion shook his head in disagreement and stepped forward. The sleeves of his loose fitted black brocade shirt were strenuously pushed up his forearms that he crossed as he stood alongside the commander. "I must still disagree, Commander Blackley. Ravenhall's army is a scratch on the skin compared to the size of the units they are sending."

"Yes, but, they could provide some... irritation to our enemies while we prepare our own attack." Sir Marion said.

Prince Elion shot a red eyed, tired glance at the Master of Armor. "We will not sacrifice an entire lands army, Sir Marion. Ravenhall does not even know who marches to them."

Sir Marion casually shrugged at the thought of sending thousands of soldiers to a slaughter. "If we need to sacrifice them for our bigger cause, then we should, but we do not need to. What I mean is for Ravenhall to surprise Lord Digarius' soldiers. The hilly landscape around Ravenhall provides a unique terrain to fight upon for those unfamiliar of each bump in the ground. We will easily know the path they will take, and know where it is they will camp along the border, so we send out Ravenhall in the cover of the hills and surrounding brush to ambush them while they wait for their command to move."

The king leaned over and moved figurines around on the table, displaying units and potential outcomes- alternating between shaking his head and nodding it as he did so. "If executed with precision, Ravenhall should be able to hold back their soldiers temporarily, buying you enough time to come to their aid, but the ambush must be a success." King Ivan looked at his heir. "You shall be quick to deploy your soldiers and make haste as you move. This will be your first war and my hope is to make it a swift one."

Prince Elion's brow furrowed and lips pursed as he counted the soldiers on his imaginary battlefield and considered the outcomes that could arise in more detail. "With the Sebern forces now joining them, once all armies converge in due time, we would become outnumbered- even with our hope of few casualties. We will need to call for aid, we should have already prepared to do so before it got this far."

"How long until Odessin's Dragon Army could arrive?" King Ivan asked.

Father Figgins stuck his chin in the air and stepping forward to place himself close to the king's side. "Even if they were to head straight to the bloodshed, their mountains and land require more time to navigate than ours, at the quickest, we would see them at the close of summer. And we have just begun to say goodbye to the spring."

"That is all to say, if they would join us." Commander Blackley added.

"You say that as if they would have a choice. While Prince Elion's wife may still house herself in the smoking mountains of Odessin, she is the future queen. Her father's do not need reminded that this is their daughters future throne we are protecting." King Ivan replied forcefully.

"What of Aishar? Could we call upon Her Majesty's home?" Commander Blackley asked.

King Ivan looked at his Hand, still standing far too close to him. "What do your logs say?"

Father Figgins opened the book he held, a small logbook containing information of each of the six kingdoms: census data, army, and land size, and, most important at this time, travel times by various avenues between countries. "Given the time it takes to sail an army through the Ringhar Sea, it would be two knots less to get them here and onto the field." He paused. "That is with the hope that Lord Priscius would obey your request and act with urgency, Your Majesty."

King Ivan bit back the distaste in his mouth. "Write to Odessin in haste, send our fastest bird, and request their troops at our doorstep at once while we prepare Prince Elion's army to leave within a few days' time. Notify Lord Williamson of what is coming for his doorstep and to prepare to attack on the borders of Ravenhall."

"If I may, Your Majesty," Sir Marion spoke up. "As Father Figgins stated, the Isles could get here much faster than Odessin, and our sails are much faster than most logbooks say. There is also the debt of honor owed to your House for your aid in the Aishar war. Perhaps it would be wise to call upon that."

"Time is essential, father." Prince Elion added. "You and Lord Priscius may not have friendly disposition, but the alliance is there."

"No." King Ivan quickly replied and waved off his room of advisors. "Calling upon the army of the Isles is a last resort. Go. Now, quickly."

***

Sister Ora walked down the aisles of the Hall of Archives, pulling random books from shelves to skim through quickly to see if one would catch her interest and quell her boredom.

None did.

Occasionally, as she looked down at the pages of the miscellaneous book in her hand, her downturned eyes would find themselves drawn to where Sir Loren stood a few steps away. Most of the time when she glanced over, his stance would be transfixed upon her, a guard ever so dutiful in his oath, but on occasion, she caught him turned towards the shelves and his head hunched forward to read the spines of the books, as it was now.

She walked towards him, the fingers of her hand running along the spines of the books on the shelf before stopping just a few inches from his figure. As she did, Sir Loren turned to her. Through the slits in his helmet, his ocean blue eyes locked with the amber depths of hers.

Sister Ora had quickly discovered that Sir Loren was extremely dedicated to his sworn duty of keeping his eyes on her, so much so that just a few days after Emaline was sent away and his presence replaced hers, on one particularly maddening and anger-filled day, Sister Ora had queried him on if he was also tasked with watching her piss and bathe.

Sir Loren had replied by telling her, in his flat and factual tone that he always spoke in, "Only if you would desire my audience for such things."

It was then that she decided she perhaps did not need to be so harsh and miserable towards him as she had been from the beginning. It was also then that she found her entertainment in finding ways to aggravate him, to see when and how she could make his stoic demeanor fall.

"Do you get a chance to read often, Sir Loren?" she asked gently as she turned to the book that had caught his eye and pulled it from the shelf.

He stood straight and took a step back. "No, m'lady."

"Why not?" she asked.

"As a soldier I only ever gained the ability to learn to read maps and the like- the necessities for war. Reading is a privilege I was not allowed to have."

She creased her eyes. "Back in Ayeshire it was part of basic training for soldiers to learn to read, even at a basic level, so that they could write correspondence, read and recite war history, and keep logs of information."

He shrugged, "Things are different here, my lady."

"Well then." she looked down at the blue book, the cover painted with gold writing and dragons. "I think you might like this one. I have not read this particular edition before, but it is of the legend of Glenolyn Alvaria and her siblings during the War of Conquest. A retelling of the war." She flipped the pages mindlessly, "Have you heard much of their legends?"

"Just the normal amount one like myself would be taught, m'lady, which is not much outside of bedside tales."

She continued flipping the pages, her eyes catching on the images of the Alvarian dragons that children of the kingdom dreamed of riding and adults hoped to never see in the skies. "They say that after the war was won the dragons split across the kingdoms and now lay asleep, waiting for their time to reign again. Baethorn's three green tails split across the southern green lands- creating our rivers and forming the Ina Gulf. Gredort's scales of ice broke off across the north and laid their mountains in a permanent state of winter and Glenoyln the Great's dragon of gold, Vinicarius, sleeps under this very Keep guarding the throne and its rightful ruler."

"That is only three."

Sister Ora looked up, a smirk breaking her solemn face. "I thought you did not know much of this legend."

"I do not know much of it, but I do remember the tales being of four."

"Carishna the Unforgiving gained her name by the vengeance she swore upon the sea and the sands of Aishar after their krakens ripped her and

Riomiar from the sky, pulling her dragon into the water to be lost to the waves forever. Carishna went insane hiding in the mountains of Odessin; Dragon Tower was her prison first before anyone else's. Do you believe what they say of the mountains in Odessin? That they smoke with the fires of Riomiar's lost eggs that Carishna hatched in secret?"

Sir Loren shrugged, "I believe if the legends are true, then the mountains would have woken up by now. What do you believe?"

She fiddled with the book, flipping it back and forth between both hands and looking down as she did so. "I do not believe what I think matters much, Sir Loren."

She sighed and placed the book back on the shelf before clearing her throat. "I believe I am done here. It is a nice day out and I would like to go on a walk around grounds before my lunch with Her Majesty."

Sir Loren nodded before stepping aside to allow her to pass. "As you wish."

The two left the Hall of Archives and walked along the outer walls of the castle, taking in the last few breezes of spring and breathing in the sun and salt air around them. As they walked around the extensive Keep, she took quick notice of unfolding chaos as King's Guards and common soldiers carried parchments and ran about the castle and out the many exterior archways with urgency. As they passed the Place of Arms, half armored, and some without any armor at all, soldiers stood in differing groups, the same level of urgency taking over their unheard conversations.

"Sir Loren, what is happening? Why are all those soldiers gathered?"

He remained silent and continued walking.

They made it only a few steps in silence before Sister Ora stopped mid stride and sharply turned to face him, attempting to appear intimidating despite the fact that if she looked straight forward, her eyes would meet his chest plate and not his face.

"Sir Loren, I asked you what was happening. Tell me."

Sir Loren looked down at her, nervously flexing his hand that he rested on his sword's pommel. "If I could tell you anything, I would. If I knew of anything, that is."

He stepped around her and continued walking their path, his pace unusually fast. Eventually her stunned state dissipated, and she joined his step as they made their way inside the closed walls of the castle.

Their paths quickly collided with Sir Marion and Father Figgins, both stern faces looking determined and focused as they whispered among themselves and exited the long hall holding meeting rooms and advisory council chambers. Despite their focus, Father Figgins did not let pleasantries or courtesies slide.

"Good morning, Your Highness." Father Figgins said as they met, bowing at the neck.

"Oh, I am —" she began.

"She is no highness yet." Sir Marion cut in, his words and face cold and sharp.

"Ah, you are correct, Sir Marion. My mistake. Some of us in the castle are simply a bit overly excited at the upcoming nuptials... and solidified alliance that is to come from the vows." His eyebrows cocked up at his last few words. "Tell me, my lady, has a date been set yet?"

"Uh, no. No, we have not yet set a date. Prince Percy and I have both been quite busy since we hit shore. But, Her Majesty and I have a late lunch today to go over details and plan. In fact, that is where Sir Loren and I are off to." She chose each word with careful consideration.

"And have you heard much from home?" Father Figgins inquired.

A sharp question that Sister Ora found odd in the moment, but the feeling was quickly dismissed.

"Not much, no. It seems that many from home are quite busy with their own duties and have not been able to write." She did her best not to show the sorrow she felt at the limited letters she had received and, of the parchments sent to her, the few she could not bring herself to open or respond to.

Perhaps it was her disappointment and grief in how she was treated before saying goodbye that prevented her from reading the letters bearing Lady Montarian's seal or the one's sent by common bird and sail boat and signed by her dearest friends.

"Well, things *are* getting quite a bit busier for us all. There is much to do in this kingdom. If you shall excuse us, Sir Marion and I have important business to attend to."

He set his cold, bony hand on her shoulder. "Do keep me updated on the wedding, my lady. I look forward to joining the Houses in ceremony."

He sharply dropped his hand, squeezing her arm tightly before doing so, and walked past her with no more acknowledgement. As Sir Marion passed by, he paused and fixed his dark and narrowed eyes intently on her.

"If your old House does not write to you, perhaps it may be wise to let them go. For your own good." He threatened. "And do let me know if Sir Loren is not living up to your... needs. The safety of the royal family and the throne are of the most importance to myself and the King's Guards. I would hate for trouble to arise under our watch."

Sister Ora crumpled her forehead in distaste and leaned away from him, taking a step back towards Sir Loren. Sir Marion smirked before eyeing them both and swiftly walking away.

Once the two men were out of earshot, she turned to Sir Loren. "I have only met that many a few times, but he always manages to make me so deeply uncomfortable. Has he always been so... like *that*?"

"Sir Marion did not become one of the greatest gladiators from Aishar or the kingdoms Master of Armor due to his kindness or softness." Sir Loren said as they began walking. "There are two things he is well known for; putting women on their backs and men in their graves."

She eyes him up and down as hey walked side-by-side. "And are you much like him, Sir Loren?"

"Like what? A seasoned killer and a well- known rake?"

She managed to let out a small laugh. "If you would desire to put it in those words, then yes. Is that how all the men and women of the King's Guard are?"

"Many, but not all." He replied flatly.

"And are you many?"

His normally straight-forward tone turned to sarcasm. "Well I do not believe that it is very lady-like of you to ask a man about what he does when he takes his armor off."

She paused her walking and turned to him, leaning in closer than she needed to. She inhaled as she looked up at the slits in his armor; steel, musk, and cigar smoke filled her senses. "Never said I was a lady, now did I, Sir Loren?"

She turned and laughed as she walked away, hearing a heavy breath escape from him just before his armored footsteps echoed on the stone behind her.

***

Queen Onetta, Princess Arminda, Sister Ora, and a few unfortunate jewelers and dress makers were gathered on a dining terrace surrounded by the warmth and cooling breeze of fresh afternoon air. The three women were seated in a row by one another, staring at jewels and fabrics draped on the table while the makers nervously attempted to aid them in the meticulous and never-ending decision making.

Sister Ora pulled at her hair and twirled it in her fingers. Without looking up from the display of jewels, Queen Onetta lightly swatted at her hand and tutted. "You will ruin your hair and make yourself look like a peasant doing such things. Now, please entertain us with your choice."

"I guess, well, I guess I prefer this one." Sister Ora timidly said as she pointed to one of the tiara and jewelry sets.

While still embellished with jewels who's worth would pay to feed multiple families in the kingdom, the set was one of the more subtle pieces on display. Centered on the diamond covered silver headband were smaller diamonds set in laurel wreath border framing one larger diamond. The necklace that matched glimmered with a band of diamonds set in a similar style.

Queen Onetta scrunched her face abd frowned. "Do you not want something more, prominent and regal? Such as this?"

The queen held up another tiara, one covered with large diamonds and wine-red rubies whose grand peaks would sit high atop the wearers head.

"Mother, I think that we must remember that this is what Sister Ora will wear on her day, not us, and allow her to pick something of her taste." Princess Arminda shot a look at Sister Ora who sat struggling to hide her look of distaste over the gaudy piece.

Queen Onetta sighed and carelessly dropped the tiara onto its padded cloth.

Sister Ora looked over the table scape covered in countless decisions she had to make. Decisions on the cake, her dress, her jewels, the feast, and more all had to be finalized, and yet, she and Prince Percy had not yet reached a decision on when they would wed; a decision she knew would be made for them too soon.

"Your Majesty, I truly did mean what I had said before about these decisions. I have never planned a wedding before, especially a royal one, and am perfectly content with you making any choices you see fit."

"Yes, I am well aware of that. I know these things are of *no* importance to you, but—" she raised her hand and snapped it at one of the aids standing nearby, causing them to hustle over with their fabric swatch book. "—you *are* the bride, and this is *your* day. There are some decisions you will have to make despite your lack of care to do so." The queen snatched the fabric book from the servant without a glance in their direction and began flipping through it. "Decisions such as when you will wed my son. Tell me, have you two made that choice yet, or shall that be thrown onto my lap as well?"

The queen stopped flipping through the book, now analyzing Sister Ora's face that had paled as her mouth hung open.

"Mother!" The princess' voice shot up.

Queen Onetta casually raised her hand to her daughter, a signal to her to be silent. The queen leaned in to the paling and panicking bride-to-be. "I know that common girls like you must dream of finding true love and being whisked off of your feet by some handsome man who promises a happily ever after." the entire balcony jumped as she slammed the fabric book closed. "But this is not some fantasy world; it can be unfair and it certainly *will* be cruel. Love is not needed to survive it. You may not love my son, and you may never grow to love him, or he you, but you will love the comfort and power that comes with being his bride."

Sister Ora opened her mouth to reply to the queen's angry glare but her reply was hushed by the movement of Queen Onetta's eyes to the spot behind her.

"Yes?" Queen Onetta snipped at the vassal that stood waiting during the spectacle.

The female messenger bowed, apologizing for the interruption as she straightened. "My apologies, Your Highness, but Prince Percy has requested the company of his betrothed for a promenade in the gardens this day."

Relief washed over Sister Ora at the chance to escape, already standing up as she spoke. "Well, it would be quite uncouth for me to turn down an invitation from Prince Percy."

"That it would be, Sister Ora. Please go enjoy the rest of your afternoon with my brother." Princess Arminda jumped in, giving her a look to hurry her escape before she was drawn back into the fold.

Sister Ora curtsied to the princess and queen, promptly turning to escape. "Your Majesty and Your Royal Highness, please excuse me. I hope we can continue our planning at another time."

She rushed off in the direction of the gardens, Sir Loren dutifully and quietly in tow beside her. After some silence, Sister Ora broke the quiet.

"Sir Loren, do you enjoy serving the royal family?" she asked as she led him down the pathway, changing her pace to a more casual walk as they made their way out of ear and eye shot of the queen and princess.

He shrugged. "It does have its benefits, and is much preferred to my prior position."

"And what was that?"

"A soldier, like all the King's Guards once were."

She nodded. "Did you like being a soldier?"

"No." His reply was harsh and sharp.

"Why?" she asked, confused by his sudden emotion.

"I was barely a man before I was sent off to my first battle and I lost many friends, most much too young to be fighting. Several I lost right in front of me. I helped bury them all after the fighting was done."

She stopped. "I am sorry, Sir Loren. I forget myself at times."

He turned to her, his voice was soft and reassuring. "It is alright, my lady. I do not mind your questions and our talking."

She smiled at him before breaking her gaze to look down, her hands in front of her with her fingers pulling at her nail beds. Sir Loren gently lifted a gloved finger to her gathered hands, not touching her, but showing her he noticed her nerves, before dropping his hand back to his side. She clenched her hands and stopped her fidgeting, quickly turning and leading them to the garden entrance where Prince Percy sat reading.

Upon hearing her steps, the prince looked up and gave a small smile, then stood to greet her.

"As soon as I heard that you were with mother and sister planning the wedding, I knew you must be in need of a swift rescue. I apologize for not getting you myself, but I knew my mother would then trap us both to talk of vows and flowers."

A small laugh escaped as she met with him. "I owe you all my gratitude, Your Highness. If I had to spend one more moment speaking of jewels and fabrics, I would have more seriously considered throwing myself off that balcony."

"And if I have to make any more small talk about this wedding to anyone, I may join you in your jump." Prince Percy jested, bringing out a larger laugh in them both.

As his laugh left him, the prince turned his smile to her and watched the crinkles in her eyes disappear as her own smile softened. After a moment, he recouped himself and cleared his throat, dropping his smile and staring ahead, then gestured his arm out for them, and their envoy of guards, to begin their promenade. The two walked in awkward silence for a bit, unsure of what to say to one another. Their limited conversation never lasted long and much of the time they had spent together at meals was times for quiet reflection and thought for Sister Ora.

Interrupting the beginning of her thoughts, Prince Percy took a low breath. "Sister Ora, I know this situation is not ideal, but I do want you to know that I do care for you."

At his words, both stopped and looked at one another. Her eyes widened at his words, but she quickly blinked her shock and worry away.

He continued, trying to hold her gaze but repeatedly breaking it to look anywhere else. "It may not be a feeling of love, but I do care for you. You are a good person from what I have been told and what I have seen. I will do my best to be a great husband and... and a father if you so wish it. I do not wish for us to grow to hate or loathe one another as so many in our situations often do. But I do not hold out hope for love to ever blossom between us, that is a rarity in royal arrangements. I still hold onto my promise that our marriage will at least be that of friendship... at least from me."

She smiled and bowed her head. "And I offer you the same in return."

"Truthfully, however, I am just not sure how to begin a friendship when we were declared betrothed before we had a chance to say hello to one another."

She nodded and loosened a breath. "Neither do I."

He smiled at his feet and glanced about the space again, finding fascination in the greenery and stone pillars around them. His hands tightened and loosened with one another where they joined in front of him. "I wanted to apologize to you for my upcoming absences and inability to swoop in to the rescue again. I will be quite a bit busier with new duties around the castle while my brother and his swords head off. Father asked me to take his place on the council while he is away."

She stammered. "What?"

"Oh, it is just the King's Council, truly nothing to be worried about. I—"

"No, no your brother- I mean Prince Elion, he is leaving... now? With an army?"

The second heir cocked his head. "You did not know? Has no one informed you of what transpired today? Lady Montarian and Lord Torrin have raised their armies against the crown."

She choked down the panic attack, promising it time to manifest later. She quickly shook her head and calmed her breathing and her tone. "No, no, of course I knew. I just did not know they were taking leave so swiftly. So much transpired today."

Prince Percy smiled a broken half smile and nodded. "Today did carry with it a lot of news I am still digesting myself. With our own army leaving our walls, my new role on my father's council, and Ravenhall being sent to defend their land, I find my mind in a thousand places all at once."

She could not hold back the worry in her eyes, the emotions they carried always overly expressive and easy to read for those who watched them.

Prince Percy spoke again. "I am sorry. I feel as if we have not gotten much past our first hellos and now this is happening. I promise you that once this is over, I will give you all my time, if you will have it."

As she absorbed his words, his announcement, his worry, his promises, her mind shifted back to the unopened letters on her desk, the ones she now regretted being too hurt and broken to open, the ones that may have carried more than apologies she hoped for. She ached to rush back to her chambers and find her quill and a bird to carry the prince's words across the Gulf, to warn and save her home.

But she needed to know more of what revenge the king and his council wished to seek.

She softly laid her hand on his arm and smiled. "Yes, Your Highness I would like that very much. We have a life to build together, and we should know much more about one another than we do before we begin it. When is Prince Elion leaving? I do wish to know just how much time we do have left."

She moved her eyes from his stare down to his mouth, then back up again. The subtle movement of her eyes on his face brought heat to his and he stammered before collecting himself. "Unfortunately, we do not have much," He set his hand on hers, still delicately resting on his arm. "He is to leave in two dates time. They are finalizing details of importance but the march to Ravenhall is long and we must be swift. I do hope you know how truly sorry I am that this is occurring, but my family did not see another option to respond to what is happening. We must protect ourselves and our people, it is our duty."

Tears brimmed her eyes as she began sniffling, her words broken up between tears. "I do understand, and I hope you accept my apologies for my tears, as I worry for my countrymen and all the losses we all will face."

"Please do not apologize for feeling sorrow or pain over what is happening." he brushed her tears away with his thumb, leaving his hand on her face to hold her there. "I too wish to weep over the losses that will occur. I only pray that those you and I both love are not lost in this war and there is a quick end to all of this. I wish peace to be brought to our people swiftly."

She lifted her hand to rest atop his on her face. "I do wish for that, too."

The two, alongside their King's Guards, continued their walk along their path around the castle gardens. As the sun began moving through the sky, the prince excused himself from their promenade to attend a meeting, leaving Sister Ora and Sir Loren on their own again. At his leave, she finally allowed herself a moment of raw emotion. Her shaking hands found refuge on her chest as her heart pounded with a mix of guilt, sorrow, and anger. She felt a strong hand rest on her back and she looked up to meet Sir Loren's eyes, softened behind the harsh and cold metal covering his expression. His free hand gestured out to an empty stone bench nearby, guiding her to sit. He stepped away, feigning interest in a tree as he turned his back and allowed her to weep.

Her tears ran dry in quick haste and her breath returned as the air shifted from a light afternoon coolness to the beginning breezes of a sunset chill. She collected herself as best she could, knowing her presence would be due shortly at another dinner where she was expected to act elegantly and finely. She rose from the bench, sniffling and clearing her throat and approached the still turned Sir Loren, who had woven plucked pieces of tall grasses together into a braid. He turned to her and nodded once as they left the secluded garden spot and made their way down the path to the main castle.

After long moments of aching silence, she cleared her hoarse throat and spoke. "Do you think we will be alright after this war? Those of us who survive it?"

Sir Loren did not respond as a tear fall from her downturned face and they continued walking.

Finally, he sighed and replied. "I cannot offer you any lies, only honesty, my lady. No one who survives a war is ever alright again, no matter how well the scars heal."

"Oh." She let out, lowly and broken.

He continued. "The only comfort I can offer you is my oath as your King's Guard. I will live by my oath, and, if needed, I will die in upholding it if the war were ever to come here."

She stopped and turned to him. Her damp eyes traced every ridge and line in his helmet, attempting to bore through the metal that hid his expression in hopes to see if his face looked as broken as his words sounded.

He was normally so quiet, so stoic. Talking only when she prompted him to and being so precise with his responses. In their short time together, she had not once been able to confirm if Sir Loren was capable of expressing emotions or had them at all.

Mistaking her silent tracing of his face for confusion, Sir Loren leaned in and continued. "When I first put on this armor, I swore an oath to protect whoever was in my care with my life and to fight to the death for their protection." He took a gentle step forward to her. "My oath means that I swear my life to you, my lady."

Chapter 21

Lord Taylian Montarian shifted back and forth in his mother's throne-like chair. The wood grain where he rubbed his thumb was worn from ages of the same gesture done by those who sat before him. The cushion below him was thick and soft, his body only taking up the center of the pad; he felt as if he had sunken deep into the worn fabric, his body too small and not fit for the size of the chair.

"My lord?" the townswoman in front of him asked. "What say you to our request, sir?"

He straightened up and cleared his throat, looking down at her rom his seat at the head of the hall. "Apologies, ma'am, I was merely considering all options in front of us."

Her head cocked to the side and her old and sun burned face crinkled. "Regarding the chickens?"

Father Robb cleared his throat beside the young lord, their eyes meeting in a side glance for a brief moment. "Lord Taylian is correct in his contemplation of what to do. While we apologize at the attack of your livestock, simply sending hunters out to kill any potential beast responsible is costly and could be quite disruptive to the natural order of nature."

"Sir, this is the third time this moon phase that it has occurred in the south town." She pleaded. "Something must be done for our farms; sheep have been slaughtered; chicken coops left with nothing but feathers behind."

Lord Taylian pushed his body up in the oversized chair, "Fences."

"What? she replied.

"Build fences along the forest border. Reach out to the proper Journeyman Houses for aid to build stronger fences and barriers between the south town and the woods. And please advise them to reach out to our family for compensation for their labors. By the end of the season, if you have not seen a reduction in your losses, return and we will aid in another way."

She scanned Father Robbins for a response to the young lord's order, then, seeing no emotion from the older man, turned her eyes back to Lord Taylian and bowed her head. "Thank you, my lord. Thank you."

Father Robb scribbled on the parchment in front of him and handed it to the townswoman as she approached, stamping it with the Montarian seal before passing it off to her.

"That is the last of the labors today, my lord." Father Robb said as he packed up his supplies, the door clanging closed behind the woman as she left. The guards around the room relaxed as the room emptied, their posts still guarded but their posture more casual. "You fared well for your first time in these duties."

Lord Taylian leaned back in the chair, letting his body sink into it again as he sighed loudly. "I forget that so much of my mother's duties involves such things as... livestock disputes and *taxes*. Do so many normally complain of such trite things as their taxes?"

Father Robb chortled. "Yes, they often do. But I must remind you, the problems of your people are not trite, no matter how much you may not be able to understand them. I am afraid lord and ladyship is not all exquisite dinners, speeches, and grand war glory."

Lord Taylian stood beside his chair, his hands feeling the carvings of the chair. He stared longingly at the carvings of leaves and woodland creatures, at the crest chiseled at the highest point of the chairs arch.

"What eats at you, m'lord?"

He swallowed. "Has Digarius struggled with this? When mother and father would leave for duties outside our borders and he had to fill for them? Did he find such things hard to do?"

"Ah." Father Figgins said, setting down his supplies. "He struggles with his future duties in his own ways. As does your mother with hers."

Taylian's brow crumpled in disbelief. "I don't know about that."

Father Robb stepped forward and rested a comforting hand on his shoulder, "Your family is made of people, Lord Taylian, not infallible gods."

He scoffed. "Yes I know that, Father Robb."

Father Robb dropped his hand and walked back for his supplies. "Oh you do? Might I offer you advice then, my lord?"

Lord Taylian shrugged turning to the small crackling fireplace behind their line of tables. "Of course. You are my advisor at this moment, Father Robb."

"Well then, I would perhaps advise finding what makes *you* happy in life. You are of age; you are one of the few blessed to not be tied to a Divine House, you are smart and talented. My lord, you have options." Father Robb bowed as he made his way to a side door. "Attempting to become your brother, or your mother, or a warrior like your father, they are not your only options in this life."

***

The dining hall in Sandhill House was brought to light by large iron chandeliers spanning the length of the space. Thick lines and puddles of spent candlewax coated the iron around the lit ivory towers, with old streams of wax teasing the bottom of the chandeliers, threatening to drop off the edge if they were not taken care of.

It was a neglected cleaning duty that irked Lady Lydia Bromlyn the moment she noticed it and caused her to nitpick more so than usual; each setting of dining ware, each speck of dust, and even the salt stains imbedded in the very foundation of the fortress that had once been flooded were the center of her ire. The dinner had been delayed due to her frustrations and the houses new guests quickly scarfed their food the moment they were allowed in the hall. Lady Lydia spent much of the dinner working to distract her guests from what she deemed an ill kept mess of a home.

The hearty fireplace formed of sandstone crackled with flame, casting shadows along the lower walls and warming up the diners from the evening chill that whistled outside. Hung atop the mantle laid two broadswords, crossed over one another below a large banner of the Bromlyn House crest- a towering stone bridge holding back waves. Above the crest, the house words were stitched: Thou shalt not falter. Thou shalt not fail.

Lord Digarius sat crookedly in his seat across from the banner, gazing upon it each time his eyes looked forward. He took a long, deep sip from his wine and his eyes glared over his cup at the words pushing their pressure on him.

Thou shalt not falter. Thou shalt not fail.

Phantom cries and screams of death filled his ears as the words bore into him, the crackling of the flame transformed into the cracks of impacting weapons and every beat of breath around him was the tallying count of how many of his men one mistake would take the life from. Time was running out before they would meet their first battle and he would lead his army to victory, or to their deaths.

Thou shalt not falter. Thou shalt not fail.

"Digarius, dear, are you listening?" His mother set her hand on top of his, her voice just above a polite whisper so as not to disrupt the rest of the conversations occurring around them.

He cleared his throat and adjusted himself in his seat to sit properly. "Sorry mother, what was it you said?"

"I had asked if you heard much from your father at all."

"No, I have not heard." His voice ghostly and distant as he replied. "Aside from notice of his arrival at the castle, the birds have been quiet as of late."

Lady Belva sat back in her seat, her concern and worry still watching over him as she spoke. "I hesitate to believe that no news is good news when it comes to times such as this, but for the sake of my heart and our hope, I will choose to believe it."

"And we shall carry your hope and thoughts with us as we continue onward to Ravenhall, Your Grace." Sir Rainey's sharp and blunt tone took on an air of assurance as his words carried across the table to her.

"Do not forget to leave some hope here for our men, since we will not be left with much for ourselves." Lord Bromlyn muttered in irritation as he sloppily grabbed the decanter of wine and tried to pour more into his already well-filled cup.

Lady Belva snapped out of her worry, "I encourage you to quell your sharp tongue and slow your drinking, Lord Bromlyn, as you seem to forget not only who is in your presence today, but whose House your colors fly under."

He dropped back in his chair and grunted before gulping more wine, holding eye contact with her stern stare. Aside from the noises of the fire, the room was tensely silent as everyone awaited a response from either party.

"My apologies, my lady." he took the glass from his mouth, and swished it around in his hand before gulping more down again.

For the remainder of the meal, the conversations turned to awkward and unnatural cuts from topic to topic with harsh emptiness between each jump.

"The weather certainly has helped the fields I hear. The farmers seem quite thrilled with the extra rain." Lady Lydia smiled and nodded at each guest as she spoke.

"Mmm, yes, but I do hope it calms so the fields do not flood downhill." Lady Belva said.

"As do I, we are hopeful for a prosperous season in the fields. We doubled our rhubarb crop and are hopeful our berry bogs produce exceptional this season, so long as the rain comes back before the frost ruins the vines. Isn't that right, my lord?" Lady Lydia shot a look at her ego-bruised pouting husband.

"Mmm... yes" he grunted out before shoveling a fist of food into his mouth.

Lord Digarius threw back his glass of wine as one would a sharp shot of whiskey, his eyes meeting the fireplace flame and following stray embers as they ascended in the air and died out before breaking completely free.

Thou shalt not falter. Thou shalt not fail.

***

Lady Belva Montarian hastened her steps on the stone as she sped to meet with her son before he locked himself in his guest chambers for the night.

"Digarius!"

Her hushed shout and echoing steps caught his attention quickly and he turned his swaying walk to her, meeting her in the middle of the hall.

"I need us to discuss your plan to be on the front when you meet with Ravenhall. As the acting Lord Commander you can order Sir Rainey or your other officers to lead the fight while you command them from a more prominent, *safe* position. I cannot—" She stopped as her voice began to crack, taking a breath deep as she looked down at her near trembling hands. Her eyes fell to her wedding band and the stones laid in the ring next to it, each stone representing each of her sons.

"Mother, if I am asking my soldiers to risk their lives and fight for justice, then I will bleed next to them each step of the way." He wrapped his hands around hers. "Standing on the sidelines or behind a wall of armored men while our people bleed for our country is the type of Lord I wish to be."

"I know, It is just—"

He cut her off. "You and father have taught me how to lead, and now you must let me do so."

She moved her hand to rest on his cheek. "You are not my sweet little boy anymore, are you?"

He let out a long breath, the air that escaped hitching for a moment. "No. I am afraid that boy has had to grow up quite a bit."

"Aye." She nodded in understanding. "Promise me just one thing, darling. Do not lose that sweet little boy inside of you. He is still there; I see him often when you allow it. Do not let this war take him."

He set his hand over hers on his cheek.

"I must go. It is late and we are leaving at first light."

***

Eight thousand troops, supplies, and war horses were hard enough to keep moving without the added troubles from unexpectedly poor ground conditions that kept plaguing First Sgt Emaline and her fellow officers.

The horses and carriages within their caravan had been moving slower due to the flooding conditions of the land they passed through and several stops had to be made to free wheels from mud or to forge new paths when more flooding cut off their planned routes. The marshy bogs near the Ayeshire-Sebern border, natural and man-made bodies of water for farming, had flooded due to the excessive rain that also made their traveling slow and non pleasant.

Despite this, the troops did their best to keep their own morale up, some could be overheard telling tall tales, reciting old legends, or talking about what- or who- they would busy themselves with after the war was won.

But most took turns joining in on old war songs led by the bards traveling with them.

"Centuries of old,
long, long ago
this land once was hollow
paid for in the blood
of names we still know
Carefully we go
down the same path they sowed
giving goodbye to the loves
we left behind

And if our destiny is to end

in that same song of blood

then we shall all sing together,

crying out for one last time"

As the soldiers recited the old battle hymn, Emaline's own quiet singing was disrupted by the hastened splashing of hooves approaching her from behind.

"Corporal Lancel, what is it?" she asked as the rider met with her pace.

"A raven, First Sergeants." The urgency in her voice, paired with the worried look on her face, caused Emaline and her fellow First Sergeants to stop abruptly and signal for their brigades behind them to do the same. She took the note, the parchment creased and smudged against her gloved hand as she unrolled the words.

The king knows all. Ravenhall to find you. King's army sent.

Her head shook back and forth rapidly as she read and re-read the message. Her anxiety tuned out the voices of concern and curiosity around her. "Do we know if either Lord Commander has been notified?" she snipped at the Corporal messenger.

"I'm afraid all that all I know is what you do. A messenger scout brought this to us from the Sandhill House, I do not know if any others received a raven as well."

Emaline passed the message to the officer on her left allowing him time to look it over. "Did they speak on if Lord Digarius had arrived or left Sandhill House yet?"

"He had already left by the time the raven was received, First Sergeant. His soldiers were out of sight on the other side of Tower Bridge."

Do not falter. Do not fail.

The words rang through her head as she cut out the noises around her. The ringing of the words continued as her hand sat on her lap tracing the ridges of the imaginary coin in her hand she deeply desired to find her comfort that soothed her each time she ran her finger over the coin; the only item left with her when she was dropped off at the orphanage. The echoing of the words only stopped when it turned into a piercing screech in her ears that set her body on fire and shortened her breath. Her mouth felt as if it was sewn shut; the fear of vomiting or screaming locking her jaw.

Do.

Not.

Fail.

Her horse paced back and forth, the stress of the tightened reins in her hand making her steed believe it needed to move. She turned her horse to scan the entirety of the soldiers behind her. There were too many to move quickly.

Emaline's grip loosened on the reins as she turned forward and brought her hand to the pouch at her side and squeezed it tight, feeling the faint outline of the small coin and other trinkets inside. She calmed herself the best she could, the words on the coin she carried finally quieting in her mind.

"Did they send a message to his army?" her breath came out shaky, but more controlled than it had been.

"I apologize, but they did not say."

She nodded and forced out confidence and calmness. "We should cut our path short. We cross the river border and head west to lend quicker aid and hope to cut off the attack. Do we have a bird trained to Lord Montarian?"

Corporal Lancel gave a grim look and shook her head.

"His Grace will need to know why our army will not converge with his as we had planned."

The First Sergeant beside her added in. "Corporal, send one of your scouts to find Lord Montarian and Lord Torrin's presumed army and notify them."

The corporal nodded and spurred her horse to run behind to her messengers.

Another officer asked. "What else is there we can do?"

Emaline shook her head in woe. "There is nothing more we can do for our brethren. We must prepare to lend aid the moment our eyes meet theirs on the battlefield and hope we do not arrive to their ending."

CHAPTER 22

The light overcast offered the slightest pardon from the muggy heat the Ayeshire army was trudging through. The bright sun had radiated down the entire morning and early afternoon and would have made their armor hot to the touch had they not had their green capes to drape over the metal and protect it from the heat.

The hills and valleys surrounding the borderlands of Ravenhall and the northern Sandhill House lands were lush with thick green grasses and the sporadic bundle of woodlands and stray trees, the heavy rains that had disrupted the dry summer gave the foliage enough water to return to the lushness the hills were admired for.

The border they would camp at was nearing close, less than an afternoon's pace away, and Lord Digarius' nerves insisted on sending scouts ahead to track along where the banners turned to blue-green and ravens replaced the stone bridge on the cloth.

Sir Rainey had not agreed with his approach of continuously sending scouts ahead since they cleared Tower Bridge. Their colorful disagreement was the first, and his hope the only, time Lord Digarius had to play the nobleman title card to end the discussion.

While he agreed that Sir Rainey had valid points with his concern over scouts being spotted and alerting any potential enemy to their position, Lord Digarius believed the risk was worth the worry. To compromise, their scouts were sent out in civilian attire so that, if spotted, they would appear to be everyday men out for a ride.

Light breezes carried the music of the vale around; mumbles and grunts of hot tired soldiers, huffs from their horses, and faint chirps and caws from ravens and other birds in the distance. Rain soaked grass scented the air. From the steeper hills ahead, the wind carried another sound- the hurried hooves of a lone horse.

Lord Digarius studied the hillscape, working to find where the horse would appear. "The Northwest hills." Lord Digarius addressed the Command Sergeant whose gaze was searching as well.

"One of your scouts, Lord Commander?" Sir Rainey's eyes strained to tell from the distance.

Lord Digarius squinted, patting himself to find the viewing scope he believed to still be carrying, "I believe so, not sure what any other lone rider would be doing heading this way."

He signaled to the army to stop. The now familiar rushing rider had quickly closed the distance between them and wasted no time on pleasantries or formalities.

"Ravenhall is here, Lord Commander. Their army is not far off, almost straight ahead on our path. I'd say a few hours and they will be right atop us."

"What? How many?" he questioned sharply.

"Looks to be at least six thousand, I counted so quickly to rush back here, but I believe my numbers to be true."

"Did you see any of their scouts about? Were we spotted?" Lord Digarius's tone quipped again.

"Not that I could tell, sir. I did spot a few of their scouts heading this way as I was coming back, but I stuck to the trees. They are still a way away. We have some time."

"How did they-" Lord Digarius shook away his curiosities. "Never mind."

"Lord Commander, I suggest we hurry over the hills and take the high ground, come straight down on them. We outnumber them by a few thousand; it should take no time at all to meet them where they stand and fight." Sir Rainey said.

Lord Digarius looked around, noting a tall field of grass with bundles of trees to the east of where they stood on the flat, mostly bare valley that acted as the greeting space before the endless hills. He eyed the rolling green ahead and traced the unsteady grounds.

"No. Once we leave this valley there will be nothing left but hills for miles. We cannot fight on that, especially with little time to prepare. Let them come down and meet us in the valley." he ordered.

"What? Lord Commander I *must* advise against this." Sir Rainey shot back, jerking the reins of his horse as he shot his words.

"Give your Lord Commander a moment, Sir Rainey." Lord Digarius continued contriving his plan internally, acknowledging the officers that had gathered to listen when his orders were ready.

"They have taken us by surprise, with hope to either ambush or draw us into their terrain. We will allow neither to happen." He began. "We shall borrow strategy from the ancestors today. There was a battle I recall from my studies; one that occurred in Odessin before the land knew its name. It took place in a valley surrounded by a hellscape of jagged mountains and stones, a landscape much like this before their lands burned into deserts."

The Lord Commander hastily recounted the ancient battle and the tactics used, ordering officers and readying each unit for their part in the plan.

As the units scattered and prepared, Lord Digarius continued to question how this was coming to be. Ravenhall was still a dozen days away for a marching army and the lands and roads leading to the center of their lands were vast and plentiful and yet, they were marching directly for the path they had chosen.

He brushed his concerns and questions away, saving them for another time and kicked his horse forward to address his soldiers. He paced his horse back and forth along the line of soldiers awaiting the battle. He searched his mind for words he had practiced for the inevitable moment he would find himself leading an army, speeches he wrote in his mind starting when he was a young boy, hopeful and innocent to the realities of his future lordship and the blood-soaked reality of war.

It was different now.

Finding the words to address real men and women who live and bleed was not as easy as curating grandiose speeches when the sword at your side was a child's toy and the soldiers in front of you were friends feigning themselves enemies and allies.

"When we departed Sandhill House and made our way to these lands, each of you were informed of the truth of why we stand here today, why we chose treason over complicity. At that moment, we gave each of you a choice: turn back for home, or swear yourselves to our cause, to a more just future. This moment, this day, is where we create that future." He smirked. "Where we become legends."

Cheers erupted as he continued shouting and pacing his horse along the lines. "Today is not the day that we become those legends through our deaths or our loss. Today is not the day that we hand our lives back over to tyranny or to the king!" Today is the day we become heroes through *strength*! Through *triumph*! Through *victory*!"

The army continued their cheering, with more vigor and many clanking their swords against their shields and thrusting their weapons in the air. Lord Digarius surveyed the gathering of armor and steel one last time. He let only his pride and strength show as he unsheathed his own sword and shouted back at the cheering mass, running his horse along the entire length of the army before swiftly dismounting and leading his foot soldiers to their hidden position.

As they settled into their hiding among the tall grasses and bramble to the east, a galloping mass crested the hill.

The sun, almost as if on cue, pushed through the clouds; its rays beaming down directly upon the upcoming battlefield like a spotlight illuminating a stage. The Ayeshire army held steady in their positions below on the widespread valley as the Ravenhall army broke the horizon. The billowing flaps of both armies banners counted down the anxious seconds until the bloodbath would begin.

The Ayeshire forces stood just out of reach of enemy longbows. Metallic stomping and movement echoed downhill as the Ravenhall soldiers moved aside and brought forth armored archers. Ayeshire made no movement and held their line as a rain made of arrows fell upon them.

Shields of stags formed a roof above the soldiers as a few lucky arrows flew far enough to clash onto the shields. Their metal tips bounced off the thick metal and fell to the ground around them. The clanging of metal arrowhead to metal shield was brief, as most of shots fell significantly short of the wall.

"Steady! Hold!" Sir Rainey commanded.

Adrenaline rang throughout the wall of soldiers, all working to restrain their energy and hold their positions. Still atop the hill, the archers moved forward and loaded their bows. The roof of green shields rose again as arrows hit the Ayeshire shields, more than last, The clamoring from the rain of weapons grew louder and steadier above their heads.

When the last arrow landed upon them, Sir Rainey shouted again. "Now!"

First Sgt. Barton's archers broke through, leaping from beneath shields held for them, bows already knocked with arrows, and ran forward. Mixed among them were shield-bearing soldiers holding their shields above, offering protection to the bowmen alongside them.

"Ready!" First Sgt. Barton ordered. The archers drew their bows and crouched under the protection of shields. "Fire!"

The shield bearers dropped to their knees as the bowmen stood up, found quick aim, and fired before dropping down under the shield bearers to prepare their next arrow. Arrows penetrated Ravenhall soldiers' bodies, bounced off armor and shields, and pained shouting echoed throughout the valley. First Sgt. Barton looked onward at the enemy lines, lines barely changed, and took in the forward movement- a quick escalation of events that had not been predicted to occur so swiftly.

"Back! Now!"

Her company of archers and soldiers fled back to the lines behind them as Ravenhall descended the hill. Their calvary had not come to protect them yet, leaving their backs turned and unprotected. As the archer's retreat began, Sir Rainey called the calvary forward. Archers traded their long bows for shorter bows and melee weapons, and others retreated to position themselves in front of their reserves.

The initial clash of soldiers came in a few short breaths. The Ayeshire flanks making quick work of folding their enemy in on themselves and pushing them forward to battle with the rising hill at their back.

From the grasslands, soldiers sprang from the ground, clamoring to their feet and making no effort to be quiet or careful. Dark-armored Ravenhall soldiers jerked in shock and panic over the surprise, those green enough to let their attention be taken met their deaths without their knowing.

Bodies fell atop one another as Lord Digarius's soldiers made their first strikes upon the Ravenhall troops. The ambush aided in pushing their dark-caped enemy against the hills they came from.

Disjointed and disrupted commands came from the Ravenhall officers as they scrambled to respond to the unforgiving attacks and ambushes.

Almost fully surrounded, the Ravenhall company under the focused attack began to disintegrate and thin. Across the battlefield from Lord Digarius' soldiers, Sir Rainey's regiment continued pushing, forcing the enemy troops to fight and fumble on the slopes of the hills. Soldiers tripped and fell over fallen bodies and uneven terrain; no mercy or pause was given to allow them to catch their footing or adjust their strategy. Fallen soldiers were ended where they laid begging and struggling. Lord Digarius urged his soldiers to push harder to close in on those who remained standing.

As they enclosed, Ravenhall sent another calvary down in frantic hope. It was to no avail, as their mounted soldiers were quickly absorbed into the encircled chaos of the battle and many horses trampled and tripped over fallen bodies and soldiers engaged in too close of combat.

Horns blew from the top of the hill; the call for retreat came too late, those who were left standing to fall back were so few.

No calls of surrender accompanied the horns screaming for retreat.

Lord Digarius pulled his sword from the body of the soldier he impaled and threw their body to the ground. He darted his head around the field of screaming death in search of an Ayeshire horse to throw himself upon. He made no command of those around him to follow as he swiftly swung onto the horse's back and kicked it forward up the hill to follow the retreating soldiers.

Every soldier wearing his banner followed him, leaving a trail of bodies in their wake as they chased those fleeing, following the visions of bloodied capes bearing the raven crest of the House they would now claim.

***

King Ivan slammed his fists on the table, clenching them so hard that his arms shook from the tension. His chest heaved as he glared down at his fists; his anger and disbelief growing with every breath he forced out of his lungs.

"How in the *hell* did this happen?" he spit through gritted teeth; his jaw aching from clenching it so stiffly. He stood and turned from the table. "How did that rebel scum manage to take *our* ambush?"

"It seems we have underestimated the Lord of Ayeshire's son, Your Majesty." Sir Marion said behind the king's turned back. Where the king's rage spun haphazardly throughout the room, Sir Marion's calm demeanor danced as he lazily leaned against a wall. "The boy may be inexperienced, but he has shown us quite quickly to not mistake that for weakness."

"And we have now handed him Ravenhall." The king mumbled under his shaking breath. He ran his trembling hand through his hair. As he turned back to his council, he hid his hand behind his back to cover the shaking of it. "This ambush was meant to hold them off until we reached their men and buried them all. It has now done nothing but embolden them and make me look weak."

Father Figgins spoke from his seat, evenly and slowly. "This is only a temporary setback, Your Majesty once Prince Elion and his soldiers meet with them, they will be easily wiped out and put in their places."

"And if not," Sir Marion took his seat next to Figgins and relaxed back in his chair, "we can show them what Aisharians are willing to do."

"Snarky comments will not win a war, Sir Marion. Besides, Aishar has not even been called." Prince Percy ended his comment with a glare at him, causing the cocky smile Sir Marion bore to disappear.

Sir Marion slowly sat up in his seat, maintaining eye contact with the second prince as his eyes darkened. "Well looks like someone's stones have finally dropped. I am sure your betrothed is thankful it finally happened before your wedding night."

The king rolled his eyes. "Let us not waste time we do not have making catty remarks at one another and instead use it to plan how we are going to cut this boy and his army off."

Prince Percy nodded and took a deep breath as he pinched the bridge of his nose and sat back, feeling the aches of another headache come on.

"In less than a fortnight Prince Elion and his men will meet with the army that defeated Ravenhall and what has been will then be erased." Father Figgins said. "Our scribes here can send word to them of what has occurred to allow them to be better prepared for what they will find."

"And what this Council should focus on is a new response when all three armies met afterward." Prince Percy added with hesitation. "Father, perhaps we should call upon Lord Priscius."

His father grunted.

"I know your and uncle Tyrrian do not see eye to eye and are no friends, but this war will not be swift. Odessin *will* take time to get here. We need all that we have ready for a long war." The prince dropped his hand in his lap, hesitating again and his next words edged in guilt. "And we know Ayeshire lands have less protection right now."

Sir Marion returned to his sly, relaxed manner as if their tense exchange had never occurred. "Perhaps I underestimated you, Second Prince. Your

Majesty, we should allow the war to play out as it is on the land and prepare to take it to the waters right at the enemies front door. Call upon our gladiators to take their land so they have nothing to return to when we defeat them. Take away their hope, leave them nothing."

King Ivan looked about the room, his hand rested on his face and his elbow on his chairs arm. His pride continued to whisper disagreements with the logic he felt in front of him. He slowly moved his eyes to Father Figgins. He shook his head. "Write to Lord Priscius, request his presence at once and call in our debt."

The king sat up, his hand resting on the table gently to steady him as the pangs of craving began to take their h old. "And someone, find out where the fuck my Odessian army is."

CHAPTER 23

The roaring fires in Saoirse Castle did little to keep out the chilling air that came down from the northern mountains of Craigie and were never able to warm the stones that were often whipped with piercing winds that came from the cliffs of The Whistling Ridges that the castle of freedom stood upon. The bones of the castle remembered the rebellion that sparked within its walls; it still whispered the tales of those in the past who yearned to break free and rule themselves but had failed. It, like a resentful god requiring obedience, still demanded its inhabitants to choose freedom or lay themselves upon their own battle axes.

Sat upon the heavy stone throne in the center of the throne hall, clad in leather armor and warming her body in heavy furs draped over her back, sat Lady Kathilla Edgel, her ice-cold blue eyes glaring down at the foreign messenger daring to stand in front of her. Her deep red hair was pulled out of her face, with braids on either side of her head helping set her hair into ponytails decorated with leather wraps and small bones.

To her left stood her two children, clad in similar furs with statures of equal muscle and intimidation. Her eldest child, Gladys, had the same rich red hair and blue eyes as her, while her son Barron's red hair was muddied with brown from his father's side.

Throughout the room stood men and women of Craigie, all gathered to hear what the messenger from Odessin had brought to them. Lady Kathilla sat back in the throne with her elbows on the arms of it, her hands clasped together in a ball in front of her face, blue eyes glaring forward. She crossed one leg over the other, the long knives strapped to her boots glinting as they caught the light and the eye of the shaking man draped in orange.

She smirked at his reaction to the knives and made sure to look down at the heavy battle axe she had leaning against her throne before looking back up at him.

"If this is a message of your wretched countries surrender of the lands that are ours, it is long overdue, but we shall hear it. If it is anythin' else, well," she smirked again, her rhotic accent emphasizing vowels in the unique ways of their land. "you'd best at least entertain me to make listenin' to you worth my while."

The Odessin messenger opened the rolled-up parchment in his hand, clearing his throat as he read, his hands shaking so much the parchment risked ripping in his grip. Despite his nerves, his dialect was smooth but quick, and he emphasized each word with meaningful intent as many from Odessin did.

"The Six Kingdoms of Victarius are wrought with treason and face the beginnings of another devastating war. The kingdoms of Ayeshire and Sebern have chosen treason against the rightful king of the golden throne and are set upon destroying our kingdom. His Royal Majesty, King Ivan of House Scott, First of His Name, Lord of the Six Kingdoms, and, Their Graces, Lord Nesima Mete, Blood of the Unforgiving, and Lord Shaital Pathis, hereby order the alliance, or complete neutrality, of Craigie and its people during this time."

"Oh, well then. If it is by the order of *His Royal Majesty* and their graces then we must listen to it." Lady Kathilla responded, each word riddled with snark.

The messenger darted his head around the room, confused at the reaction, then looked back at her, surprise and relief beginning to show on his face. Sarcasm and snark were not common in the desert country, Odessian's were often a serious people and said what they meant and meant what they said.

Her voice reverberated off the stones as she slowly stood up. "When in the *fuck* have I ever let a man, let alone a *fuckin' king*, tell me what to do? I am *Queen* of the Stone Throne, the blood of Sir Wallace Nealson and Balnar the Brutal. My blood bows to no king."

She spit on the floor at his feet. "You people continue to forget my blood."

Sir Wallace Nealson led Craigie into their fight for freedom that ignited The Great Civil War. Upon losing the war, Sir Nealson sacrificed himself to ensure that his people's surrender would not end in their deaths as well. His execution was the most gruesome in known history, the king wishing to make him an example no one would want to emulate.

After being held in the stocks of the capitol for several days, he was then slowly disemboweled, left in the public stocks again to rot and be picked at by birds before being hanged, beheaded, and drawn and quartered in front of citizens and his own family. His ruined remains were thrown into the sewers outside of the King's Keep, where legend spoke of his ghost haunting those who dared enter the depths of the castle and would take revenge on them for what was done to him. His execution was not only gruesome and cruel, but of complete darkness and evil because King Lucarius ordered Sir Nealson's own men to perform each part of it.

His descendants, including Lady Kathilla and her children, never offered a moment of forgiveness to any person who sat upon the throne and bore the same crown that killed him.

"Come here messenger boy." she growled.

The Odessin messenger timidly moved forward. As he stopped in front of her, she gently took the message from his hand and rolled it back up, tighter than it had been before. She held it to his face, gesturing for him to grab it from her hand.

He reached out his shaking hand and, as soon as he did, she snatched it, closing it tightly in her fist.

"You can tell *your* king to take this message and stick it up his ass, so long as he can fit it in there alongside the stick that he fucked himself with and left in there long ago."

His jaw shook as she stared him down. She broke her glare when she heard a trickling noise and looked down between the two. The fine silk doublet he wore was now wet at the crotch and a pool of piss started at his feet. She laughed and meet his wide eyes again, pulling his face closer to hers and then carelessly shoving him.

He stumbled onto the floor, barely saving himself from falling completely, and stammered back.

"Go back to your desert, you poor soul, and do not come back." she said as she returned to her throne.

"I-I-I-I will not, Lady Edgel, not if I can help it." he said as he backed away.

"*Do not call me that.*" she snapped, slamming her hands into the stone arms of the throne, "I am a *queen*, regardless of what your king says."

"Yes, yes, of course, my apologies."

As he continued backing away, he nervously kept bowing and avoiding her glare. After the doors of the hall closed and the messenger ran as fast as he could back to his horse outside, Lady Kathilla took a large chug of beer from the stein that was set on the ground beside her.

"It would have been wiser for them to have told us nothin' at all." she casually said to the room.

Barron turned to his mother. "And why is that?"

"Because we now know that they all will be distracted with killin' one another. Lady Catherin's heartfelt message and request for aid and this new message prove to us that we have an opportunity."

Gladys continued her mother's thought. "An opportunity to take what is ours that was stolen so long ago."

Lady Kathilla smiled at her daughter as she stood up. "Exactly, while they are all off fightin' with one another, the borders will become weak and Odessin will be far too busy suckin' the cock of the king and doin' whatever he demands of 'em."

"And The Falls of Glinton, and all of the souls that still walk the Land of a Thousand Waters, will belong to Craigie, as they always should have." Barron smiled.

Before the Great Civil War reshaped the continent into six kingdoms, Craigie, known then by the same name, flew their banners over the land that was now split in half with Odessin, once known as Odenbiur, and whose borders stopped at the edge of their smoking mountains. The Land of a Thousand Rivers was once holy for ancient reasons lost to time and fire, but found a new divine status when the Great Civil War ended on its lands during The Darkest Night, the night when all the stars fell from the sky and the rivers of water turned red.

"Aye." Lady Kathilla addressed the room. "If we cannot have our freedom today, we shall have our holy land and gain our freedom tomorrow. Our time has come to answer the call of The Vahar and bring back our gods, our freedom, and our magic. No more shall we keep to our mountains and cold, forced to feign acceptance with oppression, no more shall we pray in secret, no longer shall we dishonor the Vahar who ride their steeds in the sky and have shown themselves to be restless on their mounts among the stars.

"We shall watch as they kill one another over the throne of gold they forged with stardust and our ancestors' crowns. We shall watch, and then we shall strike and take our land back." She found her battle axe and raised it in the air. For those in the room who held a drink, they followed suit, all others unsheathed their weapons; large swords, battle axes, and war hammers now held high in the air.

"Freedom. Honor. Glory." Lady Kathilla shouted, emphasizing each word.

"Freedom! Honor! Glory!" The room shouted back, jerking upward their weapons and drinks at each word.

"Freedom! Honor! Glory!" she pounded her chest.

"Freedom! Honor! Glory!"

The three words were chanted again and again. Excitement ran through the crowd and electrified them all. The stone of Saoirse Castle reverberated and hummed in agreement, pulsing with excitement itself.

Chapter 24

"What is it you and your impending war truly aim for, sister?" Lady Lydia Bromlyn asked non chalantly.

The two sisters sat in her receiving room, decorated to mirror the rooms at Middleton Landing, enjoying one another's company over tea and their respective work; Lady Belva reading parchments of news and scrawling strategies and potential plans in her private journal, Lady Lydia alternating her attention between her stitching and household planning.

Lady Belva flicked her eyes up at her sister across the table, her quill stilling for a moment. "What do you mean?"

"What is it you desire from this war you have begun? When it ends, how will we all know if you have won?" she set down her stitching and stared at her older sister.

Lady Belva set down her quill and sat up to meet her gaze. "You know why this war began, Lydia. The king has well pushed himself into tyrannical territory and he must be unseated."

"And once you and your husband's army rip through the land you'll what? Find yourself in the king's seat then? Is that the plan? For you to have his crown?" Lady Belva moved to speak but was stopped as her sister snipped and shook her head. "You not only rule over our entire country, but you now sit in my home and demand to take over my husband's chair, taking for yourself what little we have. Do you not have enough power already? Must you have more?"

"Where does this accusation come from? I am taking *nothing* from you or His Grace. I am the Lady of Ayeshire, I do not have the luxury of sitting here in this stone house," she gestured to the crafting work on the table. "stitching pillows and kerchiefs and wasting my time!"

Both sisters took a sharp inhale and turned away from one another.

"So I am a waste to you. And here I thought my worry was baseless." Lady Lydia mumbled and threw down her stitching.

"That is not what I meant. Lydia, I apologize." She pinched her brow and muddled through her mind for more of an apology.

"Not only did you get father's adoration and his seat, but a husband that loves you and three boys who admire you. And now when this war is over you will have a crown."

"Is that what you truly believe this to be? Some grab for power of mine? Do you truly think so little of me that you believe I would begin a war for a comfier throne? This is not a war to take what is his from him, but to seek justice and do what is right for our people. Once the king and those who rule alongside him are forced to step down, we will work together as a kingdom to find one worthy of taking his seat. I have no desire to be a queen."

Her sister did not reply.

Lady Belva firmed her jaw and furrowed her face in anger and sadness. "You do believe that of me. Where along the line did you lose faith in me? Was it before you sold yourself off as a teenager to marry Lord Bromlyn for his power and rip a hole through mother and father's hearts? Or was it sometime after, where you realized your mistake and let your husband's distaste for our family change your views on us?"

Lady Lydia's jaw shook and tears crawled down her face that she kept turned away.

"You greeted me with such joy when I arrived, for a moment I felt like family again, like sisters. We do not even see one another on holidays or in polite gatherings, what has happened to our bond?" Lady Belva's heart cracked as she spoke.

Lady Lydia wiped the tears from her face with the back of her hand and sniffled. "You got your happy family and you forgot about me. Perhaps in my loneliness I have grown as harsh and cold as the salt stone of my house. And while I grow old here, fussing over the mundane duties of this role I asked for, you gain more."

"I am not gaining more from this. I am not taking a crown. I do not want it." Lady Belva reassured her.

"Then who will sit on the golden throne if you win this war?"

"My Lady, a message from Lord Digarius." A messenger scout tentatively stood in the doorway. He timidly moved forward and placed the letter in front of her, bowed, and moved to leave. "Apologies for interrupting."

With urgency and no care, Lady Belva ripped open the parchment, her eyes racing across its words and her head shook. "Ravenhall was successful in surprising our soldiers, but, Lord Digarius was able to fight them off and gain their surrender."

She turned to the messenger retreating from the room. "Excuse me, how did Lord Digarius not know of the attack? We received letter here of it, and sent the fastest hawk to Lord Digarius and a horseback messenger to the eastern soldiers."

The messenger scout raised and dropped his shoulders, "Yes and that hawk was mine, My Lady. The day after your letter was sent, she returned with no response attached to her talons."

"Sister, please excuse us." Lady Belva turned back to Lady Lydia, asking her to take leave from the room.

She reluctantly bowed her head and got up, leaving her own receiving room behind for her to use. Lady Belva silently nodded towards the open door, prompting the messenger to close it behind her departed sister.

Lady Belva stood up, lightly wringing her hands. "Do you believe that your hawk was received by my son?"

"She is trained to fly between myself and her other handler that is with Lord Digarius- trained to go nowhere else or to anyone else."

"Then how did my son not know of what was coming for them?" She snapped before catching herself.

"I'm not sure, m'lady. I'm just a messenger."

Lady Belva sat down again, her mind running through each quick suspicion and worry that it could find tucked between its crevices and in her darkest thoughts. She glanced to her writing journal, recalled many of her strategies and plans for the war, political alliances and possible outcomes if each were to go south, outlines for what her army and her allies should do in any given situation. She over planned and overthought for much of the mess she had begun.

Tucked below the journal, her eyes caught on the old parchment that Sister Ora had sent to Middleton Landing that Father Robb had sent onward to her at Sandhill House. The letter that contained warning that could have saved many lives had it reached the right eyes on time.

"Give me one moment, please." She murmured as she pulled out her quill and scrawled out two separate letters. She hastily grabbed a hot candle from a sconce on the wall, using its dripping wax to seal both shut and stamping her seal atop the hardening wax.

She brought both over to the messenger. "You are to hand deliver both of these envelopes to Father Robb in Middleton Landing. Do not send a bird, do not send another messenger, it will be you. If he does not receive them, it will be your head I will have."

"And then what, m'lady?" he asked as he took the parchments.

"I trust Father Robb to get the second parchment to her and to find a crafty way to enact the plan within them."

She grabbed the hand of the messenger, holding it tightly and crumpling the papers. "Father Robb will know if my seal is broken, he will know to have your head and force our men to ask you questions in *very* unsavory ways to find out what you know or who you told. Do not open them."

"I'm, I'm just the messenger ma'am." He shook and nodded before bolting from the room.

***

Lord Digarius sat at the table in his tent, his crunched face and rigid posture illuminated sharply by the candles and lanterns placed intermittently around the interior, many had long since run out of wax and did nothing to break up the blackness. A full goblet of wine sat in front of him next to maps and documents he had given up analyzing hours ago. He casually held his hand on the base of his wine goblet, using his fingers to mindlessly turn it on the tabletop while staring at his tent's entrance.

The background noise of the battle camp was still that of joy and victory celebration; his soldiers outside gathered around various fires to keep the night chill at bay, with many well imbibed soldiers giving grand toasts as an excuse to pour more drink, hollering over friendly displays of strength in wrestling and horseplay, and a sporadic bunch singing off-key drinking songs.

How did they know.

He looked back down at the marked map in front of him; trade lanes leading to Ravenhall from the south and the southeast marked in ink and vast in number. The dozens of routes that spanned off of Tower Bridge had the heaviest ink stains upon them.

How did they know our path.

His lost thoughts were disrupted as the entrance of the tent was thrown open, bringing in more noise alongside a stumbling Sgt. Barton.

"Lord Commander, are you not joining in our celebration?"

Lord Digarius kept his eyes in place, still staring mindlessly in the same spot on the map as before.

"I do not feel the need to celebrate when our victory cost so many lives and our battle should not have yet happened." He finally looked up at her. "I can understand that after traveling for so long past many lands, our army would not go unnoticed even staying on friendly lands, but what I cannot understand is how they knew of us quickly enough to meet in the valleys, the *exact* valley we were marching on."

Sgt. Barton straightened up and shook her head to attempt sobriety. She shrugged. "I'm not sure either, sir. We did not take a main road; they should not have known."

He rubbed the scruff on his face as he grumbled slowly. "Yes, it seems no one seems to know how this could have happened."

Sgt. Barton stood awkwardly at the entrance of the tent as he continued his quiet contemplation for several moments, seeming to forget her presence. Finally, he cocked his head up at her.

"Sorry, Barton, did you need anything?"

"No sir, I did not."

"Huh, ok. Well, you are dismissed." he casually said as he nodded once and picked up his wine glass, drinking the entirety of it quickly.

"Yes, sir." she added before turning and leaving, her drunken state even more uneasy and confused.

Lord Digarius set the empty glass back down on the table, a few droplets of wine dripped down the side and along the stem of the glass, puddling onto the parchments below. He watched as a thick drip of wine slowly made its way down the glass, muddling with the rest onto the messages stacked below it.

"It appears we are not the only ones with listening ears across enemy lines." He mumbled as he ran his hand along the wet wine, staining the parchment red and smearing the lines they had crossed and the ones they were yet to.

***

The valleys on the edge of Ravenhall lands were not made for fine hunting or for hiding from what was carried on the breeze. Rations and days old cured meat sizzled over fires and their smells were not potent enough to cover the foulness of the bodies buried nearby or the scents of broken flesh being tended in Healer tents.

Crackling fires, clanging pots and equipment, and the broken sounds of healing soldiers made up the midafternoon sounds of the Ayeshire camp built near the battlefield many died upon. There were no longer any noises of celebration; the light of the day gave memory once again to what occurred on the field the army rested upon, and painted grief where wine and drunken cheer once stained cheeks.

"Lord Digarius," Emaline eagerly greeted as she strode across the edge of camp. Lord Digarius turned and opened his arms as she approached, smiling warmly as the two met in a friendly embrace.

"It is so good to see you, my friend." he said as the two pulled away.

"You as well. I am glad you are well after what occurred." she grabbed his shoulder, jostling it as she spoke. "Congratulations on your victory on the battlefield, my lord."

The officers gathered around replied to her praise with a raise of their mugs and cups and a half-hearty 'aye'.

"A victory and a fight that came as quite a surprise to us all. My joy in our victory is dampened at the thought of all we lost."

"How many were taken?" her upturned tone changed to match the solemness of his.

He let out a heartbroken sigh before responding, then lifted his head and looked over his shoulder across the camp to the valley they had fought in. "Almost two thousand of our bravest are still being buried and burned in mass graves just outside of the hill's crest. There is no room nor time for us to bury them properly with the honor and ceremony they deserve."

"And how many of Ravenhall's?"

"Three thousand. The remaining surrendered after we followed them off the battlefield. They agreed to defend Ravenhall in the name of Ayeshire as part of their surrender. Our banners now hang in their halls."

There was no triumph in the way he spoke.

"And you believe they can hold against the king with just that?" she asked.

The two casually walked through the camp, observing familiar faces greeting one another after being apart, supplies being fidgeted with and unloaded from wagons, weapons and armor being repaired and checked by their bearers and blood being cleaned of the armor and weapons taken from fallen friends.

Lord Digarius shook his head. "No, I do not, but having their alliance is instrumental and this unexpected clash may have sped up our strategy in the end. A strategy that has seemed to have changed in other ways without my knowing."

His last few words took on accusation and defense as he turned to her while they continued their walk. Her face showed no signs of malice or understanding, only confusion.

"While I am happy to see you today, why is it you and your men have arrived without my father's alongside you? Did my father change our plans and not notify me? Or did you decide to stray without orders?"

She stopped her walking as his last question hit her. "We had to change our plan, m'lord. As soon as we received the message from Lady Montarian about Ravenhall's planned ambush, we made as much haste as we could here, hoping to make it in time to lend aid. I sent a messenger to your father to let him know we would not be rendezvousing with them because of this."

"A message?" his words were sharp and hushed. "You received a warning about the attack?"

Her face fell and crinkled again. "Why yes, m'lord. We were notified that the king learned of our plans and sent Ravenhall to ambush before you could take them. Did you not get notice as well?"

He shifted his gaze around, still keeping his voice low. "No, no I am afraid we did not. We had mere moments to prepare for the battle before it began."

"So not only did the king find out quickly about our plan to fight at Ravenhall, but you never received a messenger bird warning you of what was coming?" she paused. "How curious."

"Not curious. Devious. I am beginning to fear quite deeply that I cannot trust my own countrymen. Whether the deceit lies at home or in this camp,

I do not know, but I do know that there must be a turncoat among us." His eyes shot to hers, then flicked up and down her silhouette. He scrunched them, pondering his suspicions of who could have deceived him so easily.

Emaline did not notice his looking as she scanned the camp, ensuring that no one meandered too close to hear their words.

"What is it you propose we do, sir? Perhaps it would be wise to wait for Lord Montarian and Sebern to arrive, to hold for them to tell us what to do. Our plan was to rendezvous together before moving west again anyway."

He shook his head quickly. "Everything has become a mess so soon. It may be another moon phase before my father's army would arrive. We were supposed to have more time to gather, but we do not. The war was not even supposed to begin now, Emaline. We were tasked with waiting here, not fighting." He swallowed a lump in his throat and shook his head again, his gaze on the ground to avoid any judgement he felt owed.

After a moment of pause, Lord Digarius lifted his head with a deep breath, his crossed arms unfolding as he set his hands on his hips. "Word will spread like wildfire in camp of your knowledge of the ambush and rumors will follow soon afterward of why your men were notified and not mine. We must find the snake; take actions outside of the plan they may have already told the king of and act quickly before His Majesty would find out about the change. And keep our eyes fixed to everyone around us."

"My lord, I am not sure changing our original plan so quickly is wise."

He stepped close to her, her words wafting by his ear and not being heard. "Emaline I am asking you not only as your Lord Commander but as your friend, no one must know of this conversation."

She curtly nodded. "Alright, my lord."

"I need your oath."

"You have my oath and my sword, Lord Commander." she bowed her head.

Lord Digarius responded to her bow with his own. "As you do mine."

They both turned at the sounds of other officers making their way to them.

"First Sgt. Kingery, a pleasure to see you again." Sir Rainey greeted, exchanging salutes as they did so. "I assume Lord Commander has caught you up on what you have missed?"

"Yes, that he has, sir."

"Good. I have briefed your officers as well, and I am certain that soon everyone else will have been caught up by dinner." Sir Rainey paused for a moment, managing to find a way to make himself stand stiffer than he already was; an awkward look on his face. "We missed you on the battlefield. It would have been a more triumphant day to have fought alongside one of my strongest."

She gave a soft smile to her lifelong mentor.

"It would have been the highest honor to have fought pauldron to pauldron with you in our first battle of this war. We will be even more victorious at our next one, and I will be there to revel in the victory alongside you all."

Lord Digarius cut in to address the gathered officers. "We have sat long enough for too many days in healing and in wait. We are planning to leave in the morning and not to wait for our Sebern allies. We must not delay and give our enemy any advantage over us. My father and Lord Torrin's army will meet with us farther out on the field as we ensure that the king's army is held off and away from these lands."

Officers exchanged side glances and crumpled looks, but none questioned his firm tone and commanding stare.

"Go. Inform the rest of the soldiers of this; our reunion today will be short lived. When dawn breaks, we will move to bring our fight to the king's door."

CHAPTER 25

Prince Elion stared up at the tent's ceiling where the stripes of the red and white fabric met at the tip of a heavy support beam. He sighed in contempt as Jeffrey moved in closer to him and ran his fingers along the prince's bare chest, drawing circles and tracing lines over his old scars. The sheets on the large bed were haphazardly strewn over their bodies, the bedframe, and the floor. Behind the bed they had made a mess off, hung the crest of Britia; a large banner carrying the same crest draped down the pole in the center of the tent.

"We cannot keep doing this, Your Highness." Jeffrey mumbled against Prince Elion's shoulder.

"Mmm... you are probably right." Prince Elion murmured before shifting to lay facing him, placing his palm on his clean shaven and smooth cheek, and nuzzling his nose. "But we are quite good at it."

Jeffrey's response was muffled by the prince's lips pushed against his as he wrapped his hand around Jeffrey's neck to pull him in tighter. Prince Elion pushed himself on top of Jeffrey, elongating and deepening their kiss as he placed himself between his legs. He pulled his mouth away, trading his deep kisses for soft brushes down Jeffrey's neck and chest.

"We have told ourselves we would end this countless times and never seem to do so." Jeffrey sighed.

"Mhmm" the prince hummed into Jeffrey's chest, his hands brushing down his sides, past his hips, and to his limp cock. Prince Elion continued kissing his soft torso, and his hand began stroking, already feeling Jeffrey harden in his grip.

Jeffrey grunted and breathed out. "You are married to someone else- to a woman. We should stop."

The prince looked up, his lips still grazing the skin on his pelvis, just inches away from where his hand was holding him. "The entire kingdom knows that our arrangement is simply a marriage for heirdom and nothing more. Lady Easter and I agreed long ago to not pretend it was anything but that. She has her lovers I'm sure, and she knows I have you. But, if you truly would like me to stop, I will."

Jeffrey gazed down at him before letting out a groan and shaking his head. "Mmm, do not stop."

Prince Elion gave a devilish smile and moved his mouth downward to meet with the stroking of his hand.

"*Fuck*." Jeffrey groaned as he felt the warmth of the prince's mouth around him.

Jeffrey's gasping and moaning quickened in pace as the prince's mouth and hand did, too. After several moments of pleasure filled gasps, Jeffrey's breath hitched, his body pulsed and tingled with climactic intensity. He shot his hand down to tangle in the unkept curls on Prince Elion's head, holding his mouth in place as Jeffrey pushed his pelvis up, pushing his cock in and on out his mouth in short jerks as he ascended into his ecstasy.

"Fucking fuck." Jeffrey gasped as he let go of the prince's curls and let his body fall back onto the bed. Prince Elion crawled up and pushed their mouths together in a quick kiss, then moved his lips to growl into his ear. "Turn around."

"Yes, Your Highness." Jeffrey teased as he turned around on the bed, leaning on his hands and knees in front of him and gripping the headboard.

The prince spit into his hand, remains of Jeffrey's cum and his spit coated the hand that he brought down to his own throbbing cock. He lightly stroked himself as he watched Jeffrey spread himself in front of him.

His biceps and chest shuddered in pleasure, he worked hard to control his breathing as he stopped his stroking and positioned himself behind Jeffrey, moving his free hand to wrap around the back of Jeffrey's neck, firmly holding him in place as he smacked his body against his and pushed into him.

***

Prince Elion threw open the tent's flaps and strode across the encampment, his head held straight, and his shoulders drawn back. Under his arm he rested his helmet, the gold and silver armor of the gilded metal glimmered in the morning sun. Each strip of metal on his body twinkled and shone brighter than the rest of the army, setting his status among them.

"Where is she?" He asked no one in particular as he continued his storm through the campsite.

Soldiers and aids around him shuffled quickly; officers jumping to join him in his walk, aids jumping out of his way, and others running to busy themselves with their tasks.

"I said, where is she?" He asked right as he met with a line of soldiers guarding and holding down a woman in worn-out Healer's clothing; her white apron stained in blood and dirt.

The heir to the throne stared down at her, running his tongue across his teeth and setting his jaw firm. His eyes darted up and down her scraggly and pale body.

"Do you confess to what you have done?" he asked down his nose.

She cried out. "Please, my lord. My family needed fed; I needed a job. I meant no-"

A slap broke across her face and she screamed in pain.

"He is your prince, not your lord." a soldier beside her sneered as he set his hand back on his swords pommel.

"I apologize, my prince. I meant to no harm, I just wanted to help."

"I empathize with the desire to lend aid, but the law is the law and treason must be punished." he took a subtle step forward. "Abandoning your Divine House and choosing your own fate is treason not only against the kingdom, but against god. You lied about who you were and stole the sigil of another to lie your way into our camp and into a new life."

"I was born in the wrong House, I am not meant for minstrel work and art, I am meant to heal and help. *I am a good Healer.* Your soldiers have seen the ailments I have been able to treat. I can do so much more for the kingdom if you just let me" she begged.

"The law is set and you broke it. It is His will, God, and His Majesty's, that those who commit treason and betray His Will be punished and face righteous judgement."

"Please no." she cried.

"The law is the law." the future king repeated.

She sniffed and met his dark eyes. "I do not ask anything of you, Your Highness. I only ask that God understands my heart meant not to create sin nor commit treason. That if The One True is as kind and merciful as we say he is, that he offer me that mercy."

She set herself down on her knees, falling from the soldier's loosened grip and hung her neck out, flinching as she heard the metallic shear of the prince's sword unsheathing.

"And for the sake of those you leave behind and have damned to the hells for your betrayal, let us hope He grants it, for, by law, I cannot." Prince Elion spoke with no malevolence or anger, only by law and fact.

The ground beneath her fell into shadow as he stepped beside her.

"In the name of His Majesty, King Ivan of House Scott, First of His Name and Lord of the Six Kingdoms, I, Prince Elion of House Scott, Heir to the Golden Throne, Lord Commander of His Majesty's Royal Army, sentence you to die. As is His Will, so shall it be done."

Prince Elion took a quiet breath as he swung and his sword broke through her neck.

Her head stilled on the ground as he stepped back to the squire that waited nearby. The squire held out a towel for the prince as he approached, using it to clean the blood off his sword. The first blood of war he had drawn had not been of an enemy, but of an attempted ally.

As the prince cleaned off the blade, the prince faced the truth that the first blood of war he had drawn had not been of an enemy, but of an attempted ally. The dawning of that truth broke through the steel covering his body and pushed into his heart.

As her body was taken away, Prince Elion sheathed his sword and addressed those still gathered. "Our fate is our duty, and our duty is our faith. If we forsake our duties and choose others, we not only turn our backs on the law, but on God as well. His Will is law and we are to be true to it. Understood?"

"Aye" heads nodded in agreement and understanding.

"Return to your labors, we leave when the sun reaches its peak."

***

"Thank you, my boy." Father Robb said to the sweat and nerve coated messenger standing in front of his desk. He waved his hand in a gesture, requesting the two wax sealed parchments from him.

"Did you open them?" he asked as he inspected the untouched, perfect seal. He looked up and cocked an eyebrow in jest.

The messenger shook his head and stuttered., "No, I did not. I swore to her I wouldn't, and I didn't."

"Well, she sure worked you into quite a tizzy, must be something of big importance for her to have you shake like this." Father Robb jested as he cut the letters open with a knife. Before the top letter was fully opened his eyes began scanning her words. Father Robb rested his elbow on the table and covered his mouth with his hand as he finished reading her first message. He folded it closed and cleared his throat as he straightened in his seat. "Leave. Now. You were never here."

"Glady." the messenger replied before turning on his heel and running out the door, closing it hard behind him.

Father Robb hunched forward and struggled to stand, his back popping and stiffening as it did quite often in his old age. He hobbled over to the open-doored balcony, running his hand along the smoothness of the tele-scope sitting out on the balcony. He found his rest against the stone ledge that pointed in the direction of the Ina Gulf in the distance. He watched the waves beat against the docked ships, the empty water further out begging for sail boats to brush along its surface.

Fishing boats dared not go out too far past the shoreline anymore and public and private merchant ships were shut down from crossing to Britia. The king had just sent a scathing letter accompanied by an embargo on all goods and services between the two countries. Trade ships that had been on their way to his city were met with royal ships handing the captains copies of the same letter and forcing their return. The original letter sent to Middleton Landing had been written in clear haste, the wording and signature sloppy for His Majesty and his councils standards. When he read it, Father Robb swore he felt the rage in each pen stroke and the flames of the king's anger heating the paper.

He tapped his pointer finger on the smooth stone ledge and pressed his lips into a firm line. "How will we get to her if we cannot sail to his city nor trust a message via bird?"

He ran his gaze along the waters, the distant shoreline becoming clearer and closer the farther east he looked. "And who could Sister Ora trust with-out question?"

His tapping finger paused, remembering a conversation his mind had thrown away before the departure of their armies, when his old mind was focused on too much to take in every word and promise thrown at him. He turned too quickly, his back stiffening and spasming at the quick movement. He huffed as he walked to reluctantly find his walking cane.

"*Damn back.*" he cursed as he made his way down to the docks.

Chapter 26

Sedrick had found a few moments of peace amid his mundane workday, tucking himself away from the main work on the Middleton Landing piers and standing in solace leaning over a banister with a hidden book. Gulls busied themselves in the sky and on the pier around him, hunting for fish to snatch from the shallow waters or from the nets and boxes on the dock. The call of the gulls and lapping of the waves against the algae covered posts dulled out the sounds of those ending their workday down the pier from where he stood. The sea breeze flickered the pages of the book secretly held in his hands as he used the worn wood as a desk to rest the book on.

Despite the controversy that could arise if the wrong person were to snatch the book from his hands and learn of his poetic prose, Sedrick did not care about any potential punishment for his sins. He had already faced the worst punishment possible when he was a young boy caught reading and writing when he was supposed to be learning his sailing knots.

When you have nothing left to lose and have already survived the darkest acts of what your own family is willing to do, threats of damnation become empty and unheard words.

There was also often a plethora of bureaucratic paperwork involved in reporting someone to the government and church, and very few had time to sit in hard chairs in dingy offices when there was too much important work to be done.

Sedrick stood deep in thought, so lost in his mind that he did not hear the footsteps approaching.

"What do you think you're up to now?" Father Robb teasing voice asked from directly behind him.

Sedrick jumped back into reality and quickly closed the leatherbound journal as he turned around. "You scared the hells out of me, Father Robb, sneaking up on me like that."

Father Robb chortled more, completely satisfied with himself. "Apologies, son. I couldn't help myself. I saw you so lost in thought and figured you would not have even heard me if I had yelled." he nodded his head towards the poorly hidden journal. "More of your prose?"

"Yes, but, it is not done yet. I just can't seem to get it right." Sedrick mumbled as he combed his hand through his hair, shaking his head and pondering aloud.

Father Robb shrugged and moved to sit down on the nearby bench, gesturing for Sedrick to follow. He sat with a huff and grunt. "Well, read it to this old man."

"Oh no. No no no. You do not want to hear this drabble." he said as he sat down beside Father Robb.

"Oh, but I do. I always enjoy your words and envy that talent that I've never known myself. Despite all my epochs reading and writing, I never could manage to gain a talent for poetry like you have." Father Robb paused. "God truly gifted you with beautiful talents outside of the House he put you under. Perhaps in this new world you may pursue them."

Sedrick's eyes flickered with hope as he shifted closer to Father Robb. "Do you truly believe that? That after the war things could change so much? Even the word of God?"

Father Robb grunted. "What we keep forgetting is that the words we hear from holy men are not directly from the mouth of God, but our interpretations over time and generations. In all my epochs spent kneeling in pews and speaking behind pulpits, I have never once heard Him tell me to punish one for taking up innocent hobbies or interests; to put a nail to the hands of those who write when they are not meant to, to take a life when they had not harmed one."

"But that is what the church says His Will is." Sedrick argued.

"His Will is ancient and complex, and we are but simple men attempting to interpret and understand it. The Old Way, the way we diverged from hundreds of epochs ago, asked only that we live a life of honor and purpose, to guide ourselves down a path worthy of salvation."

"But the New Way was born because we wandered too far from His path, and here we stand, with firmer paths and ways to honor His Will, with Divine Houses determining our worth and our futures." Sedrick countered.

Father Robb slowly nodded his head, his tone introspective and contemplative. "Yes, and here we are."

"Is this what you came here to speak to me about?"

Father Robb kept nodding as he continued his ideological debate internally, forgetting for a moment the real conversation in front of him. "Oh, no, apologies, you know how I ramble at times. I came here because I have a task for you, my boy."

Father Robb turned and peered up and down the pier, ensuring there were no listening ears nearby. "Well, specifically, Lady Montarian has a task for Sister Ora, a way she can help us." he pulled out the second parchment she had sent alongside his, the wax seal still unbroken. "I need you to get this to her. We cannot trust a bird to get the letter to her, for all we know the king and his men read anything she is sent, and Her Grace needs someone who both she and Sister Ora can trust inexplicably."

"Why me?"

"You came to Lord Digarius and I before he left and pledged yourself to the cause. You asked us to allow you to lend aid in some way and that you would do what is asked. You said, let's see if I remember your exact words, that you did not wish to lie around and do nothing, that you could not sit idly by." he paused and shrugged. "And we need someone who can go unseen by those who might be watching, but who is well known and trusted by Sister Ora."

"Father Robb, I don't know, I am but a simple sailor."

"Oh quiet those words, you are much more than that." he quipped and let out a quick breath. "But I believe for this task, it may be in your favor to pretend you are just that."

Sedrick pinched his brow. "Please speak plainly, Father Robb."

"Lie, Sedrick. *Lie* your way to her and get her this letter. The king does not always have eyes on the Gulf nor along every piece of land it touches, find a way to get across and to her. Perhaps travel inland where his eyes struggle to see, stalk in the night and find your way to his front door."

Sedrick sighed rubbed the back of his neck. "What is it they are even asking of her?"

Sedrick reached for the sealed letter and Father Robb pulled it back. "The less we all know the better, unfortunately. I myself do not even know what is in this envelope, and you are not to either. Sister Ora is to retrieve specific information for us and return it to you, and you return it home. It is very important and that is all you or I are to know for now."

Sedrick sat in contemplation, his elbows rested on his knees as he crossed his fingers together and held his head down. "And this task, this *risk*," he looked up at Father Robb. "this is how I will help make the world a better place? A place where no child would be beaten and exiled by their own family for being who they truly are? Can you promise me that?"

"No. But I can promise you that it is a step towards that possibility." he held the envelope out for Sedrick.

"All the books you have given me over the epochs have made me too hopeful of a dreamer, Father."

Father Robb smiled and handed the envelope to Sedrick. "I know, that was the point."

***

Sedrick jerked the thick braided rope in his hands, securing his boat to the dock with just a few flicks of his wrists and twists of the rope The light waves bumped the boat rhythmically against the wood as he finished tying the rope to the dock's cleat. He let out a small grunt as he stood up and stepped to the back of his boat, unloading his small cache of supplies and gear.

The small port town and outlying area were unfamiliar to him; a simple small village named Burnsley that he picked on a sailing map due to its small nature and location along the Gulf. As his row boat made it to their shores, his quick observations made it clear that it was a underprivileged town, lost in the shadows of the grandness of Isilria and the stones and turrets of The King's Keep that sat just a few days away.

It was early in the morning, his secret sailing done by the cover of night in hopes to go unnoticed under his guise as a simple fisherman coming from another town. The eeriness of the dark waters had only made his sea sickness worse, giving him a headache and stomachache he could not rid himself of despite his healthy dosage of the medicine that Ephraim prescribed him long ago.

Sedrick tossed his bag of clothes and supplies on the dock behind him and reached back to unload the boxes and nets of fish he had caught on his sail in. The dock currently held just a few other fishing boats of various sizes- many empty with the crew nowhere in sight and several covered with tarps stained by rain and the elements- an unusual sight for a fishing village. Speckled along the dock were a humble number of others unloading and loading their measly catches- early morning risers hopeful to catch what they could before the shoreline was riddled with competition.

A few boats down, an older man with sun aged skin and a scraggly white beard was fiddling with a canvas tarp cover. Like most fishermen and dock workers, he wore clothing made for hard labor and work, not for leisure or fanciful events. The man peered over at Sedrick as he untangled the tarp and tossed it over his boat, hollering to ensure he caught Sedrick's attention.

"Gonna be a hard time comin' soon, innit?"

Sedrick turned as he set his net of fish down. "Sorry, sir, what do you mean?"

The man reached into his coat, pulled out a smoking pipe and a match to light it. As he began puffing his tobacco, he walked to Sedrick, his eyes crinkling as he looked him up and down. "Harder for us to make a livin' with all these damned new rules and sanctions. Can barely take our boats past the shoreline now and we all know the best fish swim in the deeper waters of the Gulf. Makes a hard livin' for a fishin' town like ours."

"Oh, right, right." Sedrick mumbled.

The man puffed his pipe again, then took it out of his mouth and looked down at the fish Sedrick had unloaded. "You got lucky not getting' caught out that far. You're probably the last man to catch them kinda fish, might get you a good coin if you're careful. Towns desperate for more than the common trout by our shores."

"Well actually, I am heading up the way." Sedrick pointed towards the direction of the king's city. "To try to sell them at the markets up in Isilria, think I will do much better up there where more coin flows."

"You'll be fightin' with the catches they're still getting' in from the sea where there's no restrictions- lots of exotic sea creatures and fish to compete with. Might not be as easy to make that king's coin." the man smiled kindly. "Just a friendly note for ya, don't wanna dash your dreams, but things aren't as bright as they once were."

"Thank you, good sir, I appreciate that." Sedrick paused for a moment before continuing. "The docks seem real quiet today, quite unusual- even with the king's sanctions."

"Hard to find a desire to work when your livelihoods been attacked. Many have tried findin' new jobs, rest already movin' on to other towns. Others been headin' to the king's city itself to find work." he lowered his voice. "Or cause problems."

Sedrick held his tongue but his face gave away his curiosity at the man's words.

The man exhaled the smoke filling his mouth. "Not many of us are real keen on sending' our daughters and sons off to war, but, if the king's willin' to pay and put us to work, help us feed the family we got left, just like anyone else, that's more than enough for some of us to want to side with him." He inhaled and puffed more smoke again. "But not enough for all."

"And what about you? Why are you not going to the king's city or leaving like anyone else?" Sedrick asked.

He narrowed his eyes and stepped forward, his yellow and chipped teeth gritting. "Because I ain't givin' up what little I got left, and I sure as hell ain't gonna celebrate shit with that king unless it's his funeral."

Sedrick's eyes bolted open. "Sir, are you not worried about the wrong person overhearing what you are saying?"

"What's the king gonna do if he finds out? Behead me? Put me in a cell? Either way, I'd be dead or fed; can't be worse than the fate he and his family have left us all to. And all he's done for us in return is tax us all to hell when he spends too much of the money we give him, send our loved ones to die in a battle for his ego, and then throw us a party hopin' we will forget that his boot is still on our neck." The fisherman shook his head and scoffed. "Most of us are tired of lickin' his boots these days, especially now that almost every family is either bein' ripped apart by being sent to fight or their livelihood being squandered by new rules about who we can and cannot do business with."

"I did not realize so many people here were fed up with what he has been doing." Sedrick confessed.

The man pointed a crooked finger at Sedrick, his pipe in his mouth muffling his words a bit. "That's what they want, for all of us to be too busy and ignorin' one another, not able to take a minute to think or talk... or fight."

Sedrick nodded, continuing to avoid saying much and focusing his thoughts on how to get out of the conversation and be on his way swiftly.

"So you gonna tell me who you really are and what you're doin' here?" the man asked before puffing more from his pipe.

Sedrick did not reply.

"I may not talk as nice as you, or be as smart as you, but it don't mean I'm dumb. I've worked on this dock longer than you've been walkin' and I've never seen your face before. You come sailin' in with fish not found on our part of the shoreline, you don't sound like most of us from this part of the land, you got a bag of clothing and supplies that don't belong on a normal fishin' trip, and when you weren't lookin' I saw books in your bag. You ain't just some fisherman. So, who are you?"

Sedrick quickly weighed the few options he had in front of him and reluctantly replied with some of the truth. "I am a traveler, just trying to survive what is coming and do what is best for myself and those I love."

"And what awaits you in the king's city?"

"I told you. Trading my catch for coin and trying to find more work, just like the rest of us."

The fisherman stared at Sedrick and continued puffing his pipe. Around them, the few other dock workers and fishermen ignored their conversation, continuing with their own tasks and conversations. "Well, come on, we ain't got all day. You'll need a ride there if you want to make it before your ice box melts and spoils your catch. My cart is up the way, was headin' west to do some tradin', but I will take ya west as far as I aimed to go."

The fisherman turned, snatched one of Sedrick's bags, and walked away without a response. It took Sedrick just a few strides, even with carrying the heavy load of the rest of his supplies, to catch up to him.

"The name's Royland, Roy for short. Best not to tell me anythin' about you or what you're really doin'. But in case things go south and you need to come back here and find me, you'll need a bit more than to tell folks you're lookin' for the talkative old man at the docks."

Royland threw Sedrick's bag into a horse drawn cart at the end of the dock, turning to him to prompt him to load the rest of the supplies and hop in. He snapped the horse's reins, nodded his head at the other men left behind on the dock, and mumbled to Sedrick as he settled into the cart with him.

"And also, you might want to find yourself a better cover, son." Royland mumbled. "Not a very good liar."

CHAPTER 27

T he rolling hills of Ravenhall had taken up the traveling northern horizon for several days.

Lord Theodus Montarian received quick word from racing messengers
that their plan for secrecy had failed and that the eastern Ayeshire forces
they were set to rendezvous with had changed paths to lend aid in the
surprise battle against Ravenhall. A thin fog snuck around the base of the
hills; the ghost-gray clouds swirled and slithered between the humps in
the ground and softly blanketed the dew-covered grass at soldiers feet,
enveloping their steps in its gentle phantom grasp.

Lord Theodus' anxious steps scattered the fog that nipped at his heels.
His nerves and frustrations over being left in the dark on the battlefront had
spread among his soldiers and Lord William Torrin's.

Lord William stepped up to his cousin, prompting Lord Theodus to pause
his pacing.

"A messenger just came back." Lord William said. "Bearing news from
Ravenhall. Your son was victorious, Ravenhall now flies your banners."

Lord Theodus replied, not giving his son's first victory any attention.
"And what did they say of his army? Where are they?"

"Theodus, I first am going to remind you that our soldiers are watching
and listening." His voice was calm and even. "And that you have spoken
before of your pride in your son and confidence in his abilities."

Lord Theodus' jaw tightened and his eyes twitched. "What happened?"

Lord William took a calming breath. "Lord Digarius left some of his soldiers behind to aid in defending Ravenhall and to ensure it does not fall while he is gone."

"*While he is gone?*" The Lord of Ayeshire snarled.

Lord William gave him a look to remind him of his tone. "Yes. The last news that those at Ravenhall heard was that Lord Digarius, alongside the eastern battalions that were meant to rendezvous with us, have left to confront the prince's army."

It took every effort in the lord to not explode. He could not help his voice rising. "On their own. They are to fight the *royal fucking army* on their own."

Lord Theodus began franticly pacing again, not caring for those observing his emotions. "I taught him better than this, he knew better than this."

"And at his age you were a perfect soldier and never made mistakes. So I can understand why this is infuriating to you." Lord William said flatly despite the sarcastic intent his words were dripping with.

"William, do *not*. I have made my fair share of mistakes as well, but not like—"

Lord William cocked an eyebrow and shuffled his feet.

Lord Theodus stopped his words and chose new. "We must ride immediately, save him from his mistake. If he is thinking with his mind and not his ego or pride, then he knows to hold once they spot the lion's banners. He cannot win this battle on his own."

***

The light lapping of Lake Lahere and slow beating of lion crested red banners were the only noises breaking the stilled silence of the Britia army lying in wait for the Ayeshire troops approaching. Prince Elion sat atop his steed alongside his second, Commander Blackley; both faces stoic, cold, and painted with impatience.

Prince Elion's armor stood out among the rest of the armor decorating those around him; where theirs was strictly built for taking hits and protecting the wearers body, the prince's was also built to showcase his status on the battlefield. The chainmail that laid underneath the silver plates was forged of the same gold that trimmed the plates and the tassets on his waist. On his left shoulder was a decorative, but still protective, pauldron molded into the shape of a lion's roaring face and the visor and helm of his helmet had a band of pointed arches circling his head, creating a crown when he put the visor down.

The officers of his army wore armor and helmets that differed from their foot soldiers to signify their ranking on the field. Their capes were red with the Britia crest stitched in gold that matched the forged metal of their shoulder pauldrons. The rest of the soldiers' capes matched the officers, but the only gold on their bodies was that of the thread that made up the crown and lion crest of their capes.

Green banners gradually made themselves visible across the barren field, closely followed by heavy lines of mounted and walking soldiers. Across his own lines, Prince Elion took easy note of the tension picking up and bodies shifting. He squandered the growing emotions and edginess with one firm word.

"*Patience.*"

The men and women around him settled.

"Let them come to us, as we planned." he added.

The breezes from the lake on their left picked up, flapping the banners more rapidly. The Ayeshire army stopped at the edge of the lake, just out of range of either army's farthest shots.

Prince Elion's jaw tensed and twitched as his enemies held their movement at the edge of the lake for several minutes.

Commander Blackley spoke up. "Perhaps we charge early to draw them in, let them believe they've pushed us back to get them in front of the lake."

Prince Elion subtly nodded. "After Ravenhall, it is likely that Lord Digarius will be overly cautious to not fall into any potential trap."

"And our sitting here waiting for them does look like what it is." Commander Blackley replied.

They turned to one another and nodded.

"Forward!" Prince Elion shouted, snapping the lid of his visor closed. "March!"

The prince's unit obediently marched forward. To his far-right, the hooves of his horseback flank overpowered the footsteps of the foot soldiers behind him. Prince Elion raised his right fist up beside his head, prompting the soldiers behind him to stop.

"Prepare the long bows." he commanded. His officers shouted the required orders that triggered the unit of bowman to knock arrows to their laxed bows.

The prince raised his right arm straight up and dropped it in a forward arch. "Fire!"

Ayeshire responded to the rainfall of their arrows with their own; enough hitting their targets to make a mark while many, just like those from the prince's army, hit quickly raised shields or bounced off armor.

The noises of impact of the horseback unit colliding with one sent against them called to Prince Elion.

"Left flank! Forward!" he ordered; sending forward the foot troops near the lake shore. He waited several counts before ordering the anxious foot soldiers to his right forward at full speed.

When full impact was almost upon the outskirts of the battlefield, he sent his remaining soldiers and himself, into the center of the fold.

The red caped horseback soldiers met with the Ayeshire troops first, flanking them as they pushed inward. Ayeshire quickly steadied themselves against the classic battle tactic.

Prince Elion and his soldiers, some on horseback but most on foot, took after the soldiers centered on the field and moved to pull them forward to fight along the lake front. His army pushed hard to little avail against the encroaching Ayeshire lines that held their newly gained ground fiercely, barely giving any steps to the Britia forces.

Prince Elion continued to charge forward, sword drawn, his path directly aimed at the distracted fighting foot soldiers in front of him. The slits in his helmet narrowed the focus of his vision, but did not stop him from catching the movement of green and silver racing for him on horseback. The prince pulled the reins as he nearly collided with the horseback soldier and swung across the shield they had attached to their side; the force of the impact knocking his opponent back and making their horse stumble.

Their mount caught their feet as they pushed the white horse forward to retaliate with their own strike, the arch of their sword aiming to slash across the exposed gold chainmail at Prince Elion's neck. Their swords collided, sliding off one another before disconnecting.

Their mounts seemed to engage in their own fight, pushing and shoving at one another, leaving both soldiers slightly unsteady in their movements. The prince tightened his reins as hard as he could to force his horse to rear and startle theirs. He let go of his grip on the reins as his horse came down beside them. As his horse's front hooves met the ground, he drove his sword down into the slit of exposed skin at the soldier's neck.

Prince Elion ripped the sword from their blood streaming neck, splaying their armor and white horse with their blood as their body fell to the ground.

"Do not let them break our lines!" he shouted. "Push them!"

The words had barely fallen from his lips before he kicked his horse and aimed for the soldiers whose attention he had caught.

***

Emaline charged forward on her mount, doing her best to push away the sounds of bones cracking and fallen soldiers shouting under her horse's hooves. She navigated through the field of carnage, unable to avoid damaging the bodies of the fallen as her horse found her footing and directed them towards those pushing against the unit she was commanding. Emaline threw down the broken sword in her left hand, leaving her with only one to wield.

Two Britia foot soldiers ran for her as she turned to lend quick aid to nearby struggling allies. With swift ease, she arched back her sword and knocked the weapon out of the first soldiers' hand, the end of her sword colliding with his helmet, knocking him back from her. The second soldier was too quick with his strike, but instead of aiming for her, he swung his blade across her horse's chest.

The horse screamed as Emaline held back her own.

In her quick thinking, she threw her feet from the stirrups and jumped out of the way of her falling horse. Emaline regained her bearings in time to raise her sword as the attacking soldier jumped for her. When their swords collided, Emaline reared herself back and slammed her foot into their chest, breaking them and their weapons apart. She turned and drove her sword through the exposed neck of another running for her, letting her weapon fall to the ground with their body.

"*Do. Not. Yield!*" she screamed at her soldiers as she stood alongside her fallen horse and opponents. She ripped the sword from the fallen soldiers neck and stole theirs as well; marched onward with new anger and determination boiling her blood.

She flew towards the closest Britia soldier, striking at him with her right sword that met with his in the air, then slicing along his lower abdomen with her left. Before he hit his knees, she was already marching onward towards the next fighter, her pulsing heart the beat of a war drum.

***

Prince Elion had dismounted his horse, abandoning it and sending it back across the field. He found more comfort defending himself on his own two feet. His right-flank soldiers had finally broke into the opposing lines and scatted what remained while his soldiers centered on the battlefield with him were bearing the larger brunt of the battle now. Their torn apart plan finally finding itself again.

He retreated several strides back from the immediate fighting to find Commander Blackley.

"Call the red calvary! Bring them *here*." The prince shouted at his second, then turned at the sounds of steps sprinting for him.

Prince Elion stood his ground, allowing the two enemies to make their way to him. As they met with Prince Elion, he crouched and swung across the closest soldier's legs to bring them down. He threw his body back to deflect the swing of the other incoming soldier, causing them to stop their steps right behind the prince. Prince Elion reached for their shoulder and held them in place as he drove his sword through their back where their armor plates had a gap.

The first soldier moved on the ground in an attempt to rise. Their efforts were fruitless as the prince stepped beside them and crushed their sword-bearing arm with his foot then drove his sword through the side of their ribs.

The wave of his calvary forces approached and rapidly tore through the stubborn lines of the Ayeshire army, finally giving Britia the advantage they needed to push the fight to where they originally planned for it to begin and to end. His calvary ripped apart the soldiers that had once held their ground, turning the bright white stags upon their banners and capes into bloodied prey as the prince's fighters encircled those still standing.

***

Lord Digarius brutally shoved, cut, and pushed his way through the armor surrounding the broken flank he was desperately still attempting to lead. To their back, Lake Lahere called to them. The land around Lord Digarius was crawling with the prince's loyalist soldiers relentlessly butchering his troops. His entire body ached from the fight and from the panic he could no longer keep at bay.

"We cannot break through, my lord!" Emaline shouted as she fought to get to him, her remaining soldiers behind her. "All that we have left is here now, alongside you."

"We are significantly outnumbered, Lord Commander." Sir Rainey shouted over the screams and grunts of the battle. "We must retreat if you wish for your House to live."

Lord Digarius threw down the body of the soldier he had driven his sword through. He quietly choked out. "These lives are my burden to bear. I did this."

"Lord Commander! What do we do?!" Emaline shouted again, striking down another soldier. "We need orders!"

Lord Digarius took a deep, broken breath. "Fall back! Retreat!"

He held his place as he watched what remained of his army stagger and stumble back to where they came in.

"Every last one, every last one was because of me." Lord Digarius whispered before retreating.

CHAPTER 28

The walk along Isilria's high market took Sister Ora and Sir Loren across a high walkway that overlooked where the waters of the Ringhar Sea fed into the Ina Gulf. She swore that if she squinted and strained her eyes hard enough, she could see the shoreline of the country she dearly missed. The breeze wisped around the loose waves falling down her back and shoulders and made the loose skirt of her jewel blue dress dance under her; the edges of the short train billowing along the stone pathway at her feet.

"Quite a sight of beauty." Sir Loren said from beside her.

Sister Ora averted her eyes from the blue waves and side glanced at Sir Loren. His helmet was not turned to the sea that had captured her own attention, but in her direction. He quickly averted his gaze and turned to look out onto the sea.

Sir Loren cleared his throat. "The sea. It is quite beautiful. How it draws your eye to it and calms yet excites at the same time."

Feeling as if her breath was blown away in the breeze, she took a new one and replied in a soft voice. "Yes, the sea does that to me, too."

Time melted away, as it so often did when one could not help but steal forbidden glances at another. But just as quickly as it melted away, it swiftly came back.

"We should be going. I did want to stop by that bookkeeper's shop before we left." She broke the silence and hurried into the small crowd of people carrying on with their afternoon errands.

The bell above the shop door rang as Sister Ora opened it and stepped inside.

"Good afternoon, miss! Welcome to Oswald's Books and Curiosities! I am Oswald, the curator of this establishment. What brings you in today?" the plump and joyful man behind the counter shouted at her. Oswald was adorned in beautiful silks and fabrics, his hair was lavish and wavy and his ears adorned with jewels.

"I am just browsing today, good sir. I was visiting the high market to browse for wedding supplies and try some of the famous baked goods from the bakery down the road." She met with him at the counter and smiled. "And I heard from other shop keeper's that you had the best book selection in the high market and wanted to confirm for myself."

The door pushed open and Sir Loren's body filled the frame of it.

Oswald smiled at her before shooting his eyes up then away from Sir Loren who stepped up behind her. "Of course I do, my lady! But I shall say, I am surprised by your visit given you must be from the castle. Are the grand archives within The King's Keep lacking? Their shelves are the best stocked in the entire country from what I have been told."

"Oh, they are not lacking in the slightest, but I do love to visit other collections." She turned and looked about the space, noting a mezzanine tucked in the back bearing more shelves that appeared just as overstocked as the ones on the first floor, but with more than just books. The shelves overtaking the first floor were crowded with books of all colors and sizes, some neatly placed on shelves and clearly well organized, but many haphazardly set upon wooden mantles with seemingly no order to them. Stacks of books on the clerk's counter and the floor around it created a fortress of literature for Oswald to tuck himself behind.

For a place so filled with words and worlds one could lose themselves in, it lacked people for it to whisk away.

"Have you had many visitors today? Or lately? It is quite sad to see such an exquisite collection of books without any patrons to look over the pages." She asked.

"Oh, just one or two browsers today, I believe one is still lurking around here somewhere. It is hard to sell much besides elementary children's books or religious texts. Even here in king's city not many can, or have the time, to read." Oswald frowned and kept his keen eyes away from the presence of Sir Loren.

"How disappointing." She mumbled.

He nodded in agreement. "That it is, my lady. Feel free to browse around, I am sure there is something here you would like."

She glanced at the pin on his chest, the same Scholar pin she and others born in her Divine House would wear.

"Mr. Oswald." she began to ask.

Oswald raised his hand. "Just Oswald, my lady."

"Yes, Oswald, may I ask you something?" she nodded at his chest. "About your pin?"

His friendly and relaxed demeanor drained away as his body stiffened, he began stammering and stuttering.

"I am asking of pure personal curiosity, my apologies for the fright." She assured him. "You are of my same Divine House, born under the book and quill constellation, yet you are the proprietor of this store, something that I understood as only being possible for those born in the House of Merchant."

"While, on the surface that is true, that this is only possible for those born under the House of Merchant, laws and texts do have differing interpretations." she rumpled her brow at his explanation. Oswald continued, "Scholars are keepers of books, yes?"

Sister Ora nodded. "Yes."

"And here I am," he gestured to the store. "being a keeper of books. Under law and under the code of the Scholars, my store, by technicality of the words we uphold, is legal. It took some verbal sparring with the church and lawmen, but the law is the law, and they could not deny it." He gave a satisfied smile at himself as he set his hands on his hips and straightened up.

Sister Ora chuckled. "How clever."

Oswald nodded. "Knowledge is very powerful."

She smiled and dismissed herself to browse the shelves. Behind her, she heard the clinking of metal as Sir Loren followed close behind.

She wanted to extend her time outside of the castle for as long as she could. Her cover of attending the high market to speak to local bakers, tradesmen, and curators about her upcoming nuptials, to bring the people of the city into the celebration, as she had told Prince Percy, was either well received or, her comings-and-goings were not cared about enough to warrant a denial of her request from the royal family.

As the loathing at her inevitable return to the castle grew, she mindlessly pulled books off the shelves to try to find one able to distract her and keep her here. Behind her, Sir Loren's boot hit a pile of books stacked on the floor, knocking them all around and startling Sister Ora. He grunted and bent over to restack the books, shaking his head as he did so and cursing under his breath.

"This store is quite crowded, far too much for me. I'll be at the door if you need me, my lady." he said before making his way back to the front of the store, kicking another pile of books on his way.

She laughed under her breath and turned back to the shelf in front of her. A small collection of romance books greeted her, a rare sight as pleasure reading was not common among common people. Poetry and prose books adorned with flowers and vines were beside the books of love, several of the titles unfamiliar to her and bound in ways not common for the modern bookbinders of the continent.

"He is quite a collector." she mumbled as she pulled out a book from the shelf with no title or writing on the spine. She broke into a hushed laughter as she opened the book to a random page and, finding a lot of heartfelt entertainment in the sketches and descriptions, continued her browsing of its pages.

Her entertainment was quickly taken from her as the chime of the bell above the shop door rang out and footsteps entered.

"Oh! Your Royal Highness, such a pleasure to have you in my shop." Oswald's voice boomed. "Two visits in one day from members from the castle. I am ever so lucky."

Her heart jumped into her throat as she fumbled to close the book and put it back, only to drop it and have enough time to pick it up before the royal guest rounded the corner to her aisle.

"There you are!" Princess Arminda greeted at the end of the aisle, a beaming smile glowing across her face. "I had heard you had taken it upon yourself to come to town and run wedding errands and wished to join you, and, I come bearing news."

Sister Ora curtsied as the princess approached, trying to hide the book in her hands. "Your Highness, my apologies, had I known you had wished to join me I would have extended the invitation, how rude of me to not ask." she said as Princess Arminda approached; her voice stammering as she fought the parched dryness of her throat.

"Do not apologize, Sister Ora. I felt the same as you, desiring simply to be out of the castle for some time. What book is it that has seemed to spark such interest for you?" Princess Arminda asked as she snagged the book and began flipping through the pages.

"No it's..." Sister Ora's words faded as the princess' face scrunched in discomfort the more she continued to flip pages.

"Is this what I... Sister Ora I mean— " she cleared her throat. "— I am sure my brother will be completely, umm, satisfied, with you as his wife without you needing to resort to anything in this... book." The normally perfect and unbothered princess avoided eye contact as she handed the book back.

Sister Ora looked down and glanced at the title surrounded by roses and, now that she took more than a moment to look at it, flowers subtly drawn in the shapes of various genitalia: *A Most Pleasurable Marriage: A Lover's Guide to Pleasure in Matrimony.*

She set the book back on its shelf, her embarrassment begging to rise and show on her face.

"Is this one of your wedding errands you wanted to run on your own today?" Princess Arminda asked, still avoiding looking at her.

Sister Ora turned to the princess. "Let us just pretend this did not happen, shall we?"

"I would love nothing more than to never think of you and my brother in those positions displayed in that book." She said as she linked their arms and walked them out of the aisle. Her tone shifted from jest and joy to a solemn quiet. "Besides, we must be off to the castle, my father is putting on a celebratory feast tonight."

"Oh, for what?" Sister Ora asked as they made their way out of the bookshop.

"We received word this day. My brother's army won their first battle and are taking back our land. The losses were high, but it was worth the victory."

"Oh." She whispered in response. Sister Ora feigned needing to adjust her eyes to the sunlight as they came outside. She dipped her head and closed her eyes for a moment. When she opened them and looked around, others eyes were upon them, many more menacing than the ones that had greeted her when she landed on the city's shores.

***

Prince Percy leaned over in his dining chair to whisper in Sister Ora's ear. "Are you alright?"

She pushed the food around on her plate, her stomach empty and craving the luxurious dinner piled in front of her, but her emotions making her choke on each bite she attempted to take.

"Yes, yes I am fine. Just not hungry tonight."

"I'm sorry." he whispered.

She turned her head to him. "Sorry for what?"

"Yes, Prince Percy, what is it you are apologetic for?" Father Figgins chimed in from across the table. The Hand had ended his conversation with the king, both of their gazes upon the young prince now.

His lips thinned into a straight line as he sat up, not removing his gaze from the smirking sneer of Father Figgins.

"Percy?" his father said.

"I am sorry for the lives lost. For Sister Ora losing so many of her fellow countrymen, many who she may have personally known, to this war. I am sorry that she must sit here and celebrate their deaths alongside us when I am sure she would like to mourn."

He glanced at her, her head downturned and eyes staring blankly at her plate.

King Ivan let go of his glare at his son and slowly turned his head to her. "And are you sorry for our victory, Sister Ora? Do you wish to mourn?"

She looked up at the king, then at Prince Percy. Her mouth fell loosely open, but no words came out.

"Your king asked you a question." Queen Onetta said from behind her wine chalice, her tone flat and bored. "Your future father-in-law would like a reply."

Sister Ora's fingers ripped at her nail beds as she gathered them in her lap. She turned to the king and spoke quietly and timidly. "No, no I do not wish to mourn."

"Speak up, dear, I am an old man and have trouble hearing when one mumbles." The king said.

She cleared her throat and fidgeted in her seat. She spoke more firmly, staring down at her plate, "I do not wish to mourn. There is no need."

King Ivan smiled. "And why is that?"

"*Father.* " Princess Arminda cut in sharply, attempting to stop the oncoming inquisition.

"Silence." He snipped much too harshly at her before turning back to Sister Ora. "Well?

A sharp breath came from her, but no breath returned to her lungs as she picked and ripped more at her hands and her eyes bore holes into the table in front of her.

"Stop it." Prince Percy demanded, shoving his hands against the tables edge, and standing up. "This is ridiculous. Despite our countries opposing sides, those are still her people and demanding she celebrate their deaths is despicable. She should be allowed to mourn death just as much as we are allowed to mourn the death of our own."

"You will not demand silence from or speak in such a way to the king." King Ivan hit back, slamming his hand down onto the table and standing up across from him.

"I am not demanding that of a king I am *asking* it of my father." Prince Percy attempted to reason with his angered father.

"I am the king first." King Ivan corrected as he jabbed his finger in the air at him.

"Just like grandfather was, yes?" Prince Percy snipped.

"Do not dare to— "

"Enough!" Queen Onetta shouted then composed herself. "This is no way for the royal family to act. We will not shout at one another like some ill-mannered peasants. We will not speak to one another in such a way. Have some decorum or make your leave. Both of you."

King Ivan wiped his hand over his mouth, a light bloodied sore at the corner of his lip reopening and drawing a small line of blood down his face as he moved his hand that flaked with dry skin. He glared at his son, then sat back down with a forceful thud.

King Ivan gestured his hands in the air as Prince Percy took his seat as well. "My apologies, all."

Prince Percy turned to his shaking betrothed beside him, her body shrinking in on itself, "My apologies as well."

***

Sir Loren set down the tin tray of food on the empty dining table in the barracks dining hall. He sat alone facing the wall, only removing his helmet once he had ensured no one was seating themselves beside him. The food looked better in the dark; the greasy pile of what appeared to be potatoes looked more appetizing next to the white boiled duck meat when you could not fully see the lack of spices or care put into the dinner.

"Food seems to be getting worse. I remember the days we once dined like the king." A King's Guard mumbled at the table behind Sir Loren's back. "Was part of the reason I took this fuckin' job, the pay, the whores, the food. Not much better than the army grunts we used to be now."

The King's Guard beside the man grunted in agreement. "Heard His Majesty is sending all our money to that war. 'Reallocating tax payer funds' is what I overheard someone sayin'. Meanwhile my mother and her neighbors had to pay to fix the cobblestones in front of their homes since the king's collectors said there were no funds for it. Meanwhile I bet your brother and the other blacksmiths are doin' mighty fine, eh?"

The mumbling guard replied in better words than before. "He just bought himself a nice new horse, a young mare perfect for leading his cart. Won't have to rely on that old half-lame one anymore." He took a gulp of beer, "War is good for some of us it seems."

Sir Loren listened and quietly chewed the duck meat and washed it down with the water in his stein. Finished dinner plates behind him clattered as the two King's Guards finished their meals and moved to leave.

"Sir Loren, we're heading out for the night now that the night's guard are posted. Heard the House with Red Doors on the main strip has some new women waiting for us." the talkative first guard said.

Sir Loren continued eating, ignoring them.

"Oh he don't want to come with us, he's got a pretty little whore of his own, yeah?" the other guard said as he came up behind him and jostled Sir Loren's shoulders. "That Prince Percy is gonna be one lucky man once he gets her in bed soon. Maybe you should give her a go first, make sure she is ripe and ready for your old charge to handle."

Sir Loren pulled his body away from his grasp, replying in a flat tone. "Do not speak of the royal family that way. It is treasonous to do so."

"Oh come on! It is nothing compared to what others are saying. Just a joke even."

Sir Loren went back to his dinner and shook his head.

The me continued their egging of him. "You've been a dog of the king for fifteen epochs, learn to live a little! Pull out that stick up your ass about your duty and your oath and enjoy your life. What's the point of being a King's Guard if you don't enjoy the benefits of it?"

Sir Loren slammed down his fork, turned his head to the side and glaring up at the men egging him on. "I did not take my oath of duty to enjoy priority treatment at pleasure houses or attention and praise from others, I took it because I believe in the cause and what it asks of me." he turned back to his meal. "My oath is my life and I am no good man if I use it for my own gain, or if I break what I swore to the king."

CHAPTER 29

Lord Theodus Montarian stormed into the large tent in the half constructed war camp. The canvas flaps flew back as he marched to stand at the table covered in papers, small models, and maps. He slammed his helmet down and whirled around to face his son timidly following him inside.

Blood was still stained across both of their armor suits as Lord Theodus began shouting, loud enough for all those outside of the tent to hear, but who would say nothing of what they heard.

"Half of our soldiers, Digarius. Half of our soldiers are *dead* because of your utter fucking stupidity!" Lord Theodus ran his hand over his head, wiping sweat, dirt, and blood across his bald scalp. His tone stayed sharp but lowered in volume. "What in the hell were you thinking going into that battle without us?"

Lord Digarius didn't reply as his father stood stone-faced and livid across the tent. He let out a broken sigh and shook his head, trying to find the reasoning and rationale behind his deadly choice that made so much sense before the slaughter.

"You were supposed to be our people's next lord, not their shepherd that led them to their slaughter." the Lord of Ayeshire's brimmed with disappointment. His head shook as he looked at his son. "You are not ready. I believed you to be ready to lead our people, but it is very clear to me now that we both are quite naïve about your capabilities."

His words cut through the air and struck Lord Digarius so deeply he felt as if his father had swung a sword or fist at him instead of a few words. He stepped forward as his father turned towards the paperwork on the table. "Father, I- it was a mistake. I believed it the right thing to do, leading our forces forward instead of waiting for them to take an advantage on us. I made a mistake and for that I will grieve the remainder of my days."

Lord Theodus slammed down the papers. "You do not get to make mistakes. You do not get to fail. When you do, people *die*... As you have so clearly discovered."

Lord Digarius swallowed the lump in his throat and pushed his eyes shut, hoping to prevent the tears he felt from falling. Instead, the blackness he saw was filled with images of the slaughter that took place just before he and his remaining soldiers fled from the unrelenting masses of Prince Elion's army.

The reprieve they received from the violence of the battlefield was momentary as they limped towards the edges of Ravenhall to recover and tend to their survivors. The moment his father and Sebern's army met them, they tore out with a fierce determination to return Britia's bloodshed. As the armies crashed into one another, Ayeshire and Sebern's combined forces of nearly fourty thousand tore apart much of Britia's remaining twenty-five thousand, reducing the prince's royal army by an estimated third and pushing them back to the shores of Lake Lahere.

Lord Theodus sighed and rested his hands on the table, "I know the pressure is unbearable at times. Living up to the legacies that lived before us, holding others' lives and fates in our hands, it is... sometimes enough to make this old man buckle a bit."

He pulled out a chair at the table and motioned for Lord Digarius to do the same. They both sat down, Lord Digarius sitting straight up on the edge of his chair and his father leaning back, his body as limp as it could be underneath the metal he still wore, and one elbow resting on the table.

"I was barely younger than you when I was given my first heavy command in the Sebern army. Thirty-two epochs ago at Broken Tower. I was the officer requested to lead our forces and end the fighting that Craigie and Odessin were at again- to be the looming force backing Broken Tower and threaten them into laying down their swords. I have never told you, nor anyone else, what truly happened that day. There are whispers, yes, but we kept it quiet between the families as best we could." He found a stein sitting on the table near a small barrel of beer and poured himself a glass, taking a large swig of it before he continued.

"While it was not I who swung the sword myself, Lady Edgel has yet to rid me of blame for her husband's death and I still see the look of hurt in Lady Torrin's eyes when she looks my direction, knowing it was one of my men who took her brother's life that day at my order. I should have commanded my soldiers to lay down their arms once Odessin laid down theirs and much of Craigie were beginning to surrender as well. The battle had begun to cease as demanded, but instead I decided that Lord Edgel needed to learn a lesson and see what would happen if he continued his rampages for land. He wouldn't give up or take a break form the fighting. Someone had to send a message to him."

Lord Theodus took another drink and a long breath. "And now, to this day, I live with the blood and pain that my mistake and my ego caused. Outside the families and those in the battle, we changed the narrative to protect what we could, to prevent a trial and judgement against our actions of striking surrendering men. It was not hard to get many to believe that Lord Edgel was the one who would not stop fighting, he was a ruthless man, but that lie sowed much division and broke many friendships. It was a necessary evil to protect many people."

Lord Digarius let out his own deep breath. It was well-known that his father was one of the leading officers in the battle at Broken Tower, the ugly scar that tore alliances between Craigie and Sebern apart, but details were never documented of how Lord Edgel died, of what Lord Montarian did, and how much blood was relentlessly shed.

Nor of the war crimes his father led his men to commit.

He could no longer meet his father's eyes as he moved to rest his elbows on his knees and asked. "What happened next?"

"Your grandfather conceived a creative plan to cover what happened; history forgets words that are not written, and it was his words that married his daughter to me, creating a firm alliance between Sebern and Ayeshire, and ridding my homeland of me. Some say it reward, some say punishment that I had to leave, but Lord Vegaria did not care of that when he brought me here. He said he saw the stag living deep in my heart, and that I was to be of importance to Ayeshire someday."

"Is that the truth to why mother took your name instead of you taking hers?" Lord Digarius asked.

"It was her idea, to show all that she stood beside me. It did break her father's heart to know the Vegaria House ended with him. He refused to call her by our name until his dying day. I think he hoped she would change her name back to Vegaria and keep the ancient house alive."

"And she gave that up to stand alongside you, knowing the truth of what occurred?" he finally flicked his eyes up at his fathers. Where Digarius' were sharp and narrow, Lord Theodus' were round and soft, saddened with memory. "If you are asking if she knew the truth, the answer is yes."

He shook his head in disbelief. "Why did the north never retaliate?"

"They knew they were outnumbered. Odessin would have gladly fought alongside Sebern and Ayeshire would have as well." Lord Theodus shrugged. "The north would have been lost had they gone to battle." Lord Theodus shot his head back down at the ground, shaking his head quickly and with anger, his words clipped and sharp. "As you live with your pain and regret over what you did, so will I."

Lord Digarius reached across the table to take the stein from his father's hand and drink from it himself. "There is also some news that I must tell you while we still have privacy, that may explain why I left for battle so quickly and changed our plans without your knowing."

His father furrowed his brow. "Oh?"

Lord Digarius pushed the stein back across the table towards him, gesturing for him to fill it. "You will need a stronger drink than ale for what I am about to tell you, but this will have to do for now."

Lord Theodus filled the stein to the brim with beer and set it back down, waiting for the news that required something stronger.

"There is a mole amongst our me A loyalist in our country's colors. Some-one has been feeding information to the king about our plans and every step we take in this war. That is how the attempted ambush at Ravenhall occurred and how we have lost so many already. The way the battle at Lake Lahere ended, it should not have gone the way it did, despite our smaller numbers."

Lord Theodus closed his eyes and sighed deeply. He pushed his chair back and walked across the tent to grab two bottles of brandy from a straw filled crate, setting one in front of his son and popping open the other for himself. He took a large swig from the bottle, not bothering to find a glass. "Do you know who it is?"

Lord Digarius took a heavy swig of his own.

"Yes. And they have been alongside us before this war even began."

***

"You fought more valiantly than any man or woman I have ever seen, First Sgt. Kingery." Lord Cossius said as he jumped down off his horse, tying its lead on the pole next to where Emaline stood with hers.

"Thank you, Lord Cossius." Emaline replied as she began unsaddling her horse. "Although, after what occurred at Lake Lahere, I do not know how much of that praise I have quite earned."

He stepped beside her, setting himself between her and the railing the horses were tied to. He ran his hand along her horse's neck as he spoke, "From what I heard on the ride back, you took down men twice your size without so much as a stumble. And fighting with two swords, that is quite impressive, and not a common fighting technique. Where did you learn that?"

Emaline finished unstrapping the saddle and pulled it off her horse, then handed it to Cossius, nodding her head towards the railing behind him. His confusion at her gesture left him as he rested the saddle on the post for her. "I had to teach myself different, more unique, fighting techniques growing up.

War camp was hard for me, and others like me; sometimes we became the punching bags." She paused at his scrunched eyes, then returned to focusing on removing her horse's tack.

She sighed, preparing herself to retell the same story that so many felt she owed them, as if her talent and skill were not enough on their own without her trauma and pain painting the picture for how she became strong. "I'm an orphan, dropped off at the war camps before I was old enough to truly train. The orphanage in the country that I was left at didn't have much money to spend on food and we often went hungry. I was scrawny and small. The letter the orphanage aids were given said that my father gave me up quite young; he had already lost my mother in war and couldn't bear to lose me in one, too."

She ran her hand softly down her horses neck, untangling and resetting her mane as she traded the bridle in for a halter to tie the horse up with. She continued as she spoke, "The other orphans and I were easy targets for hate among the others."

"Why?"

"We were young, underfed, and defenseless. They enjoyed picking on us and making us feel like we were not good enough because we were not wanted by our own parents, or our parents left us in death. To survive, I did everything I could to become better than all of them; prove them wrong, prove myself wrong, and make something of myself. I had no choice."

She finished hooking the halter together and tied it on the post by the saddle. "I had to be twice as good as the rest to get even half the credit, so I made it my goal to be even better than that."

Lord Cossius held a long pause. "I understand."

Emaline scoffed and looked him up and down. "No, no you really do not. No offense, m'lord, but this world is built quite different for you and I. Always has been and always will unless things actually change this time."

"So you do not believe that this war will actually change anything?" he crossed his arms and looked down at her.

She shrugged. "I must hope it will, otherwise, all these deaths are meaningless. I just wish it would stop taking so much bloodshed to make the world what it can and should be- what people like your father and the Lady of Ayeshire are *supposed* to be making it be for all of us."

"My father is an honorable man and great leader, and when I inherit his title, I will be just as honorable and just." his reply was overly firm and stern.

Emaline scoffed, turned, and began walking away, loosening the armor's straps on her chest plate as she took her first steps away. "I never questioned anyone's honor, m'lord. Quite interesting that you felt so strongly that you needed to defend it."

Lord Cossius held his station as she walked away. He shouted at her back. "You implied dishonor, that is why I felt so inclined as to defend it."

She turned back to him, shrugging nonchalantly. "If I wanted to insult you or your father, I would have."

He blinked and jutted his head back in shock at her bluntness. "Then what are you saying?"

A frustrated short sigh escaped her at having to continue talking to him. "What is this war for?"

He pursed his lips and crinkled his face. "For our freedom against the tyrannical king."

"And in this freedom what choices in life will people like me have? More than what we do now?"

He did not reply.

"Exactly." she paused. "The king is unjust and will be a true tyrant if he is allowed to reign, yes, but what of us? When this war ends where does that lead us common people? Right back to where we were before, just with someone nicer standing above us? I will do what I must for justice and what is right, but in the name of freedom, no one has told me or people like me where that truly leaves us and how our lives will be better for this war."

She shrugged and raised her hands in a gesture to the war camp around them. "And I am on the front lines of this war and left in the dark about the future. So, tell me, the honorable Lord Cossius, what does freedom look like to those you will rule over?"

***

"Yes, we will make room in here for them. Come come, bring them in." Lady Belva Montarian urged the healers and aids carrying in cots of wounded soldiers to the overflowing medical tents and buildings at Sandhill House. A bandaged and blinded soldier was set on the worn in cot in front of The Lady of Ayeshire.

Lady Belva rearranged the pillows and moved the blanket. She rested her hand on the soldiers face, looking into the bandages covering where her eyes were. "Do you know where you are?"

She slowly nodded, then raised her hand to rest on Lady Belva's wrist. "Home?"

She gently squeezed her face, acknowledging her touch. "Almost. You are at Sandhill House. What village are you from?"

"The settlement outside of Wolfsden is my home."

Two healers met beside Lady Belva, gently requesting her leave so they could lend aid to the injured soldier. Lady Belva stepped aside as the healers introduced themselves to the soldier. As she moved to drop her hand from the soldier's face, she held on to her wrist.

"Ma'am, please, I have no one, can you please stay for a moment?"

"Of course." Lady Belva replied, sitting down next to her and holding her hand. "They're going to remove those bandages now and tend to your face, alright?"

The soldier gently nodded, feeling the healer's hands at the sodden and bloodied bandages covering her face.

Lady Belva could not help the twitch in her body at the exposed broken flesh and empty eye socket.

The soldier looked forward, their remaining eye's pupil non dilated by the light. "Not too pretty am I, ma'am? They got me good, sliced open one eye so bad they had to take it out, the other one nicked enough to lose most of my vision in it."

She squeezed the soldier's hand as the healer's brought rags to her face doused in medicine and began talking among themselves about their treatment plan.

"I am so sorry this happened to you." Lady Belva said.

She shrugged. "It was a risk I signed up for. Well, I guess I didn't really sign up for it as much as be born for it. But if what we're fighting for is a better future, I'll gladly fight under the stag banners again if I could."

"It greatly warms my heart to hear that." Lady Belva's face held a quivering smile.

The soldier winced as medicine was brought to her eye socket and her wound was cleaned. She tried her best to talk through the pain to distract herself. "You know my cousin is a soldier too, we rode in together when we thought the call was for war games and training. When the banner was raised for true war, he found me. This was my first time going into battle, I just turned seventeen last season, and I was scared out of my wits. But he said he met Lady Montarian once, told me she was a nice woman and a true leader, that us going into battle at her call was nothing to be frightful of, but proud of."

Lady Belva held back the choking lump in her throat and the tears fighting to stain her face.

"Have you met her?"

"Hmm?" Lady Belva asked as she cleared her throat.

"Lady Montarian. Have you met her before? I heard she is here at Sandhill House."

The healers shared a look with Lady Belva but kept quiet as they began placing new bandages on her face.

"I have, yes." she softly replied.

The healers continued putting the new bandages on. "Well, I hope if I do meet her, she is as kind as the rumors say she is, that fighting for her is worth it all." She choked up. "I had my whole life ahead of me, ya know. I'm not sure what I will get to do for the rest of it now that I'm *this*."

Lady Belva patted her hand. "You will not be forgotten, nor left behind."

"That is all well and good, but how am I to feed myself, to have a family if I have no work? Am I to be a non-forgotten hindrance for all my days?" the soldier squeezed Lady Belva's hand.

Lady Belva attempted to speak, but her mind forced her to remember the ships of wounded and deceased soldiers who returned to her shores after the Aisharian Civil War, she recalled the blood on her hands at sending them to aid in their war, the same questions coming from those soldiers who had been forever changed. She recalled the winters past of armies leaving for Wolfsden when traditional wolf hunts in the mountains brought back words of mysterious men within the cold and dangerous landscape coming down the mountains to fight and the three winters that followed of fighting off giant men covered in furs and speaking languages not known by any.

The Lady of Ayeshire sighed and moved to prepare herself to leave. "No, you will not be a hindrance, nor will you have to worry about feeding your family or finding a life to live. I will ensure that. We will take care of you, as you deserve."

Chapter 30

Princess Kalia dangled her bare feet off the ledge of the garden fountain, splashing droplets of water around with her toes as she kicked back and forth. Small splashes of water hit the pages of the book in her hand every so often, blurring the ink in the spots they hit. Beside her, with her feet firmly on the solid ground outside of the fountain, sat Sister Ora with her own book open in her lap.

"F-foh-foh…"

Sister Ora leaned over towards Princess Kalia to peer onto the page and set her finger along where the sentence was printed. "What are those mischievous little red animals that your father hunts with his hounds?"

The young princess pepped up. "Oh! Foxes! Fox. The fox is the sih-sihm…" she let out a frustrated groan and dramatically threw her head back the way children tend to do. "Sister Ora, can you read to me instead? It sounds so much better when you do it."

She chuckled. "Well I think you are doing a fantastic job, and besides, I have already read that book to you a thousand times. Reading it once more to you will not help you learn."

Sitting on a bench a few feet away, stitching patterns into silk fabrics alongside Queen Onetta, Princess Arminda softly chimed in. "Sister Ora, perhaps you should enlighten us with the book that has entranced you so much that you have buried your nose in it this entire morning."

She fiddled with the corners of the book's pages, nervously looking down. "Oh, no it is simply just a book of poetry. That is all."

"Well, we all have been known to enjoy poetry as well. Please, sister?" the princess asked again.

Sister Ora's lip twitched at the casual use of the familial title. She sighed then glanced down at the page that she had been stuck on for quite some time, completely entranced and in love with the simplicity of the poem etched onto the pages. "Well, alright...

Shall death come calling at my door,

I will answer it with glee and contentment,

so long as before I go,

I first get to know the taste of your lips and the sound of your voice when you first wake.

Only then will my heart know what it truly means to live,

and to love."

When she finished, she glanced up and saw Sir Loren's helmet- once facing straight forward like the other King's Guards standing by- turned and locked in her direction. Their gazes met for only a moment before Princess Kalia broke the silence.

"Well, *that* was a sad poem."

"No, it was not supposed to be sad. It was a declaration of the depths of the writer's love for his lady, how he is so deeply mad for her that the only thing that would make his life whole before he was taken from the world would be loving her. And *that* is certainly not sad at all."

"I agree, it was not sad at all, and certainly something we all can hope for in our lives." Princess Arminda's face turned from sweet to solemn as she finished speaking; remembering how all three of the adult women in the garden, and inevitably her little sister one day, would likely never experience a love like that.

"We do not get to wish or hope for such trivial things, girls- do not waste your breath. That is not the type of freedom granted to us." Queen Onetta finally spoke up, sharp and pedantic, her fingers around her needlework becoming stiff as she spoke and continued stitching. "We must instead use our time to hope to be good mothers, acceptable wives, and leaders for others to look to. Find your happiness there, do not hope for it in love, you will not find it."

The queen pulled the string she was threading tight, so tight it snapped.

The three girls shared a concerned look and Princess Kalia had stopped playfully splashing her feet in the water, uncertain what to do.

"Mother are you alright?" Princess Arminda asked. "Today is supposed to be a day of joy, Uncle Tyrrian and his gladiators are making their way inland. I thought you'd be happy for your people to be visiting."

The queen slowly took a deep breath and set down the needlework in her lap. She looked up. Her face showed no tension that was felt there just a moment before and instead held the unemotional regal demeanor it typically bore, her tone now firm and orderly.

"I believe we have enjoyed the garden enough for one day, and if the sundial is correct, we should be getting ready to greet the Lord of Aishar and his convoy. Come."

***

The waters of the Ringhar Sea were littered with Aisharian ships sailing in and dropping their anchors; unloading soldiers and supplies onto the smaller ships heading into the shallower waters and the primary ports of Isilria.

The cream sails of the battle carracks were so large one could spot the ships with ease long before the flapping of the sails could be heard. The sailing caravels, while much smaller and sleeker in design, bore the same cream sails adorned with the crest of the Isles of Aishar and the long-lived House Priscius that ruled over Castle Red. The crest was proudly painted on the sail of every ship, so boldly large that no one could mistake who was aboard.

The Aisharian crest served as a reminder of the invincibility and immortality of the people of Aishar- the single kingdom to survive the Alvarian

War of Conquest. The kraken battling back ocean waves depicted the fierceness of their people and the legends they took as more than lore.

Much like their ancient guardians in the sea, Aisharians believe they will always rule the waters and are a proud people, so proud that they embroider and engrave this crest onto as many goods and products as possible with many warriors and citizens branding and tattooing it onto themselves as well. From the seals on their bottles of rich dessert wine, to their ships sails, noble and common clothing, and weapons, all are reminded of the greatness of Aishar.

The Lord of Aishar, Tyrrian Priscius, marched toward the top of the city to the steps outside of The King's Keep, surrounded by dozens of his personal Aisharian gladiators, all of whom were wearing light armor of gold and leather and crest embroidered capes.

Deep red sleeveless tunics peaked out from under their golden chest plates and shoulder guards, with small armor plates secured around their forearms- not as a defense, but so that they could use their own arms as a weapon to hit and deflect enemy strikes with. They all walked with their helmets tucked under their arms to show they did not fear those who may attempt to attack, and their faces were littered with scars to show the fights they survived and battles won.

Lord Tyrrian Priscius stood centered among the group. Like those marching around him, he wore no helmet and had little armor covering his heavily muscled and scar-covered body.

The moment Lord Priscius stopped marching, his convoy halted as one. The group of gold and red clad warriors faced the royal group standing before them: King and Queen Scott, Princess Arminda, Sister Ora, Prince Percy, Father Figgins, and their guards covered entirely in metal.

They did not bow to the king.

After a moment of quiet observation and stern stares shared across the group of royals and nobles, Lord Tyrrian stepped forward and bowed- just barely at the neck and more of a nod- in greeting to the king. His amber eyes glowed under the glare of the sun and its rays bounced off the tiny bits of grey that peeked out from his black locks and his shortly trimmed beard.

"Your Majesty. May I present my Lord's Guards- the finest gladiators in the Six Kingdoms." His voice was smooth, deep, and rich with the accent that was common tongue of Aisharians.

At his mention, the gladiators behind him raised their fits to their hearts, then bowed in unison and returned to attention immediately. King Ivan scanned the group behind Lord Tyrrian and stepped down from the steps he and his family had stood waiting on. He folded his gloved hands in front of him, their thick leather embroidered with the same lion and vine filigree that was on his deep red and gold stitched tunic.

"Your Grace, it has been quite some time since the great tyrant of Aishar visited the continent. It is quite a sight to look to the waters and see the fine ships of the Isles decorating our sea."

Lord Tyrrian smirked and looked down onto the coastline, his voice holding an air of calmness and riddled with pride and smugness. "It is always a beautiful day when the greatness of Aishar is seen."

He turned back to the king, the flicker in his eyes catching on Queen Onetta as she stepped down to stand beside her husband. He firmed his strong jaw at her presence, then bowed to her, deeper than he had the king. "And having you so close to the throne is perhaps the greatest reminder of the strength and power of the Isles, my queen."

A small smile threatened her lips, "And seeing you, Your Grace, is a pleasure and reminder of my home. I do miss the Isles every day that I wake, almost as much as I still mourn my the loss of my dear sister."

He let out a deep breath and sigh. "Losing Lady Maia was a day of such sorrow on all of Aishar. The sun does not shine as bright on our sands with her gone." His tone turned cold and smooth, "But, reminiscing on those we have lost is not why we have sailed all this way. From what we were told, it appears we have a rebellion to stamp out."

King Ivan replied with a stern aggravation. "Yes, we in fact do. Which brings to question where the rest of your soldiers are? While I see many ships, this number cannot carry all your gladiators. If we are to end this war and end it quickly, we need all the bodies and weapons at our disposal."

"I must remind you, Your Majesty, one Aisharian fighter is easily worth half a dozen of your armor covered soldiers." he scoffed. "And if they are being asked to sacrifice themselves for the cause of a king, that king needs prove himself worthy of their valuable lives."

The king's face turned red, his words hissing out loud enough for those closest to him to hear, but not loud enough to be heard by the observers gathered down the pathway. "I do not need to prove myself worthy. *I. Am. Their. King.*"

Lord Tyrrian shuffled his feet and cocked his chin up. "And I am their sworn lord. Their Blood Rite swears their loyalty to the Isles and to the one who rules it. They listen to only me. If I asked each of these men and women to slit their own throats, they would do it without a moment's pause. If I ordered each of my ships on your coastline to fire upon the city, they would only ask when they should stop. If I were to wish it, we could sail back to our riches, our women, and our homes and let you all kill one another in your war while we flourish and thrive as we always have."

He paused for a slight moment before making his final point, his delivery growing curter and sharper with every word. "They are here because I ordered it, and I ordered our arrival because those who rule the waters will always be loyal to those who rule the lands; and, at this moment, King Ivan Scott, First of Your Name, *you* are the one who rules the lands."

"And with your help, Lord Priscius, my father will continue to rule and the relations between our two countries will continue to be beneficial and peaceful as it always has been." Prince Percy stepped forward; his tone overly kind in his attempt to quell the anger. He stood beside the king, who had turned his head away and took quick and harsh inhales. The king's hands shook and he gripped them together tighter to stop their tremoring.

Lord Tyrrian sized up the prince as he turned his attention towards him. "Ah, the dutiful prince and our next king, keeping the peace it seems."

"Actually, this is Percy, our second son. Prince Elion is off with his soldiers now, already winning the war." Queen Onetta replied.

"Ah, well, you must forgive me. It has been much too long since I have had the honor of laying my eyes on any of you. The last time our families gathered you boys were barely men and when you traveled to the island of Thelimor in your studies, you did not visit our castle." He took another breath and cocked his head. "It is such a shame that none of your heirs have truly experienced the greatness of where your mother's line still rules strong, from where your blood was first made."

He made a pointed glance down at Princess Kalia, still standing behind the group on the steps beside Princess Arminda.

Princess Arminda met his glance with a glare and replied, stepping forward in front of her sister. "It is quite a shame, and we would be honored for you to show us, and our people, of the greatness of Aishar while you are here, in hopes of one day truly seeing it for ourselves."

Lord Tyrrian smiled. "And it will be my pleasure, niece." The lord raised his voice to ensure a show for the audience around them. "And there is no need for such formality is there? We are all family here, are we not?"

He meet the stare of King Ivan.

"Yes, we are, and we shall dine and drink like family tonight. Come, let us step out of the sun." King Ivan turned immediately and left for the castle, abruptly putting an end to any further conversation and attempting to insert his dominance and authority.

***

The welcome feast was immaculate. The fare scented the entirety of the castle more than any feast the royal family had had before. The dining table was adorned with traditional Aisharian delicacies and favored dishes. In place of gamey meat hunted in the forests of Britia were fish and exotic sea animals brought in from the Ringhar Sea; cubes of pink fish salted and sprinkled with seasonings laid in bowls beside steamed greens, crab claws and tentacles stuck out of bowls filled with broth and savory red spices, dark brown and charred chicken laid in beds of yellow cubed fruit and grains, whole fish with grilling marks were piled on large platters surrounded by pink, purple, and green fruits brighter than any seen on the inland.

The once heavily filled platters and generous servings had been well picked over by the guests finishing their final plates before the course of sweets arrived.

Bottles of the infamous Aisharian dessert wine sat aerating on a large buffet table nearby as the family finished their last bites, all while eagerly awaiting the rich delights of Aisharian desserts. Bronze metal trays sat in front of each family member. On the trays were cubes of white sugar and small bronze metal mugs. On the table beside the grand dining hall holding the dessert wine, stood three Aisharian aids in front of metal legged stations filled with hot sand.

The aids carefully watched the long-handled metal cups centered on the hot sand, waiting for the dark coffee to properly heat before bringing them to the royal family.

An unfamiliar sense of peace and relaxation had befallen Queen Onetta as the meal went on, a feeling many noticed, but did not question. She patiently answered Princess Kalia's questions on the unknown dishes, even diving into tales from her own childhood spent enjoying the same meals.

"Tell me, Sir Marion, how does a gladiator as lethal as you survive knowing the blood of battle is not on you but on others?" Lord Tyrrian asked.

Sir Marion, a guest invited at the requested demand of Lord Tyrrian, replied. "I satiate the need in other ways, my lord. You know as well as I, that battles are fought on many fronts, not just on the field. And my services are currently needed here."

"Will you be joining your fellow Aisharian gladiators on the field when we march?" Lord Tyrrian asked.

Sir Marion nodded once, his tone still cool and casual. "If you demand it and desire it, then I am pledged to do so."

King Ivan cleared his throat.

Sir Marion's eyes flickered to the king. "Or if His Majesty orders it, of course."

Sir Marion sipped his wine and left his eyes on Lord Tyrrian down the table from him.

"Your Majesty, please do not take offense to Sir Marion's words. Aisharian gladiators swear a blood oath to the Isles when they win the Blood Rite, his oath was cemented in his life long before he came here under your service." Lord Tyrrian casually waved off the king.

"And Sir Marion, the Master of Armor and head of my King's Guard also swore an oath to my service when he was brought here. Is his oath to you truer than mine?" the king eyed Lord Tyrrian, who glared back.

"Well, as I said, his oath to the *Isles*," Lord Tyrrian corrected, "is written in his blood."

Both men cocked their heads and glared as they lifted their respective chalices of drink. Lord Tyrrian flicked his gaze to the overly ornate stitching of pure gold on the king's gloves, an unusual accessory to wear for dinner.

King Ivan noticed his staring and promptly set his cup down, returning his hands to rest on the table where the view of them was obstructed by the ornate décor and leftover platters.

"So, what exactly is the Blood Rite?" Prince Percy piped up amid the growing tension.

"Only those who survive it may know, just as those who swear their blood to the Isles are the only to know the words of the blood oath." Sir Marion answered, leaning back and relaxing in his chair, his cup of wine almost empty as he watched his lord and the king. "Being half Aisharian, Prince Percy, you have a right to go through the trials of the Rite yourself if you so wish. Although, most of us are closer to the youngest princess' age when we are sent to it." He looked over at the young Princess Kalia who looked about the room in childlike innocence and confusion. He continued. "Perhaps she would like to do it one day, it is her right by heritage."

"How old were you when you... survived this Rite?" Prince Percy asked. "I've attempted research about it, but there is not much written of it."

"I was twelve, Lord Priscius ten I believe." Sir Marion nodded in his direction. "We do not write of the Rite. As we said, only those who survive it may know of what it entails."

Princess Kalia spoke up, still entirely confused by the tension of the conversation. "Did you have to kill anyone uncle Tyrrian?"

"Kalia!" Queen Onetta loudly hushed.

She shrugged. "What?"

"Do not ask such questions." her mother snipped.

Lord Tyrrian chuckled. "Maybe one day you will know, but we cannot speak of it."

The two Aisharian men shared knowing glares at one another as the coffee bearing aids came to the table, pouring steaming liquid into their empty cups.

"Lord Priscius, as your king, knowing both of us are nearing, certain ages, I must ask. You have no wife. Lady Maia died over twenty epochs ago, she bore you no children, and you have no heir. The stability of your country relies on you having an heir, and therefore, the stability of my entire kingdom could be in question if you have no heir."

"Is the stability of your kingdom not already in question?" Lord Tyrrian shot back as he lifted the cup of hot coffee to his lips. "Or is this war simply for fun?"

King Ivan's fist tremored in front of him, and his jaw squared. He took a harsh breath, almost as if he had lost the air in his lungs, and expelled the air as he spat his words. "You need an heir, Lord Priscius."

The lord slowly sipped his coffee, enjoying the flavor and richness, and set the cup down before replying to the king. "You forget our laws differ from yours. While yours speak of heirdom rising only from birth and bloodline, our allow for honor to choose if blood is not available, or it not worthy. When one, such as our own queen when she was but a lady of the Isles, gains a title higher than their current station, they are permitted by law to choose the one who takes over their lesser title, so long as that heir is of their bloodline or of noble honor that has proven themselves worthy of their title." he nodded and picked up a sugar cube and plopped it into his coffee. "The same rules apply to those without blood heirs and who hold any station. All of that to say, while I have no wife who bore me children, I do have an heir."

Queen Onetta caught herself on the edge of a shocked outburst and returned to her coffee.

"Who then?" King Ivan demanded to know.

Lord Tyrrian smirked and shrugged. "In due time they and you will know."

King Ivan fell back in his seat, pissed and defeated, and demanded the dessert wine that had yet to be served.

Down the length of the table, observing the conversation that constantly paraded around arguments and outbursts, Sister Ora leaned to Prince Percy and whispered. "Why do your father and uncle hate each other so?"

He joined her in her whispering. "Even before my father was forced to marry my mother when he was just a prince, he has held ill-will towards Aisharians. He never could stand their arrogance, pride, or desire for power, which is ironic as the very attributes he hates about my uncle are the exact same that my uncle despises about him."

"Aisharians are a notoriously proud people, that is not something that should be shamed or frowned upon." She added before taking a bite of her layered pastry covered in a dust of cocoa.

"Yes, but you and I both know the history of The Old Continent and Aishar's invincibility during The Conquest. Despite the peace treaty that formed many ages later uniting them with the kingdom, my uncle and all the lords before him still believe that they hold more of a right to rule than anyone else, that they are not to be second to any king."

Sister Ora nodded as he spoke. She swallowed the bite and washed it down with a sip of wine. "And you believe them wrong for feeling such a way?"

Prince Percy's eyes cut into slits. "What do you mean?"

She shrugged. "You are half Aisharian, yes? But also half Britian. If many Aisharians feel this way, how do you feel?"

"I —" he cut himself off and hushed his tone again, but sharpened his words. "I am a prince of the Six Kingdoms. My feelings and my loyalties are to upholding the monarchy and the kingdom." He turned back to his dinner and drink, ending the conversation with abruptness that surprised her.

CHAPTER 31

The thick mud of the marshland that made up the outskirts of the Land of a Thousand Rivers did not hide tracks easily, nor make traversing the land swift, but it served the Craigie scouts, Lady Kathilla, and her son Barron well in other ways as they hid among the boulders and tall grasses. Their dark fur hooded cloaks and leather clothing blended them into the surrounding environment.; any movement of theirs would likely appear to the spotter as an animal walking among the boulders, trees, and mud, or, if they were quick in removing themselves from the line of sight, appear as a mistaken glimmer of movement that would be dismissed.

Several yards from where they hid, across multiple trenches of bone-chilling cold water that turned into flowing rivers after winter snow and ice thawed in spring before settling into the current slow flow of summer, lay an Odessin watch camp guarding their side of the holy lands border.

Over time, attempts at seizing more land on both sides of the border had become the expected norm between the two countries fighting for control over every river and every blade of grass that their people deemed divine. As the fighting went on, camps were raised on both sides and guards added to prevent victory from ever occurring and to, consequently, continue the painful and bloody stalemate that lasted generations.

When the attempted seizing of camps were successful, or skirmishes lasted for far too long, soldiers from House Lisarian of Broken Tower in Sebern would aid in finding peace and forcing soldiers of both armies to lay down their swords and return their camps and people to one another.

Lady Kathilla lifted her head slowly, the snout of the wolf pelt on her head sniffing the air as she scanned the outlying crest of land with her viewing scope. She noted the count of guards and soldiers walking about and resting at the outpost. Two groups sat around separate fires, cooking food and conversing, and more walked alongside the small creek that ran at the edge of their camp, while half a dozen paced atop the roof of the small stone building.

Their leisure of a lazy afternoon was evident in how they held themselves. Many of the outpost guards leaned casually against the walls of the building, some playing small games with one another or sharing a flask, completely unaware of what laid out just beyond their field of vision.

"Come on," she mumbled as she focused her scope at the closed doorway of the building, "someone open the damned door already."

She moved her scope from her eye and turned to face Barron, crouched behind another rock formation near her, his own scope long left unused. Their eyes met as she angrily shook her head, disappointed and frustrated. They had been out for much of the day scouting, careful to avoid being seen and waiting on this final task to conclude before finalizing their plan of siege.

The sounds of shouting in the camp caught their ears and they turned their attention back to their target.

From the camp, a soldier shouted for the change of guard, prompting the soldiers atop the building and those walking along the water to exchange places with those resting inside. The clear shot of the building entrance blurred with the oranges and golds of the long tunic uniforms they wore; the Dragonscale chainmail that protected their torsos creating a long line of bright scalloped metal the Craigie scouts could not see through.

As the outlying guards sauntered to the end of their shift, the creak of the door echoed.

"Fuck, move out of the way." Lady Kathilla hissed under her breath. "One, two, three," she counted the jumbled mass of bodies leaving the protection of the fortress walls. "... ten."

The door shut with a loud clang as the last guard went inside. She turned to Barron, nodded once, then jutted her head backwards, motioning for the group of scattered scouts to make their way back to their own camp.

***

"Were you able to see inside at all, Barron?" Lady Kathilla asked as the groups converged together around the hearty campfire at their border camp.

"No, I got half a glimpse once but could not make out anythin' through the passin' bodies of guards." he tightened his lips into a thin line and shook his head as he gestured to a nearby cook for a stein of hot mulled drink brewing over the fire.

"From what I could see, ten came out, and ten went in. Another dozen were gathered 'round the two fires. We should assume they have more inside, more than likely a few hands worth more." she shook her head. "Although, it is odd, a camp of that size usually has more at their stations this season. I do not like dealin' in uncertainties, but that is all we have at this time."

"Gladdy," Barron turned to his sister as she sat down and settled in beside them, "did your scoutin' bring good news t'day?"

Gladys' face fell flat, showing irritation at her brother's use of her childhood nickname. "Good news, no, but we do have more certainty on what lies to the east and west. Hundred men stand throughout the eastern camp; the western camp held the same from what news my other scouts delivered. This season, they also would normally have double that. Their numbers are thinned and accordin' to those at our eastern border camps I met with, they have been thinned for a bit of time now."

"The ground and waters thawed long ago, if they were sendin' more men as they always do during the high season, they would have done it by now." Barron's voice lined with impatience. "We should begin attackin' *now* and takin' over these camps while we have the advantage."

"You are always so quick to emotion and action, brother. *Calm yourself* and think for once before you wish to act." Gladys calmly corrected as she walked to the fire and began picking at the roasting meat skewered above the flame. She nodded at the cook as she turned, requesting her own stein of hot drink.

"I do not need to calm myself, *sister*. Some of us do not need ages to contrive a plan, some of us prefer to act instead of just thinkin' of doing so." he quipped as his hands gripped his drink.

Lady Kathilla rolled her eyes and corrected her children. *"Enough.* You two are just as stubborn and bull-headed as your father was.. Barron, it is not yet an opportune time to strike. Barely a moon phase has passed since we were warned of the war, was it not?"

"Yes." his reply was flat.

"And it would take over a moon phase for their army to move far enough from our border to ensure we have enough time to begin our attack to where they could not retaliate quickly, yes?"

"Aye." he said into his cup.

"Then please, explain your reason for believin' that the Odessian's lack of resources at this *one* section of our border, that has been thinned for barely any time, means that they are already far off in war and distracted enough for our land to be taken back?"

His response faltered as his body shifted uncomfortably. "I just... assumed."

Lady Kathilla stood up and jutted her chin out at him and those gathered around her. "We do not fight based upon assumptions or emotions, doing so will not lead us to our freedom, but to our *death*. It is what ended your father's life, and many before him. We will not be so stupid as to repeat our country's failed revolutions."

"Then what do you advise we do? Sit and wait even longer to take what is ours?" he snapped and jumped up.

Lady Kathilla's cold blue eyes struck ice through Barron as she glared; her eyes ordering him to quiet his tongue and to sit.

"We will take what is ours. But we will do so when victory is sure. If we attack now any battles won will lead to a lost war. Madam Fury is not a woman whose army is to be tested or toyed with; she will send her soldiers back here to lay slaughter to us in seconds if we act with too much haste."

Lady Kathilla recalled her few and far between blood-soaked battles against the leader of Odessin's Dragon Army, Lin Furia, titled Madam Fury like her ancestors before her who held the title. Believing themselves to be the embodiment of the dragon's fury, their family name was not born of paternity, but of naming, choosing "Furia" as their surname and naming each leader of the Dragon Army Madam or Master Fury. Madan Fury took to heart her lineage, born from the blood of Carishna the Unforgiving, and born from the blood of her dragons, she was as unforgiving as Carishna before her, and as fearsome as any true dragon. When she was brought into battles large and small, few enemies came out the other side without her blessing.

Lady Kathilla sat back down and grabbed her stein, taking a calming breath and sip before continuing, "The moon has not crossed our skies for enough time to know where she and her Dragons are. Once we know, and we scout the rest of these lands, we attack and give no mercy to those thieves."

She held her eyes to the flames, reminding herself that the fire in front of her was for cooking game and warming drink, and not the fires of Madam Fury's Dragon Army burning her people alive on the battlefield.

Chapter 32

"Your Highness, we have apprehended the townsfolk that you requested." Commander Blackley informed Prince Elion as he stepped inside the tent.

The prince stood behind his desk, his hand rubbing through the length of his rough beard, and replied firmly. "Bring them inside."

The commander called for the guards and in quick moments the tents entrance was filled with noises of protest and struggle as three individuals were hauled inside and tossed carelessly forward towards the feet of the future king.

Struggling to stand straight and gain their bearings were three citizens; an elderly man shaking from fear or age- or both, a brown-haired middle-aged woman who stood sternly, and another woman whose eyes were as red as the tent's fabric with cheeks flushed in the same hue.

"It has been brought to my attention that you and many others from Clardin no longer allow room and board at your establishments, or food and drink to our soldiers. Is this true?" Prince Elion asked.

The shaking old man spoke up, his voice as frail as his body and each word stammering from fear. "Your Highness, we have offered plenty of aid to your soldiers. We have helped tend to wounds, given shelter when possible, but our taverns have been run dry multiple nights in a row, and our food supplies keep being dug into just to support their hunger at our establishments."

"But why have you stopped? These soldiers are owed a debt for their sacrifice for you. Are they not?" The prince looked down at him as he spoke.

His face and jaw set firm as he held his shoulders square and his hands met behind his back.

"But we need coin to continue to live and feed our own families. Our town was not built to host a resting army, Your Highness."

"So, you wish to bleed us dry? Empty the army's coffers?" Commander Blackley barked as he stepped forward behind them.

"We are asking for what is fairly owed to us." the short-haired woman spoke up. Unlike her elder counterpart, there was no tremble or hesitancy in her voice as she spoke in a tone that resembled an order, not one of respect addressing the future king. She turned from Commander Blackley to the prince and sneered. "*Your Highness.*"

Prince Elion took a step forward. "Is this how you speak to your future king? In sneers and firm orders?"

"No, no, Your Highness." the stammering elderly man said. "We apologize and meant no harm or ill intent."

The red-eyed crying woman reached for her assertive counterpart to stop her as she stepped up to the prince. "We deserve our compensation and your respect. A true leader would give both without requiring that we request it."

Commander Blackley moved to put himself between her and Prince Elion. "You do not speak to the future king in such a way." the commander barked at her, spitting on the ground at her feet.

"Commander, that is enough." Prince Elion ordered, his tone finally taking on emotion. "All of you, that is *enough.*"

The tent fell silent at his order. In the quiet, his mind filled with the words of his father spoken to him throughout his life and his lessons.

You cannot show weakness, you cannot be soft.

You must be firm, you must be strong.

He recalled his father's specific words spoken in private when Prince Elion showed hesitancy about the path his father had them both walking firmly down.

When it comes to the throne, there is no line that is too far to cross.

He felt his chest and shoulders become heavy with intense weight as the pressures of his father and his future crown bore all their weight down on him in this moment. He met the eyes of the townspeople; the man still scared and tired, the woman glaring at him from behind Commander Blackley's back, and the crying woman shivering where she stood.

"Have you spoken in such a way of the crown in front of others? With ill words and sharp tone?" he asked the woman.

She raised her face so that she could look down at the prince. "Yes I have. But the words I have spoken have been of truth and my tone deserved."

"And have you two also spoken in such a way of the crown?" Prince Elion looked over her shoulder at the others.

The old man lowered his head and nodded. The crying woman only continued her tears.

Prince Elion firmed his jaw, swallowing the hard lump in his throat, ensuring there would be no hesitancy in his voice or crackle of doubt. "Defamation of the crown is against the law. Were you all aware of this?"

"Yes."

"Understood. Commander Blackley, execute them for crimes against the crown. Then, display their shame in the streets for all the rest to see. Show their fellow townsmen what happens when your loyalties do not lie firmly with the throne, when you disrespect the His Majesty."

"Your Highness, please, we all have families, *children*. And he is but an old man, a grandfather, do not do this to us. Please!" the third woman, who had not stopped weeping and shivering since they walked in the tent, cried out as she tried to make her way to him, clawing from the grasp of the guards now holding her. "Please, do not make my boys orphans!"

"*I* am not, that was entirely your doing." he turned his back and closed his eyes, swallowing the lump in his throat before he hardened his words again. "Take them away, immediately."

After the soldiers and three deemed traitors left, Prince Elion strode to the large decanter of alcohol on his desk and drank directly from it long into the night, too drunk and angry to bother calling upon Jeffrey for a distraction from his battling thoughts and morals, to drunk and angry to question the orders he had given.

The law was the law, and upholding that was the heir's duty, no matter what it did to his soul.

CHAPTER 33

Lord Rener Torrin rubbed his eye as he walked through the camp to the southeast of Ravenhall and met his family and other leaders for too early of a breakfast. He sat down with an ache in his back and neck, blinked dramatically, and hoped the circles under his eyes would disappear after a hearty meal.

"You did not sleep?" his father asked as he swallowed his bite of bread. Lord William Torrin signaled for a cook to bring a plate for his second-born and pushed a cup to him.

"No." his voice croaked. "Each time I left to sleep the stars fell in more bursts. I strained all night to count their fall and to read what they spoke of."

"What did it say?" his father asked, gulping down crisp water from his cup to wash down the hard and stale bread they had been given.

"Thank you." Lord Rener mumbled to the servant as they set his plate down. He looked down at the small plate of food and shook his head. "This star fall occurs each summer, although, it came a bit late this season. They are the tears of heroes, falling from the sky with messages from our ancestors."

"And what did our ancestors have to say this season?" Lord Cossius asked.

"They fell in hundreds, in large bursts that one could miss if they blinked too much, and these bursts only ended when the sun rose and I could not see them anymore. In the past, they had fallen in high number, but for long periods of time and ended well before dawn." he shook his head as he spoke.

He ripped the crumbling bread apart and soaked it in the meat stew to soften it, then rested his elbows on the table and joined his hands together to rest in front of him. "Our recent battles have occurred in such a way, these past two knots since Lake Lahere. We have sparred back and forth quickly with Prince Elion's army, neither becoming a victor and nothing of note occurring outside of more losses. Our battles line up almost exactly with the star fall, whether by happenstance or by the stars plan."

He continued his pondering internally as he began eating the soaked bread, more palatable and soft now that it had soaked for some time.

His brother looked at him. "So, the stars are saying to continue this war in such a way?"

Lord Rener crumpled his face. "No. I believe they are saying the opposite. The star fall, or in this case our battles, were in short fast bursts that would not end, and perhaps may continue throughout this day and tonight."

His father nodded in understanding. "The stars make a point. A war can drag on for quite some time if it is fought in such a way."

"Exactly." Lord Rener replied, his mouth half full of food.

The heir to House Torrin chimed in again. "Exactly what? I don't understand."

Lord Rener and his father shared a flickering look with one another, Lord William replying instead of his son. "Cossius, the stars are telling us, our *ancestors* are telling us, that we must plan to fight this war in a bigger way if we wish it to end. These small skirmishes will not grant our freedom, only something larger can."

"Meaning a larger attack? Something more substantial?" he replied.

Lord Rener leaned back in his chair and crossed his arms, staring at the ceiling of the open walled tent as he pondered longer. "Battles are not only won on the battlefield, brother, as we know from our past. Lord Montarian has informed us that Lady Montarian has many plans in motion, that there is more she is doing off the battlefield to ensure our victory, but they are things she cannot put in writing. Perhaps her plan, whatever it may be, will be the key to ending this war, and perhaps, we must find a way to strike on the field in a larger way as well."

**

Sedrick politely excused himself through the crowd, keeping his head and voice low as he worked his way through the mass of people gathered outside of the seafront outdoor theatre in Isilria. He had arrived in the king's city two knots ago, his travel slow and monotonous as he traveled via traveler cart, foot, and borrowed horseback to make it to the city.

His forged paperwork provided by Father Robb had gotten him a job at the docks within the lower parts of the city and that money in turn gave him rent in a small fish-scented room above the fish market. But neither had gotten him close to Sister Ora to hand her the classified letter he kept in his breast pocket.

At the thought of the letter, he moved his hand inside his light jacket, confirming by his touch that it was still safely on his person. She was kept under lock and guard with the rest of the royal family, his first sighting of her being from a far distance between onlookers watching the Aisharian gladiators and Lord Priscius ascend the hill outside the castle to greet the royal family. There had been to many golden armored gladiators and silver-clad King's Guard between the two for her to even catch a glimpse of him, let alone stand beside him and be given the letter.

The smell of saffron, paprika, and smoke danced in front of him, enticing his mind to pause at the bustling and street food carts gathered under strings of paper lanterns and banners near the entrance of the grand theatre. His stomach grumbled in disagreement as he shook his head and worked to make his way past the carts.

He paused as traffic became congested and his ear caught a conversation beside him.

"His Majesty and His Grace did a fine job with this distraction. Throwing money at our merchants to supply fanciful attire and décor for today and donating food supplies to our food carts and asking for no money in return." the man speaking paused his complaint and addressed the food cart vendor in front of him. "Two of the grilled meat skewers, please."

Coin and food were exchanged as Sedrick gave up his attempt to leave the food carts behind and stood behind them in line. His coin was light, but his hunger was heavy enough to forget.

The man continued as he moved to the side and he and his partner began ripping apart the meat skewered on a stick, between bites his female accomplice grumbled out in a moan. "He continues to feed us like this then he can do whatever he wishes."

Sedrick handed the merchant a brass coin in exchange for the same faire the two beside him were enjoying. He stepped beside them to continue listening, their attention focused on their own food and their care at his presence nonexistent.

The man smacked his lips as the rich brown sauce on the meat covered his mouth. "With these Aisharians in town, my shop has never been busier. Can't be upset by that. How fares your house with red doors, mistress?"

She smiled and laughed, throwing her head back a bit. "The last time my staff was this tired and well worn, not to mention weighed down by this much coin, was the night before the army left for war."

The man laughed as Sedrick's appetite turned sour and he shoved his way through the crowd to the theatre. Behind him, he heard the man's last words.

"Coin is the true king. If His Majesty keeps it running, I'll stay happy."

***

"Well, you two are quite the sight for royal eyes." Queen Onetta beamed as Prince Percy and Sister Ora walked down the theatre steps to the royal viewing box centered among the massive entertainment space.

Sister Ora curtsied at the queen; her typical velvet and cotton dress dyed in rich jewel-toned blues and greens was replaced with a silk and chiffon dress of deep red, the style a mixture of Aisharian and Britian high society style and the color that of the royal family. A dress provided by Lord Priscius himself, part of his gifts to the royal women.

Prince Percy leaned forward and kissed his mother on the cheek, then Princess Arminda, his bicep leaving Sister Ora's grasp as he moved, the elaborate gold and dark grey brocade fabric leaving behind an emptiness as she stood on her own.

The emptiness did not last long as he joined beside her again, his shoulders rolling and his arms adjusting to the movement of the stiff and ornate tunic he wore. He held his hand behind her back as he guided them to their seats among the family in the only shaded space in the entire theatron.

The theatron that surrounded their private space could hold a great gathering of spectators and was elevated with over twenty rows of stone built seating that wrapping halfway around the large orchestra pit overlooking the sea. The royal viewing box sat closest to the ground and was centered off the stage to allow the royal family and their guests the best viewing of whichever performance was to take place- be that of blood or of the arts.

When needed for a theatrical performance, the orchestra stage would have a backdrop hung on the long stone and wood frame jutting from the sides to best set the scene. Today, however, the Ringhar Sea and the cityscape of lower Isilria both served as backdrop for the performance. The backdrop frame held small flags alternating between the Aisharian and Britian house colors and sigils.

Sister Ora settled in her seat, with the prince to her left and the king and Lord Priscius to his side. In the row behind them, Princess Arminda, the queen, the rest of the King's Council and aids were seated. As she looked around to take in the sight of all the people gathered in the theatre, she noticed the diverse variety of those gathered. Many appeared to be everyday citizens of Isilria dressed in their finer clothing for the affair and, a rare occasion, many differing Divine Houses and guilds intermingled jovially with one another.

Soldiers and citizens of Aishar were seated among the crowd as well and easy to differentiate from the Britian's by their style and how they carried themselves. The masculine citizens wore bold tunics bearing the Aisharian crest and many of the feminine dressers wore thin fabric dresses with dramatic cuts and slits- a fashion not common among feminine dressers in the mainland of the Six Kingdoms of Victarius.

The crowd continued buzzing lively, drinks clinking and coins exchanging among gamblers, none seeming to feel the tension and effects of what was occurring to others outside of the city walls.

Sister Ora's mind ended its wandering abruptly as she met the eyes of one audience member, standing firm and tall among seated and laughing observers. His dark jacket and broad stature a focal point of attention among the lighter clothing of those around him. She held back the gasp and tremor in her body. A shaking breath quietly came from her lips as her eyes softened and asked for permission to paint her face with tears

Sedrick.

Their eyes locked and her mind raced as she froze in place, stuck staring at him from across the large space. Her lips trembled as she let a faint smile form, hoping that across the space between them, he would see it. A smile broke the corner of his own as he sat down and nodded once at her.

A glaring heat bore into the back of her head as she remembered the other eyes that may be around her. She carefully glanced around and met with the scrunching and curious stare of Princess Arminda.

Sister Ora feigned another smile, "It is quite nice to see so many faces gathered here, is it not?"

The princess' look of curiosity and intrigue vanished as she responded, "Yes, it is quite nice."

Ora turned back forward in her seat, and glimpsed over at Prince Percy leaning towards his father, his elbow set on the arm of his chair with his face gently resting against his half-closed hand as he listened to his father speak.

She did her best to avert her gaze quickly forward, observing the crowd again as she listened delicately.

The king spoke quietly, but his gestures were wide. Prince Percy nodded at his whispered words and sat straight in his chair. He huffed. "We cannot even enjoy one afternoon without there being some contention."

The crowd around the theatre began to settle as a man, dressed in luxurious deep orange robes with embroidered golden krakens patterned all along the fabric, stepped into the middle of the orchestra to address the crowd.

"Thank you, thank you, all. Alongside the food and rich drink you all have enjoyed here today, His Grace, Tyrrian Priscius, The Lord of Aishar, in his generosity to the people of Britia, has also gifted us the honor of experiencing more of the greatness of the Isles with a showing of our finest form of entertainment; a gladiator showcase."

The crowd cheered. Hollers and whistles erupted the loudest from those in Aisharian attire. As they continued to cheer, Lord Tyrrian rose from his seat, a prideful crooked smile on his face, and raised his glass of wine in the air, with many in the crowd raising their glasses and steins in return, continuing their applause.

In his own seat, King Ivan had a not-so-subtle look of annoyance, but was quick, at the nudge of Prince Percy, to trade it in for a fake show of happiness as His Grace sat back down next to him and offered his glass to cheers with.

The announcer continued, "And we would be remiss to not show our gratitude to His Majesty King Ivan Scott, First of His Name, Lord of the Six Kingdoms. Your hospitality and alliance allow the abundance of Aishar to flourish and peace to be true once again."

Spectators cheered again, with differing levels of enthusiasm compared to the prior announcement as King Ivan stood, his left arm holding him steady as it trembled slightly underneath his weight. He firmed his stance and raised his glass in cheers again, quickly sitting as the crowd quelled their applause and the announcer continued.

"Today's honored champions are both valiant fighters and warriors with endless victories on the battlefield and in the stadium. Ladies, gentlemen, and all else, may I present to you, the finest fighters in all of the Six King-doms, Sir Sagial, the Head of the Lord's Guard of the Isles of Aishar, and Sir Marion, Head of the King's Guard and the Kingdom's Master of Armor."

From separate sidelines, the two announced fighters stood under cloth covered canopies. Underneath both canopies sat tables covered in food and drink and the final fittings of the armor that both men would wear. As their names were announced, they walked out towards the edge of the orchestra circle where a vast display of weapons laid out for the gladiators.

"As honored guests, His Majesty King Scott has given Aishar the honor of choosing their weapons first." the speaker paused and turned to Sir Sagial and nodded.

Sir Sagial wore the same armor that the Aisharian Lord's Guards wore when they were welcomed to the city. He was thickly built, and his tanned, scarred face showed only anger and determination as he stepped forward to select his weapons. Without hesitating he grabbed a large sword from the display, sheathed it at his side, and pulled down one of the spike chains, coiling it up around his arm and resting it at his shoulder, then stepped back to his spot beside the announcer.

"Sir Marion. You now may choose from the remaining weapons."

Sir Marion tilted his head to the side, slyly smirked in response, and nodded before stepping to the display. He did not wear armor standard of a King's Guard or of his home. Instead, he wore a large, dark leather belt that covered much of his lower abdomen with a leather and silver armor tasset falling along his pelvis and upper thighs. His matching chest plate covered only his left pec, shoulder, and upper arm, leaving exposed much of his muscle and the scars covering his skin.

Like Sir Sagial, he took no time in making his decision. From the display, he pulled down a long ranseur and a heavy morningstar club. For a moment, he stood at the display, both weapons in either hand, and easily whipped the club around at his side, making a figure eight motion repeatedly before taking his place again.

Applause erupted in anticipation and excitement as the fighters stood to face one another. Neither man wore a helmet yet, opting to take in their applause and cheers first before facing one another.

Sir Marion looked at Sir Sagial, then threw his ranseur spear down as an aid approached him with his helmet. He used his free hand to put his helmet on as Sir Sagial returned the gesture by roughly putting on his own, then unsheathed his sword, the spiked chain now coiled and hanging on the left side of his waist.

Without waiting for the official announcement to commence, Sir Sagial yelled and charged forward, slamming his feet into the ground so intensely it would shake the ground alone if the audience cheers were not already echoing throughout the stone.

In fast response, Sir Marion lunged and swung his club in the air, blocking the sword and shoving it back at the charging gladiator. The weapons clashed for just one moment and quickly separated, both being brought down to the sides of their wielders who separated at the force of impact.

As Sir Marion stepped back, he swung the club behind him, bringing it overhead with excessive strength as he stepped forward to meet the movement of Sir Sagial.

Sir Sagial met his swing with one of his own, bringing his sword overhead and blocking the strike, clashing their weapons again; a loud ringing breaking through their noises of exertion. Both men shoved their weight into their collided weapons, grunting in fury as neither let up or moved. The metal of the weapons grinded together and scraped as their eyes met through their helmets and fire and fury bore into one another.

Sir Sagial let out a large, growling grunt as he let off the pressure of his sword and shifted his weight backward, using his mass to lean back and kick Sir Marion in the chest, sending the warrior backward.

Sir Marion recovered from the kick so quickly it was as if it did not occur, only letting out a few heaving breaths before charging again. He swung his club sideways with such expertise and speed, it colliding with Sir Sagial's side before he could block or move from the strike.

Sir Sagial stumbled after the hit, giving Sir Marion an opportune moment to arc his club to strike his other side. His hit landed at the top of Sir Sagial's chest plate, it brushed off with ease as Sir Sagial turned his struck shoulder away and brought his sword up and around, striking down the club at the handle as Sir Marion prepared his third strike.

Sir Sagial used the momentum of his swing and quick recovery to strike again and slash his blade down across Sir Marion's body, the tip of it cutting into the leather armor on his shoulder and barely missing slicing open his chest as Sir Marion arched his body backward.

Sir Marion caught himself and straightened, rushing forward to strike Sir Sagial's raised arm. His spiked club collided with Sir Sagial's hand, the spikes tearing into his skin and bone and forcing him to drop his blade.

Sir Sagial stumbled and hunched over, holding his bloodied and battered hand as applause and gasps erupted from the seats. Worried gamblers shouted curses at their prized fighters and rambunctious citizens cried for more violence.

The king himself could not hold back his emotions as he cheered from his seat.

The crowds' noises overtook Sir Marion's senses and fed his adrenaline as he circled around Sir Sagial, waiting for his opponent to collect himself and fight.

"Fight, you weak fucking man." Sir Marion hissed down at him between his teeth then beat his chest with his fist. "Give me a real fight."

Sir Sagial breathed heavily as he straightened himself up, turning his head over his shoulder where Sir Marion stood a few paces away. He reached his bloodied hand across his body and grabbed the chain looped on his waist. The metal clunked to the ground as it was unclasped and Sagial turned to face the encircling predator, the chain and its spiked blade end scraping along the stone as his chest heaved with unfiltered rage and bloodlust.

Sir Marion's calm and cocky demeanor only added to Sir Sagial's rage.

He raised his hand and begun swinging the chain, gaining momentum with each flick of his wrist as he worked to prepare to throw and strike with it.

Sir Marion stayed where his pacing had stopped, his arms held straight out to his sides, begging to be struck down.

Sir Sagial moved, throwing his arm in Sir Marion's direction and letting go of the chain as he aimed for his opponent's chest.

Sir Marion lazily leaned backward at the assault, the chain missing him and only scraping the tiniest slit of skin on his side.

Sir Sagial let out a roar and charged at him; his aim careless as he pulled the chain back to himself and threw it again, not to impale, but to slice his opponent open. While careless, it was effective enough to draw blood as it slit a long line upward on Sir Marion's exposed chest and knocked his head to the side; the spiked tip scraping the metal on his face.

From his spot standing beside the royal viewing box, Sir Loren stepped backward, almost colliding with the guard standing behind him. He turned his eyes to the viewing box, noticing Sister Ora's gaze, before shaking his head and straightening himself to gain his solid composure again.

Sir Marion paced back and forth after Sir Sagial's successful strike, laughing between his hisses of pain. He ran his free hand across the cut on his chest, brushing at the blood that had trickled from the tear and spread it across his sweating chest as if it were war paint.

New cheers came from the crowd as Aisharian's began stomping out and chanting a familiar war song. Sir Marion and Sir Sagial's beating adrenaline mirrored the rhythm of the chant.

Sir Sagial stood steady in place and sent the chain in circular motion again, letting out more length and bringing it overhead as if he were preparing to lasso an escaping wild horse.

Then he lunged.

Sir Marion brought his club forward and ducked his upper body to the side as he swung his weapon in front of him. The chain wrapped itself around the club, catching Sir Sagial off-guard as Sir Marion jerked the club backward, throwing him to the ground.

The chain fell from his grip with heavy force as his body was pulled forward, catching him off balance and bringing him to the ground. Sir Marion threw down his club as he strode for the half fallen Sir Sagial. As Sir Sagial worked to pick himself up, Sir Marion swiftly picked up his almost forgotten spear, not missing a step as he moved forward.

Spectators cheered more in hopes that Sir Marion was about to deliver the final blow. Cheers of "finish him!" and demands for blood made themselves clear above the general shouting. Spectators rose from their feet if not already standing, all hoping to get the best view of what was to come.

Sir Marion kicked Sir Sagial in the gut, sending him back onto the ground and knocking his helmet off as he met the stone. Sir Marion paced around his body and spit at him.

"Get up and pick up your fucking sword." he yelled as he kicked the sword to Sir Sagial. "I told you to give me a real fight."

Sir Sagial rose to his feet and grabbed the scattered sword, disregarding his helmet that laid beside him.

Both men stood panting and tensing each muscle in their bodies as they waited for the other to move. After several bated breaths of anticipation, both moved to attack. Several quick strikes were dealt, each hit being met with the defense of the other and none meeting their desired target. During a split second of reprieve, Sir Marion switched the hold of his spear, his old grip of holding it in the same fashion as one would a sword, to gripping it along the length of his forearm to allow himself to take wider and more fluid swings.

He struck Sir Sagial across the face, drawing a deep red line across his cheek, nose, and slitting open his eye. The pain pushed Sir Sagial back again where his step met his forgotten helmet and brought him back down to the ground. Sir Marion gave no hesitation as he swung at him again as his body met stone, cutting open the other side of his face.

Sir Sagial stopped on his hands and knees, his sword clattered on the ground beside him.

Sir Marion stormed to his side as applause came so loud that the harshest crash of ocean waves would be ignored. The stomping and cheering of the Aisharian war song continued, picking up in final pace as the blood poured out of Sir Sagial's face and into a deep puddle on the white stone.

Sir Marion swung his spear around, gripping it in both hands and drove it into the side of Sir Sagial's neck. The spear ripped through bone and ligament slowly as Sir Marion stepped forward to his body and pushed Sir Sagial onto his side. He twisted the spear every few inches as he drove it deeper into him, the cracks and breaking of bones and tendons snapping and blood bursting in squirts and flashes.

The ground around Sir Sagial's ripped apart body knew no other color but red.

Sir Marion stood over him, holding the spear in place as if he were waiting on a wild game to take its last breath after the hunt, needing to hold it in place so it did not escape. He watched as Sir Sagial's eyes lost life and red bubbles formed and popped in his mouth, choking for air and spitting blood.

Sir Marion ripped the spear from his neck, taking chunks of flesh with it and splattering both of their bodies with more blood. He stepped onto the fallen gladiator's side, shoving Sir Sagial's body onto his back.

As Sir Sagial's dead eyes lost their last bit of color, Sir Marion looked into them and threw off his own helmet, ensuring that his defeated opponent's last vision was of his face.

Sir Marion flipped the ranseur around and drove it through the heart of Sir Sagial's chest, his small chest plate having moved from its place of protection during the attack. The last drive of blood from his body painted them as the audience drowned out Sir Marion's heartbeat that filled his ears.

Even those who had hoped for Sir Sagial's victory could not help but to show excitement and emotions over the display. Screams of disgust and horror were heard in the crowd of cheers. Many of Britia screaming at the gore and shock of the fight ending in death, being used to fights between knights within their country ending in surrender or draws.

Sir Marion's chest heaved as he panted and blood and sweat dripped down his moving muscles. He smiled down at the dead eye and maimed face of Sir Sagial, his eyes filled with a carnal excitement. The blood on his face and lips left a metallic taste in his mouth as he licked his lips before finally raising his head to the cheering crowd.

A primal scream leapt from the depths of his chest, inciting more applause and stomping and clapping of victory. He marched to the royal viewing box where emotions were heavily mixed between excitement and shock.

He bowed briefly at the royal family before stepping away to his canopy, not bothering to wait to be addressed or dismissed by them.

"And that is what Aisharians consider entertainment?" Sister Ora questioned under her breath.

"Showcases such as this are a favorite of my uncle's and prior lord's. After some time, it became a favorite to Aisharian citizens as well, so long as they were in the stands and not the pit." Prince Percy replied to her rhetorical question.

She scoffed and shook her head as two men dragged Sir Sagial's body away, leaving a large trail of blood behind.

"No wonder they call him Tyrrian the Tyrant."

Prince Percy leaned to her to whisper. "This is nothing compared to the real reason he was given that name."

She met his eyes, their noses now just an inch apart from one another.

She whispered. "And what is that?"

"I know you are a strong woman, but I do not know if it is something a lady should be told." his eyes darted between meeting hers and looking down at her lips as he whispered. The smell of wine was suddenly prominent on his breath.

"Did you not promise to do your best to keep nothing from me?" she whispered as her eyes captured his again.

He took a pausing breath before leaning away from her enough to place air between them.

"As you know, about twenty epochs ago, when you and I were quite young, the Isles of Aishar was caught in their civil war. My uncle Tyrrian and his twin brother Armen had begun warring against one another over who should be the rightful Lord of the Isles; a fight they had been in since they were born. Lord Priscius was born just a minute before Armen, and there had always been argument over if that one minute truly made him the rightful heir or not. After losing too many soldiers and turning the sea red with the help of his allies aid, Armen was defeated."

"So, he got into a war with his brother and now is deemed some violent tyrant?" She scrunched her face.

"No, it is what he did to his own blood in response." the prince took a large gulp of wine. "Instead of executing him for his crimes, Lord Priscius stripped him naked in front of a crowd in Castle Red's square and he... cut off his cock and stones so that he could never again have the courage to go against him. And then once the healers made the bleeding stop and Armen could walk, he was paraded around town with them hanging around his neck."

Prince Percy grimaced and took another gulp of wine as he slowly set his hand on his lap as if he were still checking to ensure his were still attached.

"And as if *that* was not enough for Lord Priscius, he forced his brother to serve as a noble aid to him so that he would not go a day without remembering which of the two was the true lord and which of them was no longer a man." he paused and turned to her. "My uncle's words, not mine."

She tilted her gaze past him and down at Lord Tyrrian who had made his way down to the edge of the pit where Sir Marion also stood. Both men were laughing with female spectators and leaning against the stone railing that framed in the orchestra and separated it from the first row of the audience.

Sir Marion had removed his chest armor, now wearing only his armored belt and sandals, and held a towel, stained in red, in his hand. Most of the blood had been wiped from his face and chest and an Aisharian woman was leaning against the railing close to him, tracing her hand along his fresh cuts.

As she moved her finger back and forth on his chest, he grinned and bit his lip before pulling her into a deeply passionate kiss, his hand aggressively gripping the back of her neck and bunching her hair in between his fingers.

Lord Tyrrian seemed to not notice, or care, as his attention was diverted to the two other women gathered by them. He traded his attention between the two, neither of which seemed to mind sharing his affection. Lord Tyrrian had stripped himself of the confines of the elaborate jacket he had worn earlier and rolled up the sleeves of his buttoned blouse, exposing his forearms as well as his neckline where the buttons were undone.

The brown-haired woman- who appeared to be a citizen of Isilria based upon her attire- traced her fingers up and down the vein that ran along his exposed forearm. The black-haired woman wearing a short dress like the other Aisharian women, continued to lean dramatically forward against the railing to allow the low-cut neck of her dress to fall open even more as she laughed and smiled at everything he was saying.

Lord Tyrrian leaned forward between the two women to whisper. As he leaned back to standing, the three held devious glances and both women exchanged nods of agreement and newfound looks of lust with the lord and one another.

Once both men were done with their exchanges, they left their women behind for the moment, knowing they would finish what they had started later, and walked back to where the royal family still sat.

"Your Grace, you seem joyful about your loss in the ring." King Ivan snarked as the men approached.

"Ah, you seem to forget, Your Royal Highness," Lord Tyrrian replied as he leaned over the rail and snatched the decanter of wine and two glasses of wine from the table. "Sir Marion is of the Isles and is Aisharian, by blood and by creed. He may have represented your throne in the fight, but he still showed your people of the strength of Aishar in his victory."

King Ivan balled his gloved hand in a fist and glared at the Lord of Aishar.

Father Figgins interjected, quickly but carefully jumping from his seat. "One might say then, that *both* our countries have won today. What better way to show our alliance to our people than through an equal victory to-day?"

Queen Onetta stood from her seat behind her husband and stepped forward, placing one arm on his shoulder, and holding her glass in the other. "I could not agree more, Father Figgins. Let us toast to today's victory, and soon, to another on the battlefield." She gave a forced smile as she looked around, encouraging the group to raise their glasses in toast.

Lord Tyrrian was the first to raise his glass in response, looking at the queen with a coquettish grin and nodding his head to the side, "Yes, let us toast, my queen."

Everyone gathered in the viewing box stood and raised their glasses, including Sister Ora, and gave a heartfelt cheer. Sister Ora imitated their emotions, her eyes moving about the crowd still gathered, meeting the eyes of Sedrick between the moving bodies of celebrating citizens.

He reached into his coat pocket, the edge of an envelope peeking out from the fabric and his finger tapping on it as he locked into her stare.

CHAPTER 34

Gerald ran down the hall of the Middleton Landing fortress and burst into the council chamber room where military officers, Father Robb, and Lord Taylian Montarian were gathered. Sgt. Pell, the officer in charge of the Ayeshire soldiers left behind in the Landing, abruptly ended his sentence at Gerald's intrusion.

"Sgt. Pell, my apologies." Gerald's voice was heavy in breath. "A group of hunters near Clear Point have spotted Aisharian sails taking over the waters outside of the king's city. They sent word via bird back to our stations."

The officers exchanged looks and waited for someone else to respond.

Sgt. Pell replied to Gerald's eyes darting around the silent room. "Your hunters words come later than our spies birds, and later than Lady Montarian's orders of what to prepare in response."

"Oh." Gerald replied, defeated and embarrassed now at his intrusion.

"But what our own messengers did not know yet were how many ships we have to worry about. Did your hunters have knowledge of this?" Lord Taylian asked.

"Yes. Two caravels and a dozen carracks were spotted."

An advisor beside Father Robb cut in, "That many ships could hold the likes of four thousand men aboard if they push their comfort aside."

Sgt. Pell put down the papers in his hand and leaned forward onto the table, glaring at the map that held outdated information on military movements of their allies and enemies. He sighed and picked up several discs painted with the kraken crest and carelessly dropped them into place within the waters around Isilria. He glared down at the discs, counting the potential casualties this information could bring swiftly to their lands.

"Lady Montarian has requested our aid in creating more weapons, increasing our supplies here at the Landing and sending forces to the battlefield to trade in broken blades for new and refill our archers arrows. They are doing what they can on the front lines, but their forces are smaller than before and need our aid." Father Robb explained as Sgt Pell adjusted the battle map. "We also have word confirming that Odessin has been enlisted and their Dragon Army is due to the capitol in some time. Unfortunately we do not know when."

"With Aisharian gladiators now close to the battlefield, and soon Dragons with weapons of fire and worse, we need more than simple swords and arrows." Lord Taylian said. "Gerald, you are good friends with Healer Ephraim, who has proven to be a master of their guild and beyond. Perhaps this request would be best coming from a good friend instead of an order from their ad interim lord."

"You speak of weapons akin to magic?" Father Robb asked. "Such as Dragon's Breath and Hellfire?"

Lord Taylian replied, "Yes, I do."

"My lord," Gerald started, "those weapons are beyond the comprehension, and legality, of many."

"Perhaps they are, but this is war."

***

Gerald stepped hesitantly into the building just off the main street of Middleton Landing. Glass and metal lanterns hung on the walls and illuminated tabletops, brightening shelves that were lined with bottles of various sizes containing mysterious liquids, botanicals, what appeared to be remains and bones of animals, and powders that Gerald dared not to touch. Shoved and stacked in any overly organized manner among the items were books, journals and scrolls perfectly rolled and set in their cubbies behind the counters.

There was not a speck of dust to be found in the Healer's Guild house- a sign that Ephraim and their compatriots had been hard at work.

Healers and apprentices were scattered about the multi storied building, some in rooms with patients with ailments that needed healing, and some on their own studying or combining substances together. None bothered to stop or question Gerald as he walked past the front counter and through the back halls towards Ephraim's office.

Gerald stepped in the doorway and watched Ephraim for a moment, who had yet to notice his presence. They stood on the other side of a large desk, stewing over a book full of sketches and words unfamiliar to Gerald. Ephraim's buzzcut and barely-there stubble had grown long and shaggy over the past few knots and their attire held little life in it.

Gerald and Ephraim had barely seen one another since the Montarian's called for their banners to be raised, their once frequent friendly visits and conversations halted by the looming future and guilt Gerald held over being left behind at The Landing while their friends were off in battle. With the return of wounded soldiers in large masses, Ephraim had been overwhelmed with more labor and the Healer house had been well overrun with patients day and night after battles had begun.

Friendly interactions were a luxury they had no time to afford to indulge in.

"Leaf." Gerald gently said as he broke his quiet observation.

Ephraim snapped their head up and smiled softly. Their face showed the weariness and lack of rest they felt; their sharp features shadowed by the bags under their eyes and lack of care they had taken of themselves as of late.

"Gerald! How are you?" painted joy came out with each word, then swung into quick worry. "Are you ok? Is something wrong?"

"No, no, no. I am fine. I just..." Gerald looked down as he finally stepped into the room and gently closed the door. "I am here to ask you for your help."

Ephraim paced the room as Gerald briefed them on their prior meeting and the ask that was given of them. Frustration peaked quickly as Gerald spoke and Ephraim took in what was being asked of them.

"Gerald you must remember that weapons are not my expertise and that was a choice I made many moons ago to never *be* my expertise. I am not like the herbalists and scientists of Odessin who spend all their time concocting dangerous chemical weapons, I spend my time learning how to help and heal the world, not hurt it." they intently met Gerald's eyes. "I swore an oath when I chose this path."

"I understand, but there must be some sort of sorcery or science you can think of that can help in the war and end it quickly- to save countless lives that would be taken if this carried on for too long."

Ephraim hesitated. Their guilt for being safe at home and not at the war battled with their personal code and values. Saving lives by taking others was a scale that did not balance, and committing unethical acts in the name of justice did not justify the blood.

Gerald stepped forward, closing the gap between them, the desk now the only thing separating them. "Leaf, please."

"No."

"Leaf." Gerald begged.

"No. *I will abstain from causing harm and only heal. I will protect life, not take it. I will prevent pain and sickness where I can.* That is only a portion of the oath I swore when I made it my calling to use my gifts to heal and save lives. Killing, and aiding others in creating more death, does not protect life, it takes it."

"But ending this war quickly by creating these weapons *would* save lives in the end. You would help prevent this from dragging on and hurting more innocent people!"

"You are asking me to create chemical weapons that will burn the skin off of a man's bones or burst them into flames so quickly the night sky will darken around the flames." Ephraim hissed. "Unlike you, I do not come un-questionably to every beck and call that Lord Digarius or his family shouts at me. My oath presides over any noble order given."

"Excuse me?" Gerald snapped. "I am not some damn dog of theirs. I follow Lord Digarius and the Montarian family because I am loyal to them."

"Do you know what it is they are asking of you... of me? Hellfire is so potent and dangerous that the slightest mishandle would kill everyone within its vicinity. It lights everything it touches in blue flames that erupt so hot and high that everything is consumed in seconds. The mere fact that it kills so quickly is the *only* technicality that prevents the use of it from being considered a war crime. And the proposal of Dragon's Breath, that alone should have caused you to pause in accepting their demand for my aid."

They held a heated and hate filled glare, any friendship and kindness evaporated.

"This is not my war." Ephraim said.

"It is everyone's war." Gerald jabbed a pointed finger against the wood of the desk's surface. "Look outside your office, it is overrun with those who have fought against the king and our battlefields and cemeteries are haunted with fresh souls lost because of this."

"And I will not add to that." Ephraim moved to walk around him, then paused at the door. "I have patients waiting. You know the way out."

CHAPTER 35

Q ueen Onetta casually strolled along the flower beds with guards keeping their distance behind her. She stopped on occasion to pluck a rare weed or imperfect bloom from the beds and toss them behind her for a garden keeper to pick up and dispose of later.

She was delicate with her movements each time she leaned into the garden beds or shuffled off the clean stone path, careful not to get dirt or debris on the ivy green fabric of her dress that matched the stems and leaves of the greenery around her. The soft fabric was decorated with rows of tiny jewels threaded along her waistline and adorned with long semi-sheer tulip shaped sleeves; a dress made to match her meticulously kept gardens.

She followed her memory to her favorite part of the gardens; the long flowerbeds filled with rainbows of iris, the national flower of the Isles of Aishar and her favorite bloom.

While breathtaking, the long beds of foliage were no comparison to the rolling rocky hillsides and fields of iris' found in her homeland.

Standing among the beds, distracted and smitten by the flora himself, was Lord Tyrrian Priscius.

He glimmered in the light in a long saffron gold robe cinched closed at the waist with a thin brown belt. The style of attire left a sliver of his bare chest exposed. Sheathed at his side was a golden sword, not displayed for decoration as many high nobles often wore them for, but for use against any enemy that dared to try him. His Lord's Guards were nowhere to be found, and, knowing his strength and power, not needed in such a place. Their absence an indication of the lack of threat he felt.

He was everything the Isles glorified molded into one man.

"Your Grace. You and I appear to both miss the Isles and came to look for a piece of it here. Would you care for company for a moment?" The queen inquired as she stepped beside him.

Lord Tyrrian looked up from the deep and vibrant flowers as she greeted him, smiling as she gracefully walked to him.

"A man would be most foolish to not desire your company, Your Majesty." he held out his arm for her to hold onto as she met with him and they began a slow walk around the gardens. "Although, I would have enjoyed it much sooner. If I were to think too hard on it, I would wonder if you were avoiding my presence since my arrival. We have not seen one another outside of our needed gatherings and family dinners."

"Then it is a benefit to our family's friendship that you have not thought much of it. I have been quite busy even before your arrival, my lord. Avoiding you has not been my intent."

"Hmm." he darted his eyes down at her as they continued down the path. The queen's stare steadfast and forward despite the intensity of his sidelong glance.

"Are you enjoying your stay? Everything is to your liking, I presume?" she asked.

"Yes, everything is quite nice. Although, I still quite prefer home. Castle Red and Aishar are always where I most desire to be."

"Yes, I still find myself often watching the waters and thinking of Aishar; the sand, the shores, the beauty." her polite tone dissipated as her feelings came to the surface, "I do quite miss it."

"And yet, you do not visit me or the Isles. Your home and your people made you who you are, and you have chosen to leave us behind without a second thought." He replied; his voice holding no emotion.

She scoffed and turned her head away. "I am queen now; my duties keep me busy. You know I cannot simply set my sails any time I would desire to go home."

"Is this not your home now, Your Royal Highness?" snark heavily lined each word as his mouth quirked into a small smirk.

The pair abruptly stopped walking, her posture and mannerisms careful to not make it appear as any sort of scene to those who looked in their direction. Queen Onetta jutted her chin up at him.

"Aishar will *always* be my home, no matter where I lay my head to rest or break my fast. Aishar is my home."

"And I repeat, you do not visit, nor do you send your children- children of Aishar- to visit. Aside from the beds of iris' lining this very garden, there is nothing within the walls of this castle that honors the Aisharian culture- *your* culture. You have appeared to erased who you are, so much that even the accent you once held has slipped from your tongue and now you sound no different than the man you bed."

The slap of her hand against his face clashed in the air and started the birds from their trees.

As she adjusted the rings on her stinging hand, Lord Tyrrian put his own hand against his face, wiping the drop of blood the metal on her fingers drew from his dark skin. His eyes darted up and down her body as he bit his lip and grinned.

"There she is." he quipped.

She hissed. "I have done what was needed to hold onto my power, to *survive*, to blend in and be who I was told to be. Erasing so much of who I was, who I *am*, was self-preservation." she stepped within inches of him. "And you of all men know I chose none of this. I had no hand in crafting this life that I am to live."

She looked about the garden, they shifting eyes of nosing onlookers demanding her attention and decorum. She grabbed his arm and turned him forward on the path, continuing their promenade as if there was never a disruption to their civility. They walked in silence until they reached the end of the beds of iris'; Lord Tyrrian halting them this time as his eyes caught on a row of ginger red blooms. The same rich red that made up the stones of Castle Red and sands around the islands.

He plucked a stem from the bed. "For you, my Onetta."

He held the flower up between the two, and she caught her breath. Her expression filled again with the anger it had just lost. His amber eyes held her gaze and darkened as his lips curled into a troublesome pirate smile.

"We have spoken of this before." she hissed in a whisper. "You cannot call me that, not here, not anymore."

Her eyes darted around frantically, hoping the guards and the gardeners did not hear what was said or sense the new type of tension building between the two.

Lord Tyrrian stepped even closer, dropping his hand holding the flower, leaving nothing between the two but their breath. He leaned in, his warm breath caressing the side of her face and neck as he spoke.

"Perhaps then, I shall whisper." the heat from his voice and breath washed over her skin as his beard brushed against her bare cheek.

Her chest rose and her pulse thumped throughout her body as the growing heat in her veins rivaled that of the sun.

"How I have missed you." his lips tickled her cheek.

Queen Onetta swallowed the large, dry lump in her throat and let out a deep breath, looking anywhere and everywhere but in his direction. Her chest heaved up and down as he stayed leaned in and her mind wandered to every place it should not go; as it recalled nights she laid in her bed alone with her wandering hands that could never find the spots his always did, to other night where his hands roped in her hair and covered her crying mouth as she trembled with every movement he made. To nights long gone yet not forgotten.

"What we once had ended almost a lifetime ago when you were to wed my sister and soon after, I to the king." Each word struggled to come out and her thighs clenched tight against where her heartbeat throbbed most from.

She pulled her face away from his.

"Did it? End then? Because I very much remember a night here in this very castle, the day after King Andrius's funeral eight epochs ago. You had spent the day crying with your husband and the night crying out my name."

"Tyrrian, that is *enough*. We cannot do this again. *I* cannot do this again. You loved my sister, and I must be loyal to our king. There is too much at stake for us to be reckless as we once were. We have duties. We have obligations."

He shrugged.

"You are right, over time, I did grow to love your sister and she was... an adequate wife. But there never was and never will be a substitute for you." his eyes danced around her face as she continued shaking her head and avoiding his looks. "Every day that you walked the halls of Castle Red while your sister sat at my side, the already thinning thread of my dignity grew more fragile. The only distance between us that was enough to keep us apart was the ocean and your husband's crown."

He stepped forward as she stepped back. "And now that I stand right here, I can tell you that all that time, the distance, and titles, are barely holding the line between us." He stopped and shook his head as he let out a breath, "But if you truly do wish me to stop, I will grant your wishes the respect they deserve."

She did not respond and after a long pause of heavy breaths, she reached to grab the iris still in his hand, the stem crunched and broken from his grasp. "It would be a waste for this flower to be plucked and simply thrown away, and I always do enjoy a fresh bouquet on my bedside."

She walked past him and kneeled in front of the flower bed to pick other iris' and catch her breath. He stood behind her, clutching his hands lazily behind his back.

"How is Princess Kalia? She will turn eight this winter, and has begun her schooling, yes?"

Queen Onetta became rigid. "Your *niece* is doing quite well."

"Turning out much like her father?" he inquired.

Her hand stopped where it held the uncut stem of an iris. Her tone and the flower's stem snapped. "She has much of the kindness the king once had, and in every other way, she is her mother's daughter."

She stood and adjusted her dress then glared at him before leaving him and his perfect, but infuriatingly arrogant, face behind.

CHAPTER 36

The Odessian guard grunted as he pulled the front of his tunic above his waistline, bunching the cloth at the bottom of his weapons belt as he adjusted the small shield and weapons out of his way. He sighed as he grabbed himself and began urinating on the dew-covered ground. He had not bothered to walk far away from the outpost building; the thick fog that rolled in overnight gave tall camouflage to the lands surrounding the camp and dampened the sounds one could hear in the area.

The scalemail armor on his torso jingled as he finished urinating and dropped his tunic back down. He turned to walk back to his patrolling position at the base, his limited view of the building disrupted by the swing of a war hammer meeting his face. The crunching of every bone in his skull and the grunt of exertion of his attacker was muffled by the thick fog and contained to those directly beside them.

"Good one, brother." Gladys said as she stepped up next to Barron.

"Thanks" he replied as he stood over the dead Odessian. "Thought I'd let him finish pissin' before I killed him."

Gladys chuckled. "How considerate."

The siblings turned to the Odessian camp and kneeled to hide themselves in the fog. They walked in a hunched position and moved to the camp. To their left and right, the shapes of cloaked and fur covered figures did the same. If they listened hard enough, they heard the occasional grunts of pain and the drop of a body as another one of their people took down a guard.

Ahead of them, voices broke through the thick air.

"Did you hear that?"

"No. Probably some wolves or something."

"You. Go check it out."

The siblings nodded to one another before turning to their fellow fighters, now more visible to them in the thinning fog. They raised their hands, and gestured to move in on the camp. The slowly prowling party now burst through the last bit of fog with reckless abandon and shouts. The guards patrolling outside of the building jumped in surprise before hastily grabbing the shields at their waist and positioning their spears atop the shields as they ran to meet their surprise attackers.

Shouts from on top of the building echoed over the shouting on the ground, notifying the warriors that were inside to awaken and join the fight. Atop the wall, Odessian's hurried to grab spears that laid in weapons racks.

Wooden spears with sharp metal tips rained down at the Craigie fighters.

Gladys and Barron split off from one another and began battling with the camp's defenders.

Barron stepped in the path of an Odessian charging forward. He glanced at the war hammer in his hands, lightly tossing it and twisting it around as if it were a toy as the fighter charged for him. When Barron saw the irises of their eyes, he turned and stepped out of the way.

The attacker's momentum was too much to quickly stop and their steps ended several feet behind him. Barron had his own momentum from his turn that sent him into a circle. As he finished his turn, he swung his hammer and struck the center of their back, crushing their body where it was unprotected. The Odessian toppled to the ground before realized what had occurred, their body barely making contact with the ground before Barron swung the war hammer down, stopping the swing only when their head crunched into the ground.

Barron pulled his hammer up and turned to find his next victim but was stopped with the vision of a spear flying down from the wall. Gladys stepped in front of him, swinging her broadsword, and knocking the spear off course and into the ground near them.

"Really?" she snarked at him before turning for the Odessian charging for her.

While many of the camp defenders charged forward with spears and a shield, this fighter ran forward with two long daggers, ready to strike down anyone in their path. As they made their way towards her, Gladys flipped the sword in her hand, running it along the length of her arm. Her attacker swiftly swung a dagger just as she raised her arm, using the blade of the sword to deflect the strike.

Her other hand held her shield at her side, just below the point of where their other dagger's slash was aimed. She flicked her shield arm up to smack away the dagger, the Odessian's body now left wide open as they held their daggers to their sides.

Gladys held no hesitation when their bodies broke contact and flipped her sword back to its true hold. Then used her entire body to slash it across the Odessian's abdomen, opening his body just below where the scalemail on his chest and weapon's belt stopped offering protection. As he hunched over to grab his bleeding waist, she swung her shield at his head, using the pointed metal boss in its center as a weapon to impale and shove him down.

She wasted no more time on him and drove her sword through his neck as he fell to his knees; not bothering to even look at him as she cut through his neck. She took in her surroundings as she ripped the blade from his body, seeing the bloodshed her own mother was wreaking on her own.

Across the camp, Lady Kathilla shoved forward from behind one of her fighters that had been impaled. Before the spears wielder could rip it from the chest of her victim, Lady Kathilla swung her battle axe down and shattered the wooden spear. The Odessian woman, in shock and panic, reached to grab another weapon, but her movements were not fast enough. The Lady of Craigie swung the axe across her neck with such force that her head landed several feet away.

Before the body could fall, Kathilla used her free hand to grab at the scalemail armor and used the headless body as her own human shield. Two spears flew down from the building as she began moving, hunched behind the blood soaked beheaded body as the spears pierced its back. She threw the dead Odessian to the ground, her arm now drenched in its blood as she slammed forward towards another fighter.

"Get on the walls! Now!" Barron shouted from his new position near her and charged for one of the external stairways.

His Craigie fighters followed suit, rushing up the stairs to attack. As they forged a bloodied path, they shoved bodies of their fallen allies and enemies over the rails and onto the ground below, clearing their path as they made it to the top.

Barron charged towards a soldier running for the weapons rack. His assault stopped when a heavy foot kicked him in the back, causing him to drop his hammer to the ground. He turned to face his new opponent, an already bloodied Odessian, as they grabbed at their belt and pulled out a crescent moon blade. The fighter tightened their grip along the leather wrapped curved center of the weapon and stepped back, ready to strike or defend themselves against the large northman.

Barron did not waste energy attempting to find his dropped axe, and instead prepared for a hand-to-hand fight. Both men stepped forward, Barron with his hands in hard fists, and the attacker with their bladed hand preparing to slice him.

As he swung, Barron loosened his swinging fist to grab the wrist of the Odessian's hand holding the blade, holding it firmly in place before twisting it and snapping the bones.

His free hand grabbed the blade and put it in his own; using it to punch the held fighter in the face, leaving punctures and rips in the skin as he refused to stop striking. Only when the body went limp did he carelessly dropped both the blade and the body before finding his hammer and moving to continue the fight.

But, there was no fight left to be had.

Gladys stood across the walkway, sword now hanging on her belted hip, and her blood-soaked shield loosely held in her hand, an ornery look on her face.

"Nine." She shouted at him.

Barron grumbled under his breath.

"What was that?" She jested.

Barron glared with intense irritation at his sister before gritting out his response, "Six."

"Looks like I win again."

"Eleven." Lady Kathilla's voice corrected as she ascended the steps, smirking at her children. "I win."

***

"Nothing more than general supplies and food in their carts, my lords." A soldier bearing the Sebern crest said as he approached Lord William Torrin and Lord Theodus Montarian standing near the edge of their battle camp that they stubbornly held onto at the southwestern edge of the Ravenhall hills. "It seems they were telling the truth when they said they were just passing through to look for new homes to settle into."

A pregnant woman approached them, her long dress dirty from days of travel in unfavorable conditions. "My lords, if I may speak?"

Her head was downturned and her hand shook as she rested it on her stomach and waited for their reply.

The cousins shared a look with one another. It was Lord Theodus who replied to her.

"Yes, of course, my lady. And you need not hold your head down away from us." He spoke as softly as he could to hide the deep bass of his voice and its normally loud bravado.

She tentatively lifted her eyes. "We are from small villages surrounding Lake Lahere, they bear no name, but we were proud to call them home. We know you fight for what you believe is true, just as His Majesty does, but we 'seek refuge away from the battles where we may be safe from the weapons and where our food will not be threatened in the future once the war tears apart the farmlands.

Lord William stepped forward. "And where is it you wish to find this safety? There are quite a number of you, and you are not the first we have seen pass through."

She looked down at the ground again, her head moving about as she tried to find her words. "I know this is insensitive, and may god bless me with mercy for speaking of it, and you grant me your forgiveness, but we know from what others have said that you have lost many of your own in the recent battles."

She looked on the brink of tears as she lifted her head to them. "Perhaps if their homes are no longer needed, we may earn them with our labors. And some of us do have coin, where we could buy them if you deem it so. We will be loyal to your banners if you allow it."

Lord Theodus held back his offense as he asked. "And you would give up your citizenship and be loyal to our banners just like that?"

"You know not of what Prince Elion and his men have done to our lands, to our people. He executed and hanged some of our leaders for their frustrations and demand of due payment for his army taking supplies and housing. I have family that is from Ayeshire, and others left for marriages in Sebern. They have never spoken ill of either of your leaderships. Despite the taxes and the differing weather, it—"

She keeled forward and clutched her stomach; quick breaths came from her mouth as she worked through her pain. Both lords rushed to aid her and escort her to the medical tent.

"Where is your husband? The child's father?" Lord William asked as he held onto one side of her and helped her walk.

"Dead. He was conscripted to fight in the king's army and was killed." She huffed out as they walked. "I am left with six children to raise on my own."

Lord William tightened at her confession. His memory fell to his home, to his wife and her joking threat of him leaving her behind to raise their children on her own. "And you may raise them in Sebern if you wish, even if the move is only temporary. My country will welcome you with open arms and offer you kinship and kindness. As they will the rest of your caravan."

Chapter 37

"All I am stating, Your Majesty, is that the public opinion has once again quickly begun to fall out of our favor, and we must do something of this." Queen Onetta held back her irritation and did her best to speak without emotion to the king. "The gladiator showcase and its festival last knot did well to make many in the high city happy, but word has come to me that the lower city by the docks feel neglected by our family. And the villages around the battlefields hold no complacency nor joy for our reign."

"My reign." his words and his head snapped to her where she sat across from him at the work desk in his suite.

Queen Onetta's face flickered at his anger. "Do not snap at me. I am only helping."

She scoffed. "What happened to the patience you once had?"

"Well, I guess I have grown tired of all your helping and ordering me around as if you are above me." He said, his words a slight slur despite there being no drink in his hand.

Her eyes narrowed and her hands clenched into fists on her lap. Her lip quivered into a snarl as she stood up. "We agreed to a partnership."

"*No*. We agreed to a marriage and to create heirs. *You* are the one who keeps playing above your station." He glared up at her from his seat. He softened his face in a form of defeat and spoke with tired annoyance. "Sit down, let us talk."

He leaned back in his chair and looked up at her stubbornly refusing to move. "Fine, if you wish to not sit then we do not have to continue this discussion."

Queen Onetta finally loosened her tight posture and sat back down. Her back still rigid as a pole and shoulders as square as they could be. "As I have advised before and am advising again, public perception is just as important as any victory on the battlefield. We must present ourselves as a family of the people and we must ensure that our people know that we are the ones on the right side of the war."

"And I assume that my devious queen already has a plan as she always does?"

"Yes. Several in fact."

***

Lord Tyrrian Priscius sauntered down the hallway of the castle towards his chambers. He pulled at the collar of his dark red doublet, popping open the top buttons around his neck as he twisted the doorknob and pushed the door open. A deep sigh escaped his lips as he stepped inside, continuing to fidget with the large, intricate buttons on his clothing. The subtle sound of wine being poured across the room caught his attention as he turned to close the door behind him.

Seated lazily at the rooms dining table, basking in the light from the sun pouring through the open balcony door, was Queen Onetta.

Lord Tyrrian paused beside the door, halting his steps and the unbuttoning of his shirt as he looked her over. She turned her stern gaze from the wine to him.

"And to what reason do I owe thanks for your company today?" he inquired.

"My insolent husband who continues frustrating me." she mumbled.

"Well, I shall give him my upmost gratitude at our next meeting." Lord Tyrrian jested as he began walking across the room again, now undoing the buttons at the cuff of his shirt.

"As you know well, his plans continue to fail and I am left to plot and plan to fix our image, an image he seems to hold no care about." she took a large sip of wine. "His stupidity has already lost this war and it has hardly begun."

"Do not worry yourself so much. Our council meeting this afternoon went surprisingly well and already we are putting into place a new battle plan."

She let out a short breath and turned her head away from him to look out the balcony.

"Is complaining about your husband's idiocy really why you have shown up in my chambers today, Your Highness, or is there another reason?"

"Onetta. Call me Onetta when we are here." she softly replied.

He continued ambling across the room, each step slow and deliberate. "I thought you said that what we had died long ago," he paused, dropping his voice down, "Onetta."

She ran her tongue across her teeth and took another slow sip of wine as she watched him prowl towards her.

His long fingers calmly pulled the final of his shirt buttons through their holes. His hands flexed with every fidget of the buttons and his jawline grew more rigid with every step he took. He stopped in front of her chair, looking down at her and gently taking the wine glass from her to sip and then set it on the table.

"I have changed my mind, Tyrrian." she crooned up at him; her eyes following every mass of muscle on his exposed torso..

Her body shifted as she uncrossed her legs and moved them open for him to stand between, holding his gaze with a teasing stare as she did so.

Lord Tyrrian bent over the chair, leaning in over her and delicately placing a hand on either arm of the chair around her. As he leaned his head forward over hers, she leaned back, relaxing fully in the chair, and tilting her chin up towards him, softening her jaw enough for her lips to fall open. The arms of the chair creaked under the tension of his hands tightening around them. His broad shoulders and biceps strained the seams of the doublet as he breathed deeply and intensely.

"Kneel." she whispered up to him; a small smile crawled on her lips.

She set the tips of her fingers on his biceps, delicately squeezing his muscles to command his movement.

He cocked his head, a flirtatious smirk on his face as she sat up in the chair, keeping her hands on his biceps and moving her lips so close to his that they almost touched with every word she spoke.

"Kneel before your queen." she hummed into his lips.

She slid her hands up his biceps and onto his shoulders, faintly pushing him to guide him backward and down. Lord Tyrrian obliged with no protest and took a small step back. As he finished removing his disheveled shirt, his queen leaned back in her chair. She lifted her leg up and ran her foot teasingly on his bare chest before resting it near his shoulder.

He dropped his shirt to the ground and wrapped his hand around her ankle.

Neither looked away as Lord Tyrrian turned his head and kissed her ankle, then allowed his mouth to make its way up her leg, dragging his lips along her skin in between deep kisses and light bites as his body slowly lowered to the ground with each kiss. As he made his way to her knee, he paused, resting her bent leg on his shoulder and wrapped his hand around her thigh.

He dropped to both his knees in front of her.

Both of his hands made their way up her thighs, pushing her dress out of his way. He returned his hands slowly back down her thighs before hooking his hand under her other leg to rest it on his shoulder. He gazed up at her, just barely seeing the bottom of her chin and edges of her jawline before dropping his head and mouth down to kiss her.

Queen Onetta moaned at the hot sensation of his tongue tracing slow, deliberate circles around her. Lord Tyrrian let out a deep hum and moan of his own- the kind of moan one reserves for moments when they are tasting the most delicious delicacies- and continued tracing, sucking, and licking for several moments. The grip on her thighs and movement of his mouth was guided by every buck of her hips and gasp and moan that she let out.

For only a moment, he pulled back away from her, attempting to look up at her gasping face and watch what he had done to her.

As he returned his lips to their spot between hers, she moved her hand through his hair and grasped his locks tightly to hold his head in place. At the gesture, he quickened the pace of his movements, his tongue rapidly running lines and tracing more circles in spots he expertly knew how to touch until finally she bucked forward, gasping deeply as every muscle in her body was flushed with a white-hot heat.

Lord Tyrrian offered no reprieve and continued until he felt her thighs tighten and shake around his head and her lower abdomen tremble above his head. The room again filled with her shaking gasps as he pulled away from her body, licking his lips as he stood up.

He leaned over the chair and aggressively grabbed her jaw, holding her face in place as he pushed his lips into hers and pushed his tongue to open her mouth. As they kissed, Lord Tyrrian took his free hand and wrapped it around her torso, pulling her up with him as he stood. His grip around her jaw disappeared as he used that hand to grab around her waist, crunching her rumpled up dress in the grip of both of his hands. He lifted her up off the chair and held her to his body as he carried her to the bedside.

He caught a foot on the sliver of the backside of her skirt and stumbled before finding his footing again and grabbing a fistful of the draped fabric and continuing to kiss and carry her.

Under her breath and between his lips, Queen Onetta managed to quietly plead. "My dress, Tyrrian. Do not ruin it."

He huffed, his voice gritty and hard as he set her down in front of the bed. "I will buy you a thousand new ones."

His hands ran quickly up her back and ripped it open, pulling it down her shoulders and arms. She shimmied the rest of the way out of her dress as both of their hands reached for the string on her chest tying her chemise in place. They both stopped, chests heaving as they tried to breathe.

Queen Onetta looked up at him, his hands still heavily wrapped around hers holding the ribbon. His normal glances and expressions of tension, anger, and stoicism were replaced with a kind softness as he looked back at her and his grip around her hands loosened before dropping from hers.

Queen Onetta held his softened gaze as he brought his hands up to cup her face tenderly, kissing her deeply, but not with the same intense heat as before. The intensity of this kiss was a passion deeper than simple lust. As she returned his kiss, she slipped her chemise off and moved her hands down to unbutton his pants, pulling them down as much as she could without breaking their kiss.

Lord Tyrrian guided her to the edge of the bed as he removed his hands from her face and dispose of the remaining clothing keeping him from her. He climbed on top of her, only breaking his kiss when he must to help guide her farther onto the bed.

"Are you sure?" he breathed in her ear as he hovered over her, his body barely an inch away from touching every part of hers.

Queen Onetta responded by wrapping her legs around his waist and pulled him to her. A small snicker came from them both before he shifted his weight and pushed into her fully, both gasping and moaning at the sensation. He continued slowly thrusting as he moved a hand down to grip her hip and hold her in place.

Each time her hands clawed his back and body tensed his thrusts deepened and his mouth pushed deeper onto hers as if somehow, someway, there was more his body could do to hers if he tried hard enough.

They exhausted themselves thoroughly until the chimes rang through the royal chamber halls, signaling for their aids to come prepare the family for dinner. Queen Onetta called for her loyal hand maiden to come with a new dress to her, knowing her silence was guaranteed in exchange for the queen allowing her to keep her job and tongue.

At dinner later that night, Lord Tyrrian wore a high collared doublet to cover the marks Queen Onetta left and she wore a new dress; one of the many gifts that he had brought with him for the royal family. Much later that night, after the sun set and the moon rose, they both met in one of the high turrets of the castle where no one could hear them. Queen Onetta stood leaning over the window of the tower, her dress pulled up above her waist, with Lord Tyrrian standing behind her so they both could watch the stars.

CHAPTER 38

Father Figgins looked out at the crowded pews filled with parishioners coming to worship. He raised his hands from where they rested on the edges of the pulpit and held them out, then motioned down to encourage- to order- his people to sit.

"May the grace of God, our divine creator, and his blessings be with you." Father Figgins greeted.

"And with you." The crowd repeated back as they finished settling in their seats.

"Last service we spoke of the divine love of God for all his creations, we prayed for the safety of our fellow man during this time of war, and we hoped for peace and unity to be found under His word. Through worship we came together, and through it we will come together again today as we pray for the lost souls taken in this war waged against our people, against God and against the crown.

"Today, I not only worship with you all, but I weep with you as well over our losses. But through our tears, we shall persevere. It is through our shared tears and worship today that we shall rise to the glory of God and all He has granted us in the divine destinies he weaved for each of our souls. Today, we shall pray for peace and forgiveness of our enemies over the blood they have stained our peaceful lands with."

He held a dramatic pause as his words sunk into the pews. "Let us pray."

He folded his hands over the scripture book and bowed his head, prompting the gathered worshippers to do so as well. "Oh God, please grant mercy and peace upon the newly ascended souls sent to you far too soon. Please grant forgiveness to those who have taken up swords against us and against you, for they know not what they do in their misguided actions.

"We pray that you enlighten them and their false tongues with the truth of your will. For was it not your will and plan that guided our hands and gave us the words we speak and keep alive? Was it not your will that molded the new world and united our kingdoms after the Great War?

"We ask for your forgiveness of our own sins, for none of us are perfect and free of sin, and we pray for peace and prosperity to be brought to our divided lands as it once was. Through your love and mercy, we pray. Amen"

"Amen." the pews echoed back as they too raised their heads.

Throughout the rest of his sermon he was met with nodding heads, smiling faces, and his devout followers listening intently to every word and pause of his sermon.

Outside the lavish chapel of the King's Church, if one listened or looked closely enough, grim faces of passersby spit their anger onto the bottom of the well-guarded steps, too poor and low-class to be welcomed into the divine church not built for the common people, but built by their hands. Even further down the hills of the king's city, in between the cries of beggars asking for change and drunkards and addicts lying in their own filth praying for aid to end their illnesses, a keen ear would hear the hushed whispers of animosity rising.

CHAPTER 39

The crowds of citizens moved quickly out of the way as the King's Guard and Lord's Guards marched through the streets. Walking in the middle of all the wall of steel was Queen Onetta, Lord Tyrrian, Prince Percy, Sister Ora, and the princesses.

Noticable mumbles about the king's whereabouts were constant. King Ivan had begrudgingly planned to promenade after church, but an illness took him during the final prayers and he was taken away to recover. It would not have been proper for the people to see their king recovering from vomiting and coated in sweat.

Sister Ora walked alongside Prince Percy and Princess Arminda who held onto Princess Kalia's hand. Sister Onetta conversed politely with the two about various surface-level subjects as they greeted citizens and did their best to put on the show that the queen had requested.

"How much longer will we do this?" Sister Ora mumbled to Prince Percy, putting light pressure on his bicep where her hand rested to grab his attention.

The prince continued nodding and feigning kind smiles at those gathered around them. "As long as my mother wishes, which, unfortunately, could be quite a while. And Father Figgins also insisted on this after his sermon of solidarity was so well received. They both do love to put on a show."

She mimicked the same gestures and smiles as Prince Percy as they continued onward, her eyes holding the stares of the citizens around them, her observations more detailed than the royal family fulfilling their obligation.

Citizens whispered and pointed calloused fingers at them, with several women looking at the royal family's ornate and clean clothing and then down at their own patch covered dresses of well-worn cotton and muslin. Polite smiles and waves were plentiful, but Sister Ora could not stop holding onto the weight of the glares and tension that accompanied the dingy scents of the lower city.

"If I may offer my observation, I do not believe this show is truly working in our favor." She whispered to Prince Percy.

He leaned in and whispered back. "How so?"

"Well, we come down from our castle to parade past all these people, dressed in the finest threads, full of the most luxurious foods, and Her Majesty expects greetings of celebration and adoration from people whose families have been torn apart and who appear worn, tired, and hungry themselves. If anything, we are parading about to show them how this war has not affected us while it has changed everything for them."

"We are giving them something to aspire to, Sister Ora. A symbol of hope for better days." Princess Arminda cheerily chimed in.

Sister Ora turned to look at the older princess, furrowing her brow in frustration at the ignorance of her response. As she opened her mouth to retort, she felt Prince Percy's arm tug at her hand, catching her attention.

He shook his head in an ask for her to hold her tongue.

As she was trained to, Sister Ora obeyed.

Queen Onetta and Lord Tyrrian walked in-step in front of her children and Sister Ora, the pair consumed in their own quieted conversation. In place of warm smiles and friendly waving that the younger royals gave, Lord Tyrrian walked with his hands behind his back, occasionally nodding to acknowledge those they passed by and, while she did smile softly at those she saw, Queen Onetta held her hands in front of her, offering a momentary acknowledgement to the gathered people.

"How long do you believe His Majesty will be incapacitated today?" Lord Tyrrian quietly asked the queen.

"I do not know for sure, but from what the aids said, he was quite ill and may be out until tomorrow if the Healers medicines are slow to take."

Lord Tyrrian smirked slyly as he eyed her. "Well, in his absence, I hope to once again enjoy the sight of you bent over my bed, clawing at the sheets."

Queen Onetta sharply inhaled, her heart already racing, then shook her head. "Do not speak to me in that way here, Your Grace."

"Then I shall reserve the rest of my wonton commentary for later. Perhaps during the dessert course at dinner we can step away so that I can enjoy tasting something much more appetizing."

Queen Onetta darted her eyes to meet his. Where her eyes held much more restraint from what she was feeling, his unabashedly were filled with lust and longing as they met hers. She swallowed the dry lump in her throat and returned her gaze to the crowd surrounding them as her hands- still clasped together in front of her- tightened until her knuckles were white.

Sister Ora's eyes grazed over the new street of people they paraded down. The street was narrower than the higher streets they had come down and, while clean and the homes well kept, not as well decorated or abundant in color. Her wandering eyes caught on a stray rainbow of color nestled on the side of the tan and beige stone landscaping.

Set up outside of a small shop was a flower stand, filled to the brim with various cuts of flourishing botanicals. Not only did the blooms adorning the stand itself catch her eye, but the people gathered around it did as well, specifically, one person.

Sedrick.

Sister Ora nudged Prince Percy gently, nodding over at the flower stand.

"Maybe it would help if we actually spoke *with* the people instead of simply waving at them behind the protection of our guards. It likely would make them feel a better sense of solidarity with us."

Prince Percy nodded. "It would not hurt to try, I presume." then he guiding them towards the crowds.

Instantly, people's interests and excitement jumped at their approach and quiet murmurs turned into infectious smiles and loud exclamations.

Prince Percy began shaking hands, smiling at, and greeting those gathered as if they were long lost friends. Sister Ora followed suit and accepted the many congratulations at her engagement. The two princesses joined them in their interactions, occasionally trading a handshake and bow for a kind embrace with citizens.

Queen Onetta and Lord Tyrrian, however, stood by watching from behind their guards, perplexed and watchful.

Standing beside the flower stand that caught Sister Ora's attention was an elderly couple, both dressed in similar linen clothing and wearing cloth aprons with shears, ribbons, and other small items peeking out of their pockets. As Prince Percy and Sister Ora approached the couple, the elderly woman greeted them with a genuine gentle smile that crinkled throughout her face, showing the cracks and wrinkles gifted to her from her laborious epochs.

"Your Highness, when is the royal wedding?! We cannot wait much longer!" she teased Prince Percy in the same fashion that one's own nosy, but caring, grandmother would.

"It will be soon, we promise. Sister Ora and I have chosen to enjoy a long engagement and spend our time giving our thoughts and prayers to the men and women on the battlefield instead of focusing on the frivolity of a wedding." he answered, placing his hand on the elderly woman's arm. "Now, it would not make me a very good fiancé if I allowed us to pass by this immaculate stand without purchasing some blooms for my betrothed, would it?"

"Oh!" the woman exclaimed, jumping up and sharing a look of excitement with both Prince Percy and Sister Ora, as she teased again. "You are quite right, your highness, it would not!"

Prince Percy turned to look at his betrothed, his eyes softening and showing the quiet kindness that he rarely had a chance to show these days, nodding towards the flowers to encourage her to find ones that she enjoyed.

"And what kind of woman would it make me to turn down such an offer from a prince?" Sister Ora chortled as she stepped to intermingle with the flowers.

"Have you picked out your dress?" a brown-haired little girl, with a lisp given to her by the gaps in her missing front teeth, asked Sister Ora as she looked over the flowers.

Sister Ora stopped her search and bent down to the girl. "I have not yet, but I am quite certain that whatever I pick out would not be as beautiful as yours."

Sister Ora smiled as the girl grabbed the skirt of her dress and twirled around to show it in its entirety. The dress was quite simple, and a standard style for common-born children in the kingdom; a dark grey cotton dress with ribbon lacing up the front and a white underdress with long sleeves peeking out.

"Do you think you could help me pick out some flowers? I am certain a smart girl like you would be able to help me find the best of the bunch." she asked the little girl as she continued twirling.

The girl squealed in excitement and nodded her head eagerly before jumping right in front of Sister Ora- her parents exclaiming for her to re-member her manners, which the girl chose not to hear. She eagerly pointed to different flowers, now tugging at Prince Percy's pant leg to tell him which ones would be best for "a pretty lady". He laughed at her excitement and picked her up, holding her on his hip with one arm and using his other hand to pull flowers from their jars.

Sister Ora slowly stepped back, conversing with the girl's parents nearby as Princess Arminda and Princess Kalia went to the flower stand to find their own flowers. Out of view, Sedrick stood with his notebook and pen in hand, leaning casually against the side of the building and appearing disinterested in what was occurring.

"Well, it seems she has figured out how to make herself loved by *your* people." Lord Tyrrian mumbled at Queen Onetta as they both observed the interactions from the middle of the wall of guards.

"Yes, she certainly has. She does make it hard to hate her at times. Not impossible, just a bit more challenging." the queen responded with a tired irritation. "She is learning quickly how to play her role."

"Why is it that they are still to marry?" Lord Tyrrian inquired. "The entire decision was based upon your husband's belief that a marriage would ensure Ayeshire's alliance in what was brewing, and, here we are, promenading beside one of our enemies and welcoming her into your family."

"Unfortunately, breaking off their engagement would make us appear in poor light and, perhaps even worse, I believe my sweet Percy has begun to care for her. A stupid choice. I may be cold-hearted and cruel when needed, but I am a mother, and I do not wish to take all the happiness from my children." she smiled and her eyes darkened as she straightened her chin. "And besides, she could perhaps be a useful pawn for later."

As Prince Percy handed the flowers to the florist to wrap, he whispered into the little girl's ear, prompting another excited shriek from her. He laughed heartily and pointed at various stems on the stand. "How about these ones? Would you like these?" He asked.

She nodded her head quickly, her missing tooth grin beaming across her face as she did so. Prince Percy plucked a rainbow of flowers from their jars and handed them to the florist, exchanging them for Sister Ora's that were wrapped in brown parchment. Prince Percy set the girl down to wait for her flowers, then walked to Sister Ora, a look of hope on his face as he glanced between the flowers and his future wife.

During this shopping exchange, Sister Ora continued smiling and greeting the people, sharing kindness and pleasantries as she made her way down the line of those gathered on the wall. When her eyes met Sedrick's, they both snuffed out the familiar flicker in their stares and feigned themselves strangers.

"Good morning, sir, it is quite lovely to see you here today." Sister Ora smiled before reaching out her hand to embrace his in greeting.

Sedrick bowed. "It is quite lovely to meet you, my lady."

As their hands met, Sister Ora felt the roughness of parchment rub at her palm. She pulled her hand away, balling it into a fist and crumpling the note as she hid it from being spotted.

"Your Highness" Sedrick greeted Prince Percy as he stepped behind Sister Ora, a bundle of flowers in his hand and kindness in his stare.

"If you all may excuse us, I must steal her away for the day." Prince Percy smiled at the crowd and handed Sister Ora the flowers as they turned to walk away.

Sister Ora walked with the crumpled up note in her hand and, as covertly as she could, tucked it in the neckline of her dress when she believed enough eyes were not watching. The family continued their parade down the street for a few more moments, the descending hill growing steeper as they walked. Emotions among the royal group were riding high on the events that had just occurred, but faltered at them being stopped abruptly by the guards in front.

"Make way!" a King's Guard shouted at the crowd in front of the parading royal family.

The knights surrounding the royal family tightened their circle around them, blocking much of their view of the onlookers. While they could not see much, glaring stares and menacing faces peeked out between the shoulder pauldrons of the knights and waves of tension weaved over the armored wall. Hands fell to swords as the group of citizens blocking the street did not move.

"Move! Or you will be moved!" the guard shouted again.

"Fuck the king and fuck his war!" a voice shouted from the crowd.

As the man's exclamation finished, rotten food flew from the crowd, impacting the armored guards and arching over and onto the royal family. The hard plopping and bursting of the missiles grew in number as more foul words accompanied their impact and citizens on roofs and an overpassing walkway between two buildings picked up baskets reeking with mold and rot and found more projectiles to wield

A busted tomato made its way past the guards and hit Sister Ora in the chest, shocking her so much she jumped away from Prince Percy, dropping her flowers as she detached from his side. She clutched her chest where the food hit, her hand now covered in red. She looked up from the mess to find Sir Loren among the guards, but her feet refused to move and her body began to shake as more shrieks pierced the air and more rotten food flew.

A rotten vegetable aimed for Queen Onetta, impacting Lord Tyrrian when he stepped in front of her. Another flying object hit her in the back, splattering her dress in brown mess that smelt of sewage.

A semi-liquid chunk of brown stained Prince Percy's face and another covered the front of Princess Arminda's cream dress. A scream of disgust spit from her mouth at her realization of what it was that ruined the softness of her gown and was now flying en masse onto her family.

The crowd pushed into the guards, those with free hands still throwing filth and food while the rest worked to break through the line or solid armor. In the chaos, the guards unsheathed their weapons and fought back the citizens. The sounds of armored fists colliding with flesh and bone battled with shouting and threats of death on both sides of the push and pull.

Lord Tyrrian's voice boomed orders at the guards to carve a path in the crowd for them to escape through with sword and force.

Citizens fell to their knees and clutched the slices in their skin as they screamed their final words, heavier objects and rocks flew across the aisles, and the street became stained with blood, shit, and rotten messes.

And bodies.

In her panic, Sister Ora stayed frozen in the center of the chaos, not moving with the armor that forced a path for her. As her breathing picked up at an unbearably rapid pace, a strong hand jerk at her, whipping her around. She screamed and swung her fists and jerked her body away, only to strike at a metal chest.

"It is me; we must go!" Sir Loren exclaimed.

She shook her head and remained frozen in place with tears marking lines down her face, cutting through the stains and mess on her face.

"If you will not move, then you must pardon my touch, my lady." he shouted as he wrapped one arm around her back and jerked his other under her knees to pick her up. Despite the crowds, the chaos, and the weight of his armor and of her shaking body, Sir Loren ran through the crowd without so much as a break in his breathing.

Sister Ora wrapped her arms so tightly around his neck that, had his armor not been on, she was certain she would be choking him. As he ran through the shouting crowds, shoving, kicking, and forcing a path through anyone who stood in his way, she heard him repeating a panicked whisper.

"You're okay, I'm here. You're safe."

The knights and the royal family made it up the winding streets and into the safety of the castle gates. As the doors of the hall slammed shut, Sir Loren attempted to let go of Sister Ora and set her down, but as his grip loosened, hers tightened and her crying grew more noticeable in his ringing ears. He continued to quietly repeat his words of comfort as he kneeled with her and set her on the ground.

He kept his hand around her back, and she kept hers around his neck, her tight stronger than it was before, holding him in place so we would not leave her.

"I have you, you're safe." he whispered to her, tenderly rubbing his hand on her back.

Her crying slowly stopped as she finally pulled herself away from him, just enough to raise her red and swollen eyes to look at his through his helmet. The moment hadn't even begun before Prince Percy ran over and dropped down to kneel next to her.

"Pardon me, Sir Loren, but I have her."

Sir Loren's hands did not move, and neither did hers.

"Pardon me, *Sir Loren*, but I have her." Prince Percy's tone turned possessive and hard as he glared at the King's Guard and pulled his betrothed's hands away from Sr Loren and shifted himself between the two.

Prince Percy gently held Sister Ora's face. "Are you okay,?"

Sister Ora wiped at her tears. "Yes, yes I am okay now."

Prince Percy helped her to her feet and towards the rest of the gathered family, all sharing in their shock. The halls filled with the rushing of more armored feet to join the knights standing in guard and Sir Marion's voice was heard over the crowd, shouting in anger and demanding answers before he was even within earshot.

Princess Kalia's shrieked cries echoed into every stone of the castle, no one in the family in enough of a state to comfort of calm her.

Sister Ora turned her head back to where Sir Loren and the, beaten, dirty, and disheveled King's Guards stood in a line. His normally rigid stance and demeanor was softened and worn under the harsh lines of armor. As he stood in line with the others, his chest heaved up in down and his hands clenched and unclenched at his sides. His helmet did not turn to her as it always did when she was in the room, instead, it faced the ground and did not budge.

***

Prince Percy rested his forehead against his palm, his elbow set upon the table. He avoided looking up much as the rest of the King's Council continued with the shouting mess that they called meeting. The black eye he received in the street riot still stung and, while the swelling had not been substantial enough to shut his eye or blur his vision, the bruising pulsated if he strained his vision or mind too much.

King's Guards and Lord Priscius' Lord's Guards stood alongside the wall opposite, each taking turns giving their depositions on the events and answering King Ivan's probing questions and accusations.

"Your Majesty." Sir Marion interjected from where he angrily stood in front of the King's Guards, cutting the king off from interrogating the knights more about what they, in the king's own words, had allowed to occur.

King Ivan stopped his pacing and turned his predatory glare in Sir Marion's direction.

"I can assure you that my knights abided by every word of their oaths just as I am certain that Lord Priscius' did as well. They are not the ones to direct your anger at." The Master of Armor said.

"And how would you know this, Sir Marion? You were not there." King Ivan accused. "Where exactly *were* you while my family was being attacked?"

Sir Marion mirrored the king's defensive body language and tone. "One could ask you the same question, *Your Majesty*."

"Enough you two." Prince Percy rubbed his fingers along his forehead as he interrupted.

The king and his Master of Armor kept their darkened eyes locked on one another, but neither provoked the other further.

"Your Majesty, while we all share in your anger over the atrocities that were committed against the royal family, *your* family, Sir Marion is right. Those that are in this room are not the ones to give anger to. They are not the ones who initiated the riots that killed four innocents and three of our own guards." Father Figgins said.

King Ivan took a long, deep breath to calm himself then addressed the line of guards. "Thank you all for defending not only the lives of my family, but of many of our citizens. You are dismissed."

The line of guards bowed and took their leave.

"Sir Loren?" Prince Percy called out from his chair, his tone broken and defeated.

"Yes, Your Highness?" Sir Loren stepped out of the exiting line.

"Thank you." the prince swallowed his pride. "Thank you for saving her."

"I was doing my job, sir. When I swore my oath, I swore my life to protect her- to protect any placed under my guard." While spoken so matter-of-factly, anyone who listened closely could hear the broken care in his voice when he said *her*.

"Yes well, nevertheless, thank you."

"Of course, Your Highness." Sir Loren bowed, then left with the last of the knights.

"Your Majesty, if I may suggest, perhaps we could offer some compensation to the victims' families to help them during this time." Lord Barker suggested from where he sat, disheveled and no longer quiet and reserved in the corner. His hands tapped on the currency logbook in his lap. "It would be the right thing to do, to lend some sort of aid."

The king sat down and pulled a decanter of dark liquor to him, pouring himself a glass and keeping his silence.

Father Figgins spoke to the king while His Majesty took his first sip of drink. "Perhaps it would be. If anything, our reputation could use some cleaning up, Your Majesty."

Lord Barker grumbled as he looked down at the ledger book in his lap.

"Do you take issue with our care for our reputation, Lord Barker?" Father Figgins sneered.

"No, I do not, but, could we not simply do something for our people for the sake of the act? And not have our reasoning be for our own gain?"

"Every opportunity in front of us must be seized when it presents itself. You have been silent before on your apparent care, why are you speaking now?" The Hand began to lose his calm demeanor as he spoke down his nose at the Master of Coin.

"Both can happen at once." Prince Percy said before the argument could continue. "We can give coin to those who lost family in these riots, and we can find an opportunity outside of that to steer public opinion into our favor again."

King Ivan nodded and added, "Lord Barker, how much coin do you suggest?"

"We cannot spare enough to make the loss of the life any easier, but there is enough that we could give to ease their burden while the family adjusts to the loss. A few bits of heavy gold to each family could set some of them right for a epoch or so."

"Very well. Send the families what you believe could settle them for a single season and offer them our deepest condolences, let them know we are here if they need the crown's support." the king said before he took another large gulp from his glass. He slammed it down on the table. "Now onto our reputation. This day was meant to fix that. I was assured of that. And now, we have even more work to do. Father Figgins?"

Father Figgins had set his lips into a thin line as he conjured up a conspiracy. "Does our mortician have the victims' bodies yet?"

"Yes. They also have the bodies of the seven rioters who were killed during the attack. King's Guards were sent to aid them in collecting the bodies and clear the streets of any trouble." Sir Marion replied.

"Then might I suggest we hold a funeral, or at least a wake for the victims, Your Majesty? It may serve the crown well to do so; help us appear... sympathetic. Even the simplest funeral would aid our cause, but imagine what could happen if we treated their deaths as if they were one of our own?" Father Figgins proposed.

King Ivan paused and pondered, then nodded. "Let the families of the victims know that we shall host their funerals in our cathedral in three days; that shall allow them time to finalize their home vigils and complete their mourning ceremonies. You and the church may do whatever is necessary to ensure this funeral is as grandiose as if it were for one of our own."

Sir Marion spoke up again. "What shall my guards do with the rioters who lived and the ones who died?"

"For those who lived, have them to join the dead within the hour; their souls need not be prepared for where they are going." The king's eyes darkened as he met the eyes of Sir Marion. "And Sir Marion, you and the guards under my banners and Aishar's may do what you wish with their heads and bodies. So long as what is done is an insult to their existence. This will be our last warning to those who wish to test my throne."

CHAPTER 40

Somber weeps of broken-hearted citizens echoed throughout the cathedral hall, along the balustrades and ascended the pillars; continuing to permeate the air with such resolve that, if there truly was a heaven, the souls of the bodies being laid to rest would be able to hear the lamentations over their loss in their eternal home in the sky.

In the center of the cathedral, seven bodies laid elevated on catafalques draped with elaborately stitched white and gold sheets- symbolizing the purity and innocence of the deceased. From high above, sunlight broke through the stained-glass windows, and from below, lining the stone walls along the hall, rows of candles flickered; both forms of light illuminating the shapes of the bodies and giving harsh, cold, shadows where breath had once warmed their skin with soft hues of tan and laughter once flushed their cheeks red.

The first of the bodies was an Aisharian guard. His body laid in his golden armor with his hands on his chest and wrapped around the grip of his sword- the bloodied knuckles of his hands wiped clean and patched and his red cloak strategically draped around his sides to hide the tears in his flesh that his blood had poured out of.

Alongside his body rested two King's Guard soldiers, both laid in a similar fashion with their full armor on, armor that had been polished and repaired, gripping their swords on their chests. Their helmets were forgotten and left behind, leaving exposing their faces for those who came to pay their respects. The female guard's blonde hair laid long on her neck and puddled around her face. The tanned male guard beside her had a face of bruises and breaks and the glove on his left arm laid empty and flat.

Nestled in the hands of the four deceased civilians were bouquets of olive branches, tulips, and roses; botanicals which were common and well-loved in Britia and symbolized more than beauty and fine things. Two young lovers lay next to one another, dressed in elaborate clothes provided by the crown. Their bodies laid on the same catafalque, their hands intertwined with one another.

The final two victims of the tragedy were the hardest for any viewer to see and were responsible for the deepest of cries and flood of tears that stained cheeks and the stone floors they fell onto.

The soft wrinkled face of the elderly flower vendor that offered kindness and blessings to Sister Ora and Prince Percy placed a deep, painful, ache in the hearts of those who passed by. Her husband, who survived the rushing stampede that took her life, stood at her feet, his hands gripping tight the handle of his cane and his eyes burning red with tears that had not stopped since he placed her limp body in his lap in the street and begged the sky to give her life again.

Whispered words broke out between his choking tears. "Take me instead, please take me instead."

A brown-haired girl, whose face once lit up in a gap-toothed grin and spoke in giggles and lisps, was the last body in the line.

In her hand, different flowers were placed than the others. A rainbow of picked blooms brought brightness where her pale face sat drained and cold. She wore a dress made of the finest embroidered silks and softest fabrics, a softness that her life had not offered her before.

The royal family stood on the side of the cathedral stage, watching over the crowds as they made their way through. Each of them wore clothing in shades of black, the men in long tailcoats and pants and the women in long-sleeved modest dresses with veils. The king and Lord Tyrrian froze their faces in cold looks as they stood in the first row and nodded politely at those who walked past them in the receiving line.

Tears, even in this moment, were not suitable for men of their status.

Queen Onetta's face was cold and firm as she stood between the two men, her regal nature not breaking and subtle softness only finding its place on her expression when one met with her in the receiving line.

"Thank you, Your Majesties for holding this mass and service. It means so much." a female citizen spoke to the king and queen as she found herself at the front of the receiving line queue.

The queen allowed softness to find its place in her expression. "Of course, it is our pleasure and duty to aid our people where we can."

As the woman left to move down the line, the softness disappeared, only to return when eyes were upon her again. Many citizens made their way down the queue to pay their respects to the fallen only to turn and find their seats, avoiding the line to greet the royal family and the victim's families.

"They all should be in line waiting to greet His Majesty and offer thanks, not leaving the queue and sitting in wait." Lord Tyrrian mumbled between breaks in the queue.

King Ivan awkwardly fidgeted with the high collar of his tunic, moving it back into place after scratching his neck and adding to the redness that was already hidden there. "For once, my lord, I agree with what you are saying."

Queen Onetta hushed them both as another group moved forward in line.

In the row behind the leaders, standing alongside extended family members of the fallen and honored guests, Princess Arminda comforted an elderly woman whose kerchief was stained with her endless tears. The princess held one hand to the woman's back, rubbing it slowly as she offered kindness and apologies. Princess Kalia stood beside her sister, the floor at her feet her focus.

Prince Percy stood beside his sisters and his betrothed. The second prince did his best to emulate his father and uncle, choking back tears each time they began to flow to the surface. He held his jaw tight as it trembled. At his side, his hands fidgeted endlessly, moving between being balled into tight fists to being tensely flexed open and rigid.

His gaze never left the little girl's body as it laid out under the light from the windows, the rainbow glass illuminating a portion of her body.

Sister Ora wiped at her own tears and looked to him, seeing how hard he was struggled to be as composed as his father. She reached her hand to his and held it softly.

"The flowers were quite thoughtful, and beautiful." she whispered as she squeezed his hand.

He did not respond, and she diverted her attention back to the front, keeping hold of his hand.

"I never asked her name." he mumbled out, choking between each word. "I should have at least asked her for her name."

Sister Ora turned back towards him, expecting to meet his gaze but his water glazed eyes remained locked ahead.

"She died because of us, and I never bothered to get her name."

"Amelia. Her name was Amelia." Sister Ora softly responded. "I spoke to her mother as we gathered here."

Prince Percy's lips pursed and tightened as he nodded before squeezing her hand and rubbing his thumb along the knuckles of hers. "I couldn't bring myself to do that. Thank you."

The bells signifying the beginning of Mass shattered the air; seven tolls for seven lost souls.

Father Figgins stepped forward as the bells finished ringing and took his place at the pulpit centered on the stage. Parishioners who had gathered in the pews sat as he gestured for them to and those overflowing onto the side aisles of the church stopped their conversing and stood looking at him in their gathered groups. The royal family, and families of the deceased still gathered on the stage, took their seats on either side of the chancel stage.

"May the grace of god, our divine creator, and his blessings be with you always." Father Figgins began.

"And also with you." The church echoed back.

"We have gathered here today, in the wake of such a tragedy, for many reasons. We are here to pay tribute to the lives we have lost, to show our support for the families that are left behind, and to seek and receive comfort with one another.

"Not only does each member of this congregation feel a deep sense of loss over these seven souls, but our hearts and our prayers have been drawn towards their families and we shall continue to lift them up in prayer as they work to move forward in their lives and in their faith."

He took a deep breath as he looked to the families seated near the stage.

"Our hearts ache over these lives that have ended too soon. And while we each seek our own answers about the senseless acts that ended these lives, we must each trust in god and the destinies he has laid out for all of us, and lean into and trust in his plan, even in times of uncertainty."

He turned back to the pews and raised his chin. "In moments such as this, it is vital that we set aside our differences, extinguish our hate, quell our anger, and unite together as one community, under God and His eye."

Father Figgins grabbed a satchel from under the pulpit and descended the steps towards the laid-out bodies. As he stopped in front of the body of the brown-haired girl, he pulled two gold coins out and pinched them between his thumb and pointer finger as he raised it to the sky. As he began reciting the Prayer for the Dead the crowd joined him in recitation.

"Oh lord, grant these souls an eternal rest

and let your love and grace bring them peace.

May their souls bring light to the darkness of our nights

as your stars do each day.

Through your mercy,

may they now rest.

Amen."

As the prayer concluded, he rested the gold coins on her eyes and moved to the next catafalque, the Head of the Church and his parishioners repeating the prayer for all seven of the honored dead.

Upon the conclusion of the prayer and the laying of the coins, Father Figgin walked back up and stood behind his pulpit. He cleared his throat and gazed out at the crowd as he gave the Prayer for the Mourners.

"May gods love and the peace he shall bring to our newly departed souls
bless and console us,

let the love we hold for our loss

someday fill the holes we have in our hearts.

In his name,

Amen"

CHAPTER 41

"Apply the bishop's wort and wormwood ointment to his leg just above the marked point of incision. It may alleviate some pain in the area, but it is no poppy" Ephraim ordered to their aid. They narrowed their eyes. "Why are you looking at me in such a way? We do not have time to wait. Go. Now."

"We have also ran out of that. We have Healers creating more as we speak, but it has not cured yet to be of good use."

Ephraim let out a hard breath that shook. The Healer's patient wing was over filled, and the air reeked of blood, spoils, and the scents of the last of their ointments and healing aids. Groans of pain and retching from those nauseated by their ailments rang in their ears. Ephraim ran a hand over their bearded face, the texture of the grown hair an unfamiliar feel.

"I have to amputate this soldier's leg and you are telling me I have no ointments, no poppy, no opium? If infection won't take him, he may die of pain alone." Their voice was a harsh and hushed whisper as they stepped closer to their aid.

"We have older methods; a bite of a belt and swig of liquor may be all of the aid we have for him to make it through the pain." the aid said.

Ephraim counted their breaths and closed their eyes. "The liquor will thin his blood and our tourniquet may not stop that much bleeding... Find a leather strap and have him bite on it, we must hope he is strong enough to make it through this without any alleviation."

They turned and opened the door behind them, making their way into the makeshift operating room. Inside, strapped down to the table to prevent movement was a groaning and half-conscious patient. His leg laid exposed, redness and inflation covering the skin under his knee and the tip of a bone protruding from where it snapped in half on the battlefield.

Their eyes flicked to the aids laying out saws and small knives and arranging towels around the man.

"This operation should have occurred closer to the battlefield instead of him being sent here. If better treatment had been given sooner by the enlisted healers, we would not be here having to take his leg."

The two women nodded solemnly in agreement.

"Strap the tourniquet as hard as it will go, we will begin."

Ephraim moved to the nearby water basin and washed their hands in the cooled water that had been boiled as they blocked out the noises of pain behind their turned back as the man's leg was tied more. Their aid from the hall made their way inside and spoke to the man, informing him to bite down on the leather strap they placed in his mouth.

They dried their hands and turned, making their way to the operating table that had once been a sturdy desk. They held the operating knife steady in their trained hand and began their cut just above the infection point. They continued their incision despite the muffled shouting and restrained jerking of the man's body.

Ephraim peeled the skin back and laid it over the man's knee.

"Shit." They mumbled. The infected muscle and bone that laid beneath the skin had appeared clean and unaffected. Ephraim reached for a saw.

The patient jerked hard as Ephraim began sawing through their muscles and veins.

"Hold him still!" Ephraim shouted as they stopped with the saw halfway through a bone. More blood poured from where the tourniquet had loosened during the patient's jerking movements. "Tighten the tourniquet before he bleeds out!"

Aids laid their hands along his leg as one tightened the strap in an attempt to stop the bleeding that had begun. The patient's body convulsed against their grip and his straps as he screamed and spit out the leather strap.

Ephraim dug their hands into his leg to apply pressure and stop the bleeding, pinching veins with their fingers and covering their hands with his blood.

"Towels! Now! Apply pressure alongside me."

The convulsing stopped before the aids could move from their positions. The patient's head lolled to the side and his lifeless eyes met Ephraim's.

Blood trickled onto the floor as Ephraim stepped away and wiped their drenched hands with little purpose or true effort. The pain outside the door came in on the air as more patients cried in pain, more Healers and aids rushed down the halls and shouted orders, and more tears and souls left bodies.

They leaned against the wall and hung their head as the room stilled.

"How many does that make today?" Ephraim asked in defeat.

"Five." an aid replied.

"And it is only the morning."

***

The dirty and bloodied battle map laid out on the table in the cream-colored tent where Ayeshire and Sebern leadership gathered while their soldiers rested and healed in their battle camp. Atop it, scattered wooden discs and figures displayed the locations of all the known armies and assets in the kingdom- friends and foes of the gathered leaders. Around the table, taking up various positions, stood The Lords of Ayeshire and Sebern, the two eldest Torrin sons, Lord Digarius, and Sir Rainey.

"Prince Elion's army will continue to push us back by land- especially so when their allies join. He will only gain more if we split our forces as you are suggesting." Lord William Torrin shook his head in disagreement, "We saw what occurred when a battle happened without all of our power present, we should not like to repeat that."

He glared at Lord Digarius who firmed his own stature in response.

"But we will have no land to retreat to if we do not move some of our units back to Middleton Landing and around Sandhill House territory to defend once the Aisharian fleet comes in." Lord Theodus pushed.

"And your lands will be well defended, yes, but what about my army, my men?" Lord William snipped again.

"My lords, if I may, we likely do not have much time before the fleets would attempt to take the Gulf." Sir Rainey cut in, his eyes slowly moving between the two fuming men as he stood in confused awe at their vitriol at one another. "The Isles do not enjoy waiting, they often strike quickly. I have fought against them before, we do not have the luxury of time. Lord Torrin, your army outnumbers His Majesty's at this time, and more weapons are being sent in a caravan from Ayeshire. I believe you all will be victorious if anything were to occur while we move."

Lord Rener caught Lord Theodus' eye before turning his attention to his father. "Father, we cannot split our forces. We were the ones brought into this war to lend aid and now this war is falling our shoulders while they flee home."

"Fine words spoken by a man who has barely fought since joining the lines." Lord Digarius shot at him.

"We will not be left behind to fight your war for you, cousin." Lord William said. "If you wish to take a small convoy of soldiers and yourself away from the battle to go protect your home from an attack that may never come, then so be it, but we will not fight for you without your banners beside ours."

"What accusation are you making?" Sir Rainey asked.

The two lords glared at one another across the table.

Lord Theodus shook his head. "Sir Rainey, please begin informing our soldiers. We will *not* move our army, but we shall take a small convoy to Sandhill House where we will gather better information and lend our people aid for what *will* come to our shores. Lord Torrin and his heirs will lead our soldiers alongside our Sergeants in our absence."

"Right away, sir." Sir Rainey replied, bowing before turning to leave.

"Rener, Cossius, let us inform our troops as well of what we spoke of and have them lend aid to the departing troops." Lord William ordered before the Torrin men left Lord Theodus and Lord Digarius behind. Before the tent closed behind him, Lord William turned back to Lord Thedous, nodding in respect as he left.

Lord Digarius and his father waited several breaths before speaking, ensuring there were no listeners lingering outside of their tent.

"Do you believe this will work? The deviousness?" Lord Digarius asked, his tone still quiet.

"Wars are not only fought with swords and fists, but with minds as well." Lord Theodus nodded, "Keep an eye on our messengers. After what we discussed, I am certain our turncoat will waste no time in showing their hand and confirming who they are. And then, only then, will we go through with our true plan."

Chapter 42

Sister Ora pushed aside the thoughts plaguing her mind as she stepped out of her chambers and met with Sir Loren.

Bookshop at high noon- I'll be waiting each day.

She brushed away the reminder of what Sedrick had written on the envelope he snuck to her before the riot two knots ago. She refused to reminisce over the memorized lines of Lady Belva Montarian's request of her as they walked down the hall.

Her days and nights hidden away in the castle, leaving the safety of the stone walls only once for the funeral, had been spent obediently and quietly dining at meals with the royal family or hiding in her room convincing herself that the request that was made of her as too much.

Citizens of the king's city had made it clear during their riot that they saw her as nothing more than one of the royal family members. That she was no different than the enemies she dined with

Ayeshire could win the war without her. She need not put herself in the way of danger again.

She was not made for deviousness.

Sister Ora stopped at the entrance they had come upon. She looked out through the open doorway, at the sun lighting the path ahead and the foliage trimming the open walkway.

"My lady, we do not have to leave the walls and walk the grounds if you do not wish." Sir Loren quietly said.

She inhaled and straightened her shoulders, then let out her breath and counted out the calming exhale. "No, let us go. I need to not be cooped up in the darkness any longer. It is just a promenade through the gardens."

"The castle grounds are still well locked down from outsiders. We are safe." he assured.

The two leisurely made their way to the Royal Gardens, walking side-by-side as they both had grown accustomed to doing. The late day sun had turned from a bright ball of yellow to a soft orange as the afternoon had concluded and it began to set for the day. The soft beams cut through the trees, tall bushes, and stone pillars along their path, adding more color and depth to the most beautiful part of the castle grounds.

They came upon a small side entrance to the gardens marked by an archway crawling with purple bell vine flowers wrapped around the curves of the arch. The sunshine and adequate rain showers had been quite kind to the gardens this season, including the bell flowers that now grew so heavy and lush that they draped so dramatically that one would be brushed by the sweetly fragranced petals as they walked through.

As they approached, Sir Loren's hand raise from its favorite resting place- the pommel of his sword- and move over her head, brushing the draping flowers out of the way for her as he paused to allow her to walk through first.

The walkways of the garden were busy, more so than normal, and likely due to no one in the castle having anywhere else to spend their time safely after being cooped up from the public for so long. Conversations carried throughout the gardens by High Scholars who lived in the Hall of Archives barracks and off duty servants and vassals found moments of relaxation between their duties.

The pair slowly walked the grounds, Sister Ora stopping frequently as others greeted her and attempted to bring her into conversations she wanted no say in.

A stroll of quiet contentment was not in the stars for her today.

"I think too many others had the same desire today, Sir Loren. Perhaps I should retire back to my chambers before dinner." she sullenly said.

"As you wish."

The two made their way out of the gardens, taking to another side entrance to avoid running into many others. The pathway led them to a long stone bridge that ran over a typically busy street and overlooked the city before converging with other paths on the grounds and leading to an interior hall of the castle.

As the bridge came into quick view, Sir Loren became tense and paused.

"I believe we should take another path." he said.

"Why? This pathway leads us directly there, just the same as all the others." She shrugged.

"It's just- I don't want- It would be best if -" he stuttered and stammered over his words, unable to finish any statement he started.

"Sir Loren, I am not sure what is wrong with you, but please, let us continue on."

She did not wait for any stammering response before continuing her path; hearing his armored feet come up quickly behind her before settling in-step with her.

"It's just I do not wish for you to be scarred by the sight left on this bridge." he finally spit out in panic.

"What sight are you —" her statement went unfinished as she took several hasty steps onto the bridge, looked up, and stumbled back.

The bridge posts that normally lit the way in the setting sun and darkness of night carried no flames, only bloodied and rotting heads.

Her hand flew to cover her mouth to hold in the shriek of horror and bile building in her throat. As she tried to catch her breath, the stench of rotting flesh and decay assaulted her senses and the bile in her throat grew more. She moved her hand to cover her nose to try to keep the stench out, but after two knots in the sun, the air was far too riddled with it for her efforts to help at all. Her stomach lurched as her eyes refused to look away from the sight; the rotting flesh left on the skulls stained black and dark by time and the sun, chunks of hair that remained were covered with fallen pieces of flesh and birds and bugs pecked and ripped at what remained.

As she began to feel incapable of holding in her tears and vomit, Sir Loren stepped in front of her, blocking her view. He set a gloved hand on her shoulder and squeezed it gently.

"Take a deep breath, my lady and let us move quickly past this place. I am sorry I did not stop you from seeing this sooner." his apologetic and softened tone and gestures of comfort helped ease her horror and allowed her a moment to settle her stomach as she took several deep breaths to gain her composure.

"Were these — are these the one's who attacked us?"

Sir Loren held a long pause, then nodded.

"Yes, they are. We executed them in the dungeons and their heads placed here while the city was at the funeral. The king wanted to ensure that everyone around these walls knew what would happen if they attempted to harm you all again."

"Did you help?"

"What?"

"Did you help them do this?" she asked.

He swallowed a lump and shifted on his feet, "I did, my lady."

Sister Ora swallowed the bitter sting of the bile in her throat and straightened herself. As she replayed the events of that day in her head, remembered Amelia's body lying in the church and all the others who were lost because of them, her malice against the royal family and disgust with the display of gore in front of her was outweighed by the fury she felt.

"Good." She replied sternly. "These people deserved this."

"Yes, they did." The slick and cunning voice of Sir Marion cut in from the bridge.

Sir Loren dropped his hand from her shoulder and turned, saluting Sir Marion as he casually sauntered over to them. Sister Ora turned her bubbling anger and glare in his direction as he stepped in front of the two and nodded in greeting.

Sir Marion turned his eyes down to his hands. In one hand was a small fruit carving knife; the handle of it enveloped in his closed hand, his thumb sat running alongside the dull back of the blade. In his other hand was a ripe mango with much of the skin already carved off, exposing the bright yellow and juicy fruit underneath. He pushed the blade along the ridges of the fruit and cut a large piece off as he spoke.

"All traitors and rebels to the crown deserve this fate- or worse."

He turned his head back towards the rotting heads, still buzzing with flies and crows flying back to roost and peck. He took a slow bite from the piece of mango on the blades edge as he looked at the gore.

"Don't they, *my lady*?" Sir Marion mocked as he turned back to her.

She tried to steady her face and appear unbothered by his words and attention.

He took a step closer to her and finished off the fruit left on the knife, his eyes staying on hers as he swallowed. He left his hand at his mouth and slowly kissed the juices off his thumb. A sly, crooked smile crawled across his face as he lowered his hand and leaned in closer to her, licking his lips.

"May I call you that? Or is Sir Loren the only one who you let speak to you that way?"

Her anger stayed with her and her well-ingrained decorum left her. "What you may do is step away from me and forget every disgusting thought that may be running through your mind."

Sir Marion's entire expression tensed; his eyes narrowed and darkened, and his lax demeanor became rigid at her response.

"*Now*." she growled.

Sir Marion's hand shot up to her chin, the sticky blade held along her neck as his jaw became so tense it looked as if his teeth would shatter under the pressure. They both heard Sir Loren's sword coming unsheathed

"Sir Loren stand down or I shall have you executed." Sir Marion ordered in a controlled tone, his glare still on her. "You do not give me orders, *you little cunt.*"

Sister Ora stepped forward, the blade of his knife moved into her skin. Her lip twitched into a snarl.

"And you do not threaten me, Sir Marion. You and I both know what would happen to you if you put one scar on my face." She moved her neck closer to his blade, begging him to try. She made a mocking voice filled with false fear, "Prince Percy, Your Majesty, I've never been so scared in my life. I feared for my life and I do not know what to do. Why, if it had not been for Sir Loren, I do not know what else he would have done to me."

She forced a tear to roll down her cheek.

Sir Marion growled and dropped his hand, his breath intense and deep.

He stormed off in the direction the pair had come from, and Sister Ora let out a harsh breath and brought her hand to her neck where she still felt the pressure of his blade. Adrenaline and shock coursed through her body as her mind caught up to what occurred and how she held herself.

"Where the hells did that come from?" she whispered to herself.

"Are you alright?" Sir Loren begged as he moved beside her, not giving her an inch of space from his body.

She nodded, blinking repeatedly to try to center herself in some way as she worked through the feeling of the rapid beating of her heart and intensity of her shock. "Yes, yes I am. Let us get away from this wretched place."

The two quickly took off across the bridge, her heart still pounding and her anger still seething inside of her. Beside her, Sir Loren's hands were balled into tight fists and his breath was short and harsh. Their quickened and angry pace made short work of their path to the chamber halls and their steps only began to slow once they entered the hall that held her chambers.

Every bone in her body screamed at her for acting the way she had. She was supposed to act properly, to be obedient and listen to those in ranks higher above her. Obedience and propriety had been molded in her since her mother trained her through her neglect and hateful words that forced Sister Ora into learned perfection. It had been even more engrained in her in her schooling and apprenticeships when she had learned that praise and pride were only given when she excelled at doing what she was told to do and when her presence was enjoyed when she became the chameleon each group around her asked her to be through their actions.

Especially in this place, she was not to act in such a way as she did.

And yet, she had. And for the first time in many moons, her actions had felt her own.

The pair made it to her chamber doors and she stepped inside, hesitating to let go of the handle and instead twisting it back and forth in her hand as she stood inside the doorway. Sir Loren stood in the hall, waiting for her permission to leave. She looked around her chambers, taking in how everything appeared at this time of day, when only the candlelight lit up the room.

The pile of books on her desk, all haphazardly stacked and strewn about, the plushness of the pillows and blankets on the neatly made bed, the closed curtains that often billowed in the breeze when the windows were open, and even the elegantly carved wood furniture all appeared so soft in the amber glow of the candle flames.

Her heartbeat and breath, after finally being calmed, picked up again as she heard Sir Loren's stance shift behind her. She turned her head over her shoulder to look back at him; her jaw softened and her lips parted as she looked at the cold metal helmet fixed on her.

"Is there anything else you need from me, today?" Sir Loren asked.

Her chest heaved up and down as she continued to look at him, just steps from her.

"Yes." she said so softly it was barely audible.

"Okay." he replied, his stance shifting again. His hands that had been hard fists just moments ago twitched at his sides and his armored shoulders and chest began to move more noticeably as his breath seemed to intensify to match hers.

She continued to look at him as she let go of the doorknob; her fingers slowly running over it as her hand fell to the side. She stepped forward into the room before turning her entire body to face him, her breathing still intense and deep.

"Come here." she replied softly again.

He did not move.

"But only if you would like." she added, her tone now insecure in her ask.

Sir Loren's breath picked up again. Finally, he stepped towards her, the face of his helmet still transfixed on her as it always was, and stopped in front of her, leaving only breathing space between them.

"Close the door." she asked.

He moved his hand out and gently pushed the door to close behind him.

The soft silence between the two filled the room for several moments.

"Is there anything else you would like from me?" his deep voice mumbled down at her.

"Remove your helmet. Please. I wish to see the face of the man who swore his life to protect me."

He continued to look down at her as he shook his head- *no.*

His hands moved from his side as he gently wrapped his hands around her fingers and raised her hands to touch the bottom of his helmet. As her fingers rested on it, he shifted his touch to wrap around her wrists. He let out a soft, broken, breath and nodded his head as she lifted his helmet off.

Every part of her being was entranced by the man underneath the helmet that had been hidden for too long.

The helmet fell to the ground as she ran her hands gently over his features; his soft and crinkled cheeks, square jawline, and ridges of his prominent nose were soft in the candlelight. His dark brown locks of wavy hair were flattened against hi pale skin from the helmet. Sister Ora delicately ran a hand up his cheek and through his waves, loosening them and allowing them to settle messily on top of his head. He closed his eyes and let out a breath as her fingers moved in his locks.

As she moved her hand to rest on his stubbled jawline- both hands now holding him there, she brought her eyes back to meet his steel blue admiring stare.

"Why do you always hide behind your helmet?"

He wrapped his hand around the back of hers and laid his index finger over hers, closing his eyes as he did so. He moved their fingers along the long, deep scar that ran down his forehead, over his left eye, and down his cheek. He opened his eyes as he rested their hands back on his cheek, keeping his gently wrapped around hers.

"Ah." she softly let out.

The two stayed like that for a moment, breathing deeply and staring longingly before she broke the stillness of their bodies and raised herself on her tip toe. She moved her face closer to his, her lips barely grazing his jaw and scarred cheek. Her lips paused over the scar as she softly set a kiss on it and then turned, resting the bridge of her nose alongside the side of his.

"Tell me if you would like me to stop." she whispered, her moving lips brushing up against his.

Sir Loren held his grip on her hand and moved his other to rest on her hip, bringing her body more into his, "I would never do such a thing."

The sensation of his lips grazing the edges of hers and the sound of his deep, velvet voice unfiltered by the cold metal of his helmet sent an aching heat through her. She let out a hot breath before both pushed their lips together in a kiss so long they only separated to take a breath.

At the break of their deep kiss, Sir Loren's hand broke away from hers and he reached down, grabbing a handful of her backside with both hands and pushing her fully against him as he moved his mouth back onto hers.

Her hands moved to the back of his neck and the waves of his curls. Both held forcefully onto one another as their breathing quickened and their kisses deepened. Sir Loren moved his mouth and tongue away and ran it down her chin and along her jawline and neck, offering love and softness where Sir Marion's knife one was.

As he kissed, licked, and softly grazed his teeth along her neck, Sister Ora moved her hands, down his body and to the armored tasset at his waist. She found the buckle that kept it tied to his body and undid it before throwing it the ground around him and moved her hands where it once hung, running her hand along his hardened crotch.

Both let out a harsh, moaning breath at the sensation; Sir Loren's at the pleasure he felt at her touch and her at feeling the size. He crashed his lips back into hers as she reached for the laces on his pants and undid them, pulling him out.

She was not granted a moment of touch before his grip on her body intensified and he turned and shoved her towards the closed door, using his hand as padding for her head as he pinned her against it. He broke away from their kiss and ripped off his leather gloves then reached down and pulled her dress up over her waist; enveloping her in a kiss again as he held her dress up with one hand and moved the other between her legs.

Both moaned at his touch, and it was only seconds before Sister Ora moved her hand to wrap around him, stroking him the best she could without getting in the way of what he was doing beneath her bunched skirts. Sir Loren growled into her ear before grabbing her wrists and pinning them up above her head.

"*Stay*." he ordered as his hands moved back down to pull her dress back up.

He grabbed the back of her thighs and jerked her body up, wrapping her legs around his waist and began slowly pushing into her, moving one hand from under her thigh to trace circles on her clit as he pushed in and out of her. She cared not that the hard steel of his chest and leg armor painfully pushed against her exposed skin.

She disobeyed what he asked of her and moved her hands to wrap around his neck as he continued to kiss and bite her. With every movement of Sir Loren's hips the door rattled on its frame, growing louder and louder alongside his grunts and her moans.

Then, without warning, Sir Loren stopped and pulled away, gently setting her down as he stepped back from her.

She stood in place against the door, barely able to stand as her entire body was consumed in pure sensation and her breath came short and fast. Her hair and dress were disheveled and out of place and her skin flushed in red. They both stared intently at one another before he shook his head.

"This is not right."

"What?" she stammered out in a broken gasp.

He charged forward again and wrapped his hands in her hair, kissing her again, harder and rougher than before. "I need to see and to touch every inch of you."

He guided her towards the bed, stopping at the corner of it, and broke their kiss and turned her to face the bed. His deep, hard kisses from before were replaced with soft kisses along the back of her neck as he pushed her hair over her shoulder. His hands moved to the bottom of her dress where her corset met the skirt, untying the ribbon holding the lacing in place. She rested one hand on the carved poster of the bed and reached the other one behind her head so that she could wrap her hands in his hair as he moved around behind her.

He continued to place delicate kisses on her exposed back as his fingers unlaced her dress. He moved his mouth up to meet her ear, and slowly and softly whispered as he worked, "Shall death come calling at my door, I will answer it with glee and contentment, so long as before I go, I first get to know the taste of your lips and the sound of your voice when you first wake. Only then will my heart know what it truly means to live and to love."

She let out a deep, heated breath at his words, "You remember the poem from that day in the garden."

He finished unlacing her dress and moved his hands to her shoulders, pushing the fabric down and exposing her sheer chemise underneath, "I remember everything you say."

Her dress fell into a puddle on the ground as she undid the ribbon of her underdress and turned to face him. He wrapped his hands around the skirt of the chemise and pulled over her head, tossing it to the ground beside them. She stepped out of the puddle of fabric to him and placed both of her hands on his broad armored shoulders.

He ran his hands over her body, tracing each thick curve, dimple, and line she had. The rough callouses of his hands slowly feeling every part of her.

She moved her hands over his armor; her look turning from lust to confusion as she tried to figure out how to remove the pieces. He let out a low chuckle as he untied one of the shoulder pauldrons from the arming doublet he wore underneath.

The two took turns quickly untying the armor from his doublet and, without much care, tossing them onto the pile of clothing at their feet. As the last piece of armor came off, Sister Ora moved her hands to the edges of the padded doublet and pulled it up overhead, allowing Sir Loren to toss it to the side as she ran her hands over his broad muscles and hard skin.

Her hands traced down his abs to the top of his pants, following the trail of curly hair down his stomach.

She looked up at him from under her eyelashes and went to her knees.

She undid the laces of his boots and ran her hands up the sides of his pantlegs to the hem. As she gripped the fabric in her hand she shifted forward, her mouth a hair away from where he hung erect, and pulled his pants down to his ankles. A teasing smile broke out across her face as she watched his reaction and heavy breathing as he stared down at her. She opened her mouth, her tongue licking the head of him, long and slowly several times.

His hand shot to the poster of the bed, gripping it hard. His other hand to the nape of her neck and pushed her head up.

"*Up.*" he said.

She smiled and shook her head at him. He rubbed his thumb along her lower lip. "You are not in charge right now, love."

She felt a harsh hard breath escape her lungs and a deeper heat throbbing through her. She stood up to face him and was met with several short, but passionate, kisses as he leaned forward and moved her until she lay on the bed. Sir Loren pulled back and stood between her legs dangling from the bed, her body at the edge of the mattress. He continued to watch her, his piercing blue eyes breaking through the darkness that the candles barely kept at bay, their deep harsh breaths filling the air.

Epochs of wearing armor and fighting in battles gave him a strong body, but the sharpness of his broad muscles were softened by padded contours of skin and curves.

He fumbled around at the end of the bed, kicking his pants and their pile of clothing out of his way.

Still staring at her, he licked his lips and dropped to his knees.

He kept his eyes locked on hers as he moved his mouth around her inner thighs; slowly and deeply, just as his kisses from earlier, before moving his tongue in light and quick flicks once he found the spot between her legs that sent shivers down her spine so quickly that her back arched in anticipation. He let out a devilish smile and finally let his mouth and tongue meet her clit; his tongue deeply rubbing against every sensitive nerve and spot. Each time her body twitched or bucked, he sucked and licked deeper; his hands wrapped around her thighs holding her down and his eyes staring deeply up at her and watching.

Sister Ora felt the heat building inside of her, and by the way her body responded- her stomach twitching and her shaking and sharp breaths- it was obvious to Sir Loren how close she was. He continued for a few seconds longer before pulling his mouth away and moving it along her thighs, kissing and caressing the red spots on her legs that had been pinched against his armor earlier.

She let out a short, shocked breath and shot a look down at him. His eyes were locked on hers still as he gave a small smile and bite on her inner thigh before moving back to where he was.

"Not yet." he teased.

Sir Loren played this game only twice more- driving her to the edge only to pull away at the last second- before even he couldn't take it anymore and drove her over the edge so deeply that her body jerked up and her back arched, going completely stiff as her entire body became a burning hot fire that Sir Loren did not allow to stop.

She cried out as he pushed her through another moment of intense ecstasy and pleasure. She let out several deep pants of breath, her thighs quivering and shaking as they settled down on the bed.

He made his way over top of her, his hands on either side of her head and holding him up. He brushed off the water that had fallen from her eyes with his thumb, smirking at what only his tongue had been able to do. He ran his eyes over her face again and smiled when she finally opened hers to look up at him. As she smiled back, he locked it in with a kiss before moving back away from her, kneeling between her legs.

She reached her hand up to touch his face and beckon him to kiss her again but stopped as she felt him slowly push all the way into her. She sighed deeply and her eyes rolled back as he continued to move slowly and deep inside her, both feeling every single inch of movement.

He dropped to his elbows as he moved, one hand holding her hips in place, and moved his mouth around her neck, decolletage, and every inch of her mouth as he kept pushing into her slowly. In between kisses, sharp breaths, and moans, he kept whispering one word into her ear, over and over again, not as a form of possession or ownership, but as an ask and a plea.

"Mine. Mine. Mine."

She ran her hands over his broad shoulders, thick arms, and down his strong back. The feeling of her nails along his skin and the movement of her legs wrapping around him turned his slow and passionate thrusts into deeper, faster pushes.

Every time she tried to respond to his verbal plea, she lost her breath until finally she was able to gasp a reply out.

"Yours. I am yours."

CHAPTER 43

"Your people seem to be as restless as the rest of the continent, Your Grace." Lula said to Lady Catherin Torrin as she stood behind her, brushing out her hair while Lady Catherin read the note she received.

"Yes, it appears so. I should have known it would only be a matter of time before Lady Edgel would take advantage of this war and restart her attempts again." her tone was sullen and disappointed. "It seems everyone is finding their own way to strike at one another."

Lula set the brush down and began braiding Lady Catherin's hair, pulling braided bits back and pinning them in place. "The other servants and I were talking this morning at tea about what is occurring at the border. With the Lady of Craigie and her people having taken several Odessian camps and moving closer to Broken Tower, should we fear our own towns along our border to be attacked?"

"Oh no," she replied, setting the letter down. "While there are still some personal tensions between our families, Kathilla has no real quarrel with us."

Lula set her hands on Lady Catherin's shoulders and looked in the mirror in front of them, making eye contact through the reflection. "I am glad to hear it, Your Grace. Is there anything else you need from me this morning?"

"Just some help out of this chair, if you could, please." she grunted as she turned to try to stand. "I have only three moon phases left before this baby is born but it feels as if she could come at any moment."

Lady Catherin nodded her thanks to her lady's maid as she helped her up and waddled off to the doorway and made her way down the hall for the second breakfast she was starving for. As she neared the kitchens, she heard the voice of Corporal Barclay, a soldier stationed within their walls and serving as a temporary advisor and strategist for her.

"Your Grace!"

She sighed. *So close.*

She turned around, plastering a warm smile on her face. "Yes, Corporal Barclay?"

"We have news from Odessin about the border fights." Corporal Barclay, said, out of breath and nervous as always.

"Well, yes, I am aware, I received note this morning about the camps."

"No, this. This is different." his features paled and his skin turned clammy as his hazel eyes widened.

"Well, out with it, Barclay. What is it?"

"Odessin sent word to us to warn that they are sending Madam Fury to put a stop to what Lady Edgel and her people have done. They have advised us to keep our border patrols out of it, or else Madam Fury will... well, you know what she does to those who dare cross her."

Lady Catherin's rested her hands on her stomach. "How many days until she and her soldiers arrive? Do we have time to write to our own and warn them?"

"We do. I can have a scribe write to Lord and Lady Lisarian at Broken Tower immediately, but I am certain that His Grace already knows given all of his eyes along the lines of our countries." He nodded rapidly and fidgeted with the parchment in his hands.

"Get on that quickly, please. And keep me informed of any more news." she said firmly.

"Right away, Your Grace. Should we not... should we also write to Lady Edgel and warn her?"

Her lips firmed in a line and her jaw twitched. "No. Kathilla has made this bed for herself, let her lie in it. We cannot interfere."

"Won't she be angry that we knew and did nothing?" he cocked his head, fidgeting even more with his hands.

She cocked an eyebrow at his questioning of her, but let it go. "She may, but her blood still boils over the last time we interfered in their fights without their consent and request." She let out a sad sigh. "I pray that my brother's spirit will calm her anger if she so chooses to hate us for stepping aside this time."

***

Five wolf carcasses laid across the unlit pyre, their bodies surrounded by offerings of produce and flowers, gold coin and stones. Ancient runes were drawn in blood on each animals forehead, a new rune for each of the five Vahar gods. Lady Kathilla and her children stood in front of the crowd of Craigie fighters all gathered in their forbidden worship.

The first wolf, a pelt of white and light grey, had a red swirl painted on its face symbolizing the cycle of birth, life, and death, the three realms Thirdall looked over. A straight line with two diagonal lines jutting from one side was drawn on the face of the second wolf, whose pelt was a darker grey. The rune symbolized abundance and prosperity, two blessings that Beihnur, the god of light, abundance, and prosperity gave just as much as he took when one showed themselves undeserving of his blessings.

A female wolf, whose pelt shimmered with dark and light fur, laid next with a rune in the shape of a 'p' with an 'x' in the center. Niyja's spirit laid over her offering, the goddess of love who guarded and gave all emotions and ensured the world remained balanced between love and darkness.

Two black wolves laid beside one another, the first with an eye painted between the wolves open two eyes. Altinir watched over the offering ceremony through the third eye, the god of knowledge and prophecy. A rune that appeared as a snake in a knot adorned the final black wolf, laid out for the trickster god, Qyi, who enjoyed creating chaos for their own enjoyment or when they found their worshippers needed to learn a lesson.

Lady Kathilla lit the torch in her hand using the small fire beside her. She stepped forward to the unlit pyre containing their offerings then turned to her people.

"May the light of the Vahar be upon you and may it guide you. May our cause be worthy of their blessings, may our lives be worthy of their embrace when we meet our end." She turned to the large man and woman dressed in pelts, a shaking man between them. She nodded at them, and they brought their sacrifice to her.

Barron stepped forward and poured a bottle of liquor over the sacrifices head. No scream came from their sacrifice's mouth, his tongue taken so he could not speak in disrespect to the Vahar when he was given to the gods, and his orange tunic ripped apart exposing the runes carved in his chest.

"And may our offerings be worthy of their enjoyment."

The sacrifice was moved up onto the pyre, small wooden logs making short steps to the center of the offering pyre. He stood with his head bowed and his hands tied. He did not look up as Lady Kathilla threw the torch at his body and his skin burst into flames.

He fell to his knees and his body convulsed in quiet pain as the abundant offering to the old gods lit aflame and sparks flew in the air around the worshippers taking in the ceremony.

Lady Kathilla stood close to the fire; her fur cloak discarded before the ceremony and only her leather vest and pants covering her body. She closed her eyes and raised her arms out to her sides.

A warm, pulsing hum separated itself from her pulse. Embers of the fire met her exposed skin, but she felt no burn.

CHAPTER 44

Sister Ora shifted the papers and books around the table, unsatisfied with what she had in front of her. Her searching in the Hall of Archives had proven barely useful to her task, the books and parchments she found only hinting to the information she needed.

She nervously glanced around the generously sized library. She had sequestered herself away from others, and Sir Loren's presence helped deter the most helpful or nosy of Scholars from browsing her table of research. While no eyes were upon her, her anxiety still heightened knowing one could be watching without her notice.

But the day drew closer to the lunch hour and her piles of research grew taller, soon to draw attention she could not have.

She picked up a pile of parchments and a few books she had taken from the same section and hurriedly put them back where she had found them, hoping to cover her steps. After only a brief moment away, she made her way back to where Sir Loren still stood.

Standing among the remains of her research was Prince Percy, finding intrigue in what she had left on the table.

"Oh, oh I apologize, Your Highness. I was not aware that you arrived." she curtsied awkwardly as she fumbled over her apology.

Prince Percy smiled and laughed. "It is quite alright. And I owe you my apologies for sneaking upon you. My vassal informed me that our lunch is prepared and waiting for us as you had requested. I know we had agreed upon meeting there at the noon hour, but, I thought we could walk together."

He gave her a sheepish smile.

"Of course, that would be lovely." she smiled and moved to walk in line with him, the pair followed by their guards.

Prince Percy strode with his hands clasped behind his back, alternating his glances between politely acknowledging all who passed by and looking dead pan and straight-forward. The dark circles under his eyes more prominent with each tired smile he gave.

His tired eyes and his features made him appear a ghostly shell compared to the full cheeked and bright-eyed prince she had been betrothed to in the spring. Summer was at the beginning of its end, and Prince Percy's appearance had changed with the season.

Where his curls were typically pushed back and controlled, today they fell about, looking as if hands had been run through them one too many times. His dark doublet fell just below his knees where a gold and red floral trim ran along the bottom hem and up the center, the fabric splitting open before meeting the gold buckled black belt he wore.

The same detailed fabric that trimmed the hem also made up the square collar, shoulders, and a portion of the chest in an intricate and wavy V-shape cut. While his doublet was more intricate and darker than what he typically wore, underneath it his pants and boots were the same, simple style he had often wore before.

"I saw you had out a history book and some parchments on the castle's manner. I did not know you enjoyed architecture. What was it that had sparked your curiosity?" he asked, his voice innocently curious, the type of tone one takes when making polite conversation to break stone silence.

She shrugged, keeping her eyes forward and not meeting his side glances. "I thought that since this is to be my new home, I should know as much as I can about it. At the Landing, Lady Montarian often gave historical tours to guests. I thought maybe, one day I might be tasked with something similar, and wanted to learn more."

The lie rolled off her tongue too easily for her own comfort.

He gave her a halfhearted smile. "I am sure we could arrange such a thing in the future. Although, I could probably tell you more about the castle and its history than any of those old dusty books. When my brother and I were quite little we used to run around the servant's halls and hidden passages in the castle. I am certain my mother spent most of her time in our youth asking someone to find out where we had run off to and lecturing us about hiding in passageways."

He laughed and smiled at the memory.

She replied softly a as they entered the small courtyard set with a picnic for the pair. "I would love that."

Scents of lavender and thyme drifted in the cool breeze across the grassy yard. From above, birds chirped and gossiped in the branches of the oak trees and an occasional pair would flap down into the grass to pick for worms and clippings for their nests.

Sister Ora moved to the blanket laid out on the ground, strewn with pillows and trays of food. She ignored the small stools and proper seating and plopped down gently onto a soft pillow.

Prince Percy sat down beside her, albeit, with less grace as she had in her simple soft dress.

"I must say, this was quite a lovely idea- to get away from the family and all of our duties for an afternoon lunch." he picked up a glass and poured a drink, eyeing the various foods laid on trays. "But I admit, I have not eaten in this manner before."

"This is how my old friends and I enjoyed spending our spare afternoons back in Middleton Landing. This yard reminds me faintly of the hilltop field at the forests edge where we would enjoy picnics and one another's company." Prince Percy handed her the glass he had filled for her, her tone turning soft and sad, "I do quite miss those days and my friends."

The prince swirled the wine around in his own cup, turning his stare from her to the swirls of red, "Maybe when this war is done, and wounds are healed we could go visit."

"I would like that very much."

Prince Percy kept looking down at his wine, awkwardly cleared his throat, "It is quite common after a royal wedding for the newlyweds to tour the kingdom together... as a part of their... honeymoon."

Her heart stopped and the sweet red wine she sipped burned as she forced herself to swallow it. Images seared through her mind of Sir Loren's rough calloused hands running along her body and his mouth tracing lines along her spine. They glimmered away as quickly as they came but were replaced with the bloodshed she had witnessed at the hands of the crown and her imagination filled in the brutality that she had heard her friends were facing on the battlefields.

"I am sorry, I should not have mentioned that. I know that our arrangement is not something that..." his voice trailed off as he lost his words.

"I think it would be lovely to be able to show you where I spent my childhood and many of my adult epochs. You have been so busy with your new duties and work that I do not believe either of us have gotten to share much about when we were younger." She locked eyes with him. "I do remember the start of an entertaining story about you and your brother spending your childhoods running and hiding throughout the castle, perhaps we begin there."

She softly tilted her head to the side, allowing her loose waves to fall around her shoulders and she smiled sweetly at him.

Prince Percy smiled and he recounted tales of his childhood hide-and-seek adventures with Prince Elion and later on Princess Arminda when she was old enough to run and hide with her brothers. He told her about the servant's halls nestled between the stones of the halls they walked and how their adventures went so far at time time that they ended up in dark passageways beneath the ground and found themselves outside the castle walls near small streams that ran down back alleys and in tunnels that led to the outskirts of the city.

She laughed at his enthusiastic retelling of their adventures and all the times they would come back covered in dirt and mud much to their mother's chagrin. "How is it you all never seemed to get lost? I feel as if I get lost roaming these halls, I cannot imagine knowing my direction in dark passageways and hidden walkways."

"Oh, do not assume we never got lost. We did a few times, but, after a long while we learned those places like the back of our hands. There was one time where Elion, Arminda and I decided to see who the best hider was of the three. Arminda knew that Elion and I had spent more epochs than her playing the game, so she secretly went to the bottom floor of the Hall of Archives where all our old records are kept and found the castle's plans when it was built. She memorized the map as much as she could." Prince Percy laughed as he paused to take a small bite of the finger sandwich in his hand. "She may be quiet and kind, but Arminda can be crafty and cunning, and she ended up becoming the best of us three. That was until my parents decided that these 'childish games' were no longer appropriate for our lot and threw us all back into our royal lessons and duties, however."

"I will remember to not to ever underestimate her. That was quite smart of her." she took a sip of her wine and as she swallowed, her smile replaced with a brooding look. "I faced a similar fate growing up, being forced away from the fun and adventure and made to abide by my duties. I always wished to be out adventuring and learning more of the world, hiking up my dress and running through fields and getting my hands dirty. But I was forced away to attend schooling with the rest of the House of Scholar children, sent far away from my family to be raised by the Scholars and aids at our citadel."

A small chuckle escaped her. "I swear those old crows would have tied me to my school chair if they had the option."

"That must have been hard, being taken away from your family without any choice." Prince Percy's face fell. "And here you are, forced away from them again."

She nodded as she looked down, and choked out. "Yes, here I am again."

He reached his hand across the blanket and set it on hers. "Did you get to see them much growing up or after you became a Scholar?"

She took a deep inhale and let it out. "I did not, no. I was raised by my family until I came of age, but then taken away once I was old enough for schooling. I have yet to decide if leaving my family behind was a blessing or not. My family was, and still is, quite poor. Too many epochs of hard labor left my father in a lot of pain and my mother always held harsh anger and resentment at the world- as if it owed her something grand that she never got. When I was unexpectedly born, it was seen by my mother as some sort of blessing, that I was some saving grace for her hardships and that I was what the world owed to her. She made it her job to ensure I knew that it was my duty to become successful enough to bring honor to the family and take care of them- to take care of her."

"Do you believe you have done that? Brought honor to them?" he asked.

"My father used to tell me constantly in his letters how proud he is of me and all the sacrifices I have made for the family. But, even now, my mother's words and letters consist not of her asking how well I am doing, but of her pressuring me about our engagement and what that will mean for her." she scoffed. "I swear I could sit on a throne myself and she would still look at me and tell me that I have not done enough for her, that there is more I am duty bound to do before she would ever tell me she is proud of me."

She shook her head. "My apologies, I forget myself and spoke too much and too intimately about my problems. Forgive me."

Prince Percy fiddled with the cup in his hand, "Can I say something quite improper?"

She shrugged and took another sip of wine.

"Your mother sounds like a miserable hag."

Sister Ora spit her wine out and laughed. Both continued in their laughter and Prince Percy handed her a napkin to wipe her face with. He stayed leaning in as she took the napkin from his hand.

"And she does not deserve to have you as a daughter." He said softly, his eyes darting from her gaze down to her lips where she held the tip of the wine-stained napkin.

She noticed his gaze, how his pupils dilated, and eyes softened as he looked back up at her. And in that moment her heart broke and guilt rattled her bones.

"Thank you, Percy. You have always been such a sweet friend to me."

His lips parted as if he were to respond, but he quickly closed them into a thin line as he nodded and leaned away from her.

"As you have always been to me." He quietly said as he settled away from her; one leg bent at the knee where his elbow now rested, creating a wall between the two.

"And what about your family?" she asked, trying to wash away the aching silence that now filled the field they sat in. "Do you believe you have brought honor to them?"

"I am trying, desperately hard to do so." he paused as he brought his other knee up, his elbows resting on both now as he shook his head down before looking at her. "But I am being tasked with playing a role I was not born to do, and have no desire to do, while my brother is off at war. I feel parts of myself slipping away and me having to become someone I do not wish to be in his absence."

"And what is it that you want? If not this?" she waved her hand around the space.

"I want to not have to sit in meetings and debate on how many lives we can end before it becomes too many bodies to bury. I want to not have to ask myself how many lines I am willing to cross each day- to stop being so lost on what the right thing to do is all the time. I want" he let out a small, half-hearted chuckle as he looked at his gilded clothing. "to not have to wear these god-forsaken gaudy clothes... I want... peace."

"Do you believe we will have it soon?" she softened her eyes as she met his.

"My father and the rest of the Council believe so. The Lords of Odessin will be here in a handful of days with soldiers and Aishar's new fleet will be finished soon after. It is only a matter of time before this will all finally be over." he shared a deep, pleading look with her. "You must know that I want this to end with a treaty and peace and not the bloodshed my father and uncle are aching for against your people."

She reached out her hand and rested it on his arm, rubbing it as she spoke. "I know, and I wish for it to end, too."

Chapter 45

"Your Highness?" The lady's maid called from the door.

"Yes?" Princess Arminda replied. Her back still turned as she stood at her window and sipped her coffee.

"Sister Ora is in the grand hall waiting for her guard to arrive back from the King's Guard barracks. You asked me to inform you of this."

She quickly turned around and large smile filled her cheeks. "Yes. Yes I did. Thank you so much."

Her lady's maid gave her a kind smile back and bowed before leaving. Princess Arminda made her way to the door where a King's Guard stood waiting for her.

"You, let us go quickly, please." She painted on another smile and quickly made her way down the hall. Her soft pink dress flowed in waves behind her fast steps, the train whipping in slight delay behind her as she turned corners and took shortcuts to the main hall.

"Sister Ora!" Princess Arminda joyfully greeted as she emerged from a side entrance of the main hall a few steps away from where Sister Ora stood waiting with her back turned. Her light pink halter dress danced again as she eagerly hugged her.

"I am so sorry to jump on your trip into town at the last minute, but after hearing you ask about it at dinner last night and convince my father to allow it to occur, I just had to join as well." Princess Arminda linked her arm with a still befuddled Sister Ora and guided them to the entrance of the castle. "I hope you do not mind. I needed my own escape from these walls after father trapped us in here after what occurred."

"No, not at all. Although, I was just going to walk around, get some fresh air. Truly nothing remarkable or spectacular." Sister Ora stammered out.

"Sounds quite a bit more spectacular than being holed up in here for one more minute." the princess laughed as they stepped out and made their way down through the grand archway that marked the entrance into the city.

The pair and their guards, with a few extra in tow, made their way through the streets with quick ease, the outcome of the riots and punishment of the instigators causing citizens to give them a wide berth and several deep bows as they walked with guards in front and behind them.

"Where were you off to, anywhere in particular?" Princess Arminda asked.

"I thought we could take in the view of the ocean and stop at this bookstore I have been into before. It is called Oswald's, you had met me there one time." she nonchalantly said.

Princess Arminda squeezed her arm. "Sounds lovely."

They passed by a side street, a display catching the princess' eye and jerking her, and Sister Ora as a consequence, to a halt.

A memorial of bright flowers and lit candles decorated the wall of a tan building. Princess Arminda's feet felt like cement as the two stood staring at the display of holy symbols, candles, and flowers underneath the painted names of the victims of the riots.

Both fought back tears and panic at the memories that quickly overwhelmed them.

On the street, the few people who remained about stopped and watched, quietly whispering among themselves as they stared. Tension and anxiety ran through the street. The citizens gathered worried about making any movement, the guards stepping closer to the women and anxiously gripping their swords as they stood by.

It was Arminda who moved first.

She walked to the memorial and dropped to her knees on the street, her pink dress flowing around her and picking up dirt as she knelt. She held her hands in prayer and bowed her head. She heard the shuffling of movement beside her and peeked her eye open mid prayer to see the ocean blue of Sister Ora's dress as she knelt beside her, mimicking her actions and kneeling in prayer.

"A princess and a future princess on their knees in the street praying for our losses. What a sight." A voice murmured nearby. Other voices spoke in hushed tones of shock at the two women.

The pair finished their prayer and stood, brushing as much dirt off their fine gowns as they could and turned back to the street, nodding and smiling softly at the newly gathered audience, before continuing on their way.

The group rounded the corner to the ocean-view walkway that led to the bookshop that Sister Ora had wished to visit. Her heart began racing as they approached, more eyes were upon her than before, not only those of the King's Guards but those of citizens peering at them and stopping their conversations to gawk. On a bench beside the bookshop sat Sedrick, a sandwich in hand and his eyes observing the group. He broke his brief eye contact with her before stepping inside the store.

Sister Ora's breath came in short bursts and she rested a hand on the ledge of the stone railing beside them to steady herself.

"Sister Ora, are you okay?" Princess Arminda set a hand on her shoulder.

Sister Ora fanned herself before responding. "I believe it is the heat. I feel a bit warm and faint."

"The heat?" Princess Arminda said, confused at her words as a cooling summer breeze wafted in from the ocean.

"Perhaps I should step inside out of the sun." Sister Ora said and escaped quickly from the princess' grip.

She did not wait for confirmation or approval as she swiftly walked off and headed for the bookshop. She burst through the door, drawing the attention of Oswald who greeted her in eagerness.

He clapped and jumped up. "Welcome back to Oswald's! I am so happy to see you again, my lady! What brings you in today?"

"Yes I was—"

The shop's bell chimed behind her and Oswald's eyes went wide and he adjusted his behavior, bowing properly and standing firmly behind his counter.

"Sister Ora, you should have waited a moment." Princess Arminda scolded as she stepped beside her.

"My apologies, I just needed to get out of the sun before I got any more overheated." her words rushing out of her.

"Perhaps we should get you back to the castle if you are so hot?" Princess Arminda said.

"Actually, I feel quite a bit better already being out of the sun. Mr. Oswald." She stopped herself as he opened his mouth to correct her. "*Oswald*, do you have any new books since I was here last?"

"Oswald *always* has more curiosities and items. I have a buyer that came in with the ships from Aishar and he carried with him these new books that you may enjoy." He smiled and pulled several beautifully binded books from the shelf behind him.

As Sister looked at them, she moved her eyes around the shop, observing the very observant and nervous patrons of the store- several of which had quickly decided to abandon their purchases and leave.

All except for one tall, bulking man on the second floor, with olive skin and tight textures in his short hair.

Sedrick barely moved his head to the side, his face staring at a book in his hands. He heard mumblings from below of Sister Ora thanking Oswald for his time and the princess beside her extending her gratitude and a farewell.

He cocked his head down to the counter below, noticing Sister Ora's left hand drop slowly to her side- a small slip of paper in her palm- and brushed it against the edge of a book on top of a stack in front of the counter. She held it there for a moment before turning and walking out with the rest of the group.

Princess Arminda's eye caught the corner of his as she surveyed the store from over her shoulder. Sedrick held his lax stance, feigning the attitude of a shopper intrigued by the sudden visit of nobility.

He waited for the chimes from the door to stop ringing and Oswald to go back to his work before he headed downstairs, the random book he had in his hands from upstairs still in his hands. He hastily made his way for the counter, grabbing the book on top of the stack that Sister Ora had stuck the note in.

"Afternoon, good sir." He greeted the back of Oswald as he set the books on the counter.

"Ah! Hello! Let me see what you have found for yourself today. I am always so curious of what my patrons find." Oswald cocked his head at the two books and laughed. "*Cheese and Other Fascinating Topics* and a copy of *The Dark History of Moats?*"

"Uhh, yes, well, only one of them is for me." Sedrick said, drumming his fingertips impatiently on the countertop.

"And which one is that?" Oswald inquired, writing the books and their prices in his ledger.

"The cheese one, of course... Cheese is fascinating." He awkwardly replied.

Oswald nodded his head "Can't argue with that." He handed the books back to Sedrick who handed over coin. "Have a good day son. Enjoy some cheese for me and watch out for moats."

Sedrick politely laughed as he left and made his way to the small inn by the docks that had been his home, tucking the books in close to him and not daring to open the note or appear too hurried as he left.

There were eyes everywhere in the king's city.

And even more beyond its walls.

CHAPTER 46

"If all of this is your will, please help me to understand it." Prince Percy's words choked in his throat, "I am trying so hard to be a dutiful son, prince, and man but I fear my foundation will never stop being shaken. How is spilling blood in your loving name just and righteous?"

He leaned his forehead onto his folded hands in front of him. "Please help me." he whispered as he listened to the silence of the night.

God did not answer.

The lost prince dropped his hands onto the paper strewn table he sat at and loosened a labored breath. He shook his head as he looked around the small room. The chill of the night air hung heavy in the tower room that had been the favored space for he, his father, and brother to meet in, that had been a room that held the young princes in it for school lessons and private meetings between the two when they were full of more hope than their duties would ever allow them to fulfill.

Recently, Prince Percy had overtaken more of the space than he had in the past, using it as a makeshift office and writing room to hide in long enough to recall who he had once been and what he tried to hold desperately onto beneath the cold exterior he had formed as of late.

"It is getting late." he mumbled; granting victory to the midnight silence that answered his prayers. He pushed himself out of his chair and turned to leave, bumping his hip into the table, and jostling it and knocking over his burning candle.

"*Shit.*" he hissed, jumping to quell the flames that began engulfing the discarded papers on the table. He smacked his palm against the quickly blackening parchments and tossed the wine from his cup onto them to stop the flames spread.

Another frustrated breath left him as he watched the ink smudge and blur across the red soaked and charred papers. He had stopped the flames but lost the work they contained. He collected the ruined papers and used a pocket kerchief to try to blot away the wine and save what was written on the remaining scraps.

"These are now utterly useless." he said as he tossed them to the side with his now ruined kerchief.

His eyes flicked across the cover of a black journal that had been hidden beneath the papers; a familiar binding from past lectures he had attended of scholars across the continent and lessons he had taken from past High Scholars who had taken him under their wings during his studies. He flipped open the binding, skimming the last few pages of notes he had taken.

His glancing stopped as he landed on a page dated just a few days before the late Father Penn's tyranny was uncovered and the old mentor was secretly executed for his attempted betrayal against his family.

An issue that the scholarly prince had once believed to be an issue so black and white he did not need to question it.

The prince and scholar had spent an afternoon discussing the Great Civil War and what had driven many before them to turn their backs on the status quo within the kingdom. Prince Percy had asked Father Penn for his interpretation on what would drive one to betray their fellow countrymen, and some their own families, as many throughout the kingdom had in the name of justice and freedom during that war. Prince Percy reread the scrawled notes on the page, reminding himself of the conversation, and stopped at the words he had transcribed from the High Scholar's long diatribe about justice.

He read them aloud. "Justice is the act of resistance against, and betrayal of, the status quo when normalcy upholds oppression."

He sat back down and hung his head as he ran his fingers roughly through his disheveled curls. His shoulders sunk with more weight than they could bear, and his chest heaved alongside them.

"How far we have gone in the hopes of protecting our people from much worse. We have become tyrants and killers in the name of peace and protection, and yet they have no peace and live in fear." he lifted his eyes to the corner of the room. "And it is all started because of words we fear the most that have doomed us from the start."

He held the stare of the looming stacks of locked trunks in the corner; the hidden key and combination to the oldest known only to three others outside of the room. Even with the widely unknown knowledge it contained, the fillings were so guarded that Glenolyn the Great had the artificer she commissioned, and then killed to hide what he knew of the safe, install a false bottom and a second hidden compartment within.

Hidden deep inside that compartment, underneath meaningless ancient memorabilia and old words, were the Psalms of Fire and Fury, still kept locked in the dark.

***

Sedrick walked with his back pressed against the cold stone walls of the castle, stepping onto the pathway only when necessary, and guiding himself by the light of the moon. Getting to this abandoned and unused part of the castle keep was easy- none paid much attention to those who skulked about back alleys at night- but remaining unseen in a space where none were supposed to be was the challenge that made his heart beat in his throat

The silver-white beams of the moon overhead offered the only source of light in this part of the castle's keep, illuminating the darkened pathway and casting long shadows underneath the high turrets and towers. There were no torch sconces lining the old stone walls, many of which were covered with grime and dirt, making Sedrick cringe as his body pressed against the cold, damp stones. Stone archways and tunnels broke up the exposed path he walked, and his anxious eyes played tricks on him as the night's shadows danced around in the abandoned spaces, appearing as merciless figures waiting for him, knowing the treacherous role he was playing in that moment.

He came upon the area that the coordinates in Sister Ora's note pointed to and stood against the cold wall watching and waiting. Midnight was close by, with only a few heart beats to spare, and he searched the dark space for a sign or a cloaked figure waiting for him; something to indicate he was on time and in the right place.

A few short paces away, at the edge of another darkened tunnel, was a small open doorway, the same as all the darkened open spaces he had passed by that sent him into panic each time his back felt their cold air instead of hard stone.

His eyes strained in the darkness as a tiny amber flame grew larger in the doorway and made its way to the entrance's edge. The flames glimmering grew brighter, casting shadows directly around the edges of the stone, a cloaked figure holding it in the air.

On the shadowed figures cloak was a golden crescent moon and a star patched where a burn had once been. Sister Ora pushed her hood back slightly, allowing shadows to be cast across the arches of her nose and her full cheekbones.

His shoulders relaxed and the tightness in his chest found reprieve. He darted his eyes around, down both ends of the alley, up onto the walkways above the castle walls, and, once he was convinced there were no other souls in the area, he quickly darted across the exposed walkway to the doorway where Sister Ora was hidden.

She softly smiled at Sedrick and nodded as he approached, then put her pointer finger to her lips before using it to gesture him to step inside the doorway.

Once inside the threshold she whispered so quietly, it was barely audible.

"These halls echo, and I cannot guarantee that we will not be heard."

Sedrick nodded in understanding as she reached into her cloak and pulled out several folded parchments.

"Are these...?" Sedrick quietly asked.

She nodded, her hands shaking as she pushed the parchments to him, and Sedrick tucked them in his breast pocket. They paused for only a moment before they both nodded in agreement to end their reunion before being caught. Sedrick stepped towards the doorway, glancing around the alleyway again.

"Ora." he whispered as he turned back towards her.

He stepped forward, embracing her in a deep, warm hug. They both choked on tears but held their silence.

"We will see each other again. In victory." he whispered before moving out into the night.

She nodded and feigned a smile.

Sedrick stuck to the darkened walls and tunnels as he hurriedly went back the way he came, his pace quickening to find shelter. It did not take long for him to make it out to a less auspicious part of the castle, a slummy back alley where beggars often went to piss or sleep, and continued onward to the rented room he had learned to call home.

Several paces behind him, above a darkened tunnel and well hidden behind a fat stone pillar, a leering shadow stood watching him step out onto the dirty open street. It observed as Sedrick left towards the noises of late-night taverns and red doored buildings before it turned back to where he had come from and watched as Sister Ora peeked out from the doorway to the direction Sedrick had fled

The lurker smirked devilishly as they slipped into the darkness and walked down the covered pathways atop the stone walls. Their pace hastened into an almost run as they saw a door that led to the servant's halls at the end of the walkway; the light from the interiors torch sconces creating an orange line at the crack where the door met the floor.

A few steps away from the doorway, they reached out their hand towards the doorknob only to have it snatched by a lurking shadow and twisted behind their back. As they opened their mouth to shout, a hand smashed over their mouth and a large, sturdy body pressed into theirs from behind, forcing them to walk towards the edge of the pathway.

As the phantom figure held the spy's body up against the wall's edge, the hulking shadow's hand gripped their cheek and with a twisting jerk of their head, snapping their neck with a crack. Without a second thought or care, their body was shoved onto the walkway below.

With a thud and a crack of more bones against the ground, the broad bodied shadow stepped back into the dark.

***

Sister Ora hushed her heavy breathing as she rushed through the lower tunnels of the castle, and down halls covered in old dirt and history, many of the halls long forgotten and not lit, with many others diverting off to hundreds of other hideaways to get lost in.

She came upon a less disgusting and dirty hallway, recognizing this over the rest she had passed through; the familiar ornate, but empty, torch sconces and wider walkways marking it as the main corridor the tunnels formed from. The faint outline of the door at the top of the stairs was illuminated by the only two lit sconces in the entirety of the tunnels. She hurried towards their flames framing the door and stopped at the bottom of the stairs only briefly to snuff out the candle in her hand and grab her skirts to rush up the steps.

She paused at the top and pressed her ear to the wood, listening for any late-night wanderers or servants working late. Upon hearing nothing but her own breath, she quietly turned the knob of the door and slipped out to the main floor castle.

From inside the dark hallway she had escaped, an onlooker stepped into the slit of light left by the door as it closed. They stood waiting at the base of the stairs as she latched the door closed behind her, engulfing the slim figure in darkness again.

CHAPTER 47

Sir Loren walked down the hall of the royal family's bed chambers. The occasional passerby acknowledged his presence with a courteous head bow and the King's Guard and other armored soldiers all greeted him with the standard respectful bow, his presence and theirs an everyday occurrence in this hall.

He stopped in front of the familiar arched doorway that he had spent much time in front of and behind, coming and going to gather Sister Ora and, in the privacy of night or on days where the royal family were too busy to notice, sneaking inside for their afternoon and midnight trysts He stood rigid outside the door, his fist tense and hard as he raised it hesitantly to knock.

From the other side, Sister Ora's muffled response came, prompting him to enter. He held onto the doorknob, taking two deep breaths before turning it and slowly stepping inside, closing it eerily slow behind him.

For the first time, when his eyes fell upon her, he did not hear a word she said, nor did he care. His ears pounded and rang as she stood speaking beside her writing desk.

He cut off her words. "How long have you been playing spy?"

From across the room, her posture stiffened to match his. Her back was turned to him as the leeching-cold shudder ran down her spine.

"I do not know what you are speaking of, Sir Loren." Her voice did not hide her terror and panic. The corner of her eye caught the glimmer of a knife on her desk, meant for opening letters, and she slowly set the book down in her hands, working to pick up the knife without him noticing.

"We both know that to be a lie. I found you last night, meeting with a man in the middle of the night. I thought- I thought for a moment you were meeting him for other reasons, that he was another man who you... cared about. But then I saw you passing information to him, some sort of documents. I am not sure exactly what it was, but I saw you. I remembered his face from the bookstore in town that we have visited several times at your request, and I saw your eyes meet his for too many moments at the gladiator showcase. He was there beside the flower stand the day of the riots." he paused. "I notice everything when it comes to you."

"Sir Loren you know *not* what you speak of." Her hand gripped the handle of the knife as it hovered just above the desk's surface, the view of it obscured by piles of books and parchment.

"If you are going to wield that knife against me, I do hope you know how to use it."

"What is it you are going to do?" Her voice trembled as hard as her body shook. The knife in her hand she knew to be useless against him, but she dared not drop it still as she turned to him.

"I swore an oath the day I was given this armor and made a knight of the King's Guard." he stepped forward. "I must keep that oath."

She stiffened her jaw and raised her chin as she fought back tears, attempting to appear strong and fearless against him, "I understand."

"Do you know the entirety of what I have sworn to?" he calmly spoke as he took more careful steps towards her.

She shook her head.

His response came slow, deliberate, and careful in its pace and tone, "King's Guards swear to obey the king's commands, to keep royal secrets shall we overhear them, and to defend him, and his family of whom we are sworn to, from harm with our very life." He continued slowly walking and took off his helmet, setting it down as he stepped to stand in front of her, "I have never broken my oath, in all my epochs, and I will not dishonor myself by doing so now. I am a loyal and honorable man, I must keep to my oath, each part of it."

All she could do was repeat her last words. "I understand."

He gently placed his hand on her tear-stained and trembling cheek as she tried to turn her face from his hold, "You are playing a very dangerous game. A game that is dangerous for us both."

Her eyes darted open, confusion overtaking her expression as tears still wetted her face. "What do you mean?"

"I was not the only one who saw you both that night, who hid in the shadows while you two exchanged your secrets. But I am now the only one left alive who knows of what occurred."

"What did you do?" she back away from him.

Sir Loren shook his head slowly at her. "Do not ask me questions you cannot bear to know the answer to."

She strengthened her stance, her face flushed with anger and fists shaking at her sides. "Do not think me some meek woman. If you committed some act on my behalf- *for my protection*- I deserve to know."

He paused before reluctantly giving in. "Have you ever felt a neck snap by your own hand? Because I have. That night was not the first time, and it will not be the last."

She swallowed the lump in her throat, smoothing the lines on her dress as she spoke, "I suppose I owe you my gratitude then."

"No, but you do owe me an explanation. How much of all of this was part of your ploy? Have you been manipulating and using everyone around you, or just some of us?" his tone was pained and sharp.

"You are asking if I was using you? If this" she gestured between the two. "was part of some sort of scheme?"

His gaze met hers again. "It is what you have done to your betrothed and the entire royal family, is it not?"

The muscles in his jaw clenched as she made a step towards him, shaking her head as she moved.

"No... no it was not a scheme or a lie- *we* were not a lie, Loren." she set her hands on his scarred face. "Choosing you was the only real choice I have gotten to make in a very long time."

He nodded his head in understanding before leaning down to kiss her.

"Thank you." he said, squeezing her wrists before dropping her hands from his face. "I must go. The King's Guard presence has been requested by the king, and I must arrive early."

She smiled and kissed him again. "I will be right here."

"I know you will." he replied, swallowing the lump in his throat "Goodbye, my lady."

***

"Perhaps there is another way to go about this, father." Prince Percy begged from where he sat, not caring for the onlookers in the council meeting.

"There is nothing else to do but *this*!" The king snapped back at him as he stood up. "We have given every chance for obedience and compliance and each step of the way our people have fought."

"No, they truly have not. It is *you* who has! You have convinced yourself of this out of your own fear and paranoia of what could happen if they did! What happened to fighting *for* our people's protection? To ensure long lasting peace?" Prince Percy shouted back as his arms gestured wide.

"*Do not fight me, Percy*." King Ivan snarled as he stepped inches from his son's face. "Remember your place."

"You swore an oath to our people, we all swore oaths to our people." the prince looked about the room. "Are our oaths the only ones that mean nothing and can be broken?"

Lord Tyrrian cooly replied. "Nephew, while I empathize with where your concern is coming from, perhaps you are too... emotionally tied to this situation to have an objective understanding of what we must do as rulers."

"We are talking about stopping just short of mass murder as a collective punishment to many who have not once involved themselves in our politics or this war, so you shall excuse my emotions, *uncle*. I do not take killings lightly- clearly unlike some on this council."

Sir Marion smirked and chimed in. "It will only end in death if they do not comply. Swearing fealty will save them."

Prince Percy turned to his father. "You swore to never be like him, like King Andrius or all the cruel men before him. You have poisoned your own mind and let others do the same. Father, you have gone too—"

"Mind your words, young prince, for they tread on treason." Father Figgins cut in. He leaned forward towards Prince Percy. "This council exists for the purpose of continuing the status quo and ensuring the normalcy we strive for is not threatened. There is a threat to that, and we are putting a much-needed end to it finally."

"You're right, that is what this council does." Prince Percy said, leaning back in his chair and quieting himself. He rested his elbow on the arm of his chair and sat his chin in his hand. In his lap, his other hand wrung and clenched as the meeting continued.

King Ivan finished his drink and stepped to the head of the table, standing in front of his pushed-out chair. "I will no longer allow this insolence, this treachery, and this war to continue onward as it has. We have clearly underestimated the amount of treason our own countrymen are willing to commit against the throne and I have allowed our own people to grow soft, feeble, and disobedient."

He took a deep inhale and stood straight.

"We will burn them. We will drown them. We will bury them. *All of them.* We will make them bleed and weep for mercy as we slaughter every last one of them like the vermin they are. Every man, woman, and child that dares stand in our way or hesitates to kneel in obedience will no longer stench this kingdom with their foul breath. We will set out to remind them that, while their god is merciful, *I. am. vengeful.*"

CHAPTER 48

The entire city of Isilria echoed with the shrieking of citizens struggling to survive the wrath of the King's Guard and hired mercenaries. Masses of people screamed and tried to run before being caught and begging for clemency as they were slammed onto their knees and beaten into silence. Families were separated and weeping women and crying children were given no mercy from the violence.

"It is by order of His Majesty, King Ivan of House Scott, First of His Name and Lord of the Six Kingdoms, that all are to kneel and swear fealty to His Majesty, the church, and the throne." Sir Marion casually walked back and forth in front of a long line of kneeling citizens. In his right hand he held a long, pure gold scepter adorned with jewels and a lion's head. "Those that choose to not, will meet their end on the ground where they stand."

His moment was taken as he jerked his head to a small group several paces away of guards arguing and fighting with citizens.

"He is too old a man, he cannot kneel, and he is deaf and blind. He knows not what you are asking of him, please, show him a moment of grace." A young woman on her knees pleaded with the King's Guard yelling at an elderly man and grabbing at him.

The elderly man stood shaking, leaning heavily on a cane, grabbing and holding onto the arm that gripped him. His head shot around and he signed with one hand in an attempt to communicate.

Sir Marion slammed his feet on the pavement as he stormed to the group; scepter raised at his side. As he approached, he swung the staff backward, the trajectory only pausing as it met resistance against the face of the kneeling woman pleading for the old man.

Blood and teeth splattered the pavement in front of her as her body fell to the ground and screams erupted from the crowd before they were shouted at to be silent.

"You do not demand anything from a King's Guard." he growled as his free hand grabbed her hair and pulled her upright to kneel in front of him.

Through sobs and busted teeth, the woman wept. "Please, sir I am sorry. I was only trying to help."

Sir Marion brought the bloodied head of the scepter to her face. "If you wish to be of service, swear your fealty to the king."

Her eyes darted between the scepter and his darkened, terrifying glare, the eye on her bruised and beaten side quickly becoming swollen. "I- I- I swear it. I swear my honor and loyalty to His Majesty."

He shoved the head of the lion into her face. She let out a small sob as she pursed her swollen and bloodied lip and kissed the head of the scepter before returning her gaze to the ground, covering her mouth with her hand to quiet her crying.

Sir Marion looked at the King's Guard, who stood unsure of what to do with the blind and elderly man, "If he cannot kneel, then you shall make him, or you shall cut him down at his useless kneecaps. No one is exempt from the king's demands."

***

The slamming open of the rookery door startled not only the scribe serving as the keeper of the tower, but every messenger bird nested within the turret.

"Good sirs, what is the meaning of this disruption?!" He yelled as King's Guards shoved their way into the tower.

"Shut up." The King's Guard ordered as they slammed a parchment in the Scribe's hands and shoved him aside. More soldiers crowded into the tower and rushed up the winding stairs towards the multiple levels of bird nests.

"Leave the falcons! The king's falcons may live, the rest may not." the head guard yelled as the rest overtook the stone stairs.

The tower keeper gasped and shook his head. "No, this cannot be true. The king would not order the killing of our birds. How will we communicate with our fellow countrymen? Give them news and good wishes?"

"That is of no importance to the king. You are the literate one here, *Scribe*, not I, so you should have no quarrel with believing this order. It came from His Majesty's own desk, did it not?"

The scribe ran their finger over the king's signature and sigil on the letter. "Yes but, but this is insanity, sir."

The sounds of squawking birds rang throughout the tower as the birds were snatched from their nests and their necks snapped before being thrown out the window like back-alley waste. Screams from outside rang out as the feathered bodies hit the ground outside.

The soldiers rushed their way down the steps and made their way to the next rookery. The soldier in charge snatched the parchment from the scribe and turned to leave.

"It is not insanity. It is the way of the king- and you will not question it."

***

Disordered hoards of citizens were forcibly ushered into the crowded square in front of the gallows, corralled into the cobblestone area like livestock being shoved into a barn.

There were no vendors with carts set up around the area selling their wares, drinks, and food to those who attended, the taverns did not fill up beforehand with lively chatter from citizens discussing the coming execution and their curiosities of how The Butcher would end the lives of the condemned criminals.

No one had wished to treat today as they once had, not when their own bruises and blood loss were still fresh from the day prior.

Guards closed in around the stragglers that made their way into the square, boxing them in to ensure that all would stay for the entirety of the spectacle, their weapons shined and unsheathed to warn off any unsavory behavior.

King Ivan stepped down from the royal balcony onto the stage where The Butcher, Father Figgins, and guards stood looking down upon the citizens of the king's city. A quick hush waved through the crowd, those who dared to still make a noise were quieted by their fellow man scared of punishment by the menacing presence of the soldiers and hired guards barricading them in.

"When I took my oath as your king I swore to will my power to create law and justice, to maintain the laws of God and the church, and to serve dutifully to protect all those under my reign and within the walls of my sovereignty." he paused to scan the crowd, "I did not take that oath lightly, and each day that I wake with the title of king still bore unto my name I remember those words- especially on this day. We have been forced to enter unprecedented times by those who demand violence in response to their own bloodshed."

The king turned towards the end of the stage, nodding to signal to bring out the ones bearing sacks over their faces and bondages around their wrists. The first to be executed stood nearest the king, who signaled again with one nod, and the prisoners unintelligible cries and murmurs were finally heard by the crowd as their face covering was removed and gag taken from their mouth.

A large man with olive skin and short textured hair stood on the stage, his eyes red with tears desperately crying. "I am innocent, *please*. Help me!"

His deep bellowing voice broke out into sobs, begging for mercy and help from the crowd. His broad shoulders, enlarged from epochs of hard labor, shook with every cry.

"*Silence him.*" the king gritted through his teeth.

The gag was shoved back in his mouth and he was shoved on bended knee, his cries mulled back into background noise while the king continued speaking.

"Good people of the great kingdoms of Victarius. This man before you is sentenced and judged to die according to the laws of the Church and our kingdom. This man has betrayed not only the throne and the church, but you and the souls of those e have lost in the war his allies have brought upon us. This man, and his conspirator and ally, are why many of you have become orphaned, widowed, or childless. He has aided our enemies with information and secrets that would lead to more bloodshed if not for our stopping him in time. He is the one who forced our hands to demand your nationalism in order to protect you."

The crowd's behavior began to shift. Low cheers and shouts in support of his execution, and others shouted the names of their loved ones lost in the battle, placing the blame of their death on the kneeled man whose face was covered in bruises and tears. Others dared not make noise against the king's words.

King Ivan stepped aside as The Butcher neared the crying prisoner, "May God have mercy on your tainted and traitorous soul."

Muffled under the cotton of the fabric in his mouth, the prisoner teetered back and forth on his knees and repeated as best he could, "May God have mercy on my soul."

The Butcher did not waste time or draw out the sentencing any long as he approached with his axe. Two guards approached and shoved the prisoner's head forward, forcing his neck out as they held onto him from behind, only letting go of his body when The Butcher's axe swung.

Blood splatted along the stage as his axe arced through the air. Cries rose above the chanting as the prisoner's body slumped over, the axe stuck crookedly in his neck.

The Butcher ripped the axe out of his neck and swung again, more blood splaying as the prisoner's head fell free of his collapsing body.

From above, the royal family looked down upon the deceased man. Disgust fell across their faces as his body and head were hauled away and another brought forward. The hood was ripped unceremoniously from their face and gag taken from their mouth as they were forced to their knees where the blood was still fresh.

Sister Ora's eyes widened and tears blurred her vision as the hood was removed and thrown to the side. Prayers she had not whispered in so long fell from her lips as the crowd gasped. The Butcher stepped back beside the execution slab, wiping the blood from his axe and readying it to be covered with new.

"A traitor in our own castle, who has lived and walked along us for too long. Who earned our trust only to betray it, and for what? To turn sworn allies into enemies. To betray those who took them in as one of their own, to break promises so that more blood can be spilled in their games of war."

The words of the king were erased as Sister Ora's ears pierced with ringing and the shouts from the crowd drowned him out. Screams were thrown at the stage. Her chest heaved in pain and her vision blurred into nothing but smudges of color.

She could not breathe, or think, or see.

She was useless, struck dumb with fear. Another pawn in another game. Another thing to be used for someone's gain. But this time, this end was done by her own hand.

She could see nothing but still, she closed her eyes, shaking her head in disbelief as The Butcher swung his blade high and brought it down.

She did not want to see the end.

Despite herself, her eyes snapped open as the axe was brought down. Before the darkness overtook her, the last sight she saw was the pain in Sir Loren's eyes as the blade broke through his neck and his head fell from his armored shoulders. She fell backward, stumbling as if she were to faint.

Queen Onetta stepped up beside her, digging her nails into Sister Ora's arm and holding her up. "You would be so lucky to be made a martyr. But we will not make one of you, *not yet.*"

Her body continued to tremble and numb as she felt herself being pulled away from the onlooking crowd. She shivered at the coldness of the iron cuffs engulfing her wrists as she was hauled away.

CHAPTER 49

Lord Theodus Montarian and Lord Digarius quickly dismounted their horses and handed them off to the hands outside of Sandhill House. They rushed up the walkway, avoiding pleasantries and greetings as they met with the closed doors of the fortress.

The creaking of the giant oak doors echoed against the stone walls and muffled the various voices coming from inside. Aids pointed them in the direction of Lady Belva, taking tea and conference in a receiving room.

"Belva." Lord Theodus greeted in the doorway.

She gasped at the sight of her husband and son, dismissing the patron in the room as she rushed to greet them both.

"Thank the stars you both are here." she huffed out as she closed the door behind the leaving man.

"My love, I have missed you more than I can say. And we have much to discuss." Lord Theodus greeted her as they shared a deep hug.

"You have *no* idea, Theo." she whispered as the two stayed embraced, their foreheads gingerly touching as she spoke, her head shaking.

"Mother" Lord Digarius stepped forward; his arms outstretched.

"Digarius, oh I have missed you as well." she embraced him.

"We have much we must confer on- *privately*." Their hug was quick as Lord Digarius pulled away and turned for the closed door, opening it to ensure no listening ears were outside, then closed it again and locked it with a flick of his wrist.

***

"Loose loyalties began changing this war even before it began." Lord Theodus said, now sitting at the table alongside his wife and son. "We could not risk writing to you about what we needed to discuss, and could not risk Lord Bromlyn —"

"— or any of his men here" Lord Digarius casually cut in.

"— potentially being foxes in the henhouse."

Lady Belva jerked her head in their direction, stepping forward quickly as her expression darkened. "Lord Bromlyn may be a cox-comb, but he and my sister are no traitor to our family."

"We cannot be sure how far this disloyalty lies. Outside of this room, there is no certainty of whom we can truly trust, especially when the one whose betrayal we have caught has spent a lifetime swearing their sword and loyalty to your family crest and broken bread with us as if they were our own blood."

"Yes but..." She squared her shoulders and let go of her hurt. "I will do what I must and put an end to this. Give me the afternoon and we shall all meet in the great hall."

***

Soldiers of all ranks gathered around the Great Hall, sharing drink and stories with one another- many of which were quite exaggerated as many great war stories often are. The Montarian family shared in conversation, as was quite normal for their house to do, and the Bromlyn clan also became social for the event, which many took to shock at seeing Lord Bromlyn conversing with others.

Lady Montarian scanned the gathered crowd, ensuring her people were in the right place and made her way towards their higher-ranking officers gathered near the throne and dais steps. As she approached, the officers exchanged formalities of respect for their Lady as she handed her empty chalice over to a passing servant, insisting that she did not need any more drink.

"Sir Rainey, I have been meaning to personally speak with you since your arrival. Thank you for your aid in this war and especially so in ensuring our future lord, my son, learned of leadership on and off the battlefield. You are an exemplary example that our soldiers can learn a great deal from." her tone and expression were both soft, yet stern without being overly confident, and her smile was kind, but she did not show her teeth as her lips curled upward.

Sir Rainey's normally firm face turned into the tiniest smile at her words. "Thank you, my lady. I also do believe there is much I can teach these young men and women."

"I believe so as well. Now, I cannot recall, how old were you when you swore your oath to our House?"

"Barely of twenty, my lady."

"And First Sgt. Kingery, you were about the same age when you swore as well, yes?"

"Seventeen actually, my lady." she shifted as she replied.

"Ahh, yes. Sir Rainey, you left your home of Isilria to come serve in our armies at that age, yes?"

"Yes, my lady. And at twenty-five your father granted my knighthood." he smiled with pride.

"And did you enjoy it? Serving under my father's lordship before serving under mine, where you were given the ranking of Commander of my army?" Again, she was careful with her tone; not too stern or aggressive, but not too soft to be ignored.

"Yes, my lady. Serving your family has been the upmost pleasure." Sir Rainey gave a closed lip smile and bow before taking another swig of his drink. His eyes creased into slits as he looked down at her.

Officers and soldiers gathered near became overly obvious in their eavesdropping and curiosity at the conversation with many stepping closer around them.

"That pleases me to hear. Do you happen to recall the words of the Knights Oath of Featly that you gave when you were knighted?"

"Yes, m'lady, I do."

"Well, please, do go ahead and recite it. Not everyone gets the honor of knowing a knight's oath and of hearing it. I am sure many here would love to someday be able to speak and live by those words." Her assertive tone left no room for doubt or questioning.

Sir Rainey opened his mouth to speak, then closed it as is brow creased and eyes darted around at the onlooking crowd.

"Go ahead, Sir Rainey." she said.

He cleared his throat and his chin as he spoke. "On bended knee, I swear to protect my liege and freehold, to serve for the good and truth of both, though it may cost me my life. I will place nothing higher above my duty, not even all the world's riches. I shall serve faithfully with valor, virtue, and honor, until I am called unto the stars. I give my oath of my own free-will, and swear to hold this oath, lest death claim me."

Lady Belva smiled, "And have you brought honor to this oath and our freehold, Sir Rainey?"

His head twitched at her words and his eyes narrowed again before he carefully spoke. "Yes, my lady. It is my greatest honor to have sworn this oath to your House."

"It is reassuring to hear that there is still honor and loyalty in this house. Thank you, Sir Rainey."

Onlookers noticed the tension in his shoulders soften as she smiled until her eyes wrinkled and patted his arm as she thanked him.

Sir Rainey bowed as she stepped back towards the dais stairs, the bard's music softening as she made her way up the three steps. The conversation throughout the room died out as she ascended the steps.

"In many ways, each one of you have sworn loyalty and honor to the Montarian clan and yet, when we need it the most, some of you dare to bring shame to our House and all who have died protecting these lands." Lady Belva pulled a folded letter out of her sleeve and slowly opened it, her eyes scanning the room for any notes of discomfort of tension and noting the movement of outlying guards and soldiers in the room.

"This was a letter sent to the king and his army just moments after many of you left the battlefield to come here. It not only advised the king on our army's movement, but of the numbers left on the battlefield, and at home in Middleton Landing- where many of your families are waiting for you to return." She looked at the letter while murmurs broke through the crowd, "I would read it to you all, so you know the exact words of this treason, but the day has been so long, and my eyes are quite tired."

She held a hard pause before turning her gaze towards the front line of military officers. "Maybe First Sgt. Kingery could read it for us, seeing as she knows Sir Rainey's handwriting so well."

Lady Belva held the letter out. "Would you mind?"

Sir Rainey became rigid and his face beaten red with anger as Emaline stepped closer to the stage to stand beside Lady Belva. The Lady of Ayeshire stepped down the dais steps to stand eye-to-eye with him, speaking as she took her steps. Soldiers crowded around him and along the path she walked, their hands on their swords and adrenaline tensing every muscle in their body.

"I know not of what you speak, My Lady." His voice too stern.

"We found it quite suspicious that when word was sent out about the ambush the king had planned at Ravenhall, your unit was the only one not informed- the very unit that was being ambushed, even though I myself sent a hawk and ensured it was received. The attack alongside the lack of warning was suspicious enough, but you were also so insistent that Lord Digarius not send out scouts ahead just before it occurred." Lady Belva began. "And at the battle of Lake Lahere, you again were quite insistent and sure of Lord Digarius being able to take on the prince's army without waiting for the much-needed reinforcements. Then on the field you backed your own unit against the lake instead of the open field for retreat. A strategy that led to a quicker victory over us in that battle. If it were not for Lord Digarius and First Sgt. Kingery's keen eyes and observations these past many moons, I am quite certain you would have cost our armies more innocent lives."

She dared to step closer to him, her stare not moving away from his. "I wish to put this simply, Sir Rainey. You are a murderer, a traitor, and a cheat of the worst kind. You have been found of treason and of treachery and you bring not only shame to *your* house, but the entirely of mine. A swift death would be too merciful for what you deserve, but you are *quite* fortunate that I have no time to be anything less than that today. What have you to say for yourself?"

His jaw clenched hard enough to break his teeth. "Your family has brought shame upon the throne and the Six Kingdoms. You break traditions that should be kept, you desire to shed blood over a king doing what he must, *my king*, doing what he must to keep ill-bred cunts like you in line."

Sir Rainey spit in her face. "And your pay is shit compared to what His Majesty has offered me once he cleans the kingdom of you all."

And then, he lunged.

Lady Belva did not flinch as hands grabbed for his lunging body and held him back from her.

She slowly and silently raised one hand, motioning for all around her to hold back and for the guards to let him go. She calmly dabbed the spit off her face with a kerchief she pulled from her sleeve. "One would think a man of your intellect would have something more creative to insult me with beside the same trite pub room insults I have laughed off my entire life."

She then laughed at his grimace and glare as she stepped forward again, slapping him with the back of her hand with so much force he stumbled back against the crowd behind him, none of which offered their support as he fell.

The Lady of Ayeshire turned to where Emaline stood awaiting her command. The two shared a quick glance as Emaline stepped forward and those still left around Sir Rainey cleared the area.

He gathered himself and began angrily stumbling towards Lady Belva again, spitting venom as he strode. "Ill-bred traitors to His Majesty will never—"

Emaline did not let him speak as she strode forward and kicked him in his chest, knocking him to his knees as she unsheathed one of her swords. Any attempt at more words by him was stopped with shove of her blade as it drove into the back of his neck..

His blood splattered over the soft green velvet of Lady Belva's dress and the stone where she stood. Even among the brutality taking place right in front of her, she remained stoic and unbothered, not even grimacing as some of the blood splattered onto her chest.

Lady Belva turned towards Lord Bromlyn who stood less stoic and stern than she with shock and appall on his face. "Your Grace, I thank you for your hospitality, aid, and loyalty to my House. But as you know, we have no more time to waste and many of us shall be off- including myself- at once for Middleton to defend our home."

Lord Bromlyn opened his mouth to retort before watching her gaze drop down to the pool of blood and the body at her feet,

"Unless of course, you seem to take issue with your Lady's leave?" a smirk matching hers broke out on her husband's face as he stood nearby.

"No, no of course not my lady. That bargain- it, it was a crude and roguish way to act, please accept my deepest apologies. Our House will always stand with yours."

"Good." she said.

She turned back to face the room, nodding to her husband, son, and their remaining officers gathered beside her. She moved to step over Sir Rainey's body as the clang of the doors opening disrupted her leave.

"Lady Montarian!"

Four guards bearing her House sigil moved quickly into the room, carrying a heavy trunk between them. "This has arrived with your name on it."

The soldiers all looked ill and disgusted with the trunk in their hands, the same look falling onto the faces of those they passed. Gagging faces were left in their wake and hands covered mouths as they walked by.

Stench of rotting flesh filled the room and Lady Belva's stoicism fell as the odor filled her nostrils. She covered her mouth and nodded at the soldiers as they sat the trunk down, waiting for permission to open it.

She held back the desire to throw up as the bloodied and rotting heads of two men were exposed to the room. Between them, resting on the same plush red pillow hiding the pools of blood, was a stag heart stabbed with a gold knife, a rolled parchment tied to its hilt.

Upon seeing the olive skin and coiled hair, Lord Digarius choked out. "Sedrick."

Emaline's broken whisper calmed him. "No. No it is not him. His nose is different, and Sedrick's ears were never garnished with gems. It is not him. Perhaps, it was meant to be, though."

"And who is this?" Lady Belva asked beneath the handkerchief now covering her mouth, pointing to the pale rotting head with matted curled hair atop it. She looked around the gathered observers, all shaking their heads in uncertainty.

She reached for the knife, ripping it from the stag heart and removed her hand from her mouth to uncoil the parchment with both hands. She read it aloud, "This war will not end until the heads of every Montarian loyalist are removed and gifted to His Majesty. Peace will only come from your deaths."

She unrolled the parchment more. "And we do hope your little bird will enjoy her gilded cage and sing for us as she did for you."

Her hands shook as she crumpled up the parchment and crunched it between her clenching hands still holding the small golden knife. Her jaw trembled in anger and her nostrils flared as she took fast and quick inhales and exhales.

She screamed as she stabbed the dagger into the heart in the center of the trunk, the remaining wet blood inside it splattering her hand.

She leaned over and rested her bloodied hands on the trunks edges. Her rage demanded her to scream again, but her people's presence required her to show them control. She began to stand, reaching for the lid on the trunk to close it and hide the foul contents it contained. Her shaking stare stopped where her hand rested on the lid's corner, inches from where the wood backing of it's interior had a small gap. Behind the gap in the lid was open darkness.

Curious, she pushed her fingers into the gap and pulled, exposing a hidden compartment full of parchment that fell about the floor.

Lady Belva filed through the pile; holy texts she had never seen with scratched out passages and names signed on the papers, letters attached to them of old leaders agreeing to changes, and a psalm no holy person in her time had ever spoken of in the church.

No Psalm she had ever known.

Lord Theodus stepped beside her. "What is it?"

She looked up at him, shaking her head in confusion as she stood and continued to read. "Something called The Psalms of Fire and Fury."

Her hand covered her mouth as she finished the scripture and the freshly inked note rolled up with it. She dropped her hand to her chest to hold her pounding heart inside.

"Mother, what is going on?" Lord Digarius asked, resting his hand on her arm to steady her.

She raised her head. "Prepare a hawk to fly and messenger to ride to every corner of this kingdom. *Now*."

Chapter 50

Autumnia 23, 690 AC

Hawk wings beat against the wind in the sky surrounding Sandhill House as horses trampled over weeds and mud and overtook every road without pause. Town criers ushered the townsfolk to gather and listen as others ran into gathering halls and taverns bearing news.

As the news spread throughout the city and beyond, The Lady of Ayeshire and her family prepared themselves to sail back to Middleton Landing. Lady Belva stepped out of the carriage that carried her down to the docks. Her feet gracefully met the land, and she straightened the skirt of her dress.

She looked up to the crowded dock as the gathered crowds fell to bended knee at her presence. She nodded at their sign of respect.

Before she could take a step, a man shouted. "Queen of the People!"

Another voice repeated it. "Queen of the People!"

Lady Belva did not move and the chanting did not stop as more voices joined.

Finally, she hesitantly stepped forward. Bent heads raised and continued their chant as she boarded her boat and the sails were set west for her throne.

Appendix and Resources

CALENDAR AND TIME IN THE SIX KINGDOMS

The Six Kingdom's of Victarius follows a Lunation Calendar divided into twelve moon phases.

The moon completes one full cycle every 30 days (or dates depending on one's accent and preferred linguistic style). Each moon cycle was determined to be a "fresh start" for the people, thus beginning the creation of the calendar for time telling and tracking of stars and the moon. The indication of each new phase was the sighting of the new moon. Some phases, however, would be 29 days instead of 30 depending on the cycle of the moon.

To tell the passing of time long ago before modern calendars, simple sailing ropes or scrap fabric strips were used to count the passing of each date. This method was believed to have been created by sailors who had no accurate way to tell dates outside of the rising and setting of the sun and moon. At each rising of the moon that passed a small slit was cut in the rope or fabric and after seven (a number chosen due to is believed good fortune from those who studied numerology) moon rises, those slits were tied into a knot to indicate the passing of time.

At the middle of each phase- on the fifteenth date- a specific date called a "node" occurs. This date is when taxes to the crown and tides to the church were due by citizens. Taxes and tides to the church are estimated not only by the money one made and property owned, but by the number of children and people per household.

Being born on a node was considered unlucky by common people because of the ill-will feeling of it being a tax day and additionally because any child born on the node would have to have their tides and tax due that same day or the family would be penalized and punished.

While records cannot be certain of the original intent of 12 lunar phases determining one epoch, rulers and holy men before the Alvarian age came to an agreement that aligning the single epoch into 12 phases would create unity and equality within the four seasons of change. Thus, the epoch was born.

The twelve phases on the Victarius Lunar calendar that make up each epoch are below in chronological order:

Scholus

Atonian

Vernius

Aquius

Sprit

Solius

Jilay

Lotian

Autumnia

Tember

Pyria

Delova

One hundred epochs would form a century, and one thousand would form an age.

The four seasons of each epoch are noted as beginning on four highly important dates within the calendar.

The Spring Equalias is the marking of spring, the first date after the ground has thawed from winter where the sun and the moon allow one another equal time to look over the sky. While the worship of the Old Gods of Three is forbidden, the Spring Equalias is still celebrated, but instead of being a celebration of the opposing twin gods in the sky, it was changed into a simple celebration of the seasons changing.

Solarius is the marker of summer, the longest day of the epoch where the moon rests and allows the sun more time to shine its light on the people of the world.

The Autumn Equalius occurs to indicate the longer nights beginning to rise and the beginnings of harvest season and soon, rest for many.

Lunarius is the longest day of the epoch and, while snow and frost have likely fallen before this time, indicates the season of winter and the first day that the moon allows the sun to rest and basks us all in its night light, signaling to the people to do the same- rest and recover to prepare for the long cold ahead.

There are no remaining records indicating how natives to the continent told time or tracked dates before the Alvarian Conquest aside from what was merged into the calendar. During the Alvarian Conquest, like many things, this history and culture was destroyed by the colonizers. Time before the Conquest was referred to as BC (before conquest) and time post Conquest is written as AC (after conquest).

Religion in the Six Kingdoms

The Six Kingdoms of Victarius were once a vastly diverse land of culture and religion, even after the Alvarian Conquest reshaped the lands. Religions and agnostic beliefs were plentiful and, for the most part, commonly tolerated and accepted amongst those with differing beliefs.

As history wore on and new beliefs came to life amid the ever-blending cultures of the travelers and settlers of the open bordered Old Continent, branches of doctrine were born from existing theologies. The most widely accepted and worshiped theologies before The Alvarian Conquest were that of The Old Gods of Three and The Vahar.

During and after the Alvarian Conquest, Purists, followers of The One True religion that came over alongside the dragon riding conquerors, became outspoken and many churches were built in their gods name.

After First King Lucarius rose to the throne after the Great Civil War, commandments of The One True became law, creating a dangerous landscape for those who worshiped other gods and held beliefs of different branches of theology. Soon after his ruling, First King Lucarius made The One True the kingdom's only acceptable religion, damning and punishing those who did not believe; temples were burned, religious leaders were punished and killed, and culture died alongside burned scriptures.

But, if one listened close enough to whispered words, they could still hear the freedom the crown and the church tried to burn away.

The Old Gods of Three

The great goddess Atimnial, also known as Mother, birthed the earth from a droplet of blood when she pricked her finger on a thorn in her heavenly garden. As her blood fell down from the skies it formed a solid earth where her spirit was planted into the very core of the earth alongside her divine magic that bloomed gardens as beautiful as the ones she tended above and gave life to her creation.

Upon its creation, Atimnal needed help watching over the earth as it evolved, and so she created twin children, Soluar and Devlunia, to watch over the world with her. Soluar is known as the sun god, worshiped for bringing their light to the earth each day and encouraging us to rise and grow like the flowers and food that their bright rays aid in growing. Devlunia is the moon god, whose dark embrace encourages us to rest from our labors and allow our fruits to be plentiful in our work.

The Spring Equalias was once a celebration of both Devlunia and Soluar and a festival of gratitude for the twins' work in bringing light and dark to the world and keeping balance. Solarius was the festival to give thanks to Soluar who would rise and work in more plentiful effort in the coming season, and Lunarius was the celebration of Devlunia whose darkness and chill created winter for us to rest during. Autumnias was perhaps the largest celebration of the epoch, where sacrifices, offerings, and more were given to Mother, as an attempt to pay her back for giving our earth and souls life.

In addition to the three gods, some practitioners of The Three would also give worship and praise to magical, unseen creations of Atimnial called Sprits. Believed to be fae-like, they would clean up the frost and snow from winter, wake up blooms and greenery for spring, and their blessings on fields and homes were believed to bring a prosperous and fertile epoch.

Believers of Sprits were not the only difference in how those chose to worship The Three.

Some believed that Devlunia deserved more worship than Soluar or Atimnial. Referred to as Lunarians, these worshipers would perform their ceremonies by the moon's light, specifically on nights where Devlunia was at their fullest and provide more offerings and praise to the moon god.

Those who gave much of their worship to Soluar, believed that their light was the truer path to follow in life. Called Solarists, they would praise the sun's rays for bringing blooms to life and believed that the seasons of planting and harvesting proved that Soluar gave more to earth and its inhabitants than Lunarius.

Aside from Soluar and Devlunia, demi gods and spiritual creatures were gifted to the earth by Autumnias, including: Aiquia, the goddess of water, Julis, the god of land, and Pyria the goddess of fire. These demi gods also had their own devoted followers, although not as plentiful as Solarists, Lunarians, and those who worshiped The Three.

The Vahar

U nlike worshippers of The Three whose gods were centered on the nature of earth, those who worshiped the Vahar attributed aspects of human nature to divine beings and creators they gave praise to. It was believed that the creation of man came first out of desire from the Vahar to birth a perfect creation to worship them.

The earth was born after humanity as a place for the Vahar to place their creation to watch them evolve and live using the gifts each god provided. The stars were created as guiding lights for humanity to look to and were heavenly steeds the Vahar rode around the skies, watching their creations create their own futures.

Thirdall was the goddess of life, birth, and death. Beihnur was the god of light, abundance, and prosperity who gave light and abundance just as much as he took it from those he deemed undeserving. Niyja was the goddess of love and watched over all emotions to ensure the world remained balanced between love and darkness. Atlinir was the god of knowledge and prophecy and Qyi was a trickster god- who often disguised themself as various gods, goddesses, and other beings in order to create chaos, play trickery for their own entertainment, and otherwise cause trouble.

Worshipers were known for leaving sacrifices and offerings to the Vahar gods and goddesses, from sacrifices from hunts and harvests, to sinners, true believers, and more whose blood was believed to satisfy the gods more than gold, stones, or harvest findings. Many who devoted their worship to the Vahar gods were believed to have magical and other worldly powers including immunity to death, burning and drowning, and possessing powers that rivaled mythical beasts that once roamed the lands.

Purists and other believers would whisper of worshippers of Vahar being evil or full of sin due to their believed magical abilities, stating that no good god would give a man power and that, in order to receive such gifts, worshippers had to have committed atrocious acts of hell to receive them.

A common blessing spoken by worshippers was "may the light of the Vahar be upon you". It was seen as an insult or wish for a curse to not bless one another with these words upon parting from each other as it was insinuated that, if the blessing was not spoken, then the silent one hoped the Vahar would take their blessings from the other.

The One True

The faith of The One True, whose worshippers were called Purists, was brought across the violent seas by the Alvarian children. Despite the societal acceptance of different religions, once the Alvarian's came to power, The One True became the dominant religion of the land and laws were slowly and quietly created, or dispensed of, in alignment with the churches preaching and many felt pressure to adhere to the beliefs of their new leaders.

While it would be many reigns in the future before other religions would be outlawed, the Alvarian children and their heirs laid the foundation for this future revocation of freedom.

According to all worshippers of The One True, each individual was born with a specific purpose and use in life as defined by Him when He aided in each person's creation. Worshipers were to spend their lives in service to God and finding and pursuing the destiny He had laid for them. Finding one's purpose to honor God was instrumental in life to ensure you ascended to the afterlife, honored your family, and reincarnated into your next life. Swaying from worship or straying from your path was the highest of sins and would ensure one's damnation to one of the many hells.

Those who committed the most atrocities were damned to the deepest level of hell; one that no soul would ever escape or reincarnate from. When one committed an act that damned their own family alongside their soul, they were not only doomed to this deep hell for eternity, but their eternity would be spent watching their family suffer in unending pain, often by their own hand.

Purists do not have any religious text that provides a detailed journey or cosmology of all the realms of hell, but it is commonly believed that there are different hells for different sinners, with some claiming to have visions of the damnation that awaited them if they continued on their current path.

During the Great Civil War, religious leaders of The One True shared a vision from God which stated that, at birth, each person's Divine Destiny was written according to the stars they were born under. Together these leaders wrote into history the Divine Houses; twelve Houses separated by each cycle of the moon that would determine each person's Divine Destiny at their birth.

Alongside this vision, church leaders spoke to God, and relayed to their devoted worshipers that for far too long He had allowed His creations to wander too far from His path for them and, upon seeing what that free will has allowed to occur, gave the church more definition and stricter tenants on how each person would be made to follow his Divine path.

As before, straying from this path was the most unforgivable sin that, over the centuries, became so deeply unacceptable that families would disown children and other loved ones who strayed from their path and devout leaders would punish and harm any who were caught, or believed to be, attempting to stray.

During the Great Civil War, Lucarius Rominia was one of the most prominent and devoted worshippers of The One True, believing that The Three and all other gods were false interpretations of The One True meant to distract them from their true purpose. When the Great Civil War ended and Lucarius rose into power, seized the throne, destroyed artifacts and effigies, and burned libraries across the kingdom, he, alongside his church, outlawed the worship of any other gods besides The One True. After his rise to power, the church of the Purists were granted rights to dispense justice and be judges, juries, and executioners throughout the lands the church now dominated.

DIVINE HOUSES AND GUILDS

Society within the Six Kingdoms of Victarius' operates in a caste system, with one's privilege and ranking within the caste being granted by their Divine House upon their birth. Divine Houses are divinely chosen destinies determined by the major constellation one is born under. Each House consists of guilds and classes, some with more diversity in option than others, with the guilds and classes within each house having their own self-imposed castes and classism.

Throughout history, families have been torn apart by siblings and children being born into incompatible Houses, with children born in the House of Scholar and House of Armor being required to leave their pasts behind to, for Scholars, pursue higher schooling, and for Armor-born, being sent to war training camps in their youths. Other Houses required apprenticeships or traveling for learning, but few are so harsh in their division from others as the higher Houses.

Children born in impoverished families but prominent Houses were deemed the luckiest in society, as they were able to leave their poverty behind for higher pursuits, but were also forced to leave their family behind to pursue their Destinies. Just as harsh, but less in luck, were children born into undesirable Houses with parents from Houses of prestige. Like their counterparts, these children were forced to leave their families behind to pursue their Divine Destinies, but instead of being awarded with privilege and honor, they were often made to start over while pursuing their lesser Houses and fates.

It was not uncommon or even looked down upon for expecting parents to attempt to time the birth of their children to the stars alignment, with Herbalists offering over-the-counter herbal mixes to take to induce labor, delay the birth, or, only offered by few Herbalists, stop it from occurring entirely if there was no chance for the child to be born into a House deemed appropriate for the family's wishes.

House of Scholar- Book and Quill Constellation

The House of Scholar is, for most, the most desired Houses to be born under and is higher on the social class hierarchy than others. Those born under these stars, if having worked their way high enough in status within this House, can hold as high of a social status and prestige as a born nobleman.

Scholars are destined to serve their country in books and record keeping alongside teaching or leadership positions if they so choose those respective paths. Those trusted the most often become high-ranking leaders themselves or advisors to the noblemen above them.

Most Scholars complete their schooling at the Hall of Archives in Isilria- the center of historical and religious knowledge in the Six Kingdoms. Others choose to take their lessons in their home country's capital, some with better stocked archives than others.

The highest position one can achieve within the house is High Scholar- an honor not given to many and only achieved through recognition for their labors by Lords and Ladies, or the king himself. High Scholars are referred to as Father and Mother when honored with the rank of First Scholar of their country with other High Scholars being referred to as Brother or Sister.

House of Herbs- Bundle of Herbs Constellation

Herbalists are divided into several Guilds of study including general herbalism, healing, scientific development, and during times of war, many become creators of chemical weapons (despite most chemical weapons being banned).

Herbalists aid in many day-to-day advancements and needs; from acting as doulas and medical experts to being inventors of great medicinal and scientific achievements. Many still believe the legends that the greatest

Herbalists are reincarnations of wizards of past ages who wielded magic that once ran plentiful through the Earth Herself.

Herbalists of different factions take their study throughout the entire kingdom, some taking more Druidic style paths of learning by escaping into nature while those seeking deeper and more traditional learning boarding themselves at the Citadel in the shadow of the Dragon's Tower of Odessin. Like all guilds and Houses, each country has various schools and places of learning to ensure that those walking their destined path do not have to always have to travel far lengths to do so.

House of Armor- The Warrior Constellation

Also considered one of the higher ranking Houses, the House of Armor consists of soldiers, military officers, noble guards, and for those who lack much talent and ability on the battlefield (or who have retired from combat), common guards and doormen for establishments in need of muscle.

In countries such as the Isles of Aishar, being born under the House of Armor comes with the most honor one could pray for, as many families believe that being born to swear your life to your kingdom is the most noble and holy destiny one could be granted.

House of Water- Wall of Waves Constellation

Those born in the House of Water take on duties related to the sea, sailing, and fishing. This includes the Sailors Guild, where members hold positions such as sailors, ship captains, and boat constructors. The Fisherman's Guild- the second most common Guild within this House- holds those who fish for and sell the water's creatures.

Other Watermen include sea merchants who work alongside the House of Merchant to trade goods along the waters and travel across the countries for commerce.

House of the Reaper- Field of Grains Constellation

Reapers feed the country, alongside the Huntsmen, and are responsible for the farmland across the continent. While not a House most wish to be born into (much to do with the intense physical labor and demand it would entail), the Six Kingdoms owe their gratitude to its Reapers for everything from common root vegetables and produce to olives and grapes used for olive oils and rare wines.

The House of the Reaper also includes farmers who raise livestock for trade or processing, making friendships with Huntsman who take up the butcher's knife.

The beauty of the diverse and vast lands of the Six Kingdoms is also indebted to the Reapers who may choose a life of maintaining gardens of flora and blooms instead of farms of wheat or other foods from the earth.

House of Merchant- Bag of Coins Constellation

Possibly the most encompassing House, The House of Merchant contains countless paths to choose from including becoming inn keepers, tavern keepers, traveling caravan traders, and general or specialty store merchants.

While many find simple pleasures in the diversity in choice this House offers, this House offers no formal training or education and most, if not all, go through periods of unpaid labor within merchant houses and places of business in order to find their desired path. Once able to obtain their own place of business (if not choosing a smaller path of employment within a merchant house) individuals born impoverished or within poorer communities often find themselves in deep debt to those with the funds they must borrow to continue pursuing their Divine Destiny.

House of Vassal- Kneeling Man Constellation

Those born in the House of Vassal are destined to take up lives of servitude. Taking up positions such as butlers, royal aids, lady's maids, vassals, and more. While not always believed to be an honorable or desirable House, the official position of Vassal is a position of honor within the House as those with this duty directly serve the highest of noblemen.

House of Craft- The Dancer Constellation

The House of Craft provides art and entertainment to the Six Kingdoms with minstrels, music keepers, artists, potters and other artistic and craft-related guilds and careers being held under this House. Like the other Houses, guilds exist within such as the House of Music, House of Clay, and the House of Art.

House of Journeyman- Hammer and Nail Constellation

The House of Journeyman contains guilds and jobs such as wine makers, beer makers, builders, roofers, and carpenters. This House Contains all categories of careers that aid in continuing the growth of society, day-to-day trade, and continuation of tasks that require apprenticeships.

Journeymen, once skilled enough in their craft, become master craftsmen and take on apprentices and journeymen of their own. Some travel far across the continent to find children in their apprentice epochs to take to live under their household and train in their trade. Journeymen are destined to pass their trade onto others and believe that a failure to do so is a failure in their Destiny.

House of Huntsman- Wolf and Bow Constellation

While this House is titled specifically for Huntsman, it contains guilds outside of those who hunt to feed and protect their town, including guilds related to hunting such as bowyers, trappers, fletchers, tanners, and butchers.

For some Huntsmen who choose the life of wielding a bow or fletching arrows, many are enlisted into military service to become archers and weapons makers for their country's banners.

House of Textiles- The Spinning Wheel Constellation

Those born in this House can choose to pursue a life as shoemaker, seamstress, tailor, or weaver, with the most favored and talented weaving threads for noble houses. Textile workers can often be found socializing or working with Reapers who grow cotton to weave or raise sheep to shear and trading with Herbalists who specialize in plants processed for dying textiles.

House of Iron- Flame and Anvil Constellation

Iron-born forge all weapons and equipment that their town and people may need, from simple metal candelabras to heavy metal work used to build great structures or create intricate weaponry.

Within this House, weapons makers are the most commonly chosen paths, with others choosing to smith architecture and home goods and others desiring to spend their time living lives of more peace and smelting metal for horseshoes and farm equipment.

A Brief History of The Continent

This is only a brief history of the known seven hundred epoch history of The Great Continent. This summarizes what remains of scattered records, legends, and rumors of the Six Kingdoms of Victarius and the lands they were born from. Many ages throughout history are incomplete in their documentation as there were many ages deemed unworthy of putting quill to paper by those who controlled the archivists while other ages were lost to the rage of old rulers and destruction of war and conquest.

Not all is believed to be true, and much is known to have been truly lost.

The Conquest

The Great Continent once knew complete freedom and borderless lands. A continent once open to refugees, travelers, and settlers from all over the Unknown World to come and go as they pleased, the continent was prosperous, abundant in innovation and free.

Hailing from a kingdom far across the ocean, the four bastard children of a king most cruel, King Alvarian, sought to rule over the open lands with their dragons and their armies after their father refused to legitimize their births and give them what he promised- true titles and reign over his kingdom.

Instead of staying in their homeland and fighting for their right to rule their own lands, the four golden-eyed children instead gathered their army and stole many of their country's dragons and crossed the long and foreboding ocean to the Great Continent, fly over the mountains and past the lands that were unclaimed, and take from others what was denied to them, believing their rule over the lands would bring it into a greater age.

The remaining written records of this time dispute how long the Alvarian conquerors were on the land before declaring war on its people in their fight to rule. It is commonly believed that they spared no moments in declaring their power and using their dragons for conquest. It is also just as commonly believed that they attempted diplomacy for an extended length of time before determining they had no choice but to force their rule. What occurred during these epochs, like many tales, has been lost.

The War of Conquest (3 BC- 1 AC)

Known as Glenolyn the Great, Carishna the Unforgiving, Patrius the Wise, and Balnar the Brutal, the four siblings led their army to victory in a war spanning from 3BC (before conquest) to 1AC (after conquest). Many of the natives of the land did not fight, instead choosing to follow the Alvarian's rule once war was declared, believing them to be gods while others feared their winged beasts and the destruction they were capable of. Others, such as the Isles of Aishar and the lands that would later become Craigie, fought until the bitter end, refusing to yield their people or their lands with ease.

Only the Isles of Aishar were unable to be conquered.

It is believed that after the war was won, the dragons that survived the battles split across the lands and now lay beneath the lands and mountains waiting for their time to reign again.

Upon victory, the Continent was renamed to Victarius after Glenolyn's golden dragon, the largest and mightiest of all who led them to their victory. The land was split into four countries for the siblings to rule over, the borders being drawn where their dragons laid their claim, with the Isles of Aishar remaining its own after proving itself unconquerable.

Glenolyn the Great's golden dragon, Vinicarius, retired to rest underneath the Golden City, protecting the rightful ruler of the New Continent from harm. The Golden City became the ruined and burned foundation that The King's Keep and Isilria was later built upon. Being the eldest sibling and the only one raised near royalty and court politics, Glenolyn used her talents and training to aid in creating influential allies for her and her siblings before they left their old kingdom. and, being the one who knew most of leadership and ruling- alongside having the largest dragon who dealt the final blow that won the war, Glenolyn became the first queen of the Six Kingdoms.

Patrius the Wise and his three-tailed green dragon, Baethorn, took rest on the southern green lands, using his tails and claws to create The Ina Gulf and dig streams along the lands before burying himself below the hilly grasslands. Patrius was responsible for convincing his siblings to not only leave their kingdom behind, but to conquer another. His high education and intellect made him the chosen diplomat of his siblings during their time in the conquest and during their rule, often using his mind and his words to aid in battle and strategy instead of his weapons and aiding in documenting the conquest and uniting the kingdoms.

Balnar the Brutal was the most furious and unforgiving of the four regarding their fathers refusal to grant their titles and aided strongly in the victory due to his brutal nature that mirrored the destructive habits of his dragon- Grerdort the ice dragon. While claiming the northern lands, Grerdort shed many of his ice scales along the north, preferring the chill of snow and ice that had not been there before, and forced much of the area into a permanent winter. It is believed his slumbering body is the makeup of the northern mountains of snow. Not much is known of Balnar the Brutal or Grerdort outside of their merciless battle tactics and brutal nature, a documentation of their part in history done by their own design and wishes to be known for their vicious nature and nothing else.

Carishna the Unforgiving's fate was not as kind as the fate of her siblings.

During the attempted conquest of the Isles of Aishar, her battle against battle hips built for defense was lost as ancient krakens of the sea brought down her crackling sand dragon, Riomiar, and pulled them both into the ocean. Riomiar fought valiantly against the grapple of the sea beasts and the waves, but ultimately did not take a breath again, now believed to be a dragon of the sea, forever on the search for vengeance against those who aided in her destruction and driving her mother mad. Carishna was saved from the waves by her sister, Glenolyn, but never healed from the loss of the dragon she had known since a babe. Her driving madness and vitriol led her to abandon the grand castles the siblings had claimed and she chose isolation and anger, turning the freshly constructed tower in the smoking desert mountains into her prison before it became anyone else's.

There, she sat with Riomiar's surviving dragon eggs, driving herself into madness until her death, hoping one would hatch and bring her what she lost. Soon after her death, the mountains came alive with smoke and fire, melting lands and burning forests to the east. This destructive act was believed to be the waking of her dragon eggs and many feared the three smoking mountains were the lairs for the dragon hatchlings that all thought had been lost.

The Alvarian Age 1AC- 407 AC

The Alvrian age was a peak moment in the continent's history, with the forging of new nations and new technologies and more cultures being blended together. The people of Victarius entered an age of innovation almost one hundred epochs after the Conquest ended and rebuilding had been completed. The capital of the continent was remembered by artists and architects as a city made of pure gold, so bright that the sun's rays could not outshine the city. Innovations such as plumbing, running water, and advancements in weaponry and farming equipment marked this time as one of a prosperous nature.

However, towards the end of the age, most of this innovation was lost to another war, division, and famine brought on by what became known as The Great Civil War.

The destruction from the war was so thorough that it reset most technology and cultural advancements to the beginning of time. Additionally, due to the onslaught of destruction of The Great Civil War, not much is known about the Alvarian Age or the age before the conquest and much of what is known may be that of simple legend- including the dragons.

The Great Civil War (390 AC- 405 AC) (The First Rebellion)

The heat of summer in 390 AC brought with it the beginnings of The Great Civil War. Several leaders, most prominently the entirety of Craigie, desired to declare themselves independent from the kingdom they believed had tarnished their lands, despite the innovation and evolution their civilization found after rebuilding from the Alvarian Conquest.

Sir Wallace Nealson, the leader of the northern country of Craigie, declared his country independent through a Declaration of Independence that was rejected and burned by the king before he even heard Sir Wallace's case or read the declaration. The king's disrespectful response threw Craigie into a war with the kingdom that led each country to fight to remain a union of nations or to declare their freedom and independence.

The desert lands that would later become Odessin joined Craigie in its attempts for freedom, being not a "true" nation but a dumping place for undesirables, those who the continent wished to forget, and the worst criminals of the land. The Dragon Tower was their prison and the mountains were their mines to labor in for gold and precious stones for the remainder of the continent. Generations of this treatment led the people full of rage and desires for vengeance that they deemed justice.

The fifteen epochs of war burned through the kingdom, leading to destruction of entire cities and monuments, a great plague, and famine from farmlands lost and food reserves stolen or tarnished. The countries found themselves on the absolute brink of destruction as allyships crumbled and diseases and starvation tore through armies and cities, bringing about a desperate treaty and plea for peace.

That peace was found, but not before more bloodshed changed the lands and the skies.

When every star fell from the sky on The Darkest Night and blood replaced all of the water in the Land of a Thousand Rivers, the Great Civil War had ended, and a new age began.

In the terms of peace that were negotiated, the country of Odessin was created and its people were freed, their shackles melted into armor and weapons, their prison becoming their castle. The southernmost country of Shireland, who joined the monarchy in their battle to keep the union, had new lines drawn and became the country of Ayeshire. A portion of the land of Arumina that held the capitol city made of gold became the country of

Britia, the lands to its east given its own name of Sebern- the name chosen due to their lands severing several old countries into smaller pieces.

Perhaps most notable to negotiations was Sir Wallace Nealson's torturous death and sacrifice at the forefront of soon-to-be King Lucarius' demands for peace.

After being held in the stocks of the capitol for many days, Sir Wallace was disemboweled, left in the public stocks to rot and picked at by birds. He was then hanged, beheaded, and drawn and quartered in front of citizens and many of his own family. His ruined remains were thrown into the sewers outside of The King's Keep, where legend now speaks of his ghost haunting those who dared enter the depths of the castle and would take revenge on them for what was done to him.

His execution was not only gruesome and cruel, but born of entire evil as King Lucarius ordered Sir Wallace's own men to perform each part of it.

The Great Civil War was instrumental to the Isles of Aishar as well. Their independence was lost during the war as they brought themselves into the continent's fighting, attempting to bring an end to what was occurring, knowing that the destruction of the continent would end their prosperous country as well. However, while they became one of the Six Kingdoms of Victarius, they kept all else of their history and culture, and their anger.

The Rominian Age (407 AC- 581 AC)

K ing Lucarius Rominia is declared king upon the completion of the treaties for peace. He names himself- and ensures the records of his Royal Archives name him- The First King to delegitimize those that came before him. During the war, he married Daiyin Machaera, a descendent of the Alvarians with a mighty army behind her, and she is recorded as being The Swordbearing Queen, choosing not to wear dresses or gowns, but battle attire with a sword always at her side.

Unknown to The First King until the crown was placed on his head, the ending of the war and the start of the new kingdom began the prophecy of the Psalms of Fire and Fury, an ancient prophecy foreseen by seers from the time of the Alvarian's but hidden in the depths of the castle and known only to a few minds.

"When the eye of the world has dimmed and stars have fallen as if made of rain,
Of solid gold and stardust rulers shall remain, forevermore until burned in fury and in flame.

And the world of men shall be made to begin again."

Upon his burning of golden crowns and effigies of those who fought against him, King Lucarius used the melted gold metal to form his new throne. Only after seeing the sight of the golden throne did the scholars that knew of the ancient prophecy share it with The First King, perhaps too late.

After dreaming far too much of this prophecy, King Lucarius threw himself into tyrannical power, pushing The One True religion onto the kingdom with unforgiving brute force and burned libraries and archives across the kingdom to erase records and limit the spread of knowledge that could undo his work.

The king and queen's eldest child, Constantine took the throne in 436 AC and was known as "Constantine the Cruel" due to his cruel, unhinged nature- one that often overshadowed his father's iron fist. From a young age Constantine was cruel, unbending, and unhinged to all except for his wife, Milian. For her, he would bend the knee if she ever asked. They had seven children who saw the only softness King Constantine had buried within his coldness.

His son, the future King Tomis had a reign that held no notes in records, although it was known that his father's rage was not as heavily inherited by Tomis and only saw the light when driven to such darkness. King Tomis' son, King Nicario's, most notable accomplishment was fathering the First Queen of the Six Kingdoms, Queen Oriana Rominia, who would only reign for two epochs before her brother Prince Jacquard usurped her throne and tore the country apart again just as her father began his work to rebuild the kingdom and give birth to an age of innovation.

The Royal Civil War- 517 AC- 522 AC

Queen Oriana Rominia took the throne in 517 AC. Despite her usurper brother's attempts, Royal Records still contain passages of how dearly loved she was during her short time on the throne. Called "The Good Queen" in many parchments and "The Selfish Queen" in other records that her brothers record keepers modified, her families warring brought the continent into The Royal Civil War.

During her short ruling, the queen was pregnant with child, but experienced a traumatic and deadly birth where she and her husband, King Talar Vistus, were forced to choose between her life or the life of their first son.

The choice to save her life was fatal to their throne and many of their people.

Prince Jacquard Rominia used this as fuel for his fire to take the throne, believing he would be a better ruler than she. He and the allies he had been building at court spread gospel against her, claiming she would never choose the goodness of the realm over her own life and selfish needs.

Ultimately, Queen Oriana abdicated her throne through force by Prince Jacquard and his army, choosing her people's lives over her throne after seeing the slaughter her brother laid upon their people and his refusal to yield for the sake of the realm.

Queen Oriana and King Talar then left for his old family home the Isles of Aishar, unable to sit by and watch her brother rule. Their future children, once their lives settled in the Isles, eventually married off to prominent and common houses in the Isles, with their eldest daughter marrying the eldest son of ancient house Kaliniari, forming house Kavistia, the house that brought to the world Queen Onetta Kavistia-Scott.

After forcing his sister to abdicate the throne, many who distrusted the Usurper King spread rumors that the noble line was now cursed, most choosing to believe this out of hope that a real curse would befall their new king and others swearing by the whispered words of those who called themselves seers. Whether from that curse, or out of bad luck, King Jacquard only ever had female heirs, their births coming shortly after he wrote into law that the throne can only be passed down through male heirs as he believed their kingdom would only ever thrive under the hard hand of a man and not the soft touch of a woman.

Out of heirs and time, his handful of male cousins all fought in court to take his throne under what they believed were the rules under his new law. Through conniving actions and savvy politics, the king informed the kingdom that the law was never communicated in its entirety and that it had, this entire time, stated that female heirs could inherit the throne but only if they were married first and the title passed to her as part of her husband's marital inheritance.

Laws can change quite easily when the one who needs the revision holds the pen and the power behind it.

King Jacquard's reign began on a somber and dark note and did not improve over time. While some inevitably accepted their new king, very few found peace or joy under his iron fist.

The Age of Darkness 523 AC- 543 AC

The Age of Darkness that followed the crowning of King Jacquard was an age of absolute totalitarianism, obedience, and labor putting to shame that of The First King's fits of tyranny. Labor days increased and more workers were needed to rebuild the kingdom forcing couples to bear more children or be fined for losing pregnancies or failing to get pregnant. Each corner of the kingdom became a police state with many executions and slaughters occurring, many of which were of simple people unable to pay taxes or of drunks who became bold enough to take in too much ale and speak ill of the king.

Even one comment against His Majesty would end in death.

Even one day of disobedience would end a life.

In 543 AC, King Jacquard fell ill. On his deathbed, he had a vision.

"Our families reign will end just how it began- through brute force and blades dripping in blood. The throne will burn and be reforged alongside our country-men."

King Jacquard never knew the Psalms of Fire and Fury.

After his passing in 544 AC, aids who truly felt no warmth for His Majesty added to record the names he was known as on the streets; The Cursed King, The Unlucky King, The False King.

Advisors to the former Queen Oriana who stayed behind, claiming loyalty to the throne no matter who sat upon it, kept the Psalms of Fire and Fury from him, eventually allowing the words to be spoken to his heir- Princess Leighana Rominia.

The Rominia-Scott Age 543 AC- 581AC | The Age of Unity and Rebuilding Begins

Princess Leighana Rominia married Richard Scott, the son of a prominent noble family long allied with the throne. In 543 AC, they ruled together as equals, even combining their family names in hopes that uniting as equals would bring their commonwealth to a new age and allow them to come together to truly rebuild their kingdoms and experience a renaissance age after her father's darkness.

During this time, monuments were rebuilt, strongholds fortified, and new castles and keeps built. This included the building of Ravenhall where the Williamson family was granted title and rule over the lands and when the final stones were laid for Tower Bridge and Sandhill House, lands promised to the Bromlyn clan during the Royal Civil War to ensure their alliance with King Jacquard.

The eldest Rominia-Scott child, Prince Jameston, took the throne in 560 AC at the age of 19 and slowly began to turn irrational and mad over his epochs on the throne. In 581 AC, King Jameston's madness overtook him and he killed himself, screaming from the top of his tower about voices in the night haunting and hunting him. This was seconds before he threw himself from the turret and onto the cobblestone beneath.

King Jameston's madness and suicide solidified the old rumors of the Rominia name being cursed. His heirs and relatives hoped that the curse had died with him.

The Scott Royal Age 581 AC- Current Date

In hopes that the Rominia curse would not follow them, the Rominia-Scott children stripped their surnames of Rominia, writing the Scott Royal Age into existence.

As teenagers in 580 AC, soon-to-be King Cyrus Scott, the eldest child of Mad King Jameston, married future queen Ava. However, many in court firmly believe that they remained cursed through his family blood as they were unable to conceive a single child.

Refusing to believe he or his family to be at fault, after ten epochs of marriage, King Cyrus had Queen Ava shamed and hanged, blaming her for their inability to conceive, stating it was God's will as she refused to abide by her duty and even claiming she took special herbs to prevent any conception.

King Cyrus cycled through five more wives before being able to conceive a single child with his six wife Maliana. Like her, each wife that came before her was given a strict timeline to provide a child or else she would be "disposed of". Bearing a daughter would only buy a wife a short amount of time before their time was up and he rid himself of them.

In 612 AC, Queen Consort Maliana gave King Cyrus a single son, a son whose hair and skin were quite unlike his.

That child was King Andrius, father to King Ivan Scott.

To secure an alliance with the ever evasive country of Aishar, King Ivan Scott was married to Lady Onetta Kaviastia of Thelimor in the beginnings of 658 AC. This agreement came from discussions with King Andrius, Lord Tyrrian Priscius of Ashar, and Lady Onetta's own father. All three men determined that her hand in marriage, as the new heir to the oldest House reigning over the oldest city in the world, was not only suitable for the future king, but best for all three Houses.

Battle of Broken Tower 658 AC

During an intense Odessin-Craigie border battle centered at Broken Tower, Lord Thillian Torrin of Sebern sent reinforcements to dispel the battle and, in his hope, put an end to the fighting that would not cease between the two enemy countries. The future Lord of Ayeshire, Theodus Montarian, was one of the lead officers of the army that his homeland of Sebern sent to end the fighting.

During the battle, after Odessin had laid down their arms, Lord Edgel of Craigie was recorded as refusing to yield to Sebern, leading to his death and driving a deep wedge between the generations long allyship between the two countries.

The details of the battle were never well recorded by ink or by word.

Aisharian Civil War 670 AC

AC, In The Isles of Aishar were thrown into a gruesome civil war as the Priscius twins' anger and disdain came to a head over who was the rightful heir to their fathers title of Lord. Tyrrian, the oldest twin by a singular minute, had claimed the title three epochs prior. During those three epochs Armen, the other Priscius twin, worked to divide the court of the Isles and push for his claim to the throne.

After Lord Tyrrian called Britia, who then called their allies in Ayeshire for aid, his claim to the throne was kept and his brother defeated. This war was the bloodiest and most gruesome of wars in recent history. While it lasted only one epoch, the deaths matched wars of several epochs in length.

It was unlike Tyrrian the Tyrant to leave survivors, especially those who were the face of betrayal, but he felt it more appropriate to keep his brother alive, although less of a man in anatomy, and forever left in indentured servitude to him and his court.

The Houses of the Six Kingdoms

Through the ages, there have been many noble, notable, and influential Houses, with some being lost to war and others lost through matrimony absorbing lines into one another. Many Houses were born of common families being granted titles and land or taking those titles and land for their own.

The most notable lost House in history is the Alvarian House- the name lost through the ages as descendants married to other Houses and took on many different names. Some of the Alvarian siblings and their children produced so many heirs to their lines that lineage blurred just as deeply as history itself.

Although their lineage lives on in the blood of many Houses, their name has died alongside their dragons.

The House of the Six Kingdoms

MAJOR HOUSES

House Scott of Britia

House Scott holds the longest surviving alliance with the throne, lasting from times before their lineage held the title of monarch. After aiding in the end of the Royal Civil War, the family was honored with marriage to King Jaquard's heir once his siege of the throne was successful. Their alliance, they claimed throughout the war and after, was not to a family or a name, but to the throne and the kingdom's well-being.

It was to the surprise of no citizen that the Scott family eventually added their blood to the throne's line of heirs (and then overtook the line later), it was only surprising that it took so many generations for their family to do so.

Ever strong in holding their power and aligning the continent under the Church throughout the centuries (being one of the prominent families to push for the Church's power during the Great Civil War), House Scott's sigil is that of a noble lion wearing a crown. Before joining into and overtaking the Royal line, their symbol was that of a simple lion.

Their house words are Fate. Duty. Faith. And their motto is "Your fate is your duty, and your duty is to your faith."

The principal Houses sworn to House Scott include, on paper and by tax, all Houses in the Six Kingdoms, including the freedom-fighting House Edgel, despite the words they spit at the king's name.

House Montarian of Ayeshire

For centuries, the noble House of Ayeshire was known as House Vegaria. Through the marriage of Lady Belva Vegaria to Theodus Montarian of Sebern in 660 AC, Lady Belva took the name of her husband, changing the name of the House, but keeping hold of her title over the Ayeshire throne she inherited from her father. A House of kind stewardship and servant-style leadership, the House holding title over Ayeshire has long been loved and honored by their people of whom they treat more like fellow countrymen than common people below them.

While the Montarian name was taken by Lady Belva Vegaria, the Vegaria House words and sigil were kept. Their sigil is the stag, words are "Strength. Integrity. Grace" and motto is "Find strength in your resilience, integrity in your actions, and grace in your heart."

This noble House is the longest standing ally of the Scott family, their alliance running true before the Scott family joined the Rominia family on the throne and often following the Scott family into war and aligning themselves in council chambers and meeting halls.

The Minor Houses sworn to Montarian include House Bromlyn and House Nilkimm.

House Torrin of Sebern

Never reigning as kings or queens, the factions of families that eventually made House Torrin held domain over the green and mountain lands of Sebern for many centuries, long before the land even held its own name and split up the old countries of Aruminia, Odenbiur, and Shirelind.

Built after the Alvarian Age ended, Berren Castle was meant to be a castle for retreat and leisure for the kingdom's rulers, but after the Great Civil War and the forming of new borders and countries, it became the home of House Torrin. The thick mountain stone fortress sits carved among the mountains on the rocky borders that separates The Six Kingdoms from the Unclaimed Lands.

Sebern protects and defends the Six Kingdoms from the mountain brutes that live hidden in the cold rocky landscapes, who bear down the mountains with creatures believed to be of magic lost and attempting to lay siege to lands they once held their own power over.

While holding no domain over the brutes from the mountains, many believe that House Torrin could control them if needed and call for their aid- or force them into submission and loyalty. House Torrin has never held the desire to control those in the mountains, or even those outside of their borders. With generations of effort of attempting to keep the peace on their northern and eastern borders, House Torrin adopted the motto of "Protectors of peace, keepers of justice" during the Rominian Age where their armies aided in quelling the Royal Civil War and pushing for a peaceful resolution- no matter who it would bring onto the throne.

Since the death of Lady Earla Torrin after her marriage to the late King Andrius before the couple's crowning, House Torrin has chosen to hold their distance from House Scott as much as they could without severing needed political ties or being believed to be separatists. The death of Lady Earla Torrin only deepened House Torrin's desire to hold no high titles or be much involved in what occurs in the west.

The majestic eagle rules over House Torrin of Sebern and the Minor House Lisarian of Black Tower is sworn to the Torrin banners.

House Priscius of Isles of Aishar

Every citizen of the Six Kingdoms knows the tales and legends of the untamable Isles of Aishar. They know even better that peace and civility with the brutal Isles is best for all; with history recounting the bloodshed and broken banners when the army of the kraken makes their way onto the battlefield.

The hot temperature of the Isles adds to the harsh nature of the people who claim it as their home. While not inherently cruel people- although many choose to believe this of Aisharians, the keepers of the Isles are deeply passionate of one another, their lands, history, and their culture.

Each Aisharian gladiator, like all soldiers in the Six Kingdoms, are sent to war camps as children to train and hone their skills. In Aishar, however, each gladiator must pass the Blood Rite in their youth. Survivors are the victors of this age-old ceremony, as failure did not mean a retrial, but of death. The Blood Rite consisted of many secrets. All that is known to those outside of its trials is that those who wish to not be killed, must kill and those who wish to survive, must be willing to put a sword through their allies, friends, or even family.

House Priscius was made of gladiators, with Lord Tyrrian being one of the most terrifying and merciless to make it through the Blood Rite and many battles without mercy. The pure embodiment of House Priscius beliefs- to bow to no throne, to grant no mercy to those who cross them, and to yield no part of oneself- Lord Tyrrian Priscius is proudly known as Tyrrian the Tyrant and holds no quarrels with those who use that as his name.

Kind Andrius, Lord Tyrrian Priscius and Lord Kavistia of Thelimor reached an agreement in 658 AC to create more unity between their countries and turn their basic civility into true unity. The agreement was to unite their Houses through marriage- the marriage of Lord Kavistia's second daughter, Lady Onetta to the heir to the throne, Prince Ivan Scott.

Lady Onetta's older sister, Lady Maia was already wed to Lord Tyrrian Priscius, uniting the ruling family of the waters to the oldest House in the world and the marriage between Lady Onetta and Prince Ivan was argued to be the final thread to weave their Houses together and strengthen their nations.

While agreed upon and benefiting all Houses involved, there was no joy or happiness at the union, only duty-bound acceptance.

Their House sigil is the mighty kraken, and their motto is "We are the waters".

House Kavistia of Thelimor is sworn to House Priscius in addition to having loyalty split to the throne when Queen Onetta was crowned.

House Mete of Odessin

House Mete's lineage can be traced back to Carishna the Unforgiving. Their pride in their lineage and history shows through their dragon imagery and dragon likeness in battle and in attitude. Using fire and long range, claw-like weapons and scale-mail armor and gathering gold, stones, and riches for the kingdom, the powerful Odessian noble family truly embodies that of the ancient and powerful scaled beast of the sky.

Descendents of Carishna's line refer to themselves often as "The Blood of the Unforgiving".

Their House words are Power. Wisdom. Strength and their motto is "Sow knowledge, reap wisdom" paying homage to the high value they place in higher knowledge and learning. The city surrounding the Dragon Tower contains the second-largest learning citadel in the Six Kingdoms, rivaled only by knowledge found in the Hall of Archives in The King's Keep. While this citadel houses halls of knowledge of a diverse nature, their halls most prominently see historians and herbalists searching for more advancement in their fields of study, while Scholars typically choose to finish their studies in the king's city.

House Pathis and House Furia are both sworn to House Mete.

House Edgel of Craigie

Descended from Sir Wallace Nealson's line and Balnar the Brutal who came before him, House Edgel is one of the oldest traceable Houses on the continent. This House has sat on the stone throne of Craigie since it was formed by Balnar the Brutal during the Alvarian Conquest and stayed on the throne despite Sir Wallace Nealson's rebellion that began the Great Civil War.

A father to countless children, Sir Wallace Nealson's throne was taken from his line after his torturous death and given to the well-loved and respected Edgel family of Craigie, who quickly and quietly married the throne's heir into the Nealson line to continue his legacy and keep his line on the throne.

While forbidden, the people of Craigie often pray to and worship the old Vahar gods and have been known to keep seers hidden among their people-an ancient magical people long thought lost, but simply quite well hidden.

House Edgel does not follow the standard forms of nobility and noble Houses. Forgoing the common social hierarchy of lords and ladies, House Edgel only has one leader that is titled, that being whoever sits on their throne. All others are only known by their names and their honor. This decision was made to ensure complete unity under one banner and one House in Craigie, and to unite their people as equals with one another. This was also done as a way to insult the monarchy and barb what the king's ancestors had put into practice long ago.

Their House sigil is the bear and words are "Freedom. Honor. Glory" with a common, but unofficial, saying among all of their people being "Freedom or death".

MINOR HOUSES

House Williamson of Ravenhall, Britia

One of the younger Houses, House Williamson was born during The Age of Unity and Rebuilding when Ravenhall was constructed as one of the two central points of trades in the Southeast. The marriage of Princess Evelyn Scott- sister to King Cyrus Scott- to Hugo Williamson granted the Williamson clan nobility and title and is now in its third generation of ruling over the hilly landscape of the Ravenhall lands. This noble marriage and unity were one of many new alliances constructed as part of the building of unity during this age.

The Williamson House sigil is a raven and motto is "Wardens of the land"- despite their small army tasked with protecting the mid-lands. This motto was adopted during the family's titling with their intent on building their stronghold and becoming a point of impenetrable force.

House Bromlyn of Sandhill House, Ayeshire

House Bromlyn was gifted the land of Sandhill, of which they were already stewards, during the Royal Civil War when they surrendered quickly and swore their fealty and army to the Usurper King Jacquard during his claim for the throne. For House Bromlyn's new alliance, they were given the land and title once the war ended but only if King Jacquard was its victor. King Jacquard also gave his first-born daughter Princess Caterin to the House to be wedded to Lillian Bromlyn's son, Mikarian, when both children became of age.

In 677 AC, Lord Bromlyn, wed to the Lady of Ayeshire's younger sister, made a claim for more land across the water from Tower Bridge. Due to the stewardship given to his ancestors over the land around Tower Bridge- including a slim few miles of land on the northern shore of Tower Bridge- Lord Bromlyn felt owed more land. During his claim, Lord Bromlyn deemed the land to the north of Tower Bridge too little, stating he was owed "all the land one can see from the last stone of Tower Bridge".

Before a battle could brew outside of bar room shouting, Lady Montarian brought a brigade with her to end Lord Bromlyn's plans. This visit was the last time Lady Belva Montarian and her sister had seen one another and the last time the Montarian family had crossed into Sandhill House territory.

The House Bromlyn words are "Thou shalt not falter. Thou shalt not fail" and sigil is a stone tower bridge.

House Nilkimm of Iron Bay, Ayeshire

For ages, House Nilkimm held stewardship over Iron Bay and the Spotted Isles. This family was responsible for building the ports and steads along the Spotted Isles and throughout Iron Bay. During the Alvarian Conquest, House Nilkimm and the settlers of Iron Bay refused to stand down, their smaller stature against the dragon riders and their mounts being nothing in comparison to the size of their pride and resilience. Legends state that during the final stand off of the lands versus the dragons, the dragons did not bow in obedience to those of Iron Bay, but in respect of their strength and refused to burn those who stood against their riders.

While sworn to the leaders of Ayeshire, House Nilkimm has never been a family to command and control, but a House whose loyalty was earned through generations of allyship and partnership.

Their House Sigil is an iron chain and their words are "Iron does not bend."

House Kavistia of Thelimor, The Isles of Aishar

House Kavistia is the oldest House in the known world, lasting long before the War of Conquest and being of the House that the Priscius noble line descended from. The great city of Thelimor is believed to be the oldest and grandest city in the world (often referred to as the birthplace of civilization), putting to shame the king's city. The ancient city was built of grand stone buildings carved along ocean cresting cliffs and waterfalls, ancient architecture budding from the earth and water, and a beauty not made wretched by war or conquest.

House Kavistia is a prideful and private House. Often not leaving their city or island for the continent, save for their tradesmen importing and exporting goods, they choose not to share or sell their innovative plans and technologies with others or invite other Houses and people into their grand city.

Their signal is of the sun cresting the waves of the great Ringhar Sea and is often accompanied by their words "Beacon of the sun".

House Lisarian of Broken Tower, Sebern

Sir Oryst Lisarian led the siege of Broken Tower during the Royal Civil War, known then simply as The Tower, when the reigning family over the land swore fealty to Queen Oriana. In his victory over its stewards, Sir Oryst was granted lordship and title, under one condition by the king.

Finished in 412 AC after the Great Civil War, First King Lucarius ordered the construction of the tower to watch over the borders of Craigie and keep a close eye on their people to ensure an uprising did not occur again. After the Royal Civil War and Sir Oryst Lisarian taking the land, Broken Tower, as it became known due to the destruction it took during the Sir Oryst's siege, became the point of neutrality and control over the Odessin and Craigie border battles.

To ensure the neutrality of the Lisarian line, Sir Oryst accepted the title with the condition that each of his heirs, and all children after, would marry from noble or prominent families of both Craigie and Odessin, continuing an alternating pattern for every child born for the next several generations.

Doing so created such an interwoven line of alliance and blood between the warring countries and neutral land that Broken Tower rarely ever took one side over the other, fearing creating division and war at their own dinner table.

Lord Augusta and Lady Reval Lisarian currently hold the title over Broken Tower, with Lady Reval's blood being of Craigie and Lord Augusta's blood being from both lands.

The Lisarian sigil is a tower and words are "Born from many, now as one".

House Furia of Black Fingers, Odessin

Just like those of House Mete, House Furia's bloodline is that of Carishna the Unforgiving. They are not only descendents of one of the most brutal and powerful dragon riders in history, but they also believe themselves to be descended from the actual blood of dragons.

House Furia has always held position over the Dragon Armies of Odessin, bearing much of the responsibility for their innovative weapons and dragon and flame imagery used in their warfare. Believing themselves to be the embodiment of the dragon's fury, their family name was not born of bloodline, but of naming, choosing "Furia" as their surname and naming each leader of the Dragon Army Madam or Master Fury.

Their House signal is a flame and their motto is "We are the dragon's fury".

ACKNOWLEDGEMENTS

Thank you to each and every person who helped me build this world over the course of two epochs.

A special thanks to Harley, the inspiration behind Ephraim, and the first person to hear about the original idea for this book series and encouraged me to write it.

To Aundrea, my OG beta reader and tough love bestie, who listened to every single spoiler filled plot change, gave so much feedback and made me feel like I was a New York Times Best Selling Author before my first draft was even done. You will always be the Emaline to my Ora, and the Ora to my Emaline.

To all the magical lands of far away fantasy that raised me through childhood and swept me away during adulthood, there is a glimmer of each of you in this story and forever intertwined in my being.

And, lastly, to younger me, the one who never stopped dreaming up worlds to escape to- We did it. We finally did it.

About the Author

Ever since she could pick up a pen and scribble, Kristina has always been up to something.

Kristina has been writing stories, poems, and novels ever since she was first able to form sentences and spell (most) words correctly. Throughout her life, her nose was always stuck in a book and her mind was always wandering and creating fictitious tales that helped her escape life's struggles.

She lives in Illinois with her rainbow organized library room of books and her furry friends- Benjamin and Hermione.

www.kristinambarbee.com

Photo © Bridget Shaw Photography

9 798988 617815